The Life We Almost Had

The Life We Almost Had

Amelia Henley

FOREVER

NEW YORK BOSTON

Copyright © 2020 by Louise Jensen
Reading group guide copyright © 2022 by Louise Jense and
Hachette Book Group, Inc.

Cover design by Daniela Medina
Cover image © Getty Images
Cover copyright © 2022 by Hachette Book Group, Inc.

Forever
Hachette Book Group
1290 Avenue of the Americas, New York, NY 10104
read-forever.com
twitter.com/readforeverpub

Originally published in Great Britain in 2020 by HQ, an imprint of Harper CollinsPublishers Ltd.
First U.S. Edition: June 2022

Forever is an imprint of Grand Central Publishing. The Forever name and logo are trademarks of Hachette Book Group, Inc.

The Hachette Speakers Bureau provides a wide range of authors for speaking events. To find out more, go to www.hachettespeakersbureau.com or call (866) 376-6591.

Library of Congress Cataloging-in-Publication Data

Names: Henley, Amelia, author.
Title: The life we almost had / Amelia Henley.
Description: First U.S. edition. | New York : Forever, 2022.
Identifiers: LCCN 2021053872 | ISBN 9781538754818 (trade paperback) |
    ISBN 9781538754825 (ebook)
Subjects: LCGFT: Romance fiction. | Novels.
Classification: LCC PR6110.E568 L54 2022 | DDC 823/.92—dc23
LC record available at https://lccn.loc.gov/2021053872

ISBN: 9781538754818 (trade paperback), 9781538754825 (ebook)

Printed in the United States of America

LSC-C

Printing 1, 2022

For Glyn Appleby,
With much love.

PROLOGUE

Seven years. It's been seven years since that night on the beach. I had lain on the damp sand with Adam, his thumb stroking mine. Dawn smudged the sky with its pink fingers while the rising sun flung glitter across the sea. We'd faced each other curled onto our sides, our bodies speech marks, unspoken words passing hesitantly between us; an illusory dream. *Don't ever leave me*, I had silently asked him. *I won't*, his eyes had silently replied.

But he did.

He has.

My memories are both painful and pleasurable to recall. We were blissfully happy until gradually we weren't. Every cross word, every hard stare, each time we turned our backs on each other in bed gathered like storm clouds hanging over us, ready to burst, drenching us with doubt and uncertainty until we questioned what we once thought was unquestionable.

Can love really be eternal?

I can answer that now because the inequitable truth is that I am hopelessly, irrevocably, lost without him.

But does he feel the same?

I turn over the possibility of life without Adam, but each time I think of myself without him, no longer an *us*, my heart breaks all over again.

If only we hadn't…

My chest tightens.

Breathe.

Breathe, Anna. You're okay.

It's a lie I tell myself, but gradually the horror of that day begins to dissipate with every slow inhale, with every measured exhale. It takes several minutes to calm myself. My fingers furling and unfurling, my nails biting into the tender skin of my palms until my burning sorrow subsides.

Focus.

I am running out of time. I've been trying to write a letter but the words won't come. My notepaper is still stark white. My pen once again poised, ink waiting to stain the blank page with my tenuous excuses.

My secrets.

But not my lies. There's been enough of those. Too many.

I am desperate to see him once more and make it right.

All of it.

I wish I knew what he wanted. My eyes flutter closed. I try to conjure his voice, imagining he might tell me what to do. Past conversations echo in my mind as I search for a clue.

If you love someone, set them free, he had once told me, but I brush the thought of this away. I don't think it can apply to this awful situation we have found ourselves in. Instead I recall the feel of his body spooned around mine, warm breath on the back of my neck, promises drifting into my ear.

Forever.

I cling on to that one word as tightly as I'd once clung on to his hand.

I loved him completely. I still do. Whatever happens now, after, my heart will still belong to him.

Will always belong to him.

I must hurry if I'm going to reach him before it's too late. There's a tremble in my fingers as I begin the letter, which will be both an apology and an explanation, but it seems impossible to put it all into words—the story of us. I really don't have time to think of the life we had—the life we almost had—but I allow myself the indulgence. Memories gather: we're on the beach, watching the sunrise; I'm introducing him to my mum—his voice shaking with nerves as he says hello; we're meeting for the first time in that shabby bar. Out of order and back to front and more than anything I wish I could live it all again. Except that day. *Never* that day.

Again, the vise around my lungs tightens. In my mind I see it all unfold and I feel it. I feel it all: fear, panic, despair.

Breathe, Anna.

In and out. In and out. Until I am here again, pen gripped too tightly in my hand.

Focus.

I made a mistake.

I stare so intently at the words I have written that they jump around on the page. I'm at a loss to know how to carry on, when I remember one of the first things Adam had said to me: "Start at the beginning, Anna."

And so I do.

Speedily, the nib of my pen scratches over the paper. I let it all pour out.

This is not a typical love story, but it's our love story.

Mine and Adam's.

And despite that day, despite everything, I'm not yet ready for it to end.

Is he?

PART ONE

"This will be the adventure of a lifetime."

NELL STEVENS—ANNA'S BEST FRIEND

CHAPTER ONE

Anna

Seven years before

The date I met Adam is forever etched onto my mind; it should have been my wedding day. I tucked my hair behind my ears; rather than being strewn with confetti, it was greasy and limp. Unwashed and unloved.

The plane taxied down the runway before it rose sharply into the sky, a frothy white tail in its wake. Out of the window was nothing but cloud, as thick and woolly as my thoughts. Each time I remembered the way I'd been dumped, virtually at the altar, my face burned with the shame of it.

Goodbye.

I wasn't sure if I was saying farewell to England or to the man who had broken my heart.

Fingers threaded through mine and squeezed. Tears threatened to fall as I gazed down at my ringless hand. Ridiculously, one of the things that had excited me most about my honeymoon had been the anticipation of the sun tanning my skin around the plain gold band I'd chosen. Knowing that even if I removed my jewelry to go into the sea, the thin, pale strip of skin circling the second finger of my left hand would act as a clear indicator that I was married.

That I was loved.

"Stop thinking about him." Nell clicked open her seatbelt as the safety light went out, and signaled to the cabin crew for a drink. I smoothed out the creases in my floaty linen dress and it struck me I was wearing white. Miserably I fiddled with the neckline, not embroidered with tiny pearls that shimmered from cream to lilac to pink under the lights, like the dress I had picked out. It was hard not to cry again remembering the perfectness of that day. Mum covering her mouth with both hands when I glided out of the changing rooms and twirled in front of the many mirrors. Everywhere I looked I had beamed back at myself.

"That's the one," Mum had whispered like we were in a church, not a bridal shop, but I didn't need her to tell me that. I knew it was the one.

It was such a shame *he* wasn't the one.

"It won't always hurt this much," Nell said; not that she'd know. She was usually the one breaking hearts; hers was still intact. "You've had a lucky escape. He wasn't good enough for you. Besides, twenty-four is too young to be married. This isn't the 1950s."

"If it were the 1950s, I'd have been married years ago and popped out a couple of kids by now." My throat swelled at the thought. I might have been young but I couldn't wait to be a mother. Would I ever have children? I'd thought my future was mapped out, but now all I had was doubts and fears and a mountain of wedding gifts to return.

"I can't see you slicking on lipstick and tying a ribbon in your hair five minutes before your husband gets home. And that's after a day cleaning windows with vinegar and beating carpets."

"I know who I'd like to beat," I muttered darkly.

"I'll drink to that." She flashed a smile. "And from now on, the only vinegar will be on the chips he told you that you shouldn't eat."

"He was worried about my health."

"Bollocks was he. He was worried you'd realize you're a normal-sized, goddess of a woman and leave him for somebody who didn't keep calling you chubby. Anyway, let's not give him a second thought. I'm ready to get this party started—"

"Nell—"

"I know, I know." She caught sight of my expression. "This isn't what you wanted. I'm not the one who should be here and you've no chance of joining the mile-high club now—"

"Nell—"

"But. You can either spend the next ten days crying by the pool or try and make the best of it. I know you loved him, Anna—"

"Nell Stevens." Her concerned eyes met mine and I knew she was worried she'd pushed it too far. "I just want to say...thank you. Not just for persuading me to come but...for all of it." Nell had dropped everything when I had called her at work, sobbing uncontrollably two weeks before my big day. She had kept me stocked up on vodka and ice cream while she phoned around the guests, explaining it was me who had had a change of heart. It was Nell who had talked me out of confronting Sonia Skelton when the rumors about her and my fiancé surfaced, and her who confiscated my phone at night so I couldn't drunk-text the cheating scumbag at 3 a.m. She allowed me to retain some dignity, on the outside at least. Humiliation still stung each time I thought of him, and I thought of him often, but oddly my feelings around him were tangled in a mass of embarrassment and regret, underpinned with a slow, simmering anger. I'd wasted three years of my life. Honestly, I wasn't sure it was him I actually missed or the idea of him. If you have to ask yourself "is it love," it probably isn't, is it?

Our foreheads touched and again her fingers entwined with mine. There was no need for words until our drinks were delivered. Nell dived on the miniature bottles with a "woo hoo."

"You've a lot to be grateful for." She unscrewed the gin and fizzed tonic into my glass.

"Alcohol?"

"That goes without saying. But the travel agent didn't have to let you change the name on the ticket. Now you've got someone to rub sun cream on your back without expecting to get laid, and someone to hold your hair back when too much Sex on the Beach makes you sick."

"I'm not going to have sex on the beach or anywhere else... Oh." I realized she was talking about the cocktail.

"You never know. We might meet two nice boys."

"No boys." I swigged my drink, bubbles tickling my nose. "No boys ever again."

I raised my glass, arm hovering in the air until she raised hers.

"This will be the adventure of a lifetime," she said, and we clinked. She turned out to be right.

But rather than flying away from something, I was flying toward something.

Toward him. To Adam.

I just didn't know it then.

*

By the time the coach dropped us off at our hotel on the Spanish island of Alircia, it was nearly midnight but I still called Mum to let her know I'd arrived; she'd only worry otherwise.

"We're here." I tried to keep the sadness out of my voice but Mum heard it anyway.

"It'll get easier, Anna," she said, but I knew being alone hadn't got easier for her. "Better with no one than the wrong one."

"I know." I *did* know. I'd accepted his proposal for myriad reasons: because of what I'd been through, was yet to go through, but none of them the right reason. The only reason.

Love.

I told Mum I'd speak to her soon. Nell and me hovered near the pots of exotic plants and flowers, waiting for the driver to empty the luggage hold; Nell plucked a bright pink bougainvillea and tucked it into my hair.

"It's so beautiful here," she exclaimed, but I barely registered the fairy lights twisted around the thick trunks of the palm trees that circled the pool. We wheeled our suitcases toward reception to check in. I was hot and exhausted. The gin I'd drunk earlier had left a residue on my tongue. A throbbing in my temples.

"Check this out!" Nell, typically, had abandoned her luggage and was sauntering into the bar. "Nightcap?"

"I'm shattered." I was struggling with her case and mine. "I just want a shower and my bed."

"Spoilsport." She said it lightly but I felt a pang of guilt. I knew she'd used all her annual leave this year and had taken this time off unpaid to support me. The least I could do was let her have a drink.

"I suppose because it's all-inclusive it would be rude not to," I said.

I stayed with our things, stifling a yawn and hoping Nell would order us shots as she sashayed to the bar. Instead of something we could knock back quickly, she returned with two glasses brimming with orange liquid and stuffed with pink parasols, cocktail sticks spearing glacé cherries.

"I asked for something fun," she shouted over Madonna, who was "True Blue." What was it with Spain and their fascination with English Eighties music?

I took a sip. "Jesus. We'll sleep well after these."

"You think? I can only taste the orange. You're such a light-weight. Hey, one o'clock."

"God, is it? No wonder I'm so tired."

"No. Look. At one o'clock." Nell jerked her head to her left. "He's checking you out." I couldn't help but look and when I did, I felt…I don't know, a sense of déjà vu. Familiarity. He was tall, dark and awkward, sipping beer from a plastic cup, and alone. He seemed to be alone. He caught my eye and smiled. I turned away.

"No boys, remember?" I said to Nell.

"I've you listed as being on your honeymoon?" the young receptionist with jet-black hair and bright white teeth asked.

"Yes." Nell peered at his name tag. "Miguel." She draped an arm around my shoulders. "If we could have our key. My wife and I are eager to go to bed."

Pretending we were married was preferable to going into why I wasn't and Nell knew I did have that terribly British urge to constantly explain myself, but the emotions that surfaced when I heard myself described as someone's wife zapped the last of my energy. All of a sudden it all caught up with me. The journey, the alcohol, my lack of sleep. My vision darkened and my ears began to buzz. Wishing I could sit, I rested my head on Nell's shoulder, lulled by the tap-tap-tap of Miguel's keyboard as he checked us in, words drifting in and out of reach...*breakfast*... *sun loungers...excursions.*

"Let's go, darling." Nell dropped a kiss atop of my head. Simultaneously I straightened my neck and wiped my mouth for traces of drool before I thanked Miguel and forced my feet to move. I could feel eyes burning into my back as we headed outside where the air was still warm and chirruping crickets welcomed us to their island.

The music grew fainter as we searched for our accommodation, using the scant light from the screens of our phones to make out the numbers on the whitewashed walls. Inflatable swans and flamingos rested on balconies, a signpost to the apartments with kids in them. Towels and swimwear dangled from retractable washing lines.

Stars speckled the sky and through the blackness, to our right, the sound of the waves lapping against an unseen shore. The warm air smelled of the beach.

"This is us," Nell said. She unlocked the door and flicked on the lights. "Oh God. I'm sorry, Anna."

I pushed past her, wanting to see what she saw. A "Just Married" banner was strung across the lounge, rose petals scattered on the floor. On the coffee table, a bottle of champagne and two flutes.

I was a bride without her husband. I began to cry.

"Excuse me," a voice behind me said and I spun around, wiping my eyes.

It was the boy from the bar.

Adam. It was Adam.

CHAPTER TWO

Adam

It was four days into the holiday and if I'm honest I was feeling pretty lonely. Josh had met a girl on day one and was spending much of his time massaging sun cream into her curves. She had a friend who smiled hopefully each time I caught her eye. She seemed nice enough, but holiday romances weren't really my bag.

"She's offering it on a plate," Josh had said.

But I needed some sort of connection. It all seemed so shallow otherwise.

"Worse than a bloody woman." Josh checked his pocket for condoms again. As agreed, I vacated the room, heading toward the bar. I'd hardly spent any time with Josh since we arrived—this was supposed to be our last mates' holiday before I launched myself into my new life—but I didn't mind. Generally, I liked my own company.

I was bored now though. I took another swig of beer—my fifth pint. It may be free but I had to drink twice as much as I did at home to get a slight buzz. The music was loud but that was okay, I didn't have anyone to talk to; besides, I was a bit of a sucker for the Eighties—another thing Josh ribbed me about.

If we'd met as adults I sometimes wondered if we'd have been friends at all, but Josh had been there for me during that awful time nine years ago and I don't know who I'd be without him. Where I'd be. Despite his "don't give a shit" exterior, he was steadfast in his loyalty and like a brother to me, albeit sometimes an annoying brother. I was wondering whether to call it a night, whether he'd finished hogging our apartment, when I saw her.

You know sometimes all the light in a room seems to attach to one person and they shine brighter than anyone else? That was her. Everything blurred into the background. I took in the cascade of thick, dark ringlets falling over her shoulders. Bright pink flower tucked behind her ear. Pale floaty dress skimming her ankles. She looked exactly like Star from *The Lost Boys*, one of my all-time favorite films.

Star.

And how she shimmered. My chest tightened. I waited to see who she was with, shoulders sagging with relief when I saw it was another girl.

Not that that meant she was necessarily single.

Not that I was looking, after my disastrous relationship with Roxanne had only finished a few months ago.

But still.

She sipped from a glass almost as large as a fish bowl, crammed full of cocktail umbrellas and fruit on sticks. She had a sense of humor then.

I smiled at her. She turned away but that was okay. I still had ten days left to get to know her.

And I somehow I just knew that I would.

*

The crowd had thinned by the time she left. The entertainment finished. The bar felt even emptier without her. Colder. Scrunching up my plastic cup, I tossed it into the recycling bin as I left. She was standing in reception with her friend, their backs to me, checking in. It suddenly seemed vital that I asked what time I needed to vacate my room in ten days, so I hovered behind her and yeah, I admit it, I breathed in deeply. Even then I was in rapture. Two words pulled me back to reality.

Honeymoon suite?

"If we could have our key. My wife and I are eager to go to bed," the one with short blonde hair said. Star rested her head on her wife's shoulder and I felt my own shoulders slump. The flower slid out of her hair, fluttering unnoticed onto the floor and I couldn't help scooping it up. When she left reception, I watched her go. It felt she was taking a piece of me with her.

Yeah, I know how *that* sounds. Did I mention that I was an incurable romantic?

I felt Miguel's eyes on me while I clutched the flower sorrowfully between my fingers.

Or an incurable loser.

I wasn't exactly following her, I promise. I was many things back then but a stalker wasn't one of them. As luck would have it, her apartment was pretty much opposite mine and Josh's. Identical, except ours had the giant pink inflatable flamingo Josh had bought on the first day, almost blocking our front door. I was still holding her flower and I wanted to give it back to her. I knew she had a wife, but I hoped that we could be friends. I couldn't quite put my finger on what it was about her I found so interesting but there was . . . something.

"Excuse me," I called, approaching her. It wasn't until she turned that I realized she was crying. My eyes flickered toward the "Just Married" banner hanging in their room, the champagne bottle on the table, before resting back on hers again.

"Sorry…" I was painfully embarrassed I'd interrupted such an emotional moment. What a dick move. The happiest day of her life and some weirdo was holding out a flower while idiotically standing in front of a bush sprouting at least thirty identical magenta blooms. "You dropped this."

She turned and ran inside while her friend—her wife—gave me a look so withering I expected the plants to shrivel and die. I pretty much wanted to join them.

I sloped back to my own apartment. Inside, a red lacy bra was draped over the sofa and there were noises coming from the bedroom I definitely didn't want to be hearing. My head was pounding. I swiped a bottle of water from the fridge and headed straight back out. Through the window of Star's apartment, I could see the girls shadowed in the lamplight, hugging each other tightly. Something tugged at my heart. It wasn't long ago that I'd held Roxanne in my arms but better empty arms than the wrong person in them. Besides, Roxanne was in somebody else's arms now. Somebody else's bed.

Bypassing the beach all the tourists use, I strode purposefully until I reached a tiny cove I'd stumbled across the first evening Josh had been "entertaining." It wasn't too far but unreachable by road, and without parking, toilets and refreshments, hardly anyone came here. It was my favorite place.

I settled on the damp sand, the night breeze springing goose-flesh on my arms. I wished I had someone to share warmth with and not in the way Josh was doing back at the apartment.

Something proper.

Instead of a bottle of champagne for two, I sipped from my lonely bottle of Evian for one, gazing at the creamy moon. A shooting star lit up the sky. I made a wish that I could talk properly to the girl who was already occupying too much head space.

Yeah, I was an incurable dreamer.

The next day my wish did come true, but the circumstances were awful.

Bloody awful.

CHAPTER THREE

Anna

On the first day of my honeymoon, I woke to darkness after a fitful sleep. Immediately I remembered that I hadn't got married yesterday—the pain of being dumped two weeks before my wedding day. That it was Nell lying beside me in the creaky bed that rocked each time once of us moved. It was her floral perfume, rather than the smell of sex, clinging to the stiff, white sheets. Checking my phone screen, I was surprised to see it was gone eight. Automatically I opened Facebook. Wondering if my ex was regretting his decision. It was torturous visiting his profile page, but I couldn't seem to help it. Multiple times a day.

"Unfriend the tosser," Nell had said, but it was an addiction. A wound that would never heal because I was always picking at the scab, despite knowing that what lay underneath was raw and painful, and would hurt all over again.

He'd been tagged yesterday by Sonia in a photo of the two of them sprawled out on a picnic blanket. Rather than standing at the altar, ready to love me for better or worse, he'd chosen to sit in a field. Sandwiches and crisps formed an oval around a giant chocolate cake. I wondered how long it would be until he told her she should lay off the sweet stuff. Pinch her waist and sigh she's getting chubby. I studied the picture. She had to be a size twelve—the same as me. I'd thought after all his barbed comments that it was my body that turned him off; it was almost worse seeing he'd gone for somebody the same shape as me. To know that it wasn't the outer me he didn't want, the thing I could change, but the inner me. The essence of who I was wasn't enough for him. I wasn't enough for him.

Best day ever!! Sonia had captioned her post. He had liked her comment but hadn't written a reply. Had it really been his best day ever? Better than the day he proposed? That was over a picnic too. His signature move. Suddenly it all seemed so calculated. A message that I'm easily replaceable. Easily forgettable.

Bastard.

"Charming," Nell muttered.

"Sorry, I hadn't realized I'd said that out loud. You're awake then?"

"God knows why. It's the middle of the bloody night."

"It's quarter past eight."

"Same thing."

Bright sunlight burst into the room when I opened the shutters. Nell shrieked and yanked the duvet over her head. I had to blink several times before I could make out the clear blue sky.

"It's going to be scorching," I said.

"Too right." Nell's words were muffled. "And that's just me in my bikini."

The all-inclusive morning buffet was ridiculous. Nell and I had piled our plates with crispy bacon, thick maple syrup, waffles, eggs with runny yolks, crusty bread and sachets of orange marmalade, reassuring each other that we'd swim off the calories. Not that I could swim properly but walking in water was toning. Also there was a gym here. Yoga classes. Beach volleyball. I was going to be all kinds of active.

By midday I'd been star-fished on my towel for two hours. My dog-eared copy of *Jane Eyre* lay unopened next to me. I'd been intending to reread it this week before my students began it next year, but for once I had switched off from work, from home. From everything. The sand molded to my shape, cradling me in its warmth. The tender skin around my chest was beginning to sting. It took a gargantuan effort to lever myself onto my elbows. Nell was shrieking in the ocean. Jumping over crystal waves. Screeching at a boy named Josh to stop splashing her.

I became aware of eyes on me. Making a pantomime of adjusting my hat, tucking my hair in, I twisted my head left to right until I saw him. It was the boy from the bar. I prickled with embarrassment, recalling how I'd run away in tears last night when he had tried to give me back my flower. Instinctively, I sucked in my stomach while covering my pasty sausage legs with my towel. When I'd first suggested booking Alircia for a honeymoon, the idiot I had almost married told me I needed to lose at least a stone if I wanted to look half decent in the one-piece swimsuits he always said suited me better than bikinis.

I had tried.

Picking at salad while he tucked into steak and chips; sitting in the cinema, my lap empty, while he balanced a giant tub of buttery popcorn, the smell making me salivate. After I'd been dumped though, I'd stuffed myself with ice cream to cool my humiliation and I'd probably put on those few pounds I'd lost, and more. It hadn't seemed important what I weighed. But now it did. Was the boy from the bar wondering why I was the only girl on the beach in a one-piece? Imagining that my body underneath was covered in boils? From behind the safety of my sunglasses, I stole another glance in his direction. Rather than staring at me with horror or disgust or even amusement, he wore an expression of something else. Admiration? Interest? There was no way I was up for a holiday romance, but still it gave me hope that my bruised and battered self-confidence might one day heal. I couldn't remember the last time anyone had looked at me like that. The last time anyone had looked at me properly at all.

It hit me that my fiancé had long stopped loving me, if he ever had, and for the first time I felt I might have had a lucky escape.

With a start, I realized that I was staring and he knew that I was looking at him. I felt a gentle creep of heat that had nothing to do with the sun. A pull of attraction as he held me in his gaze. Wanting to wash away the sticky sun cream, the sand clinging to my skin, all the feelings I didn't want to be feeling, I raced into the sea, thundering past Nell until my thighs were covered by the water, my bottom, my hips. The roll around my stomach that never seemed to disappear no matter how many crunches I did. Cringing at the cellulite speckling the back of my legs. Feeling horribly conspicuous in my black swimming costume amongst a plethora of neon bikinis.

Despite its perfect blue, the sea was colder than I had expected. I sucked in my breath, tasting the droplets of salty water that splashed my lips. Counting to three in my head, I plunged under the waves, slicking my hair back over my scalp when I surfaced. Bouncing on my toes, adjusting to my lower body feeling cool, the sun heating my shoulders and face. Around my legs weaved fish, larger than I had ever seen. Their silvery scales catching the light, casting mini rainbows above the waves. I trailed my hands through the water as I walked, smiling with delight as a fish brushed against my fingertips. Tomorrow, I decided I'd buy a snorkel. I could stay in the shallows and feed the fish. Not with bread—I didn't want to make them ill—but I'd bring some vegetables back from breakfast.

I strode forward. Once. Twice. Stopping to let the ripples around me settle. Watching a shoal of bream pass by, I moved once more. Suddenly there was a tugging sensation, my legs knocked from under me. At first I was confused, thinking it was someone playing a trick on me. I glanced around, realizing how far from the shore I had strayed. Panic rose. I was out of my depth. I tried to step toward the beach, using my hands to scoop back the water and give my legs momentum, but I was marching on the spot. Nell almost a pinprick on her towel. Unable to hear me shouting her name. I flapped my arms in the air. A wave knocked me off my feet. Water flooding my mouth. I was choking. Spluttering. Coming up for air and sinking once more.

"Help!" I screamed now. My voice minute against the vastness of the ocean that held me in its grip.

The current dragged me back once more. I was treading water now. Tiring. My body exhausted with the effort of trying to reach dry land. My eyes stinging with salt. With tears. My throat sore from both screaming and the salt water I had gulped.

It can only have been minutes but it felt like hours, my limbs heavy with exhaustion. The ocean bed sucking me down.

I felt myself slip under. Spiral down. Down. The clear water growing murky. For a split second I let my body go limp. Giving up. My lips parted. Water streamed down my throat. My lungs burning as they gasped for air. Unbidden, my feet gave adrenaline-fueled kicks, my arms windmilling with panic. My head burst out of the water. My whole body thrashing like a fish on a line, panic contracting each and every cell. I'd been swept even further from the beach. Why weren't there any lifeguards here? Why wasn't anybody helping me?

I was crying now. Fear causing me to shiver despite the sun. I raised my hand. My body dropping like a stone. My fingers grasping at nothing, fruitlessly trying to find something to grip on to.

But there was nothing to help me.

I plunged beneath the surface once more.

My energy drained, the fight ebbing away from me.

CHAPTER FOUR

Adam

There was something so confident about her. The way she wore a swimming costume rather than a bikini. Not caring about fitting in. Not trying to look like everyone else. Her body was curvy in all the right places. The way she covered up, rather than putting it all out on display, made her appear almost other-worldly. The word "chaste" sprung to mind and I chided myself for my outdated idealism. Romanticizing everything when I got the chance. She determinedly strode into the water, not dipping a toe in and shrieking it was cold like the other girls. Her self-assurance was captivating. It might have been daylight, but she still shone like a star. My mouth couldn't help smiling along with hers. I couldn't see what she was watching so intently, probably the fish.

There was a shriek.

The blonde—Star's wife—frolicking in the waves with Josh. He probably thought she was flirting with him.

Sucker.

My eyes flickered back to Star. She was bobbing up and down. Tiny in the huge expanse of ocean but in no way insignificant.

Josh and the blonde ran out of the sea and flopped down onto towels, deep in conversation. Again, I gazed out to sea, shielding my eyes when I couldn't immediately see her. She resurfaced. Her hands waved. I thought at first she was beckoning to the blonde, wanting her to go back into the water, but then she slipped underwater again, and I wasn't so sure. Worry drew me to my feet. Something was wrong. I knew it. She disappeared from view again. Her arms flailing as she fought to break free of the current, which now I realized had her in its grip. It was strong here, I knew from experience, but she should have been able to swim through it.

Why wasn't she swimming?

The ocean sucked her down once more, her body, her head, her tightly clenched hands. I ripped off my T-shirt, kicked off my flip-flops and pelted into the sea. Once I was knee-deep I threw myself forward, the water slapping against my stomach, my arms slicing through the water. It could only have taken several seconds to reach her but it felt like forever. Her head was barely above water, panic in her eyes.

"Just relax." I linked my arms around her waist. "I've got you." Her body thrashed wildly, heels jabbing into my shins. She didn't speak. She was whimpering like a frightened puppy. "Let your body go limp or you'll drag us both under." She couldn't weigh much, but I was struggling to stay afloat. She tried her best to stop moving but her muscles were rigid. It was like trying to save an ironing board, stiff and unyielding. I tried to maneuver her head onto my shoulder. "Relax." This was nothing like rescuing a mate in a swimming pool for my silver badge. I was sweating despite the water. I began kicking toward the shore, her slumped against my chest, her head leaning back on my shoulder. "I've got you," I said again. It was then I realized I never wanted to let her go.

In the shallows we stumbled to our feet, our arms around each other. I wasn't sure who was supporting who as we staggered onto dry sand. I was incredulous that conversation still buzzed, children still filled their buckets. Nobody had noticed that someone had almost drowned. My adrenaline was leeching from me, the memory of a few minutes ago hazy. But it had happened.

"Are you okay?"

She nodded but I knew she wasn't. She was shaking. I was shaking.

"Anna! I'm going to get some drinks with Josh. Be back in a bit," the blonde called loudly before she turned away.

Anna. She was called Anna. I wanted us to be alone but she needed comfort. Reassurance. I couldn't give that to her. I couldn't just watch the blonde leave, like a dick.

"Do you want me to tell your wife what happened?" I asked as her knees buckled and she sank onto her towel, still coughing.

"My wife? Why would you... Oh, last night." She gave a wry smile. "She's not my... I'm not..." She coughed again, rubbed her mouth with the back of her hand.

That mouth.

"It's hard to know how to explain," she said.

"I find it's best to start at the beginning, Anna?" I sat cross-legged next to her. "I'm Adam, by the way."

"I don't want to go into it all, but Nell's my best friend. We're not romantically... I'm not romantically..." She ran her fingers over the face of my watch. "I hope that's waterproof—it looks old?"

She was changing the subject. I wanted to know why she was on a honeymoon with her friend but I didn't want to push. She looked so pale and there was still a tremble in her fingers as she lifted them from my wrist.

"It'll be okay." I leaned back on my elbows, feeling the rough sand against my feet, the sun warming my skin, and hope. I felt hope.

"You twat," Josh would have said if he knew what I was thinking.

He wouldn't be far wrong.

"Thank you," Anna said quietly. We'd been sitting side by side, gazing out to sea for at least fifteen minutes—it was difficult to gauge the time; my watch wasn't waterproof and I wasn't hopeful it would ever work again. We were both lost in our own what-might-have-been thoughts. Our silence companionable rather than awkward. "You saved my life," she said.

"You'd have been okay." I sieved sand through my fingers. "How are you feeling?"

"Better. Embarrassed. I'm not a good swimmer."

"No shit!"

There was a split second when her expression hovered uncertainly before she burst into laughter. I found myself laughing too and when Josh returned with the drinks we were doubled over, my sides aching.

"What's so funny?" Josh asked, shadowed in the sun, but we couldn't tell him. Couldn't explain it. For Anna it was probably the relief of her being alive. For me? It was the same.

"I'm Nell." The blonde handed Anna a plastic pint glass of beer before she sat, curving her legs under her.

"Adam." I took a sip from the glass Josh offered me. It was weak and warm.

"Are you as smooth as your friend here, Adam?" Nell asked.

"Sadly not. Josh has all the moves."

"So he thinks." Nell grinned.

"I think I might have met my match," Josh said.

Nell raised her eyebrows. "You *think*?"

"And you are?" Josh held a hand out to Anna.

"Anna." She took his hand and he raised hers to his lips, planted a kiss.

"A beautiful name for a beautiful woman."

Nell cupped her hands around her mouth. "Lock up your daughters—Casanova is in town."

Josh's eyes were all over Anna, undoubtedly unsavory thoughts running through his mind.

"Oi. Behave." I threw a kick in his direction. He glanced at me and I gave an almost indiscernible shake of my head and in return he gave an almost imperceptible nod. He turned his attention back to Nell. He may come across as a dick sometimes but, like I said, he was loyal to me. Always had my back.

While he asked Nell if she fancied another swim, I asked Anna if she wanted to go for a walk and I tried not to read too much into it when she said that she did.

We strolled barefoot across the beach, not getting too close to the rolling waves that frothed into foam. Jet Skis zoomed toward the shore and shot out to sea again as though they were attached to elastic. I felt the prickling heat of sunburn on the back of my neck, but I also felt something else. Comfortable. Something I'd never truly felt with Roxanne, with her constant obsession with her appearance. With my appearance. Making me change before a night out if what I was wearing didn't complement her outfit.

"Shall we head up there?" I pointed to a slope that led off the beach.

In unison, we turned. Our bodies were close as we strolled,

arms almost brushing. I could have stretched out my fingers and taken her hand, but I didn't.

We paused when we reached the path. Brushing the sand from our feet before slipping our flip-flops on. Hers were silver and sparkly. Mine were from Primark, white and plastic. Roxanne would have been horrified.

A row of kiosks selling postcards and buckets and spades provided a strip of shade and we stepped into it thankfully, welcoming the kiss of warmth rather than the beating heat.

A man approached us and thrust a clipboard under Anna's nose. Pushed a pen into her hand. He tapped twice on the sentence at the top of the form written in broken English. Some sort of petition to keep open a school for deaf children. Anna glanced at the man, confused. He placed his hands over his ears.

"You're deaf," Anna said.

He nodded. Moved a hand to cover his mouth.

"You can't talk?"

He shook his head.

Anna's expression was one of sadness. "I'm so sorry." She spoke slowly. Clearly, exaggerating each word with the movement of her lips. "What do you need?"

He twisted his fingers, signing things we didn't understand.

"I can't . . . I don't know sign language," Anna said.

The man tapped twice on the sentence again, this time with force. The clipboard bowing in Anna's hands. He slid his finger down to a blank space before pointing at Anna.

"You want me to sign my name?"

He nodded. His hands making circles as though there was more.

"My address?"

He nodded again. Tapped the paper too hard. He was getting my back up now. He might be deaf but that was no excuse to be rude and intimidating.

"You don't have to—" I began but Anna had begun scrawling out her details.

Anna Adlington.

"Good luck." She handed the clipboard back to him with a smile. She began to walk on but he put a hand against her shoulder, stopping her. He rubbed his fingers together, the universal sign for cold hard cash.

"Oh, you want money!" Anna's cheeks spotted pink. "I'm so sorry, I don't have my bag. Adam...do you..."

I did have my wallet but I wasn't giving anything to this tosser with his aggressive attitude. It was probably a scam.

"No, I don't." I took Anna's arm and went to walk away but the man blocked my path.

"Listen, mate." I straightened my spine. "We're not giving you any money, understand?"

The man began to shout, angry words, and despite the language barrier I could guess what he was saying.

"Back off." I held up my palm, shielding Anna with my other arm. We hurried away.

"He lied," she said quietly. "You really can't trust anyone." I could hear the crack in her voice as she spoke and I knew she was thinking of whoever had hurt her, just as I was thinking of Roxanne.

"I'd better get back to Nell." She wouldn't meet my eye and began to hurry away.

"Anna." I hesitated as she paused. Unsure what I wanted to say. That not all men are bastards. That I'd never hurt her. Lie to her. That rejection was raw for me as well, that I understood; finding

Roxanne in bed with her boss, her legs wrapped around his waist while a band of pain tightened around my heart. There was so much I wanted to say but I didn't say any of it. Instead, I asked, "I'd very much like to have dinner later. With you, I mean. You and me having dinner together. What do you think?"

It was crazy to ask. A holiday romance wasn't on the agenda. A quick fling wasn't my style and I had plans for after this fortnight. A new life waiting that wouldn't accommodate a relationship. But still, in that moment we felt all kinds of right for each other. I didn't know then that we were all kinds of wrong for each other.

I didn't know, while I waited for her answer, that I should, perhaps, have walked away.

CHAPTER FIVE

Anna

"No, I can't have dinner with you," I had said when Adam first asked me out. But as he turned away, I caught both his "sorry" and the sight of the pink tinge of sunburn on the back of his neck and he seemed vulnerable somehow. Not brash like his friend Josh. There was no way I was looking for a holiday romance but I felt mean. Ungrateful. He had, after all, saved my life. Stepped in front of the not-deaf deaf guy when he was beginning to scare me.

"Adam, wait!" I had called. "Yes. Yes, I'll have dinner with you."

It was just one meal to say thank you. Nothing more.

We opted to sit on the terrace just in time to see the last glow of sunlight slipping behind the ocean. Fairy lights spiraled around the pergola. Candles flickered on every table. The beach was swallowed by night but we could still hear the gentle lap of waves. Taste the salt carried by the warm breeze. It was relentlessly romantic right down to the musician perched on a high stool, gently strumming on a guitar. Honeymoon-perfect, except a virtual stranger was the one topping up my glass.

Except, despite only knowing him for a few hours, Adam didn't quite feel like a stranger.

This is not a date.

I had been studying the menu for far too long, my stomach fluttering with nerves. It was natural I'd feel on edge; I'd almost drowned earlier, but each time I raised my eyes and caught sight of Adam I felt... something.

"Are you ready to order?" The waiter hovered around our table for the third time, pad and pen poised.

"I'll have a crab salad, please." I can't remember the last time I ordered anything other than salad on a date.

"You're getting a bit porky, Anna. Think of our wedding photos."

Except this... this wasn't a date and the restaurant smelled so delicious—garlic and oil and herbs. Did I really want a plate of leaves? If I *had* died today, I wanted to have lived my life. Loved my life. I wanted to be remembered for being kind and happy and fun. Not the girl who never let herself go because she was trying to lose the same ten pounds over and over again.

"Sorry, can I change my mind?" I quickly scanned the menu again. "I'll have a paella with a side order of tomatoes stuffed with feta and spicy chorizo, and could I please have some bread and olives while I wait?" I lowered the menu, my shoulders stiff with the expectation of disapproval on Adam's face but instead he smiled.

"That sounds great. I'll have the same, please."

We both watched the waiter until he disappeared back inside.

My mouth was dry. I picked up my glass and took a long drink of sangria, watching the other diners. The couple staring so deeply into each other's eyes that they probably didn't register the clink of cutlery on china, the low murmur of conversation. The elderly lady eating alone, a paperback propped up against a jug of water, eyes straining to read by candlelight. A widow? A family of at least three generations seated at a long table across the terrace. A "Happy Golden Anniversary" balloon tugging against its string.

What did these people see when they looked at me? A girl whose fiancé hadn't been able to bear spending another single day with her, let alone a lifetime? A girl having a holiday romance? The start of something?

This is not a date.

"So." Adam's voice led me back to the present.

"Sorry, I was miles away." I took another drink. Put down my glass and fiddled with the edge of my napkin. Why was I so nervous?

"Don't judge me, Anna, but…" Adam took a deep breath. "I've already chosen my dessert."

I laughed. "Me too. Limoncello and plum tart."

"Snap. I knew there was a reason why I like you. Not like *like*," he added quickly. "Not…" Now he played with his napkin.

"To friendship?" I raised my glass and we toasted, but our eyes met and an unspoken toast passed between us, to the future versions of ourselves and even then, on some level, I knew that in the days to come, weeks, months, years, our lives would be bound together.

"Tell me about yourself, Anna Adlington."

The arrival of a platter of bread and dips gave me time to think. What did I want him to know? Everything and nothing.

"I'm an English teacher."

"Primary?"

"Secondary."

"You like a challenge then?"

I met his gaze. Is that how he saw me? Fearless? Brave?

"I do like a challenge." Did I? Was I flirting? I carried on. "My dad is a teacher. *Was*. Was a teacher."

Adam studied me. He could have assumed my dad had changed professions or retired, but somehow he just *knew*.

"I'm so sorry, Anna. Do you want to talk about him?"

One thing I've learned is that grief makes people uncomfortable. Loss is a subject to be changed, skimmed over in case death is catching. Nobody wants to think about it. Talk about it. Question their own mortality. Yet Adam had covered my hand with his and was unflinching in his gaze. I knew he was seeing more of me than anyone else here could.

"Thanks, but no." I drew my hand away but I could still feel the warmth of his skin. I coiled my fingers around the cool stem of my glass when all I really wanted to do was to thread them through Adam's.

"Anna," he said softly. "I—"

"For you, señorita." The waiter placed a steaming plate of paella in front of me. "Señor."

The tension broken, I picked up my fork. "I love this Mediterranean food so much."

"Me too." Adam speared a prawn. "Josh's parents took us to Barcelona for a week after we'd passed our A Levels and when we got home I made paella."

"Was it good?"

"I didn't realize rice expands so I chucked in the whole packet—not just any packet, a huge one from a cash and carry. I was eating the bloody thing for about a week but by then the seafood had gone off and... It wasn't pretty, let's just say."

I laughed. "It hasn't put you off eating it though?"

"Nothing would put me off my food. What's your favorite thing to eat?"

"Ice cream. You?"

"Pringles. Once you pop."

It was easy to talk about the inconsequential, ignoring the spark between us. I wasn't sure if Adam could feel it too. He told me when he was growing up, he was obsessed with Eighties music and films.

"I loved *Back to the Future* with Michael J. Fox," I said. "Was that the Eighties?"

"Yep. Everyone loves Marty." Unabashed, Adam began to sing "The Power of Love" from the movie. I joined in the chorus, knowing that everyone here was a stranger, probably never to be seen again.

"So I know where you'd go if you could travel in time. Or what era anyway. The Eighties in . . ." I appraised him. "America? Hollywood?"

"Because I have film-star good looks?" Adam smoothed back his hair.

"I was thinking more about you seeing where they made movies rather than starring in them," I laughed.

"No offense taken." Adam pretended to dab a tear with his napkin. "I'd like to see America. I'd like to see all the places I sell tickets to." He caught my expression. "I'm a travel agent."

"That sounds interesting."

"It's a means to an end. I've been saving to see the world and working there has meant I can plan it all out properly, and get a staff discount. I leave next month."

I fixed my smile in place. There was no reason for me to be disappointed. It's not like I'd see him again after this holiday, but melancholy settled heavily in my stomach once I knew that we wouldn't even be in the same country.

I stretched my mouth into a smile. "Where are you going?"

"Thailand, Italy, China. India. Everywhere. I want to see it all. Everything. I'm a frustrated Christopher Columbus. Tell me something about you, Anna Adlington."

"I can play flute up to Grade 4." I watched his face for his reaction. "You look underwhelmed. Okay, you'll be blown away by this one."

Adam drummed the table with his fingertips.

"I know the offside rule," I said triumphantly.

"I am impressed!"

I knew he would be; he'd mentioned he loved football. We continued chatting about the superficial. The things that are easy to share. But even then there was something more to us. Something deeper. An affinity I was trying so hard to ignore. My rational mind kept pointing out that he was leaving in a month.

This is not a date.

"I want to show you something," Adam said after we'd split the bill. We left the restaurant and headed away from our resort past various bars. Vendors attempting to entice us inside with promises of half-price pitchers and cheap cocktails.

"Come, come. Photo. Photo." A man ushered us over to a lonely parrot perched inside a cage too small for him to spread his wings. A cage whose stench made my stomach roil. "You pay. I take picture."

"No." How could anyone use an animal this way? The bird had half of his red and green feathers missing. A chain around his ankle. He looked so miserable.

"I'll have a photo taken," Adam said.

I watched silently. Judgmentally. I had thought Adam was kind. The man placed the bird on Adam's arm and retreated, raising the camera in front of his face.

It was so quick. I barely registered what Adam was doing as his fingers worked at the chain around the bird's ankles. There was a flapping of wings and a happy squawk as the bird rose into the darkening sky.

Adam grabbed my hand and we ran—the photographer's angry voice chasing us.

A stitch burned in my side by the time Adam led me down a narrow walkway where I could have stretched out my hands and touched either of the whitewashed buildings that flanked us. At the end, there was a cove guarded by a chain fence. A smattering of padlocks clamped to the links.

"Love locks!" I rushed forward, delighted, tilting the padlocks toward the moon to read the names, the initials, the declarations of undying love. It felt good that, despite being dumped, there was still a small ember smoldering inside of me that believed in romance.

Adam strolled onto the beach and by the time I reached him, he'd shrugged off the shirt that had hung open over a T-shirt. He spread it over the sand before gesturing for me to sit. I slipped off my sandals and dug my toes into the damp sand. For a while we sat, listening to the crash of the waves rolling inland until we had caught our breath.

"That was amazing," I said when the burning in my chest had subsided.

"Maybe not," Adam said. "The bird is used to being given food and water. Being chained up. There's a chance he might not survive in the wild but I reckon he'd prefer to take his chances than spend the rest of his days in that small filthy cage. Besides, he can always come back if he wants. If you love someone, set them free and all that."

I found it impossible to let things go; I was still checking my ex's Facebook umpteen times a day. Once, when I was younger, I had a cat named Pugwash. He grew old. Sick. When I was sixteen, my mum told me that the kindest thing to do would be to put him to sleep but I shouted and I cried and I wouldn't agree to it. For days afterward I watched with shame as Pugwash limped around the house he'd once raced around with ease. My guilty ears listened to his sad mewing as he failed to make the jump onto the windowsill where he liked to watch the traffic. I knew it was best for him. I *knew*. And yet I still couldn't envisage life without him. At the end of that week I came home from school and found Mum had made the decision for me. Letting him go when she knew I wouldn't. Knew I couldn't.

"So you're a regular hero," I said. "Saving women from drowning. Rescuing birds."

"Oh, I'm far from perfect," Adam said. "I leave the toilet seat up. Toast crumbs all over the worktop. I dip the butter knife into the Marmite."

"Urrgh, Marmite. You're right. You're not perfect."

Our laughter died away and there was a change in the atmosphere as Adam asked, "So, Anna Adlington, who has made me laugh more tonight than I have in months, who are you, really?"

I didn't know how to answer that. Who was I?

"I...I don't know anymore." As a wife I would have been someone. But now self-doubt and self-loathing had filled the space where my confidence used to be. I felt the constriction in my throat as my words thinned to nothing. Adam gave me a moment to compose myself before he quietly said, "I didn't meant to upset you."

"*You* didn't." I gave a hollow laugh. Part of me wanted to tell him everything, but the sting of being jilted was too sharp. Too raw. And there was a part of me, a bigger part, that still felt it was all my fault and I was scared to admit that to him. Afraid that if he saw the unlovable part of me that I was trying to keep hidden—the part that made it easy to cast me adrift—he would run away too.

"He's a fool. Whoever let you go." He read my silence.

"If by 'let me go' you mean dumped me two weeks before my wedding, so I had to come on my honeymoon with my best friend, who pretended to be my wife to save me the embarrassment of explaining it all to the hotel…Anyway, you said if you loved someone—"

"Did he love you?"

"No." I wrapped my arms around myself, forming a physical barrier to keep all my emotions inside.

I was unlovable.

"Did you love him?" Adam's probing questions were soft and rounded rather than pointed and sharp. It didn't take long to consider my answer.

"He was there during a difficult time. My dad…his heart…"

Adam gently placed his hand on my arm. He didn't tell me I didn't have to talk about my dad the way most people did, hoping I'd change the subject, uncomfortable with my raw emotion, avoiding eye contact and shifting away.

"I felt I needed him after that and…I think…partly… I wanted to be married. To have the security my parents had, to have someone look at me the way my dad looked at my mum. I think I knew on some level when he proposed that he didn't love me, but I figured I'd never love anyone as much as I loved my dad anyway so...I was still grieving...am *still* grieving. It's been nearly two years now." I hadn't wanted to talk about it but now I couldn't shut up.

"And how's your mum?" he asked with genuine concern.

"She's...okay-ish. It's been tough but she's filling her time. This is the first time I've been away from her since we lost him. I'm ringing home every day. She misses me. She misses him."

"They're lucky, those who find it. That eternal love."

"Can love ever be eternal?" Despite the example my parents had set, I was doubtful I would ever find that.

"I think so. Yes. Why shouldn't you have absolute faith that you can achieve your dreams? Reach for the stars."

"Is that another Eighties song reference?" I nudged him to show I was done talking about the sad things.

"Nineties." He flashed a grin, teeth white under moonlight. "Speaking of the Eighties, I nicknamed you Star when I first saw you."

"Why?"

"Because you look like Star from *The Lost Boys*."

"Not because I sparkled so bright." I placed my hands against my cheeks and flashed a Marilyn Monroe smile.

"That too."

The atmosphere turned from heavy to light and back again. I was dizzy with it all. Confused with my conflicting emotions. My rational self was telling me that it was the beauty of our surroundings, the lack of everyday stress, and a multitude of other things that weren't Adam causing this tornado of longing.

My heart whispering that this was it. This was the way I should have felt when I agreed to marry someone, only I hadn't felt it. Not then.

A breeze lifted strands of my hair and Adam tucked them behind my ear.

"Star." The word melodic on his lips.

This is not a date.

I could have moved away, but I didn't. Adam leaned forward and hesitated. Waiting for me to tell him to stop. To slow down. To speed up. But my objections, my desire, my logic and my desperate need to be touched were stuck in my throat.

His mouth feathered across mine and the world fell away. He tasted of sangria and kindness, and long after our kiss had ended, I kept my eyes closed to savor it. For one perfect moment I released my thoughts that whispered this was only temporary. That soon I'd have to let him go. That one day this would be packed away tightly in the memory box labeled "holiday romance"— transient and meaningless.

Already, I didn't want to be without him.

CHAPTER SIX

Adam

Our time together had been a whirlwind. Since that first night on the beach when I'd kissed Anna, we had been inseparable. Josh and Nell were happy for us; they'd formed a friendship of their own so I was living out my very own romcom. We'd done all the touristy things: visited the volcano, the lava tunnel, the underground lake. We'd strolled hand in hand around the markets. We'd watched the sun rise and set. We'd talked about anything and everything, everything except the future. But more important than any of that, we'd laughed. Proper belly laughs that made my stomach muscles ache.

Every evening we'd eat together before retreating to the cove, where we would lie on the sand, always touching. I loved that she was so tactile. Now, her leg was slung across mine, her fingers playing with the buttons on my shirt, her head on my shoulder. I told her about Roxanne. About the itch to travel the way my parents always had. Stories of when Josh and I were growing up and we'd made a hole in the fence between our gardens so we could slip through day or night, sharing comics and sweets. Later, cans of Strongbow and porn. She had laughed at that.

44

"When I first met you and Josh, I didn't get why you were friends—you both seemed so different—but I can see how much he means to you," she had said.

"He's family." I hadn't told Anna about my parents, not wanting to evoke that look of pity, but we were almost at the end of our holiday and it seemed like the right time. "Nine years ago my parents moved to Australia."

"Without you?" Her fingers tightened around mine. I could hardly bear to look at her face but when I did, I could see a desire to understand. Her eyes searching mine.

"Yeah. Well, they wanted me to go with them. Dad's family are from there and his dad wasn't well. It's too far to keep visiting so..." I shrugged.

"But you must have been only..." Anna worked it out in her head. "Sixteen?"

"Yeah."

"That's so young. Why didn't you go?"

"I nearly did, but the thought of carrying on my education in a foreign country seemed so daunting. Josh suggested I move in with his family; I spent so much time there anyway. After endless conversations between my parents and Josh's, it was decided I'd stay in the UK until I'd finished my A Levels, but after I'd left school I wanted to go to the same university as Josh. My parents were cold people, distant. I'd never felt that close to them. They'd settled because Mum was pregnant with me but before that they'd always traveled. I felt I had tied them down. Josh and his family...I... I just belonged there. They put up with me every single uni holiday and after I'd finished my degree...Honestly, who'd want to trade the gray skies and constant dampness that is the north of England for a blazing sun and a beach on your doorstep, right?"

"Right." Anna trailed a finger over my wrist. "But now you and Josh have a flat together?"

"Yeah, just a small one. Despite our degrees, neither of us have high-flying careers. Josh temps—he never wants to be tied to anything or anyone—and I've been so focused on going away I guess I haven't really made the best of the time I've had here. You're happy living with your mum though?"

"I am, but moving back home at twenty-four feels like a backward step." Anna sighed.

"Where does Nell live? Could you share with her?"

"No. She rents a house with a couple of girls she works with. I don't think I could keep up with them. My liver couldn't anyway."

"She's certainly giving Josh a run for his money. Where did you meet her?"

"Ah. Now there's a story. We met during our first few days at uni. She was the drunk girl in the loo," Anna said.

"The what?"

"You know. In a bar there's always a drunk girl comforting a complete stranger in the toilets. Telling her she looks amazing. That she *is* amazing. That the bastard who had made her cry isn't worth her tears."

I nodded although I didn't know at all. It must be a girl thing. Still, it wasn't hard to imagine Nell determined and vocal, flying the flag for female empowerment.

"And that was your fiancé you were crying over?" I asked.

"Nah. He came later. I was crying over some random I'd met earlier that night who ended up snogging the face off of someone else. I was a bit drunk. A lot drunk. Fresher's week." Anna shuddered.

"I'd like to snog the face off you." I dove on her, covering her face in wet kisses, while she shrieked in mock disgust.

I replayed the highlights of our time together while I showered and dressed that last morning. Whatever angle I looked at it from, Anna was my perfect woman and tomorrow she was leaving. We both were.

Today, though, we were visiting the home of some literary author I had never heard of and, judging by the fact we were the only people standing in his library, no one else had heard of him either.

"Imagine writing a story that people would still read hundreds of years after you'd died." Anna's face shone as she gazed at his typewriter in awe. I didn't read books but I got it. She felt about words the way I felt about films and music. The way I felt about travel.

The way I now felt about her, but I couldn't tell her that. In twenty-four hours, we'd be nothing but a memory.

Anna glanced around the room before stretching her arm across the security rope and running her fingers over the keys. "He once touched these. Imagine how happy he must have been sitting here, dreaming up characters."

"Haven't you ever wanted to write?" I asked.

"I'd like to but I'm not sure what."

"Have you tried?"

"No."

"Everyone has something to say; it's a matter of figuring out what that something is. What book would you write, if you could?"

"A love story." Anna didn't think twice. "One with a happy ending."

"A clichéd ending."

"Happy," Anna insisted. "Listen, this board says that he never finished his last work. Or did he and it wasn't published. I can't make sense of the way it's worded." Anna frowned as she read the poorly translated sign again.

"It must annoy you when you read things written incorrectly, Miss Teacher?" I asked.

"Not at all—I'm not the grammar police," Anna said too lightly. By now, I knew her better than that. I raised my eyebrows.

"Okay, it does annoy me a bit," she conceded.

I crossed my arms and waited.

"Okay. Okay!" Anna grinned. "It *really* irritates me. Honestly, I once wouldn't go into a steak house in London because it had been named Stephens Steaks without an apostrophe."

"That's awful," I said.

"I know."

"Imagine naming a steak house 'Stephen's.' It hardly screams Wild West."

"Shut up," Anna laughed. "There must be things that annoy you?"

"People who think the Eighties were uncool."

"Oh." Anna kept a straight face. "We're back to talking about the Eighties. Again. Shame we have to go. You realize what the time is?" She checked her watch.

"No?" I said. My watch still wasn't working after its dunking in the sea.

"It's Hammer time," Anna sang as she stretched out the sides of her shorts in a homage to MC Hammer rather than a mockery, I'd like to think. "You can't touch this."

I laughed while I watched her terrible dance. "I think you'll find, Anna Adlington, that particular song was perhaps the Nineties."

"Shut up and touch this." Anna wrapped her arms around me and pushed her body against mine. Who was I to argue?

"Last night then. Is it stupid to ask what your plans are?" Josh splashed aftershave onto his cheeks. He hadn't been able to charm Nell but they were hanging out most of the time. Each other's wingmen apparently. I think the fact she hadn't fallen for him was what was keeping him interested. I zipped up the one pair of jeans I'd brought. They were splattered crimson because I'd clumsily knocked a glass of sangria over them and couldn't rinse the stain out under the tap.

"Anna and I are having dinner." We were going back to the seafront restaurant we now thought of as ours.

"You like her, don't you?" Josh asked.

"Can't stand her. That's why I spend all my time with her." I sniffed my red T-shirt underneath the arms before tossing it on the floor and pulling the last clean one from my case. I still hadn't unpacked. The wardrobe stood empty, the floor strewn with clothes. We really were pigs.

"I mean you *like* her."

I waited for Josh to follow up with a sarcastic comment, but he didn't.

I didn't know what to say. He'd only ridicule me if I told him that if I could, I'd give her everything, I'd unhook the moon. Unscrew the stars that didn't shine as brightly as her. I'd give her the entire universe. If I could.

"Yeah. She's all right, I suppose," I said, lacing up my trainers.

"Don't fall in love, you big twat." He shoved me hard on the shoulder.

I didn't tell him that I already had.

Anna was breathtaking in a long turquoise dress that floated around her ankles; ethereal and angelic and too good for me, a scruffy oik who hadn't even packed a pair of trousers or shoes. No wonder Roxanne had berated me for my lack of fashion sense.

"For old times' sake." I tucked a pink bougainvillea into her hair. "Ready, señorita." I crooked my arm and she tucked hers through mine.

We split the bill after too much paella and Limoncello and plum tart—our final dinner mirroring our first. Anna always insisted on paying her own way. While she used the bathroom in the restaurant, I bought a bottle of house red and the waiter threw in two plastic cups.

Anna linked her arm through mine. We automatically headed toward the cove. We didn't speak. It was the last time we would tread this route together and I wanted to savor every moment.

At the end of the walkway, Anna's eyes flickered to the padlocks, the way they had every evening since our first.

"I have something for you. For us." From my pocket I pulled out a lock and a marker pen.

"A love lock!" She looked at me uncertainly.

"A friendship lock." Her face fell and I mentally kicked myself. "Anna, I…"

Don't fall in love, you big twat. Josh had said. He was right. It was the wrong time for me. For her. Impractical.

Shit.

"It's a lovely thought, Adam." She took the lock from my hand. "To symbolize our…friendship. What should I put?"

"How about just 'Adam & Anna'?" Our names fit together like pieces of a puzzle.

Anna took her time, writing in cursive script, before clipping the lock onto the chain.

"Adam…" Her eyes met mine. They glistened with tears.

I felt helpless. Useless.

"Anna, I…" I stroked her cheek with the back of my fingers. She gave a tiny shake of her head before forcing a smile.

"Last one onto the beach buys breakfast tomorrow at the airport." She sprinted away from me, leaving me fumbling with the wine and cups before I could follow.

"Hey, that's not fair!"

Ahead of me, she laughed. The stretch of her arms, the vibrancy of her dress, reminded me of the bird I had unchained. For a nanosecond I contemplated leaving her there and then. Preserving this as my last memory of her. Happy and free.

Instead, I chased her. Making a production of swiping my hands toward her but each time letting her slip through my fingers.

Eventually, we flopped onto the damp sand. I unscrewed the bottle of wine and we raised a silent toast.

Unlike previous evenings we were quiet. It wasn't the time for talking.

After we'd drained the bottle of wine, we flopped back on the sand. She rolled onto her side to face me. My thumb stroked hers and somehow that was enough. We didn't make love. Not that time. We'd tried that on the beach and decided we were better off in the apartment. It really wasn't as romantic as it looked in the movies. Sand gets everywhere, and I mean *everywhere*. It was an experience neither of us were in any rush to repeat. We must have dozed, because when we woke, the sky was turning from black to gray to pink. My eyes held hers, imparting all of the things I wanted her to know. All the things I couldn't say.

The static of hope crackled in the air, invisible to the naked eye but palpable nevertheless. I brushed it aside.

It was time to say goodbye.

CHAPTER SEVEN

Anna

The turquoise maxi dress I had bought from the tiny boutique in the hotel reception fitted me perfectly, worth the last of my euros. It was our last night and I could hardly bear it. During the past ten days Adam had built up my confidence brick by brick and I was afraid my newly found self-esteem would crumble to dust once he'd gone. We hadn't discussed whether we'd keep in touch. I didn't want to. Soon, he would be traveling the world, meeting new people, and if his texts tapered off, it would hurt all over again to think he had forgotten me. I'd rather say a clean goodbye and be left with the illusion that he was thinking of me.

Always thinking of me.

The way I knew I would think of him.

I painted on a pink gloss smile, determined not to ruin our last few precious hours together with melancholy and regret.

I didn't regret anything.

It was best for both of us to go our separate ways. Imagine if I asked Adam to stay and he said yes and he resented me for it one day—and that's if he said yes.

If.

Such a small word but it contained so many possibilities. My mind couldn't help time-traveling to a future where Adam and I were married, two children, a rose-covered cottage, but it was nothing but a daydream. Even if we wanted to see each other again, how would it work? We lived four hours apart and in truth, we might not feel the same about each other once back in the real world. I gazed out of the window at the speck of glittering sea visible between apartments. This was not the real world. This was not my real life.

For the first time in days I opened Facebook. At the top of my news feed was an update from my ex—**Living the Dream**—and a photo of him and Sonia raising glasses of fizzing champagne as they shared a meal. His plate was laden with meat and roast potatoes. On hers, a salad. I felt...I enlarged the photo to see if I was mistaken, but I wasn't. I felt nothing but relief that I was no longer trying to be someone I wasn't. Without hesitating I clicked **Unfriend** because I knew with certainty that we were never friends, not like me and Adam. That was how a relationship should be: honest and fun. In the future I wouldn't settle for anything less.

"What are you doing?" Nell burst from the bathroom. A tiny white towel wrapped around her middle, arms and legs golden.

"Moving on." I grinned, turning off my phone.

"Glad to hear it. You're okay then, with this being the last night?"

"Yes." I was sad but glad I'd met Adam. "Nell, are you sure you don't want me to have dinner with you tonight?"

"Nah. I couldn't get in the way of love's young dream."

"It isn't love."

"Are you sure?" Nell stood behind me. Her eyes found mine

in the mirror. "There'll be a way to make it work, Anna. If you want to."

If.

"It's been lovely. Just what I needed. A holiday romance."

"We both know it's more than that. You're not the type for a quick fling. Life's too short, Anna. You know that. Don't let him slip through your fingers."

"It's a rebound. I should have been married now." But she knew me better than that.

"Anna." Nell waited until I put the mascara wand back in its tube. My gaze met hers. "I never once saw you look at that tosser the way you look at Adam. It's the first time I've seen you smile properly since you lost your dad."

In the mirror her eyes glistened with tears. Mine did too.

Dinner was paella for old times' sake. During the meal I turned over Nell's words in my mind. Should I fight for Adam? For us? I just didn't know if he felt the same. He was quieter than usual on our walk to the cove. We both were.

"Anna," he said as we reached the fence. "I've got something for you. For us." He pulled a padlock out of his pocket.

"A love lock!"

"A friendship lock," he said, and then I understood. He was letting me go. Disappointment was a bitter pill but I forced a smile, imprinting our names upon the padlock before clicking it onto the fence. I felt him watching me. I raised my head. He was standing in front of a backdrop of sea. The setting sun casting a burned orange halo around his head. No matter what, I would never forget him. No matter what happened tomorrow and everything after this August, I still had this. Him. Now.

I was going to savor every last painful minute. It wasn't an evening for sadness. One thing I'd learned during my time with Adam was that it felt good to be happy. We'd laughed so much together and I was grateful for that. Suddenly I was thankful for the time we'd had, the time we still had, rather than dwelling on the ending of us.

"Last one on the beach buys breakfast tomorrow at the airport," I called out, racing ahead, trailing my joy behind me like a kite.

Once I'd let him catch me, we sat drinking cheap wine that tasted like vinegar. As the sun dipped and the sky darkened, I was comfortably drunk.

We lay entwined, my fingers creeping under his T-shirt, feeling the softness of his stomach. Tracing the birthmark on his forearm that resembled a map. Wanting to remember it all.

Everything.

Eventually, we dozed on the damp sand. Our bodies always tangled together; even when we rolled over, we automatically adjusted ourselves so we were never apart. His hand on my hip. My arm stretched backward, touching his thigh.

Adam was still asleep when I woke up. I studied him. Committing his features to memory, an image I could revisit at any time.

The pale sun rose, diluting the darkness, threading pink and gold through the muted sky as night leached silently into day.

Our last day.

Time to say goodbye.

CHAPTER EIGHT

Adam

The driver hefted our suitcases into the coach hold. I took a last, lingering look at the hotel. Its whitewashed facade, the brightly colored flowers in terra-cotta pots. It didn't seem possible I'd been here for two weeks. I could barely remember the first four days without Anna. My holiday started when she had arrived.

It felt like my life had started when she had arrived.

I watched her climb onto the coach with Nell, and I followed with Josh. Already there seemed a distance between us. If my last memory of us had been me watching her as she had gazed in wonder at the rising sun, it would have been a lovely memory to hold on to.

The airport was light and bright and full of too many people. We queued for check-in. We queued for passport control. We queued for coffee. Nobody was hungry.

We sat, the four of us, until the tannoy announced the gate was open for me and Josh.

"Time to go, Ad." Josh stood, scraping his chair back. We all rose and then there was a flurry of elbows and noses that bumped as we hugged and kissed, wishing each other a safe trip.

"It doesn't have to be goodbye," Nell unexpectedly whispered into my ear.

"Adam. We need to shift," Josh said, but I didn't move. I couldn't. What had Nell meant? Had Anna said something?

The desire to sweep Anna into my arms and declare eternal love was overpowering. I could feel Josh glaring at me and I knew what he was thinking.

He was thinking I was a twat.

"Anna..."

Her eyes met mine. Her lashes coated with unshed tears. There was nothing I could say to make it easier.

The realization that I would never again feel the shape of her name on my tongue made my throat close.

I couldn't let her go.

I wouldn't.

The announcer was calling for us to board but it sounded so far away because now the world was only made up of her and me. Josh was swatting our boarding passes against his thigh impatiently, but everything felt inconsequential.

Everything but her.

The thought that I could stand back and watch her walk out of my life seemed as ludicrous as trying to fight against the tide, so instead I let go of rational thought and allowed myself to sink into the possibility of what might be.

I took her hand.

"I'd like to see you. Again. I'd like to see you again very much." My voice cracked with nerves. "What I'm trying to say is that this should be the end but I don't want it to be. The end, I mean."

"But what about your plans? Traveling?" She searched my eyes for clarity.

"The world will still be there if I don't go for another month, another year even. Or you could come with me? It would be an adventure."

I held my breath while I waited for her answer.

CHAPTER NINE

Anna

The heat hit me. I climbed out of the air-conditioned coach, jealousy twisting in my gut as a clutch of new arrivals spilled pasty and hopeful from the airport, exclaiming how gorgeous the weather was. It was unfair to the other tourists to wish that it was raining but it would have felt fitting. As though some higher force greater than Adam and me was feeling the same sorrow I felt. But above us blue skies stretched lazily; the only black cloud was the knowing it had come: the inevitability of goodbye.

We perched on hard chairs, our carry-on luggage shoved under the table, and sipped at bitter coffee.

I didn't speak. I couldn't. The past ten days had been the best ten days of my life. The thought that my time with Adam, which had felt like everything to me, might someday fade to nothing was excruciating.

The tannoy called for Adam and Josh to board. He stood. Soon he'd be walking away from me. In my head I tried out the idea of a life without him but it was too painful. I blinked back unshed tears. I wouldn't cry.

I wouldn't.

There was a round of hugs. Kisses. And then something else.

Amongst the symphony of airport sounds—the tinny speakers, the wheeling of suitcases, the whine of tired children—I heard it. The whisper of possibility.

"I'd like to see you. Again," Adam said. "I'd like to see you again very much." His palm was damp in mine. "What I'm trying to say is that this should be the end but I don't want it to be. The end, I mean."

"But what about your plans? Traveling?" Did he mean after he'd returned? I wasn't sure.

"The world will still be there if I don't go for another month, another year even."

It was everything I wanted until he said, "Or you could come with me? It would be an adventure."

Instantly, I tried to break free of his hold. "I . . . I can't." I tried not to cry. "I don't feel the same way."

He held on to me tightly and studied my face.

"Anna, if you tell me you don't want to see me anymore, I'll go. But if you don't want to travel because you want to stay close to your mum, then I'll stay."

My throat contracted. How could it be that he knew me so well, but how could I ruin his plans? His trip?

"I want to stay. I want to meet your mum," he said. "I want to hear more about your dad. All you need to do is say yes."

Tears came and this time I didn't try to hold them back. "Yes," I whispered and then louder, "Yes!"

I leaped into his arms, not a flicker of doubt that he'd buckle under my weight. Knowing with certainty that he'd always catch me.

My heart was bursting, singing with happiness and hope.

Singing so loudly other passengers stopped and smiled at the couple so smitten with each other that there wasn't a single part of her that wasn't touching a part of him. Her legs wrapped around his waist, her face buried in his neck as he spun her around. We were *that* couple. Unselfconscious and unashamed. In that moment our love was absolute. Our hopes for the future circular, no beginning and no end. Just the unequivocal knowledge that whatever life threw at us, there would always be an *us*.

I never thought of a time we wouldn't be together. As he spun me around, I felt dizzy with joy. Now I'm dizzy with sorrow. If we had known what lay ahead, would we have done it anyway?

I'm not sure that we would.

CHAPTER TEN

Adam

"You look like shit." Josh stood behind me. I was trying to shave with an unsteady hand. In a few hours I'd have to face Anna Adlington. Explain my shabby behavior.

I studied my reflection. Ten months ago in Spain my skin had tanned to a warm brown, now it was pale. Washed out. Dark bags bruised the skin beneath my eyes, a deep furrow of anxiety between my eyebrows. Pieces of tissue speckled my chin where I'd nicked myself with the razor, the blood seeping through.

I felt like shit too. I couldn't remember the last time I'd slept properly.

"Are you sure you don't want me to come with you today?" Josh rested his hand on my shoulder. "I can drive and then leave you to it. You're knackered and it's a long way."

I shook my head. Four hours. There were four hours between Anna and me. On a good day I could make the journey in three hours forty-eight. On a particularly bad day it took almost five. The distance between us was a problem. With my eyes burning with tiredness and my bones aching to rest, it seemed ridiculous now we'd ever thought that it wouldn't be.

We couldn't always see each other every weekend because I had to work one Saturday in four. When we were together, Anna was often marking or planning future lessons and when she took a break it wasn't all spontaneous, rampant sex like it should be in the first throes of a relationship. Anna living with her mum meant we didn't get as much privacy as I'd have liked. Don't get me wrong, Mrs. Adlington—Patricia—was lovely. Despite still carrying the shell-shocked look of grief that she'd lost her husband when he was only forty-nine, and the burden of caring for her own mother who was showing signs of dementia, she was kind and funny and had welcomed me with open arms. Often Patricia would stay at her mum's on a Saturday night, giving me and Anna some alone time but it wasn't the same—trying to relax on an unfamiliar cream sofa that I couldn't eat or drink on, surrounded by an unhealthy amount of cat ornaments, photos of Anna's dad staring down at us from the walls. Sometimes I just wanted my own flat. My own sofa. Eating a chicken korma in front of the TV instead of having to sit at the table, but Anna didn't have a car and the travel fell on my shoulders, which were stiff with exhaustion.

The "us" of Alircia, who'd talked and laughed and *lived*, were unrecognizable to the people we had become. We had thought we could beat the statistics, and in a way we had. There's less than a 50 percent chance of couples staying together in a long-distance relationship, and out of those couples who don't make it, the average time they were together was four and a half months. We'd made it to ten so that was a win of sorts.

The screen of my phone lit up with a photo of Anna. She was on the beach in the turquoise dress she'd worn on our last night in Alircia. She looked so beautiful my heart ached.

I rejected the call.

"She'll try me next," Josh said, and seconds later his phone began to ring. He read my face, pressing the decline button on his screen. It wasn't fair. I'd been avoiding speaking to Anna for days and she was worried. She knew something was wrong. I'd fired off the odd text, **I'm okay. Sorry busy will call you soon. Low battery**, but they were bullshit and she probably knew it.

The truth was that since I'd had the offer of a new job, I'd been avoiding her.

It wasn't like I'd sought it out. The CEO of the agency stopped by my desk for a chat. We were discussing football over a coffee when he casually dropped into conversation that he was looking for a travel consultant.

"You never did go off and see the world, did you, Adam?"

"Nah but there's still time."

"What if the time is now?"

He'd offered me the job there and then.

"You'd be creating bespoke packages for corporate clients and the wealthy. It's not too dissimilar to what you do now but on a larger, more expensive scale, but you have to know the resorts inside out. Some will want five-star luxury but others something a little more bespoke. I want you to set it up, scout out locations. Take as long as you need to source suitable accommodation, from high-class hotels to yurts off the beaten path." He paused and waited for my reaction.

"I...I'm flattered you thought of me but—"

"No buts. You'd be perfect. You're an intelligent graduate who loves travel."

I loved Anna too but I didn't mention her.

"This is a chance in a lifetime." He clapped my shoulder. "Think about it but don't take too long."

I had thought of nothing else. My dream was being handed to me with a great big fucking bow wrapped around it. What kind of fool would I be to turn it down?

I talked it over with Josh, his parents. I talked it over with everyone except the one person I should have been talking to—Anna—but now I was ready. I was ready to try something new and brave and daring.

I raised my hand to check my watch before remembering that I didn't have it anymore. My wrist was bare.

"It's eleven," Josh told me.

"I...I'd better get going."

"Are you sure you shouldn't tell Anna that you're coming?"

"No." If I spoke to her she'd guess something was wrong and this wasn't a conversation we could have over the phone.

"You're doing the right thing." Josh gave my shoulder one last clap.

As I drove up the motorway I wondered if she'd understand how much this meant to me.

I wondered if she'd love me still.

I wondered if she'd cry.

CHAPTER ELEVEN

Anna

Usually I loved spending time with my nan but today my mind was somewhere else. With someone else.

"If you need to go and be with that young man of yours…" Nan smiled kindly. Behind me I could sense Mum shaking her head in a don't-mention-Adam way.

"I'm not seeing him this weekend, Nan." I wasn't sure if I'd ever see him again.

"You'll see him soon enough," Mum said briskly. She was trying to cheer me up but it still felt dismissive. "I'm going to make some sandwiches." She disappeared into the kitchen.

"If you've had a falling-out with Adam, sort it out. Life's too short." Nan's eyes misted and I knew she was thinking of Grandad. It had been years since he had died but she still missed him. We all did. There was a pause while we were both lost in our own thoughts, gazing out at the garden, which was a riot of spring color. Nan was looking directly at the tangle of yellow and pink flowers that fought for space in her pots, but from the expression on her face I knew she was only seeing her past. I wanted her to share that with me.

"Nan?" I tucked my legs under me on the sofa. "If you'd known how much it hurt to be without Grandad, would you still have fallen in love with him?"

"Anna, you can't choose who you fall in love with. I knew that very first night we met that I'd spend the rest of my life with him."

"Tell me again about your first meeting."

"You're not testing my memory, are you?" Nan narrowed her eyes. "Because despite what that doctor who doesn't look old enough to have left school says, there's nothing wrong with me."

"I just like hearing it." I was a hopeless romantic, although I was feeling more hopeless than anything else, glancing at my phone again. Nothing.

"I was a waitress and Grandad came in for his lunch. I served him faggots and gravy and he asked what time my shift ended. It had only just begun and so he sat there drinking coffee for five hours, waiting for me. At dead on five when I'd finished, he walked over to the jukebox and put on Elvis's 'Love Me Tender' and asked me to dance. It wasn't the place for dancing, but we did, in between the tables, my boss glaring at me. Before the song had finished, I had fallen head over heels for your grandad."

Listening to their story always made me emotional but today, more than ever, I felt Nan's hope, her joy, her certainty. I felt it all in the way I had with Adam at the airport. How had we gone so wrong? I wiped my eyes.

"Anna. If it's meant to be, it will be," Nan said.

"Here we go." Mum set a tray down on the coffee table, a plate piled with egg sandwiches. The smell made my stomach roll. Out of politeness rather than hunger, I picked one up and nibbled at the crust but I couldn't eat it. My stomach was filled with an anxious sick feeling every time I thought about Adam, which was pretty much all of the time.

"I'm not hungry." I stood. "I'll go and change your sheets, Nan."

"You're a good girl, Anna. I hope Adam realizes how lucky he is."

I turned away quickly before she could read me. Adam probably felt many things but was lucky one of them? I just didn't know.

"Shall we pick up a takeaway on the way home?" It was almost six by the time we left Nan's; she was eating with Mrs. Percival, the widow from next door. I wasn't really hungry but we still had to eat. Crispy battered cod and chips doused with salt and vinegar might bring a smidgeon of comfort.

"Let's not think about food yet," Mum said.

"But it's nearly dinner—"

"I said let's wait and see."

It wasn't like Mum to snap but I couldn't imagine how she felt seeing my nan slowly begin to slip away from her, knowing that from here on in, it would only get worse. I glanced at her profile as she drove. Her jaw set. Fingers gripping the wheel tightly.

"Nan was good today, don't you think?" There hasn't yet been a time that she hasn't known me or Mum. Sometimes it was hard to believe there was anything wrong with her.

"She was. I often think the doctor's got it wrong. We all get forgetful, don't we? Walk into a room to find we've no idea what we went in there for. Am I kidding myself, Anna? She seems fine, doesn't she? Mostly." Her question dripped with a desperation that made my heart hurt.

"She does, but if there comes a time she isn't...fine...then we'll be there for her. You and me."

"I do the best I can for both of you." Mum's voice was quiet.

"I know."

"Even if it might not seem that way. I do what I think is right."

"Mum. Everything you do is right. Please try not to worry." There had been a shift in our relationship ever since we lost Dad. Often I was the one to offer reassurances. Advice. I was the daughter, the parent, the friend, the adult and the child. Everything.

We pulled up outside the house. I started to climb out of the car.

"Wait." Mum gripped my arm. "I've left my mobile at Nan's."

"Do you have to fetch it tonight?" It was a silly question. Nan might need her. Call her. I began to tug the seatbelt back across my body.

"No point you coming with me," Mum said. "Go in and have a bath or something."

"It's okay. I'll keep you company."

"No, Anna." That sharp tone again. She couldn't look me in the eye. "Go inside."

Worried, I did as I was told, clearly the child again, trying not to read too much into it. We all needed space sometimes but it felt like everyone needed space from me right now: Mum, Adam.

I slipped my key into the lock and pushed open the front door. The hallway smelled of garlic and I cast my mind back to last night, trying to remember what we'd eaten. Mentally scanning the contents of the fridge, wondering if I could pull together some sort of meal before Mum came home. Exhausted, I kicked off my shoes and padded barefoot into the kitchen.

And there he was.

Adam.

Candles flickering on the table. A vase of pale pink roses set between Mum's best china plates.

He stepped toward me and I took a step backward. He'd ignored me for days and now...*this*. Whatever *this* was.

"I don't...I...How did you..." I licked my dry lips. I'd lost the fundamental ability to speak.

"Your mum left me a key." He wiped his hands down the front of his apron. He seemed nervous.

"She'll be back in a minute." My eyes scanned the two placemats.

"No, she won't. She's staying at your nan's tonight."

"Why?"

"To give us time. To talk. I've made paella. I measured out the rice and everything. I'm afraid it's lemon meringue pie for dessert though. Limoncello and plum tart was a bit beyond my limited capability." He flashed a smile but I didn't return it. He'd hurt me and I felt betrayed by both him and Mum, going behind my back like this.

He pulled out a chair, its legs scraping against the kitchen floor, and gestured at me to sit. I sank heavily onto its wooden seat, automatically taking a drink from the glass he pushed into my hand. Sangria, of course. I set it down and filled a glass with water instead.

Wordlessly he served up the food. Vibrant yellow rice and pale pink prawns. I took a mouthful but it stuck in my throat along with all the questions I wanted to ask. I set down my fork and he did the same.

"I'm sorry," he said.

My chest tightened. What was he sorry for? Ignoring me? Or something else. There had to be a reason he'd been rejecting my calls. He spoke.

"I can't keep doing this. This traveling back and forth. Snatching time when we can. The lack of our own space."

I'd been expecting something like this. Steeling myself for it, but that didn't make it any less painful.

"I've been offered a job. A travel consultant. I'd be traveling for months initially, but after that I'd be away regularly. There's a decent salary. All expenses paid."

There was so much I could have said, but I couldn't say any of it. If I talked, I would cry and I didn't want to cry. I didn't want to ruin this for him. This was Adam's dream and I needed to support it, support him, even if I wasn't sure if this meal was a "goodbye" or a "will you wait for me."

"It wasn't a decision I took lightly. I'm sorry I didn't tell you but…"

I nodded that I understood. His eyes met mine and his were full of tears too. This wasn't easy for him either.

"I turned it down," he said quietly.

"Why?" My voice was a whisper.

"Because travel *was* my dream but sometimes we have different dreams and now, Anna, it's you. You're all I ever wanted. *Do* want."

"But you said…you can't do this anymore."

"No." He rose from his chair and walked to me. Crouched down and took my hand between his. "I don't want a long-distance relationship anymore, Anna. I want your face to be the last thing I see before I go to sleep at night. Your voice to be the last thing I hear. I want you. Properly." He dropped one knee to the floor and before he had even pulled a ring out of his pocket, I was crying.

"Anna Adlington, will you do me the greatest honor of becoming my wife?"

Perhaps if I could have frozen one perfect moment in time, it would have been that.

"Yes." I launched myself into his arms and he fell backward. "Yes!" I covered his face in kisses. His hands were in my hair, his lips found mine. My fingers fumbled to undo his belt as he unzipped my dress. It was a good job Mum wasn't coming home.

Later, upstairs, I snuggled under my quilt, raising my hand and splaying my fingers, smiling as the small diamond on my ring finger glinted under the lamplight.

"Here." Adam passed me a plate of lemon meringue pie and climbed into bed beside me. "I'm afraid it's cold, future Mrs. Curtis."

"That's okay. You're pretty hot, future husband."

I took a bite but I still didn't have much of an appetite. I thought about the way my period was late. The sickness I felt. Adam and me hadn't talked about having children, a family of our own. Our long-distance relationship had been so draining we hadn't looked properly toward the future.

I stole a glance at him as he forked a slab of pie into his mouth. I hadn't taken a test yet. Should I say anything?

If I was pregnant, he would be happy, wouldn't he?

CHAPTER TWELVE

Adam

When I proposed to Anna that night, I didn't expect that six months later we'd be actually getting married, but then I hadn't expected her to tell me she thought that she was pregnant.

"Please say something," she had urged as she'd twisted the corner of the duvet cover round and round her finger.

"I...I..." *It's the best news I've ever received. We're going to be better at this than my parents. I'm going to love you forever*, but "Holy fuck," was all I actually managed to say.

"Adam!"

"Sorry, it's...brilliant, Anna. Really. Brilliant." I hadn't realized just how happy the thought of being a dad made me until the following day when we bought a test from Boots, giggling like teenagers, before finding out it was a false alarm.

"Oh." Anna couldn't keep the disappointment from her voice. "It must have been stress that was making me feel sick and messing up my cycle."

I had hugged her closely to me, feeling like a heel. The worry of me going AWOL had caused this. But later we had talked. Properly talked. We now knew undoubtedly that we wanted children.

"We should get married first," Anna said.

"The sooner the better. This year."

So a winter wedding it was. Initially we had worried about possible snow and ice but then British summers are never predictable. You can't book the sunshine and I didn't need it to be perfect—I was marrying the perfect woman and everything else came second to that.

"Nervous?" Josh handed me a can of Fosters. It was only ten o'clock in the morning but I couldn't resist cracking it open. There were a few hours to kill until we had to be at the church.

"Yeah. A bit. It's mad, isn't it, how much has changed."

"Totally. Who'd have thought one holiday would lead to this." Josh gestured around his new flat.

"You don't regret moving?" Me and Anna had bought a two-bedroom starter house near to her mum. Josh had stayed in our old place for a few weeks but then decided to move up north too.

"Nah, I was ready for a change of scene and you might be a twat but..." He took a swig of his lager. "Someone has to look out for you. I am the best man." He adjusted his cravat.

"That doesn't mean you get to cop off with the chief bridesmaid." Despite his best efforts, Nell had, so far, continued to resist his charms.

"One kiss. If she'd kiss me just once, I'd die a happy man."

"She'd eat you alive."

"Probably. How about you? Any regrets?"

"I don't..." I trailed off.

"What's that supposed to mean? Anna's happy?"

"She's been weird the past few days. Really weird. She was so excited about the wedding but now she keeps crying when she thinks I'm not around. Every time I've tried to talk to her about today, she's clammed up."

"You think she's realized you're a twat and she's going to do a runner?"

"Don't even joke about it."

"Mate, it'll just be nerves. Anna loves you, God knows why, but—"

The ringing of my mobile cut him off. I answered it. Listened. My stomach churning as I took in the news.

Bad news.

The worst.

CHAPTER THIRTEEN

Anna

It didn't matter that my dress was creasing, my eye makeup running. I curled on my bed, listening to Adam's heartbreak at the other end of the phone.

"Sorry," I said again. It didn't seem enough. It wasn't enough.

At last we said goodbye and I stood, slowly smoothing down the crinkled fabric of my gown. Catching sight of my reflection, my sad eyes staring back at me, and I turned away from them, heading downstairs to break the news to Nell and Mum.

"Hey!" Nell glanced up from her laptop screen. She and Mum were trying to re-create the wedding crown made of flowers that had looked so easy on YouTube. I'd wanted the complete boho-beach-babe look. A nod to where we'd fallen in love. My dress was cream, the color of ocean spray, loose and floaty. Instead of heels I wore sandals, my toenails painted as golden as sand.

"Christ, Anna. This is impossible," Nell said. "There's only two hours until we have to be at the church. Are you sure you don't want me to nip to Claire's Accessories and pick you up a tiara?"

I didn't answer.

"Anna? Are you okay?" Mum asked.

"It…it's Adam. His parents didn't make their flight yesterday—they won't be at the wedding."

"That's such a shame." Mum slipped her arm around me. "They must be so upset."

"Adam thinks they never intended to come. He's in bits. He hasn't seen them in years and they promised they'd be here. *Their son* is getting married! How could they miss it?"

It was hard to understand why they were choosing not to come. My dad would have given anything to be here today. All week I'd been feeling progressively worse that Dad wouldn't—couldn't—be the one to give me away. I'd shed many tears when Adam wasn't around; I hadn't wanted to take the shine off the big day build-up, but now *this*. It felt we were cursed. Only one parent out of four.

"We can't know they never intended on coming and I'm sure they have their reasons," Mum said.

"But Mum, Adam is so upset. I don't know how to make it better for him." I felt bereft. My inadequate sorrys and "I'm your family now" just hadn't seemed enough.

"You can't always make it better for him. Nell, are you okay if I take Anna upstairs and show her something?"

"Yes."

"Forget the crown, Nell," I said miserably. It didn't seem important anymore.

"Absolutely not." Nell was on a mission now. "I'm not going to be beaten. Look, if I just tape the roses to the halo and twist in strands of jasmine, and entwine cream ribbon through it all, it'll be done. It should be easy. Fuck." A thorn tore through her skin, and she sucked her index finger.

"You're going to bleed all over your dress. Honestly—"

"Anna." Nell's eyes met mine. "I've got this." She plucked another dusty pink flower from the diminishing pile. "Right, you little bastard. If you don't behave, I'll chop your head off. I've secateurs here. Don't think that I won't."

I knew she'd pull it off.

Upstairs, I sat on Mum's bed while she lifted something out of the bottom of her jewelry box. She pressed it into my hand.

"A coin?" I didn't understand.

"Not just any coin, but the coin Grandad Harry fed into the jukebox to play Elvis the day he met Nan."

"Really?" I turned it over in my hand, feeling all of the history contained in its cold, hard metal.

"I don't know," she said. "Grandad said he asked the owner to fish it out so he could keep it as a reminder of the minute he fell in love. Whether that *is* the actual coin or not we'll never know, but the point is what it symbolizes."

I still wasn't quite getting it.

"I've never told you this, Anna, but Nan's parents disowned her."

"Why?"

"Because she fell pregnant with me before she was married."

Instinctively I placed my hand over my stomach, remembering the time I had convinced myself that I was pregnant a few months ago.

"It was a different era, Anna. A real scandal. Nan was devastated. Grandad tried to talk to her parents but they never came around. She told me she cried and cried until Grandad gave her this coin, telling her it was from the jukebox. 'I can't say anything to take your pain away,' he had said, 'but carry this coin with you and whenever you're feeling lost or lonely, give it a rub and know that I'm thinking of you. Always.'" Mum smoothed my hair from my face and cupped my cheeks with her hands. "We can't always fix things for those we love, Anna, and they can't always fix things for us, but sometimes just knowing—remembering—that we have that special person who loves us, listens to us, is enough."

"I felt I'd let Adam down on the phone. I didn't know what to say."

"Sometimes you don't need to say anything. When Grandad was laid off from the brewery, he came home and sat on the back doorstep, his head in his hands. Do you know what Nan did?"

"No."

"She gave him the coin and sat. Just sat with him, holding his hand. Throughout the years, that coin passed back and forth between them and when… when your dad died, Nan gave it to me."

My eyes filled with tears.

"And now, Anna, I'm giving it to you." She closed my fingers around it.

"But—"

"Hush. Sometimes we don't have to say anything."

And we sat there silently on the bed she'd shared with Dad, my head resting on her shoulder, until Nell burst into the room triumphantly brandishing the finished crown.

It was all going to be okay.

The second I saw Adam at the altar, the world disappeared. My arm linked through Mum's as we made the slow walk down the aisle. My heart was both light and heavy, missing Dad but grateful for Mum. Excited to become Adam's wife. His eyes didn't let go of mine until I reached him. Whispering an "I'll explain later" in his ear, I pressed the coin into his hand.

We promised for better or for worse and I don't think either of us registered who was there and who wasn't. It was him and me.

It would always be him and me.

At the reception flamenco music played while we ate the wedding breakfast: paella, and Limoncello and plum tart of course. During the speeches I drank too much sangria, expecting Josh's to be raucous and rude but it was short and heartfelt. Mum stood and spoke.

"In the short time I've known him, I've grown to love Adam. Before he proposed to Anna, he asked me for her hand in marriage; not a lot of young men would do that nowadays and I appreciated the gesture. Anna's dad would greatly have appreciated the gesture too and I know that he'd be just as fond of Adam." I nodded. "But the most important thing of all is that they love each other, and any fool can see that they do."

"Even me." Josh raised his glass.

"A toast. To Mr. and Mrs. Curtis."

Mrs. Curtis.

I couldn't stop smiling.

It was time for the first dance. We had told Josh and Nell what our song would be and why, but I'd wanted it to be a surprise for Mum and Nan. We'd chosen "Love Me Tender." Adam took me in his arms and we swayed along, intermittently kissing. After the first few bars I watched as Josh strode purposefully toward Nell. Even if it hadn't been tradition for the best man to dance with the chief bridesmaid, he would have wanted to. Nan was sitting on the edge of the dance floor, wearing such a wistful expression that Josh hesitated as he passed her. With one last, lingering glance at Nell, he offered Nan his hand. Her face lit up as Josh led her onto the dance floor.

Smiling, I broke away from Adam and beckoned for Mum to come and dance with me while Adam did the same to Nell.

I couldn't take my eyes off Adam as he twirled Nell around the dance floor and I remember now with clarity the happiness that filled me as I watched them.

My husband. My best friend.

I never thought I'd lose him.

Never thought I'd lose them both.

PART TWO

"We can't always fix things for those we love."

PATRICIA ADLINGTON—ANNA'S MUM

CHAPTER FOURTEEN

Adam

There was a pub called The Star. It was a bit of a dump but when I had first moved here, over two years ago now, the name had made me smile when I'd driven past it.

"Fancy going out for a drink?" I had asked Anna when I arrived home. "You've a pub named after you, Star!"

"I'm living the dream," she had laughed.

The floors were always sticky and the very fabric of the place stank of cigarettes, but still we came regularly with Josh and Nell to play pool. Not many pubs had games rooms anymore, or dark wooden beams that striped the ceiling. It was a contrast to the other local pubs that were part of a chain. Here, we were largely ignored by the older clientele who perched on stools at the bar, nursing frothy pints of ale, leaving us to sprawl in front of the crackling fire and chat without too-loud music or extortionately priced beers.

Tonight, Anna was distracted; she picked up her glass of orange juice and put it straight back down again onto a battered mahogany table that wobbled on its spindly legs. I knew she was thinking about her appointment tomorrow. Our appointment tomorrow. There was a lot riding on it but for now I just wanted to relax, have a good time.

"Hey." I nudged her lightly with my elbow. "It's your shot."

She picked up her cue and bent over the table, her denim skirt stretching. I couldn't help checking her out. Before we had married, I had wondered what sleeping with the same woman for the rest of my life might be like, but I was just as attracted to her as ever. More so.

Anna's tongue poked out between her teeth the way it always did when she was concentrating. She jabbed the white ball and potted a yellow.

"That would be very impressive," I said, "if we weren't red."

"Shit, are we? Sorry."

"We thought you two losers needed a chance," I called across to Josh and Nell. Nell didn't bat back one of her usual sarcastic replies. She'd been quiet all evening too. We all took another shot and then it was Anna's turn again.

"Red?" she questioned.

"Red." I tried not to get annoyed. It was only natural that she was worried about tomorrow but then she was always worried. I just wanted one night without thinking about it all.

I watched as she thwacked a red ball into the black, which in turn dropped into the pocket, awarding Josh and Nell the victory.

"That was a waste of fifty pence," I said lightly.

"Well, if the money means that much to you," Anna snapped.

"Hey." I held up my hands. "I was just kidding."

"No. I'll give you back your fifty pence." She unzipped her purse and tipped a pile of coins on the table, and there it was: her grandad's coin, which had passed between us several times since the wedding. We both stared at it before Anna scooped everything back into her purse except her grandad's coin, which she stuffed into my pocket. She wound her arms around my neck and buried her face in my shoulder.

From over the top of Anna's head I caught the furrow of anxiety between Josh's eyebrows. He was worried about the way we'd begun to bicker, but I couldn't expect him to understand the pressure we were under. He mouthed, "Drinks?" and I nodded.

"Are you Lonesome Tonight?" began playing from the jukebox—not our song but close enough—and I pressed Anna's body against mine and began to sway.

"I'm not in the mood." Anna pushed me away. It was only in my head I replied, "You never are."

We lounged on our usual sofa, watching the flames dance in the grate. Josh returned with a tray of drinks. I eyed his glass of frothy pale beer thirstily before picking up my lemonade.

"So." Nell tore apart a beer mat. Separating the layers of cardboard. "I've news."

"What?" Anna gently took the mat away and held her hand. I think we all expected from Nell's somber expression for the news to be bad.

"You know Chris?"

I nodded. *Know* was a bit of a stretch. She had brought him to play pool with us a couple of times but it had been uncomfortable with Josh glaring at him, and anyway, you couldn't play doubles with five people. We hadn't felt bad when he didn't come back; Nell's boyfriends never seem to last beyond three dates.

"I'm moving in with him."

"What?" Anna looked hurt and I'm guessing this was the first she had heard about this.

"It's all happened so quickly." Nell shrugged. "I haven't had time to tell you."

Josh stalked away and I felt his pain. He had claimed his one kiss with Nell at our wedding but there hadn't been anything between them since and I knew he was hoping that one day she would see him as more than just a friend. Minutes later he returned with a bottle of fizz and four glasses.

"It's great news." He popped open the bottle and it was probably only me who could detect the tell-tale set of his jaw implying that he thought it was anything but great.

He frothed out the bubbling champagne and we toasted Nell and Chris, telling her that we'd like to get to know him better. The alcohol went straight to my head, I hadn't drunk for such a long time. Anna barely touched hers. I knew she wouldn't mind driving home.

"You're okay about this?" Nell asked us all, but she was looking at Josh.

"If you like him, we like him." Josh raised his glass. "But if he hurts you, I'll break his fucking legs."

On the drive home my head was fuzzy. Josh and I had finished the bottle between us and a headache was forming behind my eyes.

I stole a glance at Anna, hunched over the steering wheel. Tension radiating from her.

"You can't blame me for having a drink tonight," I said.

"Can't I?" she snapped.

"Anna, it's been well over a year."

"For me too! Don't you think I miss it? No, of course you don't, you never think of anything except yourself," she was shouting, and I couldn't help shouting back.

"That's not bloody fair and you know it." I fought to regain my composure. "I want a baby as much as—"

"Do you? Do you though? You wouldn't know it from the way you were knocking back those drinks."

"A few glasses of champagne won't hurt."

"How do you know why I can't fall pregnant? How do we know?" She wrenched the steering wheel and violently we left the road, bumping down a rutted track into a clearing in the forest. It was pitch black under the towering trees. She turned to me, but instead of fury in her face, there was nothing but sadness. "How do we know?" she asked again, this time quietly.

"We'll know tomorrow." I was thinking of the appointment again with the fertility specialist.

"I'm so scared."

"Anna, I—"

"Shh." She unclipped her seatbelt and awkwardly climbed over the center console, onto my lap. She kissed me. I held her face between my hands and kissed her back, hard. She undid my belt. I lifted my hips to slide my jeans down before I unbuttoned her shirt, running my hands up her thighs, under her skirt. My fingers feeling how much she wanted me.

This. This was what I had longed for.

Feeling desired. Needed. Feeling the way we used to feel before we relied on an app to tell us when we should touch each other.

This was what I had missed.

Her.

Us.

It was four o'clock in the afternoon and my mouth still tasted like something had died in it. Our appointment was in fifteen minutes. Anna should be here by now. Her school day finished at three.

Where was she?

I checked my phone again but she hadn't messaged. Another five minutes passed and I was wondering whether I should book us in when I saw her running toward me.

"Are you—"

"Let's get inside," she said breathlessly.

We told the receptionist we were here and were told to wait on hard gray chairs that matched the gray walls and the gray floor. It looked like the place dreams came to die.

"Good day?" I wanted to distract Anna from her thoughts. I wanted to distract myself from my thoughts.

"Not really." She tucked a curl behind her ears. "You know I was worried about Jemma?"

"Yes." Jemma was one of Anna's Year Eleven pupils. Anna had noticed she'd become withdrawn and was worried she might be being bullied.

"She asked to see me after school today, that's why I was late. She's pregnant."

"Oh, Anna."

"She wants me to help her arrange a termination." Her voice was flat, emotionless, but I knew how twisted up inside she was.

"Mr. and Mrs. Curtis?" We were summoned into a room.

We sat down. Anna's hand slipped inside mine.

"Hello," said Dr. Bowman. "I have the results of your laparoscopy, Anna. We suspected from your heavy periods and the pain you experience that your failure to conceive—"

"Failure?" I couldn't help blurting out as Anna's fingers tightened around mine.

"Sorry. Lack of success conceiving over the past eighteen months might be due to endometriosis and the results confirm that it is. Do you both understand what endometriosis is?" He paused.

"Yes," said Anna at the same time I said "kind of."

"It's when the lining of the uterus—the endometrium—grows elsewhere, such as in the fallopian tubes or ovaries. The lining breaks down but, unlike the cells in the womb that leave the body as a period, it has nowhere to go."

"And this has prevented Anna falling pregnant?"

"Not necessarily, but it could well have contributed toward her fail...lack of pregnancy. Sometimes with endometriosis there is a build-up of adhesions that can trap the egg and prevent it from moving down the fallopian tube."

I glanced at Anna. Her face was as white as chalk. I could see that if she spoke, she would cry.

"So is there anything we can do?" I asked.

"Surgery to remove the adhesions would certainly increase the chance of conception. There are no guarantees, of course. Anna has age on her side and may well conceive naturally."

"We..." Anna took a deep breath. "We want the surgery."

"The surgery can cause further problems: infections, bleeding, damage to affected organs."

"We want the surgery," Anna repeated.

At home, I tucked Anna under a blanket on the sofa and made her a hot chocolate. It sat untouched on the coffee table, melting cream streaking down the mug onto the glass.

I lifted the blanket and slipped under it.

"Anna—"

"Don't," she said quietly. "Just don't."

"This isn't your fault, you know." I felt helpless knowing how wretched she must feel inside. If it were the other way round, I know that rightly or wrongly, I would feel to blame.

"I can't talk about it. Not yet. Please don't make me."

At a loss to know what else to do, I reached into my pocket and pulled out her grandad's coin. She took it gratefully, curling her hand around it.

I had thought, at that time, we would be okay. It was comforting to think that we had a good support network around us, but I didn't know then that our network would crumble.

I didn't know then what was to come the following day.

CHAPTER FIFTEEN

Anna

It was a sleepless night. In bed, I placed my hands over my lower abdomen and imagined the adhesions forming under my skin. The adhesions that were preventing me from falling pregnant. Next to me, Adam slept and I hated him for not being awake. Didn't he care? I glared at him through the gloom until my eyes filled with tears.

Of course he cared.

I knew that undoubtedly. He would never blame me, and yet I felt I was to blame. My stupid, faulty body was to blame.

Tears of self-pity flowed and I let them, turning my face into the pillow, the foam absorbing my sorrow. I was scared. Scared of the surgery. Scared it wouldn't work. Scared Adam would leave me for someone who could conceive. Every single potential problem I could think of loomed out of the dark.

By the time the gray sludge of dawn lightened the sky, I had vowed that I would not let this come between me and Adam. I wouldn't let it become the focus of us. I wouldn't let my endless fears become his fears. He was my glass-half-full optimist and I needed him to stay that way.

I wanted to talk to someone though. It wouldn't be fair to burden Mum. We hadn't even told her we were trying—not wanting that "Am I going to be a grandma?" question every month. We thought it would be a nice surprise for her when it happened. I was glad she didn't know.

Quietly, I dressed. Pulling on track pants and lacing my trainers. The cold air filled my lungs and I ran and ran until I found myself on Nell's doorstep. Here I could cry unfiltered, lay out all of my doubts before her, knowing she would listen without judgment, without trying to fix it. Fix me.

It was Chris who answered. Bare-chested, black joggers hanging low on his waist.

"Anna." He stifled a yawn with his hand. "Is everything okay?"

"Yes. Sorry it's early." Stupidly, I hadn't thought that he might be here. "Is Nell awake?"

"She probably is now," he said, but not unkindly. "Come in."

I followed him into the kitchen. The sink was piled with washing-up, most likely from Nell's housemates. She rarely cooked. Still, she'd be moving into Chris's house soon enough.

"Congratulations, by the way," I said as he filled the kettle. "It's great news."

"Thanks." He turned to me with the biggest grin on his face. "I can hardly believe it—me, a dad!"

It was a punch to the gut. I sank onto the kitchen chair while Chris carried on talking. "I know it wasn't planned but Nell will make the best mum, don't you think?"

"I . . . I have to go. Sorry, I've just remembered . . . something." I rushed toward the front door, reaching it at the same time that Nell reached the bottom of the stairs.

"Is everything okay, Anna? It's the crack of dawn!"

"I was just out for a run but—"

"A run? Now I know something's wrong. Shit. It was your laparoscopy results yesterday, wasn't it? Sorry, it slipped my mind."

"That's okay, you've a lot to think about with . . . with the house move."

"What were your results?" She looked at me with concern.

"They were fine. Nothing wrong at all."

"That's fantastic!" Her face broke into a grin. "So you could fall pregnant any day now?"

I swallowed around the lump in my throat. "No. We've decided to wait. We're so young and I want to at least be head of department before I take maternity leave, if not deputy head. There's no rush." My smile was so fake, my face in danger of shattering.

"Oh," she said. "I get that your career's important and I know you want to follow in your dad's footsteps and make head teacher, but I thought—"

"You thought wrong."

She studied me for a moment. I maintained eye contact, certain she could see all of the pain inside me.

"It's enough for us to know that when the time is right, there's no medical reason why we can't conceive," I said.

She waited for me to say something and when I didn't, she asked, "Are you sure there's nothing wrong, Anna? You would tell me if there was?"

"Of course." This time I couldn't force a smile. "We share everything, don't we?"

"Always," she said. I understood her reason for not wanting to tell me she was pregnant but it smarted.

I felt something shift in our relationship. She was slipping away from me.

She had lied to me. I had lied to her.

Everything changed from that day forward. It wasn't that I resented her but it hurt, every time she rubbed her bump, complained about backache, bad skin, morning sickness. I wanted it so badly. I wanted it all.

Alfie was born seven months later and I fell in love with him instantly. I told myself that it was enough being a surrogate auntie. I told myself not to feel jealous that Nell had made new friends, all part of the first-time mums' club that I didn't know if I would ever join. I tried to keep her in my life, but she was engulfed by sleepless nights and baby swimming and massage and yoga and a million other things that I didn't know babies needed.

Nell accidentally fell pregnant again just three months later and it was hard. It was so bloody hard to maintain our friendship that I stopped trying. I didn't know then the tragedy that waited for me ahead. I didn't know then how much I would need her after *that* day.

How much Adam and I would both need her.

CHAPTER SIXTEEN

Anna

Five years. It had been almost five years since we married. Sixty long months in which I hadn't been able to give Adam the thing he wanted. The thing we both wanted more than anything else.

We were two. We were still two. Not three or four. No pram blocked our hallway. Our lounge was impossibly tidy, no plastic toys to throw into tubs at the end of the day. The spare room housed years of accumulated junk instead of a cot. Since my endometriosis diagnosis I'd twice undergone surgery to remove adhesions and taken fertility medication. The doctor had said I *could* conceive but...

My eyes strayed to the black-and-white framed photo of our wedding day hanging on the wall at the foot of our bed. It was the last thing we saw before we turned off the lights, the first thing we saw every morning. It used to make me smile. Now it made me sad. The picture was so intimate, our foreheads touching as we'd leaned toward each other.

I felt beautiful. Now everything felt ugly. Our marriage showered in a confetti of faded dreams.

Furiously I dragged the cotton-wool pad across my skin,

removing all traces of the makeup I had worn to work. From around my neck I unfastened the silver chain I wore most days. In my jewelry box was the gold star pendant Adam had bought me for our first Christmas together. My stomach tightened painfully. He hadn't called me Star for ages. I really should have tucked the necklace somewhere I didn't have to look at it every day, but I knew that wasn't the solution. Out of sight was definitely not out of mind.

I pulled out the drawer of my dressing table. Nestled under the pile of underwear, once black and lacy, now washed-too-often-no-longer-white and bought for practicality rather than fun, it lay there like a dirty secret. Gently I pulled out the parcel, unwrapping tissue paper as fragile as my heart. Inside was the tiny lemon sleepsuit covered in bears and the brightly colored cuddly parrot we'd bought on a whim, the weekend we arrived home from honeymoon when we had begun trying for a family of our own.

"This parrot looks like the one we set free the week we met," Adam had said. "Our future child absolutely has to have it. We shall call him Percy." I still could picture us. Me carefully carrying the shopping bag as if it was as precious as the baby we thought we'd create. Adam's arm protectively around me. At home, I had sprawled on the rug, Percy Parrot in my hand, the sleepsuit spread over my stomach, while Adam had thrown logs on the fire.

"Will you still love me when I'm fat?" I had grinned, waiting for his jokey response.

"I'll love you forever, Anna," he had said as he crouched before me. My flippancy had melted away as he kissed me long and hard. His hands unbuttoning my shirt. Fingers brushing against my flat stomach, feather light. Stupid but I had thought that I'd fall pregnant that night. It felt too perfect for it not to happen. Afterward, Adam had tugged the throw from the back of the sofa and covered us and we had toasted our future with elderflower cordial. I'd been determined not to drink. Adam vowed to be alcohol-free in support.

"What do you think of names?" I had nestled against him.

"I'm rather fond of them. It would be confusing if we didn't have them."

"Idiot. How about Charlotte?"

"Too formal. Iris?" he had suggested.

"Too old-fashioned. Harry?"

"Too wizardy."

I had pushed him.

"Sorry," he had said, rubbing his shoulder. "That was your grandad's name, wasn't it?"

My phone began to ring, pulling me from that memory. It was Mum.

"Hello, I was just thinking about you. Well, about Grandad."

"What about him?" Mum asked.

"About his name." As soon as I had said it, I kicked myself.

"You're thinking about names? Anything to tell me?" Mum sounded so hopeful.

"Mum. You know we're not starting a family until I'm where I want to be in my career." It pained me every time I had lied to her over the past few years but I couldn't face her disappointment each month, along with my own. I had never told her we were trying. I hadn't told Nell. She was so busy with Alfie and Emily. Two children under five—she called it a nightmare; to me it was a dream.

"Your dad would be proud of you being made Head of Year,

but more than anything he'd want you to be happy. There is no right time to start a family, Anna."

"I know. We will one day, I prom—"

The slam of the front door saved me from making a promise I couldn't keep.

"Adam's home. Can I call you back?" I wanted to put the sleepsuit away before he came upstairs.

"It's okay. Nan just wanted me to tell you there's a program about a man who traveled the world on foot on BBC later. She thought Adam might enjoy it."

"Thanks." I had no intention of watching it. Adam didn't need another reminder of the life he'd given up for me. He was no longer working in a travel agency but in the administration department of the council. He didn't hate it but he didn't love it either.

We said goodbye and after I had stuffed everything back into my drawer, I trudged downstairs wishing Adam and I could talk about our disappointments as readily as we used to talk about our dreams, but we didn't seem to be able to. Or perhaps it was that we didn't want to. Afraid of what we'd say. Afraid of what we'd hear. Did he blame me? He must have and I just couldn't bear to listen to him say that he did. Still, as I headed toward the kitchen I vowed that I would make an effort. Instead, I found myself snapping, "Did you get the bits I asked you to from Tesco?" My eyes scanned the kitchen for shopping bags.

"Fuck. No. Sorry. Bad day. I—"

"*Every* day seems to be a bad day," I bit back, and I knew that tonight wouldn't be the night for meaningful conversations. Again.

"Hello to you too." Adam turned his back on me and washed his hands at the sink before flicking on the kettle. I crossed my arms, waiting for him to realize he'd forgotten the milk.

"One thing. I asked you for one thing," I said, trying to hold back the tears that had gathered. We both knew I wasn't talking about the shopping and I knew I should stop goading him but my hormones were all over the place, my period was due, and I couldn't help myself. I shouldn't have looked at our baby things. Again I wondered whether we should try IVF but I was so scared that it wouldn't work and equally scared that it would. Often I tried to recapture the feeling I used to have whenever I had looked at Adam in those early, heady days, but the boy from the bar had slipped through my fingers and in his place was this helpless man standing before me who looked so tired.

"Anna, it's not my fault..."

"It never is, Adam."

"Not *everything* is." His eyes met mine. "But no matter what I do, I can't seem to make you happy."

"Well then, you should leave. *That* would make me happy." I wiped my hand across the back of my mouth. The spiteful words I'd spoken in shame had left a bitter taste as they spewed from my lips. "Sorry." I couldn't look him in the eye. "I didn't mean that."

I stepped into his open arms. This was the way it went. We fought and then we made up. It was exhausting.

"If we can't have tea, wine? Thursday is the new Friday." Adam pulled a bottle of Malbec from the rack while I fetched two glasses from the cupboard. We didn't drink when we'd first tried to conceive. As time marched on, it became "just the odd one"; by two years it was weekends only. But weekends stretched from Friday lunchtime to Sunday night and soon after that it was why not take the edge off? Adam uncorked the bottle while I pushed a stopper back into all the things I wanted to say. It didn't feel like the right time.

It never did.

My nan had a yellow sofa once, her and Grandad had saved for almost a year to buy it when they had first got married. It became battered from years of family life. The springs poking through the sagging cushions. The arms worn and faded. After she had lost Grandad, Mum had worried about her living alone. "On top of everything else that's wrong with that sofa, it's a fire hazard. You must get a modern one made of non-flammable material," Mum had insisted. Nan did buy a "three-piece suite," as she had called it, but was scared of spoiling it. She refused to take off the protective covering. When I visited, I perched on the edge of my seat, afraid of splitting the plastic open. Afraid of ruining what was underneath. That was how I constantly felt now, sitting lightly on the lie that was our marriage, muscles tense, smile static. Terrified that I would press down too hard and the truth would burst out. We hadn't been able to have a baby and it didn't matter how many times we said we were enough for each other; I didn't think that we were.

Not anymore.

CHAPTER SEVENTEEN

Adam

My first glass of Malbec lasted about three seconds. I poured another. If I was drinking, I couldn't snap back. I just couldn't face another row.

Nothing I did was good enough anymore. I should have known when Anna had scrawled pink wafer biscuits on the list that morning that it was her time of the month. That I needed to tiptoe around her more than I usually did.

Five years. Five years we've been trying to conceive.

When do you say enough? Let's take a break and just be *us* for a bit.

It broke my heart that I couldn't give Anna what she wanted and yeah, I saw through her barbed "I only asked you for one thing" comment. We both knew she wasn't talking about the shopping. Despite the endometriosis, I felt entirely responsible, like I was less of a man. Rationally I knew that with someone else, someone different, I might have the chance of a family but I'd never once thought about leaving Anna. "You should leave. *That* would make me happy," she had said, but I knew she didn't mean it. I hoped she didn't mean it. I think she felt the guilt as much as me. Feeling less of a woman, but she was *all* woman. This I was reminded of each time the app on her phone beeped to tell her she was ovulating and we pounded up the stairs to bed while I tried to prepare myself mentally: ten minutes to curtain call.

We had visited a clinic to check the quality of my sperm. They had handed me a plastic pot and directed me to a room full of porn but it had been Anna I had thought about. Barefoot at our wedding reception. Crown of flowers. Laughing riotously at something Nell had said.

I missed Nell.

Josh did too. "Couldn't we start hanging out again?" he had asked.

"Josh! Nell is married now. Time to move on, mate."

"Giving up is not an option," he had said.

Had Anna given up too soon on their friendship? I wished Nell were here to help Anna through this. I thought she would be if Anna was honest with her, but she couldn't or wouldn't be, and in shutting Nell out, a chasm had opened between us all. Nell and Chris's social circle widening to include other parents, and our social circle ever decreasing.

Would Anna be happier without me? Could she conceive with someone else's sperm? Could she have a baby without IVF? Maybe we just weren't compatible in that way. It filled me with self-loathing that I could be the cause of her unhappiness. That I was walking under a ladder, black cat crossing my path—all kinds of bad luck. If I was being entirely honest, the resentment wasn't only one-way: I had given up a lot for her. My plans to travel the world. The new job I was offered. My friends when I had left my village. Sometimes I imagined standing at the airport six years before. Anna on one side, and all my hopes and dreams on the other. Would I give it all up again? No matter how much we bickered, the days, sometimes weeks that passed without any meaningful conversation, I knew that I would. Our time together wasn't all bad, it was just that the bad times were pretty fucking terrible, but every now and then I'd glimpse the Anna of old. Last weekend, for instance, we had been to the engagement party of a guy I worked with and in the back room of the pub was a pool table.

"You up for it?" I had asked her. It had been about two years since we had played.

"Bring it on." She had kicked off her heels and hitched up her tight black dress and thrashed me three times in a row. Afterward, we had danced to S Club 7, both reaching for the stars and had staggered home at 2 a.m. clutching a white plastic bag bursting with kebab and chips. We had sat cross-legged on the lounge floor, picking meat out of the pita.

"We couldn't do this if we had kids," I had drunkenly said. Had stupidly said. I hadn't meant it the way it sounded and the mood was ruined, but for those precious few hours before I stuck my foot firmly in my mouth, we had laughed. Properly laughed.

"Are you hungry?" Anna asked now but I was one step ahead of her, guessing that the salmon on the shopping list was meant to be our dinner.

"Sweet and sour chicken?" I waved the menu in front of me, a white flag of sorts.

She placed a hand on her stomach. "I don't know if I fancy Chinese tonight." She often felt bloated when her period was due. She was wearing her time-of-the-month pajamas. All baggy and worn. I didn't like to ask her if she had started yet. Didn't fancy getting my head bitten off again.

"What do you fancy?" I wiggled my eyebrows alluringly but she didn't laugh. She didn't rip my clothes off either. She wouldn't until the bloody app told her to.

"Curry?" she asked.

Garlic breath and raw onion salad.

"Perfect," I said.

After I had rung the order through, I quickly showered, scrubbing my hands that still smelled of oil—I was late home because I had stopped to help an elderly couple change a flat tire. Ridiculously it was virtually outside of Tesco, but by the time I had sent them on their way the shopping had slipped my mind.

Rummaging for a pair of clean socks, I noticed that one of Anna's drawers wasn't properly shut. There was a piece of tissue paper poking out. My shoulders deflated even further. She had been sitting here alone, looking at the sleepsuit we had bought. No wonder her mood was so foul. I wished we could talk, but what would we say? I felt to blame. She felt to blame.

The best thing I could do was act normal, knowing that the tension would pass. It always did. I changed into my jogging bottoms and sweatshirt stained with bolognese sauce. Anna wasn't the only one who had stopped making an effort. Is this how all marriages ended up? Comfort clothes. Comfort food. Finding comfort in everything but each other.

Perhaps tonight would be different. I splashed some hopeful aftershave on my cheeks as the doorbell rang. By the time I was back downstairs, Anna was spooning korma onto plates.

"Movie?" I scrolled through my tablet for something to cast.

"Nothing too slushy."

"*Up?*" I knew it was corny and I should probably choose one of the Bourne films or a Dan Brown, something infinitely more masculine anyway, but I loved the Disney story of Ellie and Carl and we hadn't seen it for ages. There was also a small part of me that wanted to remind Anna that a couple could live a long and happy marriage without children.

"Okay," Anna sighed, and I knew she only agreed because she thought she needed to make up for her snappiness to me and I didn't disagree. I took what I could get. "Just don't ask for a dog this time."

"Fine. But if I ever find a talking golden retriever like Dug, he's ours." I smiled but it made me sad we had bought a hamster rather than a dog. We had planned to get a puppy after we'd had a baby, when Anna was at home and the dog could join the household knowing where he stood in the pecking order. I already knew my place.

The movie began. I turned up the volume as Hammie spun endless turns in his wheel that squeaked with every rotation. I passed Anna the tissues because, no matter what she said, the opening scene got her every time. The lonely old man grieving for his lost wife. She snuggled up to me and I loaded another poppadum with mango chutney before I passed it to her.

As we watched the house tied with balloons soar through the sky, I stole a glance at Anna. She was my Ellie. The one true love of my life. Was I her Carl? If I was ever without her, I didn't know what I'd do. I would be the one sitting in the chair, crying over our photo albums.

"Adam?" Anna asked as Carl abandoned his quest to visit the place he and Ellie had dreamed off, instead building a new life for himself.

"Yeah." I pulled her close to me.

"Do you still believe that if you love someone you should set them free?"

My stomach twisted. What was she asking? Why was she asking?

"I think…" I considered my words carefully before I replied. "I think…yeah." In the swarm of profound words and phrases in my mind, I could only say yeah. No wonder we ate in front of the TV every night.

We went to bed and I watched her sleep because, sad as it was, I still did that.

If you love someone, set them free.

The thought of being without her formed a hard ball in my chest.

Did she want to leave?

I didn't know how to fix this. I didn't know how to fix us.

You can't, the night-time said softly in my ear.

I turned away from it. I turned away from her.

The moon fell steeply through the window onto our wedding photo, which had once made me happy to look at but now made me sad and despairing. Frustrated and angry.

It made me all of those things, and more.

You know what to do, Adam, whispered the darkness once more.

And I did know.

But could I really do it?

CHAPTER EIGHTEEN

Anna

The alarm shrilled seven o' clock. It felt like the middle of the night. Adam stumbled over to the window and yanked open the curtains but the dark winter sky outside did nothing to improve my mood. I had a raging headache from too many glasses of Malbec. The bitter taste of garlic lingering in my mouth.

"I'll go and make some tea." Adam whistled as he pulled on his slippers. His morning cheerfulness infuriated me.

"Yeah, like tea's going to help," I snapped.

"Hangover? I told you not to have that last glass."

It was precisely his telling me this that had led me to defiantly finish the bottle. Half the time I behaved like a rebellious teenager rather than a wife but I couldn't seem to help it.

"Yes, well, if you had bought milk like you promised, we wouldn't have opened a bottle at all." I couldn't seem to let anything go.

"My fucking fault! I should have known. Everything is."

"Not everything."

Most things.

He stormed out of the bedroom, swearing as he stubbed his toe against the flat-pack bookcase on the landing that had gathered a layer of dust as it waited to be built. We bought it six months ago. Our tiny house was full of half-finished projects and we argued about them endlessly, Adam insisting he would get around to things "in his own time," but he never did. He'd rather spend his weekends "relaxing" like he was the only one working full-time. He was either sprawled on the sofa watching football on a Saturday afternoon or off playing it with Josh on a Sunday morning. After a match he would wallow in the bath, groaning each time he moved. It was me, of course, who washed his sweat-damp kit. Picked the clumps of mud up from the floor.

I had grown up and Adam hadn't. Or perhaps we had just grown apart. Perhaps that was what happened when people got together in their early twenties. I had no idea at that age that one day I would enjoy meandering around art galleries, visiting stately homes. Longing for a garden I could landscape rather than the small, square box we had. I had no idea that Adam wouldn't have developed any different interests to the ones he had when we met. Sport. Dreaming of all the places he had always wanted to visit but never had. Perhaps now never would. It had appeared incredibly romantic, him putting our relationship before his own ambition, but now I wondered if we were an all-too-convenient excuse for staying. Easier. Adam had never been good at arranging things.

That wasn't quite true. On our first Valentine's day he had a star named after me—I had laughed that he had called it Star—and that night we'd trudged up the hill, wellington-booted and huddled under layers, and he'd showed me, through a borrowed telescope, my gift.

"How will I know which is mine?" I had asked.

"Because you always shine brighter than the rest."

Was it wrong to have wanted life to continue like that, to

have expected it? I knew it wasn't about big romantic gestures, it was about the small things. But Adam didn't seem to bother with those anymore either. His list of things to do pinned to the fridge had grown so long I had screwed it up and thrown it away in frustration, unable to bear looking at it anymore.

The clock glared 7:15. If I didn't hurry, I'd be late. In the bathroom mirror, my hair was a matted mess. I'd been tempted to cut it over the years, tame my curls, but each time I suggested it, Adam was so upset that I'd kept it long. It was silly, but part of me felt that if I cut off my hair, I'd be cutting off some of his love for me. Shearing away more of the girl he fell in love with.

Gray morning light spilled in through the bedroom window as I sat at my dressing table, carefully selecting my makeup. I had taken more care over my appearance since the appointment of our new head teacher, Ross. He was young and dynamic and in his last post had turned a failing academy around. It was the thought of his deep brown eyes that studied me so intently that caused me to contour my cheeks. To cover my lashes with two coats of mascara rather than one. To blend my eye shadow, my blusher, so my look was natural. Barely there. It took ages.

Downstairs, I scooped last night's curry-stained plates from the coffee table in the lounge; Adam had walked straight past them. On our wall was the framed map of my star. Every day I was tempted to take it down. It was a painful reminder of the way we used to be. But I knew if I removed the frame from the wall, I would see how the wallpaper had faded around it, the way the girl on a beach in Alircia, barefoot on golden sand, had faded away from me, and there was a part of me that wanted to cling on to her. Wanted to hold on to Adam—my boy from the bar—otherwise I'd have left by now, wouldn't I?

*

After the final bell had rung and the kids had rushed outside, Ross sauntered into my classroom. Instinctively I smoothed my hair.

"Are you rushing home?" he asked. "Pub?" We had progressed from sharing coffee breaks in the staff room to casual lunch-time paninis in the coffee shop near the school. We had grown close but this was the first time he had suggested something out of hours.

"I've got a stack of marking to do." I patted the English books piled on my desk, aware I hadn't answered the question. I busied myself tidying away my pens, straightening papers, my head and my heart battling. "A quick one won't hurt." I didn't know if I was trying to convince him or me.

The pub was quiet. I couldn't help glancing around while Ross ordered at the bar, afraid I might see somebody I know. Guilt pulsed that I was doing something wrong, although strictly speaking I wasn't. But over our lunches we had stopped talking about work and begun to talk about ourselves; we weren't just colleagues now but something else. Friends? I was kidding myself. It was a slippery slope I was skidding down.

"What shall we drink to?" Ross poured from a bottle of Merlot.

"Surviving another day?" I raised my glass.

Ross laughed. "Yes, you know what they say about teaching?"

"What?"

"It would be a perfect job if it weren't for the bloody kids."

I scanned the menu, playing it cool. "Do you want them? Kids?" I knew he didn't have any.

"God, no. I don't. I think we see the best of them—the ambition, the curiosity—but we also see the worst too. I feel privileged to help shape futures but when I go home, I want to switch off. Is that horribly selfish?"

It was horribly alluring but I didn't tell him that. Imagine being with somebody who didn't want a child. I wouldn't have to feel guilty then. I drained my glass and held it out for a refill. "We're all entitled to be a little selfish sometimes, aren't we? Not everyone wants a family."

"How about you, Anna?" He paused until I met his gaze. "What do you want?"

It was a loaded question.

"I...I don't know."

"Are you coming to the conference in Derbyshire next week?"

"I haven't spoken to Adam about it yet."

"You don't need his permission, do you? It's an education seminar. Work, Anna." But we both knew it was more than that. There was an undeniable attraction between us. An attraction that meant two nights away in a country hotel was a terrible idea. The conference was for head teachers, deputies. Not for staff at my level. He wanted me there because he wanted me and, if I'm honest, I wanted him but...

"I'm not sure it's a good idea." I had told myself it was a line I wouldn't cross but since he had asked me two weeks ago, I had shopped for new clothes. New underwear. Reveling in the what-might-be.

"It could be good for you. Us." Ross placed his hand on mine. It was too heavy. Too hot. Too everything that wasn't Adam, but I didn't move it. Knowing that even if I did, I would still feel it there.

"Anna," he whispered. "Anna. Why are you so unhappy?"

I found myself opening up to him. Not about my infertility or about Adam—that would have seemed disloyal—but about the pressure I felt to look out for Mum since Dad died. To live up to Dad's legacy as a head teacher. The worry that my nan was becoming more and more forgetful. He listened. The way Adam used to. The way he did in Alircia on the beach.

Ross wiped a tear from my cheek with his thumb.

"Sorry," I said. "This was supposed to be fun."

"I know! Fuck me, it's the last time I ask you out. It's old Maude the dinner lady next time. She looks like a riot."

I laughed and that was something that didn't happen frequently.

"I'd better go." I stood and looped my handbag over my shoulder.

"Stay for another?" He waved the bottle. It was dangerous. I should go home. "I can't drink it, I'm driving. It would go to waste otherwise."

"Okay." While Ross went to the loo, I rattled off a text to Adam, telling him there was a staff meeting after work. I had almost convinced myself it was true until Ross sat down again, not in the chair opposite me this time, but next to me. His thigh pressing against mine.

"This is nice," he said. "Sometimes I love living alone but sometimes I go back to an empty house and it feels so lonely."

"Have you dated? Since your divorce?"

"No. I was holding out until I met the right person—it's soul-destroying being with the wrong person."

"*Was* holding out?"

"We can find happiness in the most unexpected of places, Anna. It's a question of being brave enough to let it in."

I downed my wine. The warm bloom of alcohol loosened my tongue. "I want to be happy but I'm not brave enough."

"I think you're stronger than you think." Ross placed his hand on my knee.

Was I?

It would take courage to leave. Courage to stay.

Thinking of Adam, I stood. I was lost, lonely, desperately unhappy, but lying to my husband was a new low.

"I should go." I meant it this time.

"Can I drop you home?" he asked.

"Please." I directed him, not to my house but to the neighboring street, asking myself why, if it were nothing more than a friendly drink, I didn't let Ross drop me home. But I knew why.

As I unclipped my seatbelt, he leaned across and cupped my face in his hands.

"Anna."

He kissed me.

And I let him.

Adam was sprawled on the sofa. "How was it?"

"What?"

"The staff meeting?"

"Oh, that." I was caught in my web of deceit. Unsure what to say but he had turned his attention back to the TV. I curled up on the armchair, watching my phone screen illuminate as Ross texted me over and over.

I'm sorry.
I'm not sorry.
I shouldn't have kissed you.
I had to kiss you.
I want you.
I think I'm falling in love with you.
Do you want me?

It was the last one that threw me into a tailspin. Did I want him? Or was it that I didn't want this—my eyes flickered to Adam. He was fixated on the screen.

My mind strayed to Ross. His hands. His laugh. His lips. He wasn't my boy from the bar. He would be different.

But it might be better.

In the kitchen, while I waited for the kettle to boil, I splashed cold water onto my face, which was burning with the shame of my illicit kiss. The fact that I had wanted it. The fact that I had enjoyed it, entwining my fingers in his hair as I returned his kiss.

Back in the lounge, Adam held out my phone. "You got a text."

I snatched it from him, studying his face for signs he had read it, shoving my handset into my pocket like a dirty secret I was trying to hide.

Do you want me? Ross had asked.

Later, in bed, I was still examining the questions from all angles when Adam reached across to me. My entire body immediately tensed.

He pressed his lips against mine but all I felt was Ross's lips. His hands caressed my back but all I felt were Ross's hands.

"I'm not in the mood, sorry." I gently pushed Adam away. He muttered under his breath. I couldn't make out his words but I probably deserved them. The truth was I didn't want Adam unless I knew I was ovulating and even then it lacked any passion. Sex now a task to be checked off from a never-ending list of mundane things to do.

Empty the dishwasher—tick.

Try to make a baby—tick.

Was it wrong to yearn for something exciting?

Someone who excited me?

I thought about everything until Adam fell asleep and then I reached for my mobile.

Do you want me? Ross had asked.

I gave him my answer.

CHAPTER NINETEEN

Adam

Dawn was pushing the darkness aside when my phone vibrated under my pillow. I hadn't risked the alarm, not wanting to wake Anna. Not wanting her to know. Not yet. I watched her sleep, her face unguarded.

My certainty of the previous night dipped and swelled. I was changing my mind about four million times a minute.

Could I do it?

Should I?

Anna and I had been so unhappy for so long, in some ways it seemed like the right thing to do but…I wasn't sure. It was early but her mobile lit up with a text. I looked at the screen and then I knew for sure.

I crept around the house, shoving things into an old rucksack, praying she didn't wake. When I had everything I needed, I took one, last lingering look at my wife. I contemplated kissing her goodbye but instead I slipped out of the front door, closing it silently behind me.

CHAPTER TWENTY

Anna

The bed was cold and empty when I woke. The house too still. Too quiet. I wondered where Adam was. I tried to remember whether he'd mentioned going out but we'd barely spoken last night.

I reached for my phone. There was a text from Ross. It said, **If you ever change your mind . . .** I felt a momentary pang of regret but turning him down was the right thing to do. He wasn't the answer. I didn't know what the answer was.

Saturday stretched before me long and languid. It was ridiculous that during the week my alarm startled me from sleep, but at weekends I was always awake impossibly early. I got up. Once we would have relished a lie-in, fingers greasy from buttered toast, tongues hot from coffee and later with kisses. We assumed our selfish time was precious, short. Convinced that before long we would have a Moses basket nestled at the foot of the bed. A toddler to take to the park. Weekends would be spent feeding ducks, riding bikes, cutting men from gingerbread before pressing Smartie buttons into the dough. Bath-time. Bedtime. It would all center around them, the children we hadn't yet been able to bring into the world.

*

By ten I had showered, dressed, changed the sheets and cleaned out Hammie's cage while he hared around in his plastic wheel. There was still no word from Adam. I had an uncomfortable feeling in my stomach. I lit a vanilla candle before I retrieved the bills we had stuffed down the side of the microwave. I might as well do something useful with my time before he came home. The house felt different without him here. For a moment I pretended he was never coming back.

You should leave. That *would make me happy*, I had said Thursday night, but would it? I didn't feel the same about Adam when I looked at him anymore but had my shame, my guilt, clouded my vision? We never used to bicker like we did now. Would we be happier apart? Would Adam? Should I set him free? Set both of us free? It was hard not to cling to the familiar. The comfortable. I still remembered crying in my old cat Pugwash's fur, reluctant to let him go despite knowing it would be best for him. Wanting him to be pain-free but unable to contemplate a life without him.

I opened the kitchen drawer to fetch our banking folder. Instead of being under the clean tea towels I had placed there yesterday morning, it was on top of them.

Unease squirmed in my belly as I scanned the contents. Our savings account book was missing. A chill swept through me. Adam must have taken it, but why?

He's leaving you.

The thought popped into my head.

I reached for my phone and called him. His photo smiled up at me from my screen. There would be an innocent explanation. Adam wouldn't use the money we had been saving for our family.

He wouldn't just take it.

My palm was clammy by the time his answer service kicked in.

He had rejected my call.

By lunchtime Adam still wasn't home. I had rung him incessantly. I was driving myself crazy with theories because the fact was too painful to face. Adam had taken our savings book without discussing it with me.

I couldn't call Mum. She had taken Nan on a coach trip to the market Nan liked because it sold every imaginable color of wool. I hadn't gone with them because I had been feeling so exhausted, but now I wished I had. I was going frantic. After a moment of hesitation, I called Nell.

"Hey Anna! I've been meaning to phone you." She sounded pleased to hear from me.

"Have you got time to talk?"

"Yep. I'll just...Oh God, Emily, don't draw on the sofa! Alfie, stop your sister. No, don't join in. Chris?" she yelled. "Sorry, can I call you back in a sec, Anna?"

"Of course."

But she didn't.

By mid-afternoon I was climbing the walls. My stomach was cramping and I realized I hadn't got enough tampons. I also hadn't carried out a pregnancy test. Each month I played that lonely game of maybe-this-time. Every four weeks I vowed that I wouldn't do it again, but I couldn't help carrying out a test on the day my period was due. Despite the endometriosis, my cycle had remained pretty regular and it had become a ritual I was scared to break, not that it had brought me any luck but because, if I didn't carry it out, it would feel like I was giving up hope and hope was all I had.

I used to go to the small chemist at the end of the street. For the first few times the assistant had grinned conspiratorially at me while I had made my purchase. Months stretched into a year and she would no longer meet my eye as she served me. Instead of a smile, she had worn an embarrassed flush around her neck. I had learned never to visit the same shop twice in a row.

"Just these two?" The gum-chewing girl raised her pierced eyebrows at my contradictory duo of Tampax and a ClearBlue kit.

"Yes." I rummaged in my purse for money, hesitating as my fingers brushed Grandad's coin. I couldn't remember the last time Adam had given it to me and I wished I could give it to him now, so that he would know that I was thinking of him. Worrying about him.

About us.

Abashed, I scooped the bag from the counter containing my purchases and my shame. I carried my failings out of the shop, wearing my inadequacies like a coat. Over the years I must have spent over £500 on tests. There were so many things that we could have done with the money. Our bank account was on my mind again when I spotted Adam. He was coming out of the letting agents, and smiling. He was smiling, looking happier than I had seen him look in months. He had a rucksack slung over his shoulder. What was in there? Clothes? Regret stirred in my belly each time I recalled my harsh words.

You should leave. That would make me happy.

Panicked thoughts swarmed. He had taken the money from our savings and rented a house.

The boy from the bar had left me.

I opened my mouth to call him but my throat had swelled with emotion and I couldn't speak.

Isn't this what I wanted, deep down?

If you love someone, set them free.

It was another couple of hours before Adam arrived home and by this time I'd convinced myself he wouldn't be back. I had stuffed the empty box of the pregnancy-testing kit at the bottom of the bin, the way I sometimes hid pink wafer biscuit wrappers, like a shameful secret. I had been rehearsing a speech endlessly in my head, telling myself I would be calm and controlled. This moment could make or break our gossamer-fragile relationship.

"Can we talk?" I blurted out as soon as he walked through the front door.

"Me first." He looked so serious.

Don't say it.

He pulled at the collar of his polo shirt and I knew he was nervous.

Don't say it.

"I've got something to tell you. I think it'll be a shock. But..." His fingers worried at a stray thread. He snapped it off. My eyes filled with tears—will our marriage break just as easily as cotton?

Don't say it.

CHAPTER TWENTY-ONE

Adam

"I've spoken to Ross today," I said again. "Your head teacher?" I added. Anna knew who he was, so why wasn't she saying anything? Her face paled and she swayed slightly. I cradled her elbow and led her through to the lounge. I couldn't believe I had dropped the bombshell on her while standing in the hallway. Sometimes I was such a twat.

"Why? What did he say?" Her voice was barely audible.

"He said it's fine for you to take some time off."

"And I need time off because...?"

"Because." Was I doing the right thing? It was too late now. "We're going back to Alircia on Monday."

"On Monday, but that's..." She looked stunned. I couldn't read her expression. I couldn't tell if she thought it was good or bad.

"The day after tomorrow." I pulled the collar of my polo shirt away from my neck. It was choking me.

"But...How?"

"I've sorted it all out. I dug out our passports and bank stuff and everything before you woke so it would be a surprise. I've been running round all day. I've spoken to my boss, as well as

Ross, and we both have two weeks off. We're staying in the resort where we first met. Where we spent our honeymoon. We'll be there for our five-year wedding anniversary."

"But…"

"I know you think of the island as much as me. I saw your phone this morning. You've changed your screensaver back to the photo of the cove." I took her hand. "Our cove."

"I have been thinking about Alircia. About everything. But…"

"Shh." I tucked a strand of hair that had fallen over her face, behind her ear. "It's a chance to spend some time together, Anna. We need it. We deserve it. I've got our euros. I just need to confirm the travel insurance policy with the travel agents if I can't find a better deal online."

Hammie rattled his teeth noisily against his water bottle. "What about—"

"I called in to see Josh at the letting agents. He's temping there this week. He's going to pop by tomorrow and take Hammie to his place. Come on, say yes. You've been working so hard."

"I can't…Adam, Ross—"

"I know it's term time but honestly he was great. A bit shocked at first. He specifically told me to tell you that he understands and that he wants you to be happy." It was good of him to give me that message to put Anna's mind at rest about missing work.

"Did Ross really say that?"

"Yes. He's a good man."

She began to cry. "Yes. Yes, let's go."

I wiped her tears with my thumb. "You said you wanted to talk?"

For a second she looked afraid. "No. Not now."

I pulled her close to me. "We're going to have a great time,

Anna. It'll all be okay. Everything." My voice was firm, my promises strung tightly together so they couldn't fall apart.

I wouldn't let us fall apart.

I hadn't meant to, anyway.

CHAPTER TWENTY-TWO

Anna

The sea was an impossible blue. The glistening waves beckoned to us as they lapped against the honeyed sands. We had landed a few hours ago and after unpacking we'd come out for a walk. The late-afternoon heat pushed us back as we trudged up the slope toward our cove. The place I first realized that I didn't want to live without Adam. It had become more touristy since we had last visited on our honeymoon. There was a scattering of shops and bars where whitewashed houses once stood.

"Do you think our lock is still there?" I nodded toward the myriad padlocks that clamped their love onto the fence bordering the beach.

"Doubtful. They've probably got rid of loads to make way for more. It's a tourist attraction. The souvenir shop over there is selling them for ten euros." He pointed to an A-Board. "Hey." He noticed the way my face collapsed. "Don't be sad."

But I wasn't just sad because part of our history had been rewritten. I was also nervous. Scared of the things I needed to say. Scared of his reaction.

"Fancy an ice cream?" he asked.

"No. A bottle of water would be good though."

My mouth was dry, too full of the words I couldn't speak.

While Adam was in the shop, I stared out into the distance. A yacht bobbed toward the opposite island.

"Here you go." Adam handed me a bottle of Evian. "And this is for you. Us." He rustled a paper bag toward me. Inside was a lock and a pen.

"Can we do it later?" I pushed the bag back toward him.

"Anna, what's wrong?" He looked at me with such concern. Such love.

I had to tell him.

Today.

Now.

"Nothing...I...Let's do the lock. Can you write it?"

"What shall I put?" Adam removed the cap of the marker with his teeth. "Adam and Star?"

He hadn't called me Star for such a long time. It was being back here, the nostalgia making us feel nothing had changed when of course, everything had. More than he knew. Why couldn't I just say it?

"I think..." I took a deep breath of salty air. The sun was dipping over the ocean, burning a fiery red ball into the center of the sea. In the distance, a guitarist strummed a ballad. I couldn't understand the Spanish words he was singing but I felt his emotions.

All of them.

I had wanted the perfect moment and it didn't get more perfect than this. "I think you should write 'Adam & Anna' but leave a space underneath."

"For a love heart?"

"For another name."

"I don't get it?" His eyes drifted from my face, to the hand I had placed protectively over my stomach. "Do you... You're not..."

"I am."

The sun shifted once more, the sky turning coral.

Suddenly he was crying and I was crying and, although I knew it was impossible, although I knew I was only six weeks pregnant, I swear I felt the baby—our baby—turn cartwheels of joy inside of me.

It would all be all right. Without the pressure of trying to conceive. The crushing disappointment when I didn't. It would all be all right.

It had to be.

CHAPTER TWENTY-THREE

Adam

Stretching my hands toward the sky, I roared, "I'm going to be a dad!!" My elation was carried in the salty sea breeze, lightly touching a clutch of tourists snapping the sunset. They turned and smiled. Sharing my joy.

Our joy.

"I'm going to be a dad!" I couldn't stop saying it. I picked up Anna and swung her round and round, until I was dizzy with the movement, dizzy with her news, dizzy with the responsibility. "Oh God." I rested her down gently but didn't let go of her. "Do you feel sick? Do you need to sit down?"

"I'm fine," she laughed. "A bit tired but fine."

She did look pale but there was something else in her expression. Relief? She couldn't have thought I would be anything but over the moon.

"But when…How?" I sounded like a knob. But…fuck. We were having a baby!

"I found out on Saturday. It was horrible keeping it from you. I'm not…I'm not going to keep anything from you again." She looked so serious. "I thought this was the perfect place to tell you—here was the beginning of the story of us."

"And now it's the start of a whole new chapter. Part two!" I picked up the lock and pen where I'd dropped them on the ground.

Adam, Anna
&

I wrote on the lock before I passed it to her. As she secured it to the fence, I placed my hand over hers, the way I had after I'd slipped the wedding ring on her finger.

My wife.

Soon I can say my wife and child.

A lucky bastard, Josh would say.

He'd be right.

Excitement nudged me awake. Anna was still sleeping, her hair fanned over the pillow. Quietly, I pulled on yesterday's shorts and T-shirt and headed down to the shop where I had bought the love lock yesterday. I had seen the perfect gift for my wife; I just hadn't known it at the time. When I returned, a purple velvet pouch nestled in my pocket, I was hoping to slip back into bed for a cuddle but Anna was dressed so instead we went for breakfast.

"Can I get you more tea? Toast?" I asked for the hundredth time.

"I'm fine," she said again but she hadn't looked fine. I was irritating her with my constant fussing, but I couldn't help it. Last night, as she had slept, I had googled pregnancy and learned that the baby was roughly 7mm long and the size of a pea. Next week they would have doubled in size.

"Have you told your mum?" It only just occurred to me that I might not be the first to know.

"Not yet, but I'll tell her as soon as we're home."

I had a list of people I wanted to tell: Josh, his parents. My parents.

"This might bring you closer to Nell."

"I hope so." Anna's face was relaxed. She looked like a different person. "I don't want to tell the world until after my twelve-week scan though."

"We don't have to tell anyone until you're ready." I liked having a secret that just the two of us shared. "But those Japanese tourists from last night know, and the barman, the hotel receptionist—"

"You couldn't help yourself!" The corners of her mouth briefly upturned. "But if anything does go wrong—"

"*Nothing* will go wrong," I said, as though the determination in my words could make it so.

We had waited too long for this.

My wife and child.

I would lay down my life to protect them.

"Bugger. So much for a quiet afternoon."

It was only eleven o'clock but the closest beach to our hotel, Pacifico, was a riot of noise and color. Music and laughter. Red and green bunting hung between wooden poles pushed into the sand. A BBQ sizzled the scent of beef. A makeshift bar was laden with goldfish-sized glasses filled with milky pina colada, garnished with chunks of pineapple, straws and pink paper umbrellas.

"Do you want to walk the extra fifteen minutes around to the cove where it's quieter or head back to the hotel? Lay by the pool instead?" I asked.

Culture Club asked if you really want to hurt me.

"And tear you away from free booze and all the terrible Eighties music you love?" Anna gestured with her rolled-up towel. It was the only thing I had let her carry and only then because she said I looked like a donkey about to buckle under the load of sun cream, windbreak, books, camera, hats, lilo.

"An ass, you mean?" I had replied.

"An arse more like."

We spread out our towels and lay down. I idly trickled warm, dry sand between my fingers.

"Excuse me, sir? Free yacht trip?" The man in front of me was wearing a navy polo shirt adorned with a red "WLY" logo. He gestured toward a yacht.

"What's the catch?"

"No catch. It's the launch of Webster's Luxury Yachts. We've different-sized yachts available to hire for holidays and private functions. Today we're giving people a taste by offering a trip to the island over there. We'll bring you back later. There's a couple of spaces left on the yacht leaving right now. It's a beauty. There's forty passengers on board and several crew."

"Anna?"

"I'm so comfortable here."

"But we wanted to go to the island. I've never been on a yacht. It will be an experience we won't forget."

"Okay." Anna reached for her sarong. "It had better be unforgettable."

The yacht was larger than it looked from the land. On its shiny white side, *Maria* was painted in curling letters. The guests lounged on padded seats, and women in bikinis and sunglasses tilted their faces toward the sky, the breeze styling their hair. There was a small pool on board, not large enough to properly swim in but sizable enough. A waiter offered us drinks from a silver tray—champagne for me, orange juice for Anna—telling us the pool could be covered at night to form a dance floor.

"I could get used to this." I raised my glass and toasted. "To us."

"The three of us." Anna grinned. "Shall we go for a wander?" We made our way down some stairs. The doors to the cabins were open for us to explore.

"A double bed." I sat on it and bounced up and down.

"What were you expecting? Bunks?"

"Kind of. Josh would kill to see this."

"It's not quite worth dying for," Anna said.

We carried on exploring. There was a bar with squashy sofas and a flat-screen TV. Music pumping from discreetly positioned Sonos speakers. Something loud with a thumping bass.

"Want to sit?"

"No, let's get some air," Anna said. On the deck she took deep breaths. I wondered if she had morning sickness. I guided her forward until we were standing at the pointy bit of the yacht. The front. I put down our glasses before stretching Anna's arms out to the side, circling her waist before I sang that Celine Dion song from *Titanic*.

"Idiot." She rested her head back on my shoulder. The wind whipping her hair around my face—she still smelled of coconut. I slid my left hand to her stomach. Flat for now, but according to Google there would be a bump there in the next few weeks. I had never been happier. I knew this trip would be unforgettable.

"I love you." I kissed her neck.

"I love you too."

She stumbled as the yacht suddenly lurched to one side. Her free hand grabbed the railing. "What was that?"

"Dunno." I cast my eyes around. No one else looked concerned.

"Hope we don't break down," she said.

"We won't. The yacht will go on. You know what else will go on?"

"Your heart?"

"Yep. Because every night—"

A judder.

Shouting.

Two waiters pelting across the deck, trading Spanish words I couldn't understand. One loosening his bow tie as he ran.

"Adam?"

"It's nothing." But I was beginning to think it was something.

Suddenly an alarm, a shrill beeping sound that pressed down on us from all sides.

"Adam, the boat is tipping."

We watched in alarm as our glasses slowly slid across the wooden deck before they toppled into the sea.

"Come on." I took her hand. Not that a disaster was about to happen—I could see land in two different directions—but something wasn't right. I would have felt happier if Anna was wearing a life jacket. I would have felt safer if she was wrapped entirely in cotton wool for the next nine months.

The yacht careened violently. Anna crashed to her knees. "Adam?" She was panicking now. I could hear it in her voice. All around us was noise. The smashing of glasses, champagne spilling onto the deck, the beeping of the alarm. Yelling, harried words in Spanish, the crew hurtling in all directions.

"It's okay." I helped her up.

"We're fucking sinking!" someone bellowed, and instantly a child began wailing.

It was too much, the crying, the shouting, the incessant alarm.

Think, Adam.

"I'll be back in a second."

"Don't leave me." Anna was crying now. I rushed toward one of the catering staff and grabbed his arm.

"My wife, she can't swim. Life jacket?"

He garbled an answer in Spanish. His eyes wide.

"Where's the fucking lifeboat?" a woman screamed. "We're going to die!"

I wanted to tell her to shut up. That we were so close to both islands that no one was going to die, but above the cacophony of sound I could hear Anna calling me. I hastily made my way back to her but the boat was now at more of an angle and I lost my footing and crashed onto my side, pain shooting through my hip. "Stay where you are," I shouted, raising my head, knowing Anna would try to reach me. I needed her to keep holding on to the railings. I needed to know that she was safe.

I crawled. My hands slapping against the water that flooded the deck. The yacht slowly tilting; if it carried on it would eventually be on its side. I reached Anna.

She crouched down, clinging on to the railings, hyperventilating.

Next to her a teenage boy swept his smartphone around. "This is so fucking cool. My channel will get so many hits."

It was all too much. They needed to shut the alarm off. The beeping was adding to the panic.

The swoosh of a flare. Its red tail cutting through the blue sky.

I heard a splash. Someone had jumped overboard and was swimming toward the shore.

Each time the yacht shifted in the water the waves hit harder and harder. Salt water mixed with the fear in my throat.

Possessions were sliding around the deck. At my feet a teddy bear, a yellow ribbon tied around his neck.

"Any last words." The boy shoved his phone in Anna's face, filming her despair.

"Go fuck yourself." I knocked the mobile from his hand.

The people who had jumped had the right idea. We were going down fast, too fast.

"What...what are we going to do?" Anna could barely speak through her sobs.

"We're not far from shore. We can swim," I shouted over the alarm.

"But I can't—"

"But I can. I've got you." There didn't seem to be any sort of plan. We were closer to the island we had left. I could make it, even with Anna.

I was certain.

"Come on." I scrambled over the railing; the yacht was now at such an acute angle there wasn't much of a drop. "Anna?" I held out my hand. "Jump."

"I can't." She placed both hands over her stomach.

It was on me to protect her. My wife. My son or daughter. The thought was both exhilarating and terrifying. The love I felt, primal. I would get us out of this. I would.

"You can. I've got you." I wouldn't let her fall, either of them. I was Samson-strong.

"I can't...Adam..."

The alarm beep-beep-beeped in time with my heart, which was now in my mouth. What was I going to do if she refused to jump?

"Anna, please," I said evenly as my feet kicked below the surface, the proverbial swan. I stretched out my arms. "Trust me? Please, Star. For me."

She put one leg over the railing, hesitated.

"I'm so scared," she whispered.

"I know, but I won't let anything happen to you. I promise."

Slowly, tentatively, she climbed until she was on the other side of the railing. There was another lurch.

She screamed.

Slipped.

Fell into the water with a loud splash. She disappeared under a wave. I dove beneath the surface and could see her sinking. Deeper and deeper. I swam like I'd never swam before until she was in my arms. They were both in my arms. My wife and child. She struggled. Kicking her legs frantically, dragging us both down again. I broke through the surface. Again and again I fought for us to break free.

"Anna! Stop struggling!" I shouted as we burst into sunlight once more. "Relax. Relax your body. I promise you, you're safe. Star. Relax." Suddenly she became limp.

Other passengers were swimming past us now but I kept a steady pace. The island we had left a short time ago didn't look too far away but it was an age before we reached the shallows, where we stood and stumbled, hand in hand, flopping onto the sand.

My chest was on fire. Each breath hurt. It was an effort to speak.

"Are you okay?" I asked her. "We need to get you checked out. You and the baby." Even on dry land I was horribly worried about them and it occurred to me that I always would be. As a father and a husband, I should be.

"I'm okay, but...but Adam..." She covered her face with her hands and I wrapped my arms around her. Held her as she cried.

"Shh," I soothed. Over her shoulder I could see a small lifeboat crammed with people heading back to shore but there was still a person clinging to the railings of the yacht. Were they a swimmer? An adult? In my mind I saw that teddy bear, fur sodden with sea water, hopeful yellow ribbon tied around his neck.

"I have to go back."

"Adam! No!" Anna clutched my arm.

"There's still somebody on board. Say they can't swim? Think how scared you were, Anna."

"Please don't!" Her fingers dug into my wrist. "It isn't your responsibility."

"Anna, there were *children* on board."

My eyes held hers until she loosened her grip on my wrist and nodded. "Be careful."

I kissed her hard. "I love you, Star." And then I was running back into the sea. Swimming back toward the yacht.

But I was tired. My legs aching. Body slow.

I counted the strokes in my head. Slowly. Methodically. I was about halfway and the urge to rest was immense but Anna was back on the beach, alone and scared, and my arms continued slicing through the water, my legs kicking hard.

Back at the yacht I reached the stray passenger. It was an elderly woman on her knees, desperately clutching the railing.

"Jump," I called.

"I can't swim." Her voice was paper-thin.

"It's okay. I'm a strong swimmer." But the adrenaline that had surged through my veins was leaching into the salty water. I didn't know how much longer I could keep going.

I was tired.

So tired.

CHAPTER TWENTY-FOUR

Anna

Despite the sun blasting out heat, I was shivering. My teeth chattering together. My legs precarious, too unstable to support me.

Adam.

I was on my knees, too weak to stand, shielding my eyes from the brightness bouncing off the waves. Adam was nearly at the yacht. Other swimmers were close behind him, also trying to help. Tourists, the guy from behind the bar, the girl who was flipping burgers on the barbecue. The man who had thrust the leaflet about the yacht trip into Adam's hand was standing, watching. I glared at him. Blaming him.

There was a rubber-band ball of "what if" in my chest growing larger with every passing second. The elastic tightening, making it harder to breathe.

Adam.

He made it. A small, bobbing dot in the sea. He was talking to someone—I couldn't quite make out if it was a man or a woman, an adult or, as Adam had feared, a child, but they were not moving. They didn't know him like I did. They didn't trust him.

He had only been gone a short while but it felt like forever.

Please, I urged, not sure if I was willing the person to get into the water or Adam to turn around and come back. Both, I think. *Please*.

But they didn't move. The yacht shifted dramatically. Almost completely on its side. I couldn't bear to watch but I couldn't turn away from it either.

No. Please. No.

The elastic-band ball inside of my chest had exploded when I saw, with horror, what was happening. Short, sharp, snaps to my heart.

The steel pole in the center of the yacht was falling, falling directly onto Adam.

I screamed his name.

My roar was so deep, so painful, I was sure my baby must have heard it. Felt it. I covered my mouth with my hands as the pole hit Adam.

He disappeared under the water.

I couldn't breathe while I waited for him to resurface.

He didn't.

My boy from the bar was gone.

CHAPTER TWENTY-FIVE

Adam

There was a blow to my skull. The taste of blood in my mouth. Colors bright and dull. Light and dark. A kaleidoscope of pain.

Water, in my mouth and eyes.

Water, in my nose and ears.

My arms and legs flailed. I was sinking deeper and deeper. Dizzy. Disorientated. My lungs burning, chest tight.

The water morphed from blue to gray to almost black. I was spinning. Twisting in the sea, everything about to explode. My skull. My rib cage. Body burning.

Anna.

I tried to swim but I felt so odd.

Couldn't think straight. Couldn't force my legs to kick their way to the surface.

I was sinking. Heavy. A mass of pain and regret and fear.

I was drowning but, rather than my life flashing before me, there was only one thought in my head.

Anna.

I was heavy and light and here but not.

Drifting. Drifting. My arms and legs splayed.
I was weightless.
A feeling of calm washed over me.
And then I felt nothing at all.

CHAPTER TWENTY-SIX

Anna

*A*dam.

I couldn't lose him. Not now. Not when our future was at last bright and glittering with all the things we had dreamed of.

Adam.

How could I ever have thought that I didn't want him anymore? I did.

Oh, how I did.

The other swimmers had reached the yacht and were diving under, resurfacing without him.

Adam.

The beach had lost its color. Its noise. Holidaymakers static and silent, staring out to sea like mannequins.

"He's got him!" someone shouted. Adam's head surfaced and a sob clawed up my throat.

"Bring him back," I screamed, beckoning with both hands, quickly, quickly.

I paced.

One step.

Two.

Three.

Turn.

A tiger in a cage. Coiled. Ready to spring the second they reached shallower water. Ready to shower my husband with love and kisses.

At last they were closer but Adam didn't stand. Instead he was dragged onto the sand and dropped heavily.

Adam.

I fell to my knees beside him. Shaking him. Wake up. Wake up.

"He's not breathing!" Frantically I scanned the crowd. The horrified expressions. The camera phones. Why wasn't anyone helping?

"Please." I shook Adam again, crying harder. "Someone."

"Let me see." A woman kneeled opposite me, her fingers scooping the inside of Adam's mouth, before checking his neck for a pulse.

"Adam. He's called Adam." It was important that she knew but she didn't answer. Instead, she breathed into his mouth—the mouth that had kissed me goodbye. She linked her hands and pushed hard on his chest.

How can his heart have given up when it was so full of love for me? For our unborn child.

His face was pale. The sand, once golden, was stained crimson by the blood trickling from a wound on his head.

I waited for him to gasp, the way they do in the movies. For water to spew from his beautiful lips.

It didn't.

Adam.

Please don't leave me.

PART THREE

"Giving up isn't an option."

JOSH QUIGLEY—ADAM'S BEST FRIEND

CHAPTER TWENTY-SEVEN

Anna

The smell of hospitals was the same wherever you were in the world. Abrasive and clinical; disinfectant mingled with bleach, sorrow tinged with fear.

Adam hadn't woken up.

I tightly clutched the itchy gray blanket that had been draped around my shoulders, wishing it were my husband's hand that I was holding. I half ran to keep up with the trolley as it was wheeled down a corridor, bright with harsh, fluorescent light. Doctors and nurses blocked my view as they poked and prodded him, chattering away in a language I couldn't understand. They could have been saying Adam had no chance of survival, they could have been discussing last night's TV, what they'd be eating for dinner. I had no way of knowing.

I had never felt more scared.

"Where are you taking him?" I asked again. "Why isn't he waking up?"

Again, my questions went unanswered.

The trolley burst through double doors with a clatter, its wheels squeaking on lino. I tried to follow it but a pretty nurse, with a swinging high ponytail, caught my elbow.

"Please." I attempted to break free, but her grip was firm.

"English?"

I nodded.

"You come."

"But Adam—"

"He looked after. We check you okay."

I didn't need somebody to tell me I was okay. I wasn't. I was falling and breaking apart. I hovered outside the room Adam had been taken into, second-guessing what was going on inside, but my medical knowledge was limited to watching *Casualty* on a Saturday night. My grasp of Spanish non-existent.

A woman hurried past me, a tormented expression on her face, a baby in her arms. Immediately I laid my palm gently on my stomach.

"I…I'm pregnant," I told the nurse.

"Come." Her voice softer. I let her lead me away.

My eyes, throat and ears had been peered into; a blood pressure monitor wrapped tightly around my arm. My temperature had been taken. I'd had a scan. Been offered tea, coffee and a plate of fish and vegetables that had made my stomach roil. My body was clad in borrowed scrubs, too short and too tight but at least they were dry. I had been offered everything except the one thing I really wanted: assurances that my husband would be okay.

Was okay.

The family room was small and airless, the walls a dirty orange, the floor an expanse of shining white tiles knitted together with darker grout. In the corner, a red bucket speared by a mop. Here, it smelled like lemons. I sank onto a too-soft, too-low chair. My knees almost level with my chin. There was a stack of magazines on the table I couldn't read, and then a tourist's guide to Alircia, which I could but didn't. It was painful to see the photos of all the places Adam and I had visited on our previous visit: the volcano, the lava tunnel, the underground lake. There were so many things I had yet to do with Adam. So many places we hadn't been. I refused to believe he wouldn't wake up, and yet worry throbbed relentlessly at my temples.

I was longing to talk to someone. That's what they always did on TV dramas, wasn't it? Low mutters and desperation pouring down a phone line. But who? Adam hadn't been close to his parents for years. If I called my mum it would bring back memories of Dad being rushed to hospital and she would feel helpless being so far away. She couldn't fly out because she had to look after Nan. I would tell Mum soon, but not until I could hold it together without crying. She wouldn't know how to cope.

I didn't know how to cope.

It crossed my mind that I could call Nell, but there was a part of me that wanted to believe this wasn't happening. That saying it out loud would make it so. Besides, I hadn't any facts to share, speculation was all I had at that point. I veered wildly between thinking that Adam was fine, sitting up in bed and joking, to convincing myself he hadn't made it and no one wanted to be the one to tell me.

No news is good news.

It was a ridiculous saying—one that had never made sense to me—but it was all I had to cling on to. If I hadn't been told Adam had died, he had to be alive.

Didn't he?

The slam of a door roused me. Shock had beckoned sleep. I was slouched on my seat, my head resting uncomfortably against the wall. My neck was cricked, spittle crusting around my mouth.

It was a different nurse to the one who had carried out my tests. She crouched down and sandwiched my hand between hers.

"Anna." She nodded as she spoke my name.

I held my breath, waiting for her to speak.

"I can take you to see Adam now." Her English heavy with accent.

"Is he...Is he..."

"He's comfortable."

I was afraid to ask what that meant. Instead I let her help me to my feet, which tingled with pins and needles, wishing I could transfer the same numb feeling to my heart.

The hospital was a maze. We twisted and turned through winding corridors. Curious glances followed me; the visibly upset girl in the ill-fitting scrubs.

Comfortable.

That's what they had said about my dad after he had had his heart attack and then they had sent Mum home to rest. He had died four hours later, alone.

The nurse slowed, stopped outside of a door.

"This is our intensive care unit. Anna, don't be frightened when you see him."

If I had been scared before, now I was terrified.

She gestured for me to go in first. Tentatively I stepped inside. Greeted with the sight of Adam, I stumbled backward, treading on her toes.

"It's okay." She rubbed my arm. My hands were clasped over my mouth.

But it wasn't okay. It wasn't okay at all.

CHAPTER TWENTY-EIGHT

Anna

There he was—Adam—unrecognizable and yet familiar. Under a startling amount of wires and tubes he was still. Silent.

"I know it looks scary, but everything in here is for Adam's good." The nurse kept one hand on my arm. "That's the ventilator." She pointed to a machine. "It's keeping oxygen circulating through Adam's bloodstream."

"It's breathing for him? Can't...can't he..."

"The doctor will talk to you as soon as he can. That's the vital signs monitor."

"Why isn't it beeping?" I had watched my fair share of medical dramas. It was so quiet.

"Adam won't be left alone so the monitors are silenced. An alarm will sound if the readings fall outside of the set parameters."

If.

"Adam also has a catheter, and that"—she pointed to a tube—"is a CVP—a central venous pressure line..." I couldn't focus on what she was saying. I couldn't tear my eyes away from Adam, willing him to move. Open his eyes.

He didn't.

The door opened and a man with dark bushy eyebrows and a solemn face stepped inside. A man who could make or break my future.

"Mrs. Curtis." He held out a hand. "I'm Dr. Acevedo." His English was perfect. "We've carried out some tests on your husband—"

"What sort of tests?"

"A CT scan of Adam's head, chest X-rays and bloods. The CT scan indicates some internal bleeding in the brain. If someone has bleeding in the brain this can lead to increased pressure, so the main priority is to reduce the pressure from rising any more. We've sedated and ventilated Adam because this can help to prevent the pressure rising, but it isn't guaranteed."

"But what do you think? He will be okay?"

"Mrs. Curtis, it's impossible to say at this stage. What we know is Adam sustained a head injury and was underwater for more time than we'd like. The brain was starved of oxygen for several minutes. It's unclear whether Adam will have suffered any permanent damage. We're doing all we can."

"So…"

Permanent damage.

I had never felt so overwhelmed.

"But even if he…he *will* be okay?" I was asking the impossible. "He's young, and he's fit and—" Words fell from my mouth in a jumble. If I could just convince the doctor that Adam shouldn't be here, then he wouldn't have to be. I laid my trump card, "He's going to be a dad," hoping it was the thing that would make the difference. Make the doctor say, "Oh, okay then, I'll bring him round." But he didn't.

"It's impossible to predict at this stage." He caught sight of my face. "I'm sorry. I know it's not the news you wanted to hear. It's probably best that you go back to your hotel and get some rest. Someone will be with your husband at all times."

"I think…I think I'll just sit here awhile if that's okay?"

"Of course." He nodded.

"Can I…Can I touch him?" I glanced toward the bed, and the tubes and wires coming out of Adam's hand, his mouth, his stomach. Everywhere.

"Yes." His voice was softer now. "You won't dislodge anything if you're careful. Please try and rest though. It's understandable that you want to be here but you have to look after yourself. Think about your unborn child."

And just like that, he tore me in two.

"I'll speak to you again tomorrow." He hesitated at the door. "Mrs. Curtis, I hate to ask but if you could give the details of your travel insurance to reception, someone can get onto them first thing. It sounds clinical, I know, but it is necessary."

"Yes, I will," I said. I didn't have the policy but I remembered Adam saying he was booking it through the travel agent.

Somebody else to ring.

Something else to do, when all I wanted to do was cry.

Outside, a fist of darkness snatched the last of the daylight away. Adam's room was gloomy, lit only by the light from the corridor spilling through the window, but I preferred it this way. After Dr. Acevedo left, I'd cautiously approached Adam's bed, almost scared of this man I had been married to for the past five years. He was vulnerable in a way I hadn't seen him before. I had sat, watching intently, for a flicker of eyelids, for the movement of a finger, a toe, however tiny. My head had throbbed with shock and sadness and fear.

"Wake up. Adam, please wake up." My whispers had been urgent, the way they sometimes were in the middle of the night when I had thought I'd heard something. Adam would instantly spring awake and pad downstairs barefoot, in his boxers. There was never anybody there and Adam, in our first few years together, had never complained about being woken. In more recent times, he had huffed and sighed his way back to bed and I'd tetchily asked if he'd rather stay asleep and be murdered. He had dramatically rolled over, pulling the covers to his chin, telling me I was being ridiculous.

"Adam," I whispered again. I wouldn't have cared if he'd called me all the names under the sun if I'd managed to rouse him. I didn't care about any of the small things anymore, because the big thing, the most important thing, was that he woke up so we could go home. "Wake up," I whispered again, ignoring the pitiful expression on the nurse's face who remained in the corner of the room, like a statue.

But he hadn't.

I talked incessantly, reminding him that he had a life worth coming back to. When I'd exhausted our memories, when I'd been exhausted by our memories, I plucked random countries from my mind and talked about his plans to visit them. "France. You remember that's where you were going to start your trip, Adam? You were going to eat frogs' legs and croissants and visit the Notre-Dame." We had talked about it sometimes, the two of us completing Adam's dream trip before we started a family, but I hadn't wanted to leave my home. My family and friends. It wasn't only the thought of Mum living alone, without Dad, coping with

Nan; I found the thought of months living out of a rucksack daunting rather than exciting. I wondered whether Adam ever regretted not going. Whether he ever regretted meeting me. "We could go now," I offered. "You, me and the baby. The adventure of a lifetime. That's what Nell toasted on the plane when we first flew out here. Did I ever tell you that? It has been, hasn't it? The adventure of a lifetime, you and me?" We may not have traveled or done anything notable but we had made a life together, we had created this new life that bloomed inside of me.

Hours later I was quiet; I had been dozing on and off but was awake once more. Through the graying light I could barely make out his features. I held his hand, careful where I placed my fingers, and closed my eyes, stroking his thumb with mine. It could be just he and I as dawn broke. Throughout the night I had adjusted to the noises in the corridor outside, the squeak of a trolley being wheeled in the corridor, the chatter of nurses, the odd peal of laughter, relegating them to the background. It was nothing but white noise. Oddly comforting.

"Okay, mister. Hint taken. I'll shut up and let you sleep for now. You must be exhausted after all your hero antics yesterday. I can't believe you've saved me from almost drowning twice. But soon it will be time to get up. We can't all laze about in bed. Some of us are growing a life, remember? And if you don't wake up, you're going to end up with a child named Charlotte or Harry. Neither of which you liked."

I cast my mind back to five years ago. The way we thought it would effortlessly happen for us. Knitting another square in our patchwork blanket of the family we wanted to create had almost caused us to unravel. I tried to remember how it was when we were happy. But I couldn't. It was impossible to focus on anything except the here and now. The fear that I was losing him. The nagging, gnawing feeling in the pit of my stomach telling me I had caused this. Divine intervention. Wasn't that what I believed I had wanted, last week, last month, last year? To be without him? And now that I was faced with that prospect, I found myself clinging on too hard.

Too tightly.

The following day Adam was still under sedation. Still just lying there, and although I knew it was safer this way so the pressure in his brain didn't increase, I longed for them to wake him up. The nurse urged me to go back to the hotel to shower and rest, but I convinced myself that we'd only be here for one more night. That tomorrow Adam would wake and we'd both be leaving together. For the second night, I settled down at the side of his bed and tried to snatch some sleep.

My heart pounded. At first I wasn't sure what had pulled me from my fitful dreams. It wasn't the nurse carrying out her regular checks. Adam's machines were still illuminated, still silent. No alarm had sounded. Then I felt it. A cramping in my stomach. Not a niggling, time-of-the-month cramp. Or cramps from not eating properly for two days. Steel fists twisting my insides. Sweat slick on my skin. The scrubs I was still wearing sticking to me. My breath came hard and fast. I doubled over on the chair, waiting for the pain to stop. When it finally did, I cautiously raised my head. Where was the nurse? There was supposed to be somebody in the room with Adam at all times. I willed my pain-weak body to stand so I could fetch her, but the pain hit again. Winded, I crossed my arms over my stomach and dropped forward, my head almost in my lap. The spasms were intense. The way I imagined contractions would feel. My body fighting to push something out.

No.

There was a dampness between my legs. I was crying now. The pain unbearable, both physical and emotional.

No.

Waves of nausea battered me. I vomited all over the floor. Shaking, my hand reached for the emergency buzzer. I wrapped my arms around myself tightly as though I could hold myself together.

As though I could keep my baby inside.

"Please," I gasped as the nurse rushed into the room, flicking on the light. "Please. There's something wrong with me."

I stood to move toward her but the floor shifted beneath my feet. The last thing I could remember before the blackness swallowed me was trying to make a deal with God to keep my baby safe. Trading my life for my child's. Trading Adam's life.

The second I had thought that, I hated myself and I tried to take it back. I wanted them both. I needed them both.

Adam, don't die.

He was the last thing I saw as my vision tunneled.

My last conscious thought.

CHAPTER TWENTY-NINE

Anna

Curtains swished around the bed next to mine. It was visiting time on the ward and, as if they believed the flimsy piece of pale green fabric could drown out their voices, the family chattered loudly in a language I couldn't understand. Even if they were speaking in English, I didn't think I'd be able to process what they were saying. My mind was full of one thing.

I had lost our baby.

I had cried, begged, offered the doctor money to save the life that had been ebbing away, but it was too late. After examination, I had been given the option to wait and see if all the pregnancy tissue—and hearing my baby referred to as this brought a fresh bout of tears—expelled naturally, which could take weeks, or to take medicine to speed the process up to a few hours. Reluctantly, I had chosen the latter. The sooner the "process," as the doctor called it, was over, the sooner I could recover my strength, and I needed to be strong for Adam. But I hadn't been able to force the tablet down. I had sobbed, retched, shook my head over and over, but eventually the tablet had dissolved under my tongue and today . . . today I felt anything but strong.

I was waiting for the nurse to bring me some lunch. If I ate, she had promised me that the doctor would discharge me. That I could go straight to see Adam. She had checked on him twice for me, relaying that his sedation had been withdrawn. He was breathing on his own, which I thought must be a good sign, so why wasn't he waking up?

I rolled onto my side, turning away from the clock that taunted me with its slow, slow hands. On the other side of the window was a blue cloudless sky. Holidaymakers would be counting their blessings, *another day on the beach*. It was hard to believe that was Adam and I just forty-eight hours ago.

A breeze caressed my face but nothing could cool my eyes, hot and swollen from crying. Somehow, I slept.

"Anna."

Hearing my name, I scrambled to sit up, my heart thudding in my chest. Immediately thinking the worst. "Is Adam—"

"No change. I've brought your lunch."

I propped myself up on pillows as the nurse slid a tray on wheels across my bed. The plate placed in front of me was stacked with mozzarella, lettuce, thick slices of juicy tomatoes, all sprinkled with basil.

"Thanks. And when I've eaten this, I can go?"

"Yes. I'll fetch some painkillers you can take when you leave, and some more sanitary pads for you."

"I don't have any clothes." My words came out a choke.

"I'll find you something." She patted my hand before she left.

I felt sick from the medication, sick from exhaustion, sick from everything that had happened, but I cut off a small piece of mozzarella and chewed and chewed until there was virtually nothing left to slide down my throat. I repeated until my plate was empty. When I'd finished I swung my legs out of bed and unsteadily made my way to the bathroom, touching the wall with my fingertips to keep my balance. There, I dropped to my knees and vomited up everything I had eaten, bile stinging my throat. Afterward, I went back to my bed and pretended I was fine and before long, they let me leave.

Rather than rushing straight into the intensive care unit, I found myself standing in the corridor outside, drawing lungfuls of air to steady my wobbly legs.

Please.

Deep breath in. Deep breath out.

Please let him have woken up.

I placed my palm on the door and forced my mouth into something resembling a smile so he did not see how worried I had been.

"The ventilator has gone." Adam was breathing on his own. I grinned at the nurse but her somber expression pushed the smile from my face.

"Mrs. Curtis—"

"Call me Anna, please. Is he..."

Still Adam?

"I'll go and fetch Dr. Acevedo. He wants to talk to you."

The second she had gone I sank into her still-warm chair.

"Adam..." I faltered. Unsure what to say. Could he hear me? I didn't want to tell him I had lost the baby, not like this but...

I was still deliberating when the door opened.

"Dr. Acevedo." I rose to my feet. My stomach twisting itself into knots.

"Please. Sit." He gestured to the chair and I knew that whatever he was about to tell me wasn't the good news I was longing for.

The knot in my stomach pulled itself tighter.

"We've withdrawn sedation from Adam and as you can see, he hasn't woken up. That's not to say that he won't, but he's currently in a coma."

"But he's breathing on his own now? That must..."

"I'm sorry it isn't better news."

We both looked at Adam. None of this made sense to me. My pulse was galloping. I felt like I might fall.

"A coma?" I struggled to recall what I knew about the condition. It was a term I'd heard a hundred times before, on TV, in movies, but in that second I couldn't define exactly what it was.

"It's from a Greek word, meaning state of sleep. Adam's brain injury has resulted in the impairment of his conscious action. His brain is active but only at base level."

"Right. So..." I couldn't think of a single intelligent thing to ask. Coma was such an innocuous word but the consequences were unimaginable. I had never felt more frightened.

I glanced at Adam.

"But he'll wake up?" There was a burning behind my eyes, in my throat.

"Typically comas last between two and four weeks. The longer a patient is in one, the less chance they have of emerging or surviving."

"But he'll wake up within a month, won't he?"

"Mrs. Curtis." Dr. Acevedo couldn't quite meet my eyes. "Whether somebody recovers from a coma is largely dependent on the severity and cause. Taking into account the blow to Adam's head, the lack of oxygen when he was underwater, the fact he hasn't woken after sedation was withdrawn, and his test results... you need to prepare yourself. *If* Adam does wake, he may have some physical, intellectual or psychological impairment."

The thought was horrifying. "So...even..." I clenched my hands into fists. "Even if Adam wakes up, he might not be...the same?"

"Similar experiences tell me that—"

"Regardless of your experience, I don't think you've had enough time to carry out proper treatment." My voice was high. Indignant. "There must be *something* you can do."

"I wish there was, but there's nothing else we can do at this stage except keep Adam comfortable and nourished. *If* Adam does wake up, there would be further tests, of course."

I couldn't take any more of his pessimism. "If we were at home, in England, would they be doing anything differently?"

"There's nothing that can bring a patient out of a coma. It's a waiting game."

I felt I was the one who was drowning. I willed Adam to move, to sit up and rip the tubes and wires from his body. To prove this bloody doctor wrong.

But he didn't.

"Can Adam hear us?"

"It's impossible to know. Sometimes patients wake and recall conversations that were carried out by their bed. I'm sorry." He shrugged.

"So what happens now?"

"Now? I suggest you go and get some rest; you've had a rough night of it yourself. Unless you have any other questions?"

I wanted to ask, why did this happen to him? To me? To us? What would happen if Adam didn't wake up in days, weeks, months?

Years.

I wanted to know everything. I wanted to strip back the medical terminology and the science and understand it all. Adam wasn't a statistic, a condition. He was…he was Adam. My Adam. But I wasn't ready to hear all of the answers and couldn't think how to vocalize all the things I needed to say.

Dr. Acevedo hovered for a few moments at the foot of Adam's bed, picking up his clipboard containing notes that I couldn't decipher, but I knew if I could read Spanish they wouldn't make things any clearer.

"I've other patients to see, Anna," Dr. Acevedo said when I remained mute with shock. "If there's anything you need."

There was so much I needed. I needed Adam to wake up and be a husband to me, to support me through the grief of losing our child. I wanted to ask Dr. Acevedo if he could grant me those things but instead I gave the standard British response "I'm fine, thank you."

I was a liar.

But I would not cry.

I watched Dr. Acevedo leave.

I would not cry.

And then I followed him out of the door. I was going back to our apartment to ring our travel insurance company and arrange to have Adam flown back to England, where surely something could be done. It wasn't hopeless. It wasn't.

I would not cry.

The kindly nurse had given me the money for a cab and a bag full of sanitary pads, and after collecting a spare key from reception I was back in our apartment. Everything was exactly the same as we had left it. Adam's clothes a mess in and around his open suitcase. My things neatly unpacked. In the wardrobe hung the turquoise dress I had worn on our last night here when we had met. I had been planning to wear it again, to take Adam to the same restaurant.

It was freezing. I aimed the remote at the air-conditioning unit that chugged on the wall and wrapped the white cotton duvet around my shoulders.

Still, I shivered.

I had never felt so lost. So alone.

I wasn't quite sure where to start. My bag had sunk with the yacht. Luckily my cash and passport were in the safe at the bottom of the wardrobe, unlike my mobile, which was at the bottom of the ocean. I called reception and asked them to google the number of our local travel agent.

The travel agent took an age to answer. When they did, I jabbered out a condensed version of what had happened and why I needed our travel insurance policy emailed to the hotel.

"I'm sorry, Mrs. Curtis. I can only divulge booking information to the lead passenger."

"That's my husband, Adam."

"Yes. Can I speak to him?"

"Haven't you been *listening*? He's in a *coma*."

"I'm sorry to hear that."

"So can you tell me the details of the travel ins—"

"I'm sorry. I'm only able to talk to the lead passenger."

I demanded to speak to the manager, anger keeping my tears at bay. Once she came on the line I told her, with far more control than I felt, about Adam's condition.

"Oh, I am sorry, Mrs. Curtis. What a start to your break. Will—"

"Can you look up our travel insurance—"

"I'm only really meant to talk to—"

"The lead passenger. Yes, I know. But he's in a *coma*."

"Yes. Of course. Sorry. Just a moment." She tap-tap-tapped on a keyboard. "Right. Mr. Curtis booked and paid for the holiday in full and said he'd ring to confirm about travel insurance one way or the other—we don't recommend leaving the country without it—but…"

"But?" I asked with a sinking feeling.

"He never called back. I'm sorry, Mrs. Curtis. It doesn't look like you have any cover."

The bed tilted. I closed my eyes until my dizziness passed. "But…he's in hospital. I can't afford…"

"I'm sorry. There's nothing I can do."

"You must have been in this situation before? Will they refuse to treat Adam? Kick him out of the hospital?" I was verging on hysteria.

"Without insurance, Mr. Curtis will still be entitled to basic medical care but no extra treatments or tests and of course repatriation won't be covered…"

Her words hit me with force.

Repatriation won't be covered.

I couldn't fly Adam home.

My skin was covered in goosebumps. I was still sitting on the bed. Still clutching the receiver tightly in my hand. It now whirred with the disconnect tone and I put it back on its cradle.

What am I going to do?

After the conversation with Dr. Acevedo and the bleak picture he had painted, I was desperate to be in a UK hospital, but without insurance how could I get Adam back to National Health Service care? It must cost thousands, hundreds of thousands perhaps, to fly a coma patient home with all the medical equipment and at least one nurse.

What am I going to do?

Everything was wrong and I couldn't fix it. I wished my dad were still around. He'd get us home somehow. Surely the government could help? Other people must have been in a similar position before. But how long might that take?

Too long.

Fleetingly I thought of Ross. He was well paid as a head teacher and didn't have a family to support. He likely had the money, but would he help?

Could I ask him?

Exhausted, I stumbled into the shower. Wanting to feel warm. To feel clean. To scrub off the hospital smell and put on fresh clothes. My clothes.

While I lathered my hair, I thought again of Ross. Would it be fair to him, knowing the way he felt about me, to turn to him? Would it be fair on Adam to accept help from a man I had kissed?

In my mind I turned over possibilities until the water ran cold. I stepped out of the shower into a fluffy white towel.

Perching on the edge of the bed, I picked up the phone once more and made a call.

As soon as it connected, I garbled, "It's me. I need you."

CHAPTER THIRTY

Anna

After making the phone call, I had rushed back to the hospital with renewed energy. I wasn't alone. Help was coming. I had read to Adam from *Of Mice and Men*, which I was currently teaching to my class, skipping the sad bit with the dog. Adam would hate that. Now, it was late. Outside in the corridor the lights had dimmed. Eventually I dozed.

The sand was warm beneath my feet.

Adam shielded his eyes as he stared up at the sky; I followed his finger to see what he was pointing at. A parrot flapping his red and green wings soared beneath the sun. "If you love someone, set them free," Adam said.

I woke up drenched in sweat and tried to force the whispers of the dream from my mind.

I won't give up on you, Adam, I won't.

But would he give up on me when he came round? How would he feel when he learned I had lost our baby? His baby. Would he blame me the way I was blaming myself? Would he, after his near-death experience, realize life is too short to spend another five years trying? Leave me for somebody who could effortlessly conceive? I had thought we were going from a two to a three. The thought I might remain forever a one was heartbreaking. I placed my palms gently over my middle. I never got to meet the life that had been growing inside of me but it didn't stop me missing them. My stomach rose and fell with every breath and I imagined it was my baby moving under my hands.

Eventually, I must have drifted back into sleep, because the next thing I was aware of was a clearing of the throat. "Dr. Acevedo. Is everything—"

"It's okay." He picked up on the fear in my voice. "Have you been here all night? You should go home. Get some rest."

But home was nearly three thousand miles away and rest was the last thing I felt like. I rubbed the back of my neck, digging my fingertips hard into knotted muscle. The doctor made his checks and told me nothing had changed. I could tell by his tone he thought this was bad but I was grateful things weren't worse.

Minutes after he had left the room, the door swung open again.

"Mrs. Curtis?" The man hovering in the doorway had pale skin and green eyes that peered at me from behind round, rimmed spectacles. He also had a comforting British accent. His beard was speckled with gray and I'd have guessed that he was in his forties. I didn't think that I had met him before, but there had been so many people passing through Adam's room I had lost track.

"Yes." A ripple passed through me. A knowing that my life was about to change once more.

"I'm Dr. Chapman. Oliver. Can we talk?"

"Yes."

He glanced at the nurse. "Shall we go somewhere? The cafeteria?"

"I don't want to leave Adam."

"I think it would be best if we were somewhere private."

There was something about him I trusted. Perhaps he reminded me of England. I kissed Adam and told him I would be back soon and followed Oliver out of the room before spinning around and rushing back to Adam's side. I fished my grandad's coin out of my purse and left it on Adam's bedside table. If he woke, he would know I had been thinking of him.

We walked in silence. The smell of bacon drifted down the corridor to greet us and I felt a hot, fierce longing for home. For Sunday brunches in our local coffee shop, mopping up beans with thick white bread. Steaming cappuccinos in paper cups and slabs of carrot cake with cream cheese icing carefully packed in a box to take home. I was overcome with a feeling of light-headedness. I steadied myself against the wall as Oliver looked at me with concern.

"Let's sit." He guided me to a table. I shook my head when he passed me the menu. I didn't have the wherewithal to read. "You must eat."

"Anything will do." Food had lost its taste. Rather than questioning me further, he nodded and strode over to the counter, returning minutes later with scrambled eggs on toast and a mug of tea.

He waited until I had finished eating, laid down my knife and fork and pushed my plate away before he spoke.

"Mrs. Curtis." He removed his glasses and rubbed the bridge of his nose.

"It's Anna."

"Anna." Again, a few seconds of silence. "I'm so sorry about your husband—"

"Adam." I wanted to make him real, not a number or a surname. A person.

"I understand Dr. Acevedo has talked to you about Adam's prognosis—"

"I don't…understand." I was trying to be strong but nevertheless my eyes filled with tears. "There must be a way to wake Adam up?" I plucked a serviette from the table and wiped my cheeks.

"I'm so sorry but there isn't. I'm from the Chapman Institute for Brain Science." He slipped his glasses back on, hooking the arms behind his ears. "We're a research center based at the north of the island. A collaboration of scientists, engineers, mathematicians and physicists. We explore the most challenging scientific questions."

"Right." I twisted the serviette in my fingers, not sure how this was relevant to me.

"We're intent on unraveling the secrets of the brain." He leaned forward, his eyes shining. "I'm confident that over time we can improve treatments for neurodegenerative diseases like Alzheimer's, and brain disorders such as autism and schizophrenia."

"How?"

"Various means. We have advanced technology, the best equipment at our fingertips. We know the human brain has at least 133 different types of cells and each cell has a distinct function. They work together to give sensory input, motor function and ultimately consciousness. By studying subjects—"

"Wait." My tone was sharp. "Please don't tell me you want me to give you Adam to study? His brain to *experiment* on!" I leaped to my feet, my chair toppling over with a clatter. "You want to cut him up." I was furious.

"No!" He stood, waving his hands. "God, no. Sorry. I'm not good with words. Scientists often aren't. Please sit."

"I don't think—"

"Five more minutes. Please."

I looked pointedly at my watch before I sat back down and crossed my arms.

"At the Institute we're explorative. Open-minded. Science doesn't—it can't—yet explain everything. Just recently we discovered two new types of neuron in the human brain that... Sorry, I'm going off track. There are many things we understand and many things we don't. Consciousness is something we don't fully—might never fully—understand. Adam is in a coma but does that mean his mind is a blank space? Can he access his memories right now? What does he feel? Is there nothing or is there something?"

"I don't know... I..." Why was he saying those things? "Are you telling me Adam is still able to think?"

"A few years ago a Japanese neuroscientist called Yukiyasu Kamitani developed artificial intelligence to reconstruct images in a person's mind. There was a study with patients who have locked-in syndrome. Through algorithms, a computer lab was able to interpret what the mind was 'seeing' as still images. We've advanced it one step further and I think we've developed tech that will create moving images so we can observe a stream of thoughts like... like a movie is the best way to describe it. It might, and this is a might, be a way to see what locked-in patients, those with dementia, coma patients, are seeing, if anything, in their mind. If there is still anything left of them." He removed his glasses again.

"It all sounds too far-fetched. Too Frankenstein." I glanced around the canteen, expecting someone to jump out with a hidden camera. This had to be one huge prank.

"Most people would be shocked by the leaps science has made.

Cloning. Face transplants. Things that were once only the subject of bad sci-fi fiction is now all achievable. And I think we've—"

"You keep saying *think*."

"It's yet untested."

Furious, I stood, slapping my hands against the table. I leaned toward Oliver.

"You want to test it on Adam? I can't believe—"

"I wouldn't do anything without your permission, I promise. Nothing else. Just this one clinical trial. I can guarantee you it won't hurt him, and I'd share all the results with you, of course."

"Absolutely not."

"This is ground-breaking, you could—"

"Please don't tell me what I could do. Or should do. Adam is my *husband*, not some guinea pig."

"I know that. I know. Look, Anna. I can't imagine what you are going through right now but…" He fumbled in his trouser pocket and pulled out a business card. "Please just think about it." He pressed it into my hand. "We have state-of-the-art medical equipment. Adam would receive the best care, better care than here and there's accommodation for you. You'd be within minutes of his bed day or night."

"I don't care." I started to turn but what he said next pulled me back.

"I'd pay to fly him home immediately afterward." He saw my hesitation. "Anna. If there is anything in Adam's mind, wouldn't you like to know what it is?"

Me. It had to be me in his mind. On his mind. I didn't think I could bear it otherwise.

"I'm sorry. I can't help you."

Without looking backward, I walked away.

*

By the time I had stalked back to Adam's bedside, I was raging with anger. With shock. The door swung open again. "Look, I've told you once," I began, but it wasn't Dr. Chapman. "You came!" Even after our phone conversation, I wasn't sure. I was so overwhelmed with relief.

"Did you ever doubt that I would?" Arms opened and we were a tangle of limbs, hearts pressed together in a tight hug.

"Adam's . . . He's . . ."

"Shh." Soft fingers stroked my hair. "I'm here now. It'll be okay."

And for the first time, wrapped in Nell's arms, in her strength, I felt that it might be.

CHAPTER THIRTY-ONE

Oliver

Well done, Chapman, Oliver thought. *You made a right pig's ear of that.* He had never been very good at expressing himself, sharing his emotions. Clem, his wife, used to laugh at him.

"You're so awkward!"

"Totally." He had grinned.

"Completely, socially inept."

"Absolutely. But you love me anyway."

"That I do." She had pressed a finger to her lips and kissed it before brushing her fingertip against Oliver's mouth. He had nodded his head once. A silent acceptance that he knew how much she adored him. That he adored her too. It became their signal at the numerous functions they had to attend where Oliver would feel out of his depth, unable to keep up with the small talk. The politics. The bow tie around his neck feeling like cheese wire. His eyes would search out hers across the ballroom, she'd be grouped with the rest of the wives. She'd press her finger to her mouth and Oliver would nod.

Their love had been colorful and vibrant then.

Oliver slotted his Corsa into his usual space around the back of the Institute, next to the bins. A million miles from his old homecomings where his Jag would crunch up the driveway. Clem would have been shadowed in the doorway, honeyed light spilling around her shoulders, greeting him with a tumbler of whiskey and her brilliant, brilliant smile.

It was Sofia, his assistant, who greeted him now.

"How did it…Oh, Oliver."

He couldn't summon a smile.

"You mustn't lose heart." She knew him so well. "There'll be other patients—"

"I know," Oliver sighed. He didn't explain that his disappointment wasn't only because after years of hard work he was finally ready to commence clinical trials and he thought he had found a subject, but because the similarities between Anna and Clem had unsettled him. "I'm going to get changed."

His quarters were cramped. Stuffy. The air-conditioning in this part of the building broken. One of these days Oliver would get around to having it fixed but for now he didn't mind the discomfort, welcomed it almost. He supposed he felt he deserved it. Besides, he had come from nothing.

He could live off site, somewhere infinitely more spacious, but he preferred to plow every penny into the Institute. Besides, the tiny lounge that also doubled as a dining room often reminded him of where he had grown up, the kind of place he would probably have spent all of his adult life if it hadn't been for his brief, glorious relationship with Clem.

Oliver took off his tie. He rarely wore one but he had wanted to make a good impression.

It was quiet in this place he couldn't quite call home, and that wasn't only because of his stark surroundings. He missed Clem tinkling on her piano, humming along to the Billie Holiday tracks that crackled and hissed from her record player. He couldn't relax in the silence—it was a stark reminder that he lived alone—but he didn't feel entirely comfortable in the company of others either.

In the bathroom, he splashed cold water onto his face, closing his eyes against the memory of Anna's anger. First meetings were always impossible, but still, he could have handled it better. The first time he met Clem had been just as disastrous. Her father's friend was holding a benefit. His wife had suffered a stroke and he had wanted to raise both money and awareness for brain research. Oliver's boss, Mateo, had been scheduled to give a speech but at the last minute he had come down with a sore throat and asked Oliver to step in. Oliver had stood on the stage under the bright, white lights, sweat sticking the shirt to his back, his voice a stammer. He had been completely out of his comfort zone and that was before he had even spotted the woman in the front row, sparkling in a sea-green dress, thick dark hair cascading over her shoulders.

"And mermaid" had slipped out of his mouth before he corrected himself to "And moreover" and the rest of his carefully prepared presentation fell out of his mouth in a gibbering rush. Afterward she had approached him.

"That was quite a speech."

He had waited for a punchline that didn't come.

"It must be so rewarding to know you're making a difference. The world needs more people like you." There was a wistful look in her eyes. "Do you think you'll ever find a cure for Parkinson's? My grandfather had it. Such a cruel disease."

"Yes." Oliver had wanted to take her hand. To tell her his uncle had Parkinson's too and he understood, but he wasn't a tactile person and so he had tried to use words to reassure her instead, explaining he was confident that a cure would be found in their lifetime. He wanted to tell her about the exciting progress that had been made in understanding the cause of the disease. "Can I buy you a drink…" He had trailed off as she lifted a glass of champagne from the tray of a passing waiter. "Sorry, I'm an idiot."

"I don't think so." Her blue eyes had settled on his. "Tell me why you think a cure will be found."

He had begun to talk. Terminology tripping off his tongue but she had nodded along, asking him to clarify the things she didn't understand, and instantly he fell in love. He had been astonished that she felt the same.

Clem had been an heiress. There had been much gossip when they shared their fledging relationship. Oliver was branded a gold-digger. He knew what her friends and family had thought about him. The way their whispers dried up as he approached—*Oliver, old boy, super to see you*—their booming, cheerful voices doing nothing to detract from the suspicion in their eyes.

Oliver wondered what they would think if they saw him living this way. They would likely take some pleasure in his empty fridge, his creased clothes.

The concerns hadn't only come from her side.

"You might be happy now but there's no long-term future for you both," his more forthright friends had told him. "You're a novelty, her bit of rough. You'll never fit in properly to her world. She'll grow tired of you, and then what?"

But for Oliver and Clem there had been no divide, only an "us" that strengthened each time someone tried to draw them apart.

There was something about Anna that reminded him of Clem. The defiant tilt to her chin. Her loyalty to Adam. Her desire to protect him. He thought Anna wouldn't let Adam go as easily as Clem had slipped through his fingers. Here one minute, gone the next.

He knew he shouldn't, he knew he should go back to work, but he couldn't help opening the sideboard and pulling out their wedding album. Touching her photos as he'd once have touched her face. He could still smell her sometimes, the heady mix of jasmine and lime. It was as if she had just popped out. He had been left waiting endlessly for her to return.

Oliver slipped on his white lab coat that felt as much a part of him as his skin, but instead of heading back to his research he lifted a glass from the cupboard.

Anna.

Clem.

He poured a drink, not whiskey now but orange juice. He never touched alcohol.

Not anymore.

CHAPTER THIRTY-TWO

Anna

Nell didn't have any of the awkwardness I had first felt around Adam as he lay comatose in a hospital bed; she wasn't intimidated by all the equipment. She immediately held his hand and chatted to him as comfortably as she would perched on a bar stool, sharing her news over a glass of wine.

"So, the flight attendant beckoned the other one over, and whispered 'A couple have just gone into the loo together. I think...' The attendant glanced at the elderly lady I was sitting next to and lowered her voice. 'I think he's *comforting* her.' 'Oh no, dear,' the elderly lady shouted. 'I think you'll find they're having sex. It's the mile-high club. Are you a member, dear?' she asked me. 'Me and my Arthur tried once but couldn't manage it. Look, it's my arthritis, you see.' She raised her hand and tried to move her fingers. 'I'm not very bendy.' I don't know who was more embarrassed, the flight attendant or the couple when they came out of the loo to find everyone staring at them." Nell laughed. "Anyway. Alircia again! It's gorgeous outside. You're looking rather pale there, Adam. You want to haul your lazy arse out of bed and get out into the sun." She told him the football results—I hadn't thought to do that—and finished by saying that she was stealing me away for a while. "I'll look after her, and bring her back soon." She planted a kiss on his forehead.

Nell looked so tired as she picked up her suitcase. She had dropped everything for me, the way she had when I had been dumped all those years ago. Despite the distance that had grown between us, she was here.

She was always here without question or judgment.

"Is there somewhere we can talk?" she asked, and I nodded. It wasn't only Adam we needed to discuss.

At the hotel, Nell dumped her stuff in our apartment and then we headed to the restaurant for a late lunch. The buffet tables were groaning under the weight of the food. I wandered aimlessly, empty plate in hand, not quite sure what I could stomach.

"Go and sit," Nell insisted. "I'll bring you over some bits to pick on."

At the next table, a baby banged his plastic spoon on the tray of his highchair. All at once the emotion of the past few days caught up with me and I began to cry so hard, I didn't think I'd ever stop.

"Anna?" Nell set the plates on the table. "Let's go back to the apartment."

"Sorry," I said once I was settled on the brown checkered sofa in the open-plan living area. Nell opened the fridge, the lone "I love Alircia" magnet slipping as she pulled a bottle of water from the door.

"No need to apologize, God, I'd—"

"It was seeing that baby." Fresh tears spilled. "I…I was pregnant."

"Pregnant? Wait. What? Was?" Nell wiped my eyes with a tissue.

"I only found out just before we came here. I was going to tell you when we got home but…but…"

"Oh, Anna." Nell pulled me close to her. I allowed myself to break apart once more. It had been so hard trying to hold myself together. "I had no idea you were trying again."

This made me cry harder. I used to share everything with Nell but I had lied to her. "We never stopped trying." I couldn't look at her. I knew I would see confusion and hurt, but it was the guilt that would be on her face because she'd had two children effortlessly while I had still been trying for one, that I couldn't bear to witness.

"You mean…I thought…Christ, Anna. All this time? Five years?"

"Yes."

She was stunned, her mouth hanging open while she rummaged for words. "But…but then you fell pregnant. Naturally?"

"Yes. I'd only just told Adam. What will he think when he wakes up?"

"He'll feel much the same as I imagine you feel right now. Devastated."

"What if…" My voice was hoarse. "What if it was my fault?" I covered my face.

"Anna." Nell lowered my hands. "What happened on the yacht wasn't your fault."

"I'm not talking about that." I was so ashamed, I couldn't look at her. "I drank alcohol, Nell. We shared a bottle of Malbec a few days before I found out I was pregnant and then I had a couple of glasses of Merlot in the pub."

"Oh, sweetie. That wouldn't be the cause of this. Haven't you talked to a doctor?"

"She said..." I sniffed. "That it's unfortunate but these things happen."

"It's so sad but they do. There often isn't a reason."

"It's not just the alcohol." I couldn't decide whether to tell her. She waited. Her fingers linked through mine. "I...I kissed someone else, Nell. I thought I didn't want Adam anymore."

If she was shocked, she didn't show it. "A kiss wouldn't cause you to miscarry."

"But it feels like a punishment. The baby. The accident. The universe leaving me alone like I thought I wanted but...Nell, I wanted this baby so badly. I want Adam back. I love him so much."

She let me cry it out until my chest was hot and my eyes so swollen I could barely see. Outside of the window, there was laughter and chatter. Two small children carrying a giant inflatable flamingo headed toward the beach.

I blew my nose. "When I had the results of my laparoscopy, I came to tell you but Chris let it slip you were pregnant. I was so shocked. Sad you hadn't told me and, if I'm honest, envious. I wanted to confide in you but didn't think you'd have understood. When you joined all those clubs with the other mums I felt so left out, it was easier to see you less. Tell you I was busy with my career but it wasn't that. It was never that."

"You should have told me."

"I know, but I didn't want you to feel any sort of guilt that you had achieved what I couldn't. And...and because I was ashamed. I felt less of a woman. Less than you."

Nell held my hand tightly, her forehead creased in sorrow, tears pooling in her eyes. "You must have hated me. I did nothing but complain when I was pregnant; fed up with feeling my body wasn't mine. Bitching about the cost of babies. My lack of sleep. The last few years my entire world has revolved around the kids."

"As it should."

"And I *envied* you."

"*You* envied *me*? Why?"

"I haven't slept through the night in five years. Alfie wakes at ridiculous o'clock and thinks it's great fun to come and jump on our bed. Emily won't be left alone for a second. I can't remember the last time I had a poo in peace. It comes to the weekend and Chris is exhausted from all the overtime he's put in, but he has to help out with the kids because, quite frankly, I'm not coping, and I would keep thinking lucky Anna and Adam can lie in bed in peace, go to the pub for lunch, eat a meal before it goes cold. I can't because somebody else's needs always come before mine. I look at Chris sometimes and think he didn't sign up for this, and I question whether he'd rather be with someone else. Anyone else who isn't always covered in baby sick and..."

Now Nell was crying.

"Don't think that. He loves you so much."

"I can't help it." She wiped her eyes.

"I feel the same. We'd come to yours and I'd see Adam on the floor, playing with Alfie and Emily, and Adam would smile at you and I'd think is he wishing he'd ended up with you instead of me? That he picked the wrong girl that day on the beach."

"You must never think that. I've never seen anyone more right for each other than you two. Who did you kiss?"

"My boss, Ross. Just once. I've been an idiot but I've lost a part of myself since I got married. Ross gave me a chance of reinvention. Adam knows me so well. Too well. He knows what I really want and…it's been hard, you know? Watching him with your kids. He would have been an amazing dad."

"He *will* be an amazing dad."

"One day." I touched the wooden table for luck. "I'm so sorry we've drifted apart, Nell. I had no idea you weren't happy either."

"The grass is greener and all that bollocks." Her eyes were red-rimmed, the same as mine must be. "I've missed you."

"I've missed you too." I opened my arms and we hugged for the longest time.

Later, Nell headed out in search of food, returning with plates piled high with egg and chips. "All that sharing has made me hungry. Though you could use some carbs and protein."

After a few mouthfuls I put down my knife and fork but she encouraged me to keep eating, placing some egg onto my fork.

"I might have to do this in the future," I said quietly.

"What?"

"Feed Adam, if he…if he wakes up and he isn't the same."

"Don't think like that. Bloody doctors always have to prepare you for the worst."

Dejectedly, I pushed my plate away. Nell slid it back in front of me.

"One more bit of egg, Anna," she said. "You need the nutrients. God, I've turned into my mother. Speaking of mothers…"

"I know." I haven't yet told mine what has happened. "I'll ring her later. I haven't been up to telling her, knowing she'll cry and then I'll cry."

"Yes. And then you'll feel terrible that she's so worried about you. But we do worry about you. I know Adam's the one in the hospital bed but that's just left you with all the practical worries and now you've told me about the baby—"

"I'm not going to tell her about the miscarriage. Please don't tell anyone. Do you think I should tell Adam while he's...?"

"Do you think he can hear you?"

"I don't know. I met a man earlier, Oliver Chapman from the Chapman Institute for Brain Science. He seems to think that if there's anything going on inside Adam's mind he can uncover it." I recounted our conversation.

"Hmm. It might be worth hearing him out."

"Don't you think it sounds a bit..." I chewed the sore skin around my thumbnail. Should I have listened properly to Oliver? "I couldn't take it in. I couldn't make him out either. He seemed more uncomfortable than I was."

"I think scientists are perhaps a bit strange. They probably spend more time with test tubes than actual people. Let's google him." Nell fetched her iPad from her hand luggage. "Right." She angled the screen so we could both see the results. There was a myriad of links to research studies and this gave me hope that perhaps Oliver was credible. Perhaps he *could* help me and Adam.

Nell opened an article titled "Is it all over for the once brilliant Chapman?" Whilst I read, a sick feeling spread through me.

Oliver had lied.

CHAPTER THIRTY-THREE

Oliver

Oliver remembered it so clearly, the day everything changed. There had been a charity gala over on the mainland. Oliver was supposed to go but he had been so wrapped up in his consciousness research, so wrapped up in finding a way to connect to patients with Parkinson's dementia like his uncle. As he had wandered into the bedroom to change, Clem had sensed his reluctance to leave the project. She had been sitting at the dressing table, sweeping blusher over her cheeks but underneath the rose pink, Oliver knew how pale she was. She had been overdoing it lately.

She had caught his eye in the mirror. "You stay and work."

"No. I want to come with you."

She widened her eyes and they had both laughed.

"Okay, maybe 'want' is a bit strong but…"

"No buts." She had stood and draped a shawl around the shoulders he wanted to kiss. Her black dress hung loose. She had lost weight lately. This weekend he would cook her favorite meal: rack of lamb and creamy mashed potatoes.

"You catch up on your workload. I'm so proud of you. Your

uncle would be too. Don't lose sight of that," she had said, knowing his progress was painfully slow.

"I know. It's just that...all those people who would benefit if I could just break through."

"And that's why I love you. You're not driven by ego but a desire to help. Now get back to it. I'll get the schmoozing out of the way and then we'll both have the weekend free to spend some quality time together."

"Ooh! Quality time!" Oliver had waggled his eyebrows as he looped his arms around her waist, pulling her to him.

"Maybe we'll start our *quality time* when I get home." She had played with a button on his shirt. "Do wait up."

He had leaned in to kiss her before he had second thoughts.

"I don't want to ruin your makeup. You're beautiful, you know."

"You're not so bad yourself."

"Even if I'm socially inept."

"Especially because you're socially inept. I'll be back as soon as I can. I'm shattered so it won't be a late one."

Oliver had watched from the window as she climbed into the taxi. She pressed a finger to her lips and Oliver nodded once. It was the last time he had seen her without her diagnosis hanging over them. She'd collapsed that night and been rushed to hospital.

"It's cancer," the doctor had said after a series of tests.

Oliver had felt like he was falling. He had gripped her hand while he asked what the treatment plan was.

The doctor's gaze had shifted briefly to the floor before looking at Oliver once more and he had known the forthcoming news wasn't good.

"I'm afraid it's stage four so, while there are things we can put in place to—"

"It can't be. She hasn't had any symptoms..." But even as Oliver had said the words, he knew that they were a lie. Her constant exhaustion. Her weight loss. Her stomach aches. The lack of color in her cheeks. He had put it down to her busy lifestyle. Let her reassure him that she didn't need to see a doctor, she was fine, she had said.

Fine.

She was dying.

"I'm sorry," she had said, as if she'd let him down when it was the other way around. He worked in medicine, for God's sake. How could he not have known? Still, he hadn't quite believed it, was sure a miracle would somehow occur.

But it didn't.

"I'm sorry too," he would whisper while she slept.

It was frightening how quickly she had faded away. In a matter of weeks he was sitting by her bed, sleeping by her bed, while she drifted in and out of consciousness. Delirious with pain and medication. It tortured him that he didn't know what she was thinking, feeling. Did she blame him? He blamed himself. An earlier diagnosis might have made all the difference. He had been too wrapped up in his research to notice. What sort of husband was he? He didn't deserve her love. He didn't know if he still had it.

His guilt had grown, stretching his skin, pushing into his bones until his whole body ached with the pressure of feeling.

"Clem." He said her name frequently, as though by keeping it alive he could keep her alive.

He couldn't.

It was mid-morning. Outside, the sun was shining, the birds were singing. A lawnmower hummed in the distance. It was a fluffy white clouds and ice cream day. A possibility day. She had opened her eyes and focused on him. Properly focused on him. Oliver had felt a surge of hope. She was coming back to him.

"Clem?"

She didn't speak. Oliver didn't know if she wouldn't or couldn't. Instead, she had raised her finger and pressed it against her lips. It was her "I love you." It was her goodbye. He had nodded, just once, his throat swelling with pain.

She had slipped away but Oliver kept hold of her hand, kept speaking her name.

She was gone.

After Clem had died, Oliver couldn't let his constant questions about consciousness go. What happened to someone if they could no longer communicate? Could they still think? Feel? Remember? Oliver didn't want to think or feel or remember. He tried to dull his pain with whiskey but he couldn't dull his thoughts. He rattled around their huge home, tumbler in his hand, unable to settle. Unable to sleep. What had Clem been thinking in those final weeks as she had drifted in and out of consciousness? How much easier would it have been if there had been a way they could have communicated? A way he could have understood the things in her mind. It wasn't only for her benefit he wished this. He agonized over whether she had blamed him for not insisting she saw a doctor, whether she had stopped loving him. In those last few weeks when she was wracked with pain, was she full of love or hate? Did it bring her comfort, thoughts of him? Of them? Of their wedding day, barefoot on the beach, frothy waves rushing excitedly toward them as they declared until death do us part.

The alcohol soured his breath, burned his throat.

He clanked another empty bottle into the recycling bin and unscrewed the cap from a fresh one.

"It must be so rewarding to know you're making a difference," Clem had said the first night they met. "The world needs more people like you."

She'd be so sad if she could see him now.

So ashamed.

It was the newspaper article that did it. A photo of him in a crumpled, stained shirt. Hair wild and unbrushed. "Is it all over for the once brilliant Chapman?" the reporter had asked.

Could he make a difference? Be the man Clem wanted him to be? The man he had thought he was? It was too late for her, for him, but what if he could help others? He had previously researched consciousness. Should he carry on? Could he?

"I'm so proud of you," her voice had echoed from the past.

Instead of slugging whiskey into his glass, he had glugged it down the sink and stumbled into his office, waking mid-afternoon, a bitter taste on his tongue, his face pressed to his desk, papers stuck to his cheek. He vowed never to drink again. To continue to make Clem proud.

Now, as he finished his orange juice, Oliver thought about the grief he had felt. Still felt. "I can't imagine how you feel," he had told Anna but it was a lie. He knew how it felt to lose the person you love more than anyone else in the world. He had felt it too. He perhaps should have told her the truth.

He wanted to bring Anna the answers, the comfort, he himself once craved.

If only she would trust him.

CHAPTER THIRTY-FOUR

Anna

"I can't imagine what you're going through," Oliver had said to me when we met but he knew only too well. Why hadn't he just been honest? Reading the article filled me with an overwhelming sorrow. His story was vastly different to mine and yet strikingly familiar. Love. Loss. The inconceivable pain of sitting beside someone's bedside, willing them to come back to you. To recover. The helplessness. He had felt it too. All of it.

Had he and Clem planned a family? I placed my hands gently over my cramping stomach. My nan was fond of saying "You can't miss what you never had," but oh, she was wrong. Oliver must grieve for the future they had planned. In my mind he made the leap from scientist to man. No longer coming across as odd, just incredibly sad. Now I understood why he was so driven in his research. A picture formed in my mind of him sitting with Clem in the hospice, her physically in front of him but her mind somewhere else entirely, Oliver pushing his glasses onto the bridge of his nose as he tried to read her face. Her thoughts. Unable to know what she was thinking.

Feeling.

Wanting.

"They look so happy together, don't they?" In a photograph from their wedding day, Oliver was barely recognizable, not from his lack of beard but because of his beaming smile. The sea glistening behind them, the breeze ruffling Clem's long hair.

Nell scrolled down further. There was a picture of Clem's funeral. Oliver was one of the pallbearers. Her coffin balanced on his left shoulder, devastation crumpling his face.

"I think he might genuinely want to help," I said.

"Maybe. I'm going to google that Japanese neuroscientist."

Nell found an article about his work. She read far quicker than my tired eyes could.

"God, it's like something out of a film. There's something that can actually decipher the images in someone's mind. It's crazy to think all this stuff goes on and people like you and I have no idea. It sounds so futuristic."

"I don't think Dr. Acevedo believes that there's anything going on inside of Adam's mind. I don't think he believes Adam will ever wake up. He's hardly the most positive of people."

Nell opened YouTube and typed in "miracle waking from a coma" and was flooded with results.

"Look, Dr. Acevedo doesn't know everything."

There were videos of patients waking after two years, twelve years, twenty years. We watched clip after clip. Patients who had defied the boundaries of medical theories by relaying they could hear everything going on, they could think, dream, hope. Dr. Acevedo might not know everything, but Oliver...

"I can't stop watching." Nell blinked back tears. "So many people who were written off. They've all come back."

I wouldn't let Adam be written off, not without a fight. "I want to visit the Chapman Institute. Find out more. Will you come with me?"

"Try and stop me."

I reached for the apartment phone.

"Wait." Nell pulled a new mobile from her bag. "This is for you. I picked it up at the airport. I've keyed in some numbers, including Josh's."

"He'll be heartbroken when I tell him."

"Do you want me to call him so you don't have to keep going over it?"

"No—I can't keep putting everything off."

"We also need to find another hotel. While the kitchen was making our lunch, I talked to reception about extending your stay but they're fully booked next week."

"Shit." Without travel insurance, my accommodation wouldn't be covered. We had some savings left but I didn't know how long they would last. My mind flitted to the videos we'd just watched: *two years, twelve years, twenty years*. How long might Adam be in hospital?

"We'll get you both home," Nell said.

"I'm not sure how without insurance. The few thousand pounds in our bank account won't nearly cover it. Mum doesn't have any money; Dad didn't have life insurance. That's why Adam and I made sure we're both covered."

"It might be worth speaking to them? Some policies have a critical illness pay-out."

"We don't." I didn't think this was a critical illness anyway. They'd say there's hope of a complete recovery.

"Never mind. I could start a JustGiving page. A 'Get Adam Home' campaign?"

Home. One word. But those four letters brought such comfort.

"If, and it's a big if, we let Oliver get involved, he promised me a place to stay and to cover our travel afterward."

"Let me call him. I want to sound him out." While Nell arranged for us to visit the Chapman Institute the next day, I washed down two painkillers with water.

"Are you in a lot of discomfort?" Nell asked when she'd hung up.

"I feel..." My fingers strayed to my stomach. Lost. Empty. Bereft. It was too hard to articulate. "I think I'll go and have a bath. Why don't you ring Chris and see how the kids are?"

"I'll unpack and do it later."

"Nell... Call him now."

There wasn't always a later.

Several times in the bath I had almost fallen asleep but afterward I sat on the sofa in clean shorts and T-shirt, damp hair dripping cool water down my back, my mind hopping from anxious thought to anxious thought.

"What if Oliver is a crackpot?" I tried not to pin my hopes on him. "What if the trial is dangerous? What—"

"What if you tried to relax for just a little while?"

I tucked my legs under me on the sofa and rested my head on Nell's shoulder. "Thanks for coming."

"That's okay. I only wish we were back here under different circumstances, but who knows, Adam could wake up any second. We could all be on the beach tomorrow sipping cocktails."

Her fingers threaded through mine and for the first time in days I felt a glimmer of positivity, which lasted until the phone rang.

It was the hospital.

CHAPTER THIRTY-FIVE

Oliver

Oliver had been surprised to receive a phone call from Nell yesterday afternoon.

"Anna's told me everything." Her tone had been hard, almost confrontational. For a split second, Oliver had thought she was ringing to tell him to stay away from Anna and Adam.

"It sounds barmy but we've checked out your website and looked at the breakthrough that Japanese neuroscientist has achieved."

"I can talk it all through with—"

"All this research into consciousness. This progress. How come most people don't know about it?"

"It isn't a secret. Most things are out there on the web. If you're not interested in science you don't look for it—"

"It's fascinating," Nell said. "I can't stop googling. Did you know that in one study it was found that 70 percent of the participants who were in a locked-in state and doctors believed had no awareness, could actually communicate when the right equipment was used?"

"Umm, yes. I know."

"If you train an algorithm to translate brain activity, we can see the images from inside someone's mind."

"Yes. We've progressed that several steps further—"

"And there are loads, literally loads of people on YouTube waking from comas after being given a sleeping tablet. Is this something you'd try?"

"No. I think—"

"Also—"

"Nell. Would you and Anna like to come and have a look around? See the work we're doing." Oliver's palm was clammy with nerves, the phone slippery in his hand.

"We're not committing to anything."

"Of course not. Just a chat."

"Even if we agree, there will be conditions."

"Of course."

"And . . . and if you hurt Adam, I will hunt you down. I've got—"

"Skills?" Oliver cut in. "Look, this isn't a Liam Neeson movie. This is real life. Adam and Anna's lives and I don't take that lightly. I've been . . . I have some degree of understanding of what Anna is feeling right now."

It took a second for Nell to reply. "We read about your wife. I'm sorry. It's just that . . ." Nell's voice wobbled.

"The people you love are in a terrible situation and you don't know how to help them. I get it. Look, all I can say is come and meet me. Nobody is going to force Anna into anything. I promise."

"Okay. Tomorrow at ten."

They were late. He hoped they were still coming. He prayed Adam's condition hadn't changed. Immediately Oliver berated himself. He'd be glad if Adam had woken up, of course, but there was always the other possibility.

That Adam might have died.

He checked his watch again. It was nearly eleven.

Where were they?

CHAPTER THIRTY-SIX

Anna

Me and Nell tumbled from the taxi, horribly late for our appointment with Oliver. We hadn't rung to explain but I was sure he would understand.

Given the circumstances.

The Institute was a sprawling white building at the very tip of the island, the only clue to its identity a small, discreet silver sign bearing its name and logo. Behind it lay a glistening sea and a sky so blue it was impossible to tell where one ended and the other began. The heat was relentless. It built and built and now it was approaching midday, it was insufferable to be outside, but still I loitered hesitantly, knowing if I stepped inside, I would be on a path I couldn't turn back from.

"It's just a chat," Nell reassured me.

"I know but..." I couldn't put into words how scared I was that I might agree to the trial and it would work, only to discover that there was nothing going on inside Adam's mind, or that there was but not a single thought was about me. "I don't think I can go in." I sat on the low wall, my head in my hands, taking deep breaths while Nell rubbed my back.

"Mrs. Curtis?"

I looked up to see a woman of around forty wearing a crisp, white short-sleeved dress. "I'm Sofia. Are you okay?" It was only then I noticed the discreet CCTV cameras positioned high in the corners of the building. I was flustered that I'd been observed.

A monkey in a cage being scrutinized without knowing.

What was I thinking, coming here?

"Dr. Chapman is waiting," Sofia said, turning back to the building, her high ponytail swinging.

"The second you want to leave, we will." Nell held out her hand to me and I took it.

Inside it was thankfully cool. Light and bright. Shiny green plants rested on polished floors. The air tanged with the scent of oranges. I had been expecting the smell of hospitals.

"I'm pleased you came." Oliver ushered us through to his office where we sat.

"Sorry we're late. We had a rough night at the hospital and overslept this morning," I said. "Adam…Adam had…" I wasn't strong enough to say it.

"Adam had a cardiac arrest," Nell explained.

"I'm so sorry. How is he now?"

"Stable but Dr. Acevedo says…he says…" Again, I looked to Nell.

"Dr. Acevedo has given Adam a 3 percent chance of recovering. Aside from his head injury, the water that he ingested when he nearly drowned has put a huge strain on his heart and after his cardiac arrest…"

There were three bottles of Evian on the table. I picked up one and took a sip.

"He doesn't seem to have any hope," I said once I had composed myself.

"Doctors go from their past experiences. They can be very black and white."

"Do you think..." I left my question hanging.

"I honestly don't know. Statistically, it doesn't look promising for Adam; I wish I could tell you otherwise, but—"

"We've been watching YouTube. There are so many cases of patients waking up." I was seeking reassurance that it did happen. That it would happen for Adam.

"And there are an awful lot who don't. The last thing I want to do is give you false hope. I can't wake Adam from his coma, but we've finished our testing as best we can without a candidate and Adam fits our criteria perfectly. I'd love to tell you I could cure Adam but there isn't anything at the moment that can do that. What I'd like to do is to explore his consciousness and see if there's anything there. It would be ground-breaking if there is and we could develop accessible equipment that would benefit so many patients and their families. Most doctors would tell you Adam's mind must be empty of thought but—"

"Brain science research is proving that doctors aren't always right." Nell jumped in. "Can we see where you carry out your research?"

"Yes, of course. Anna?"

Stalling, I took another sip of water before I stood. My heart was pounding. I followed Oliver into the corridor, unsure what we would be faced with. Rows of cages and animals? Brains in jars?

"I won't bore you with the details today, but these are our labs." As we walked, Oliver gestured to glass-fronted rooms. I couldn't help stopping and gazing inside. Everything looked so normal.

A man perched on a stool at a bench tapping the keyboard on his laptop. There was an array of computer screens and it was nothing like I had imagined.

Breathing felt a little easier.

"How long have you been here?" Nell was asking all the questions.

"The Institute has been running for seven years, but we've only been in this building three."

As we walked, Oliver told us about recent breakthroughs his team had made. Before now I had only thought of Oliver in conjunction with what he could do for Adam, but listening I realized that the research they were doing here could change many lives.

Change the world.

"It's hard to imagine the day progressive neurological diseases are eradicated." Nell was fully engaged. "Dementia and Parkinson's seem so commonplace now. We've almost accepted them as a normal part of aging."

"I'm confident we'll see big changes." Oliver opened a door. "Perhaps not all in my lifetime but it's revolutionary, the progress that's being made. Not just by us but worldwide." He gestured. "This is where you and Adam would stay."

I stepped inside the room. It resembled a hotel. Oil paintings of beach scenes on duck-egg walls. A coffee table and two comfortable armchairs beside open sash windows. From here, we could see the sea. Smell it. Hear it. Feel the breeze. There were four doors leading off from this one. Beyond the first one was a huge bed. Machines I recognized from the hospital.

"This is where Adam would sleep."

The next room was also a bedroom housing a double bed

and a wardrobe. "This would be your room," Oliver told me. The other door led to a large bathroom with a freestanding shower and a bath. "It's important that you're comfortable, Anna. It's a difficult time, the waiting."

"We read about Clem," I said. "I'm so sorry for your loss."

"It's partly why… The work I've done with consciousness is… it was inspired by my uncle who had Parkinson's dementia but now… it's even more important than I realized because of… because of…"

He didn't go on. "Your wife," I finished for him, understanding Oliver's determination to see if something exists beyond the realms of what we already know.

"Yes. Her passing has… Research had always been my passion but after she'd… gone I had so much time and enormous amounts of money if I'm honest. I wanted to set up my own institute. This is my… my pet project. It feels so personal. Until recently it felt so unachievable. But I've had a breakthrough."

"Tell us more about your study," I interrupted. I could tell Oliver was one for convoluted replies.

"Of course." He led us through the final door. This room was colder, more clinical. I shuddered as I stared at the machine in the center of it. I knew it was some sort of scanner, I'd seen them on *Casualty*, but never one this big. There was a flat surface for someone to lie on, which would then disappear into a large circular tube.

"That looks like a lifebuoy," Nell said.

She had a point—if a lifebuoy was hundreds of times larger than usual and stood vertically.

"It's a cutting-edge fMRI—a functional magnetic resonance Imaging scanner that measures the blood flow to the brain as a proxy for neural activity. It's larger and far more powerful than the standard machine. It has stronger magnets, which means a better resolution and a faster readout. The visual cortical activity it measures will be decoded to provide a layered image that will reproduce a reconstruction of…"

"Whoosh."

Oliver trailed off as Nell ran the flat of her hand over her head in a "you've lost me" motion.

"Sorry," he said. "Basically, scientists have created a way to extract information from different levels of the brain's visual system and algorithms to interpret and reproduce any imagined images. With clinical trials so far—the work of Yukiyasu Kamitani, for example—the images are fed back via a computer and can then be viewed via the console room over there." He pointed to a small window, another room beyond it. "With the new tech in the fMRI scanner I mentioned before, I believe we will be able to see not just still images, but…I suppose the easiest way to describe it would be like watching a movie."

"So I can see on a screen what Adam is thinking?" I was incredulous.

"Potentially, yes."

"You keep saying potentially or in theory or possibly."

Oliver pushed his glasses up the bridge of his nose. I wondered why, with all of his money, he didn't buy a pair that fit. "I don't want to promise you something that I can't deliver. What I *can* tell you is that early indications are really positive but we've been lacking a test subject…" He noticed the way I clamped my lips together to prevent myself furiously telling him Adam was *not* a test subject. Oliver had been so open about his lack of social graces and I knew he didn't mean any harm.

"I've done it again, haven't I? Sorry. I don't usually work with people."

"It's a lot to take in," Nell said. "The concept that we can see on a screen—"

"There's more," Oliver cut in. "It should also be possible for someone—me in this case—to wear fMRI, compatible VR goggles, which, in theory, could incorporate any senses Adam might be experiencing. I don't want to be viewing the results solely through a computer."

"Our friend Josh has one of those Occulus Quest VR gaming headsets," Nell said. "I had a go. It was so immersive. So real. As though you're somewhere else. Is this similar?"

"It's so much more than that with the addition of sense recognition. Machines are artificially intelligent; they can't pick up on the nuances, what a person is feeling. By connecting to Adam's consciousness with the addition of these goggles, I can really absorb myself in Adam's mind—if there's anything going on, of course. I'll be able to experience—"

Taste, touch, feel.

Know.

It was all too much.

I sank heavily onto the armchair, trying to imagine Adam here. My things in the next room.

"Do you have to be in the scanner too?" I asked. "Could Adam merge with—"

"God no. It's nothing like that."

"I've seen *The Fly* and—"

"There's absolutely no danger of anyone's teeth falling out or them growing wings."

"But...will Adam..." My questions clogged my throat. There

were so many things I wanted to ask, but I was almost afraid of the answers. "Is…is it dangerous?"

Oliver fell silent.

"Is it?" I probed.

"It shouldn't be. I'm almost certain."

"Almost?" Almost wasn't good enough.

"An fMRI is safe for the majority of people—there isn't any radiation. The magnets can affect certain medical conditions but nothing applicable to Adam. I've a contact at the hospital and I'd already checked Adam's suitability before I approached you. However, as yet it's untested. Our fMRI uses much stronger magnets than a usual machine and it may carry a small risk."

"How small?"

A 3 percent chance of survival.

"Negligible. We'll be monitoring Adam's heart rate throughout for signs of distress. The person who takes part would be taking a risk, albeit tiny. It's unprecedented. We're taking an unknown leap into someone's—Adam's—mind without knowing how sharp his memories, his feelings might be. I can imagine it will be draining but I'm hoping tiredness is the only side effect."

I dropped my head into my hands. It was all so overwhelming.

"Anna, I don't want to rush you and I'm not putting any pressure on you, but Adam's prognosis…it isn't great, and given his cardiac arrest last night, well…If you want to do this, we might not have much time," Oliver said.

If there was anything on Adam's mind now, did I really want to know what it was? Mentally I drew up a list of pros and cons. He could be thinking of me, of our unborn child he did not yet know had gone. If the worst did happen, I could be secure in the knowledge that he loved me until the very end. But he could be angry with me. If I had taken the swimming lessons he always urged me to take, I could have helped. I could have saved him. He might *blame* me and the pain of that would be unbearable. But then, he might need something and I could make it easier for him. But what if he was in so much pain he wanted to die? How would I cope with that?

My mind went back and forth; the trial is a good thing. A bad thing. Not being able to decide either way.

The third thing to consider, of course, was that there might be nothing inside Adam's head. A blank canvas. That the space Adam's hopes and dreams once occupied was now empty.

At least I would know for sure.

The minutes ticked by.

A 3 percent chance of recovery, Dr. Acevedo had said.

If I didn't agree to the trial, would I regret it? If Adam... I could hardly bear to think it, but if he didn't survive, would I always be wondering? Hating myself for missing my one chance to know?

A 3 percent chance of recovery.

I was running out of time.

Yes or no. Yes or no. Yes or no.

PART FOUR

"I am a scientist, but I still believe in miracles."

OLIVER CHAPMAN

CHAPTER THIRTY-SEVEN

Anna

It is late. Nell has gone back to the apartment to sleep. Oliver has given me overnight to think things through and I sit here now, back at the hospital, back by Adam's side. Remembering.

"Seven years. It's been seven years since that night on the beach," I whisper.

I had lain on the damp sand with Adam, his thumb stroking mine. Dawn smudged the sky with its pink fingers while the rising sun flung glitter across the sea. We'd faced each other curled onto our sides, our bodies speech marks, unspoken words passing hesitantly between us; an illusory dream. *Don't ever leave me*, I had silently asked him. *I won't*, his eyes had silently replied.

But he did.

He has.

Will he ever wake up?

I stroke his cheek. His skin is dry.

My mind drifts over my memories, which are both painful and pleasurable to recall. We were blissfully happy until gradually we weren't. Every cross word, every hard stare, each time we turned our backs on each other in bed, gathered like storm clouds hanging over us, ready to burst, drenching us with doubt and uncertainty until we questioned what we once thought was unquestionable.

Can love really be eternal?

I can answer that now because the inequitable truth is that I am hopelessly, irrevocably, lost without him.

"Please wake up." My mouth brushes against his ear. "I want you. I need you."

But does he feel the same? Oliver could hold the answer to that question if I am brave enough find out. What if Adam doesn't make it and I am left forever wondering?

I turn over the possibility of life without him but each time I think of me without him, no longer an *us*, my heart breaks all over again.

If only we hadn't come here. Stepped on board the yacht.

My chest tightens.

I am back in the water. Current dragging me down. Waves crashing over my head.

Breathe.

I am kneeling on the hot sand beside an unresponsive Adam, begging strangers to save my husband's life.

Breathe, Anna.

You're okay.

It's a lie I tell myself, but gradually the horror of that day begins to dissipate with every slow inhale, with every measured exhale. It takes several minutes to calm myself. My fingers furling and unfurling, my nails biting into the tender skin of my palms until my burning sorrow subsides.

Focus.

I am running out of time.

A 3 percent chance of survival.

Gently I kiss Adam's forehead before picking up my pen and pad from his bedside table. I've been trying to write a letter to my mum but the words won't come. If the trial goes ahead, I shall insist on being the one taking part. Oliver has no right to Adam's thoughts. His emotions. He has no right to any of it.

"The person who takes part would be taking a risk, albeit small," Oliver had said. "It's unprecedented. We're taking an unknown leap into someone's—Adam's—mind without knowing how sharp his memories, his feelings might be. I can imagine it will be draining but I'm hoping tiredness is the only side effect."

It's not only connecting to Adam's consciousness that carries a risk; there are the stronger magnets in the fMRI machine, the ultra-fast processor, the software, none of which I fully understand. What I do know is that I am putting myself in danger and I need my mum to know why in case something so awful happens I never get to see her again, but my notepaper is still stark white. My pen once again poised, ink waiting to stain the blank page with my tenuous excuses.

My secrets.

But not my lies. There have been enough of those. Too many.

I want her to know everything. How I thought I didn't love Adam anymore. How I kissed another man. The baby we have lost.

Why I am so desperate to see him once more and make it right.

All of it.

I'm almost certain now I *should* do the trial, but I wish I knew what Adam wanted; a glance toward his impassive face gives me no clues. My eyes flutter closed. I try to conjure his voice. Imagining he might tell me what to do. Past conversations echo in my mind as I search for a clue.

If you love someone, set them free, he had once told me but I brush the thought of this away. I don't think it can apply to this awful situation we have found ourselves in. Instead I recall the feel of his body spooned around mine, warm breath on the back of my neck, promises drifting into my ear.

Forever.

I cling on to that one word as tightly as I'd clung on to his hand.

I loved him completely. I still do. Whatever happens now, and after, my heart will still belong to him.

Will always belong to him.

I must hurry if I'm going to reach him before it's too late.

A 3 percent chance of survival.

There's a tremble in my fingers. I begin the letter, which will be both an apology to Mum for the risk I am taking, and an explanation, but it seems impossible to put it all into words—the story of Adam and me.

Us.

I really don't have time to think of the life we had—the life we almost had—but I allow myself the indulgence. Memories gather: we're on the beach watching the sunrise; I'm introducing him to my mum—his voice unsteady with nerves as he says hello; we're meeting for the first time in that shabby bar. Out of order and back to front and more than anything I wish I could live it all again. Except that day on the yacht. *Never* that day.

Again the vise around my lungs tightens. In my mind I see it all unfold and I feel it. I feel it *all*: fear, panic, hopelessness.

Breathe, Anna.

In and out. In and out. Until I am here again, pen gripped too tightly in my hand.

Focus.

I made a mistake.

I stare at the words I have written so intently they jump around on the page. It's the harsh truth. I had thought that I wanted to live without him.

I don't.

I'm at a loss to know how to carry on. I look to Adam for inspiration and I remember one of the first things he had said to me: "Start at the beginning, Anna."

And so I do.

Seven years ago. I pause. Recalling our first week. That visit to the author's house. Me touching the typewriter. Adam asking if I'd ever thought of crafting my own book.

"Everyone has something to say—it's a matter of figuring out what that something is. What would you write, if you could?" Adam had asked.

"A love story," I had told him. "One with a happy ending."

"A clichéd ending."

"Happy," I had insisted, because ultimately isn't that what we all want? It's what *I* want.

Speedily, the nib of my pen scratches over the paper. I let it all pour out.

This is not a typical love story, but it's our love story.

Mine and Adam's.

And despite that day, despite everything, I'm not yet ready for it to end. I glance at my husband.

Is he?

CHAPTER THIRTY-EIGHT

Oliver

Oliver has spent the night pacing the long corridors of the Institute. Checking his phone. Second-guessing what Anna's decision might be. She stands before him now, exhaustion etched onto her face. As much as he burns to know her decision right away, she deserves to be treated with the consideration he had always shown Clem. With the care that Adam would give her if he were able to.

"Let's get a coffee."

Noticing Anna struggling to keep up with his long strides, he slows. He glances at her. At Nell. Wishing one of them would say something.

It isn't until she has her hands wrapped around a mug that she eventually speaks.

"I've been going through it all. The risks. The danger of trying something that has never been attempted before. How my mum would feel if anything happened to me."

"Nothing could happen to—"

"Please." Anna looks at him. Her eyes are bloodshot. "Let me finish."

Oliver gulps his coffee, washing down the words he wants to say.

"My dad . . . He died suddenly. Unexpectedly. It's a great regret of Mum's that she wasn't there when he went. It's a great regret of hers that in the period before he died, they were both so busy—he was a head teacher—and they didn't talk as often as they should have." Anna pushes the hair back from her face. "They talked. They were happy. It's just . . . Mum said she had always thought that there would be lots of time when he retired for meaningful conversations. I think . . . I know she'd understand why I want to do this, and if it goes wrong . . . I've written her a letter explaining . . . There are things that have happened between me and Adam. Things I need to know."

"I don't quite understand," Oliver says.

"I'm going to say yes to the trial. But I'll be the one connected to Adam, not you."

Oliver's stomach drops. "I'm afraid I can't allow that." It isn't only because this is his project. His dream. He now understands why Anna wrote to her mother and she is right to be cautious. There could be . . . consequences.

"Then I'm afraid I won't allow you to try," Anna says.

"Anna, I'm as certain as I can be that this is safe, but the bottom line is the new fMRI scanner is more powerful, it has—"

"Stronger magnets, faster readouts. It's new tech. I understand *all* of this."

"Then you should also understand that there could be some side effects and I can't—"

"Can't or won't? Look, if anyone is going to able to feel what Adam is feeling, it should be me. I'm willing to take the risk. What if this is the only chance there is . . ." Anna's voice cracks.

Oliver whips off his glasses and rubs his eyes. He can't agree to this.

"What if, for now"—he is thinking on his feet—"we try the trial without another person taking part. Just Adam. Without the VR goggles we'd still receive images from the scanner but they wouldn't include the other senses, of course. We can all view on screen at the same time—"

"No," Anna cut in. "I won't agree to that. We use the goggles and I'm the one with Adam. All or nothing."

"Go big or go home," Nell says.

"It's too..." Things are sliding out of Oliver's control.

"Please, Oliver. Let me try."

"Nell?" Oliver pleads. "You must see that—"

"I'd want to be the one if it were me and Chris."

"But..." Oliver has logic. Reasons. But are they excuses? What if it were Clem in Adam's position? He would want to be the other person taking part. He clasps his hands behind his head and stares at the ceiling in despair. He could wait for another suitable candidate. He should wait.

"Anna, I'm sorry—"

"Don't say sorry. Say yes. I...I messed up. With Adam. Hasn't there ever been anything you wish you could say sorry for in your relationship with Clem?"

There were so many things to apologize for; Oliver wouldn't know where to start. He should have noticed Clem was ill. He should have made her see a doctor. He should have been able to save her.

"I think...there are always things we want to say sorry for."

"And if you got that chance now? Wouldn't you take it?"

"This trial is for us to see what is in Adam's consciousness. Not what is in yours. It is unlikely you will be able to communicate with him."

"But there's a chance that I could?"

Oliver shrugs helplessly. "We just don't know."

"But we could find out." Anna touches his arm. "We could. I'm not saying you can't experience whatever it is that may or may not happen—this is your life's work—but the first time, I want that, I *need* that to be me."

Time is slow. Eventually Oliver says, "I can't say yes or no." He momentarily places his hand over Anna's. "Until you've met somebody." He stands. "Come with me."

CHAPTER THIRTY-NINE

Anna

Eva is the clinic's psychologist. Oliver will decide whether I can take part in the trial after she has assessed me. I am sitting opposite her, trying to portray a calmness I do not feel.

At school I loathed exams. The pressure of knowing that the answers I gave over the next sixty minutes could potentially dictate my future. My palms would sweat, my temples throb. This is the way I feel now, but this time there is far more riding on a test than university offers and job prospects. I am not just doing this for me, but for Adam.

For us.

Oliver has taken Nell for another coffee, promising he will return the second Eva tells him she has finished. It's all moving so quickly I don't feel ready. I can't stop fidgeting, agitated that I've already been away from Adam today for longer than I'd like.

"Are you comfortable, Anna?" Eva asks.

"Yes, thank you." I'm not. Mentally I have never been less comfortable than I am right now.

"Don't look so scared." With a French-manicured fingernail, she tucks her sleek dark hair behind her ears. In comparison my own nails are bitten to the quick and I tuck my hands under my thighs so she doesn't judge me.

"I won't bite," she says.

I try to relax. The room is cozy. The white walls and shiny floors of the rest of the Institute haven't been carried through here. Instead, the paint is the color of butter. Bright orange pots spilling with tall leafy green plants flank the door. The turquoise chair I am sitting on is soft and deep. On the oak coffee table in front of me is a jug of water and two glasses, along with a box of tissues.

Eva scrawls into a notebook.

"Will this take long?" I try to keep my impatience from my voice but I'm tired and tetchy. "It's just...my husband..."

"Of course. I'll make it as quick as I can and then hopefully we can move Adam here. We have the best equipment on the island." Again the pen scratches across paper. Again I try to suppress a scream, not sure whether this is part of the test. Whether she has begun assessing me. I force myself to be still. Quiet.

"I'm going to ask you a series of questions. Try not to think too long about the answers. There is no right or wrong." She smiles. "Ready?"

I nod.

"Are you worried or anxious about anything right now?"

The desire to tell her to sod off, to get up and stalk out of the room, slamming the door behind me, is immense.

"Sorry, Anna," she says before I can react, politely or otherwise. "This is a standard questionnaire. Some of the questions might seem inappropriate but I have to ask them. Of course you're worried. I don't mean to sound insensitive but it's important I run through these before—"

"It's fine." I just want this over with. "Yes, I feel worried."

"A little, often or constantly?"

"Constantly."

We continue in the same vein. I am asked whether I am tense. Whether I have trouble sleeping. If I'm scared I'll lose control. Whether I have chest pain. Suicidal thoughts. The list goes on and on. Sometimes I lie, trying to make myself seem more together than I am, but generally I'm honest.

Yes, my anxiety is out of control.

Yes, I feel guilt.

Shame.

Fear.

"You're doing really well, Anna," Eva says encouragingly. "That's the basics out of the way. Now, I don't want to sound like a cliché, but was your childhood a happy one?"

"Is this relevant to Adam?"

"It's relevant to you. Whether the trial is a success or not, we need to ensure that you're able to cope with whatever happens."

"I've coped so far."

"It's procedure. I'm aware some of it feels patronizing and I apologize."

"It's not your fault, it's...I'm tired. I just want to get back to Adam. My childhood was fine." It's my adulthood that has turned into a living nightmare.

"And your parents were together during your formative years?"

"Yes."

"Happy?"

"Definitely." It's my most truthful answer so far.

"Are there any events from your childhood you think I should know?"

"Umm, no."

"Are you sure?"

"What's your definition of childhood?"

"Tell me what's on your mind and I can decide whether it's relevant."

"My...my dad died when I was twenty. Not exactly a child." I had felt like one though.

"What happened?"

"He...he had a heart attack. It was very unexpected. The hospital said he was stable. They were hopeful but...he died later that night. On his own." I shift in my chair, my heart racing. She picks up on my increased agitation.

"We'll get you back to Adam soon, don't worry, and the hospital has Nell's number, don't they?"

"Yes." It doesn't make me feel any better. I should be with him, not here dredging up my painful past.

"How did you cope with your dad's passing?"

"It was hard. I had to be strong, for Mum. It was..." My voice wobbles. "It was such a shock. He'd always been there, you know? Always able to sort anything out. If my car broke down, if I was short of money, if I just needed a hug and some reassurance I was lovable. He was *there*. And then he wasn't."

My tears are hot, I gulp them back down. I'll be strong for Adam the way I am strong for my mum. Eva studies me for a moment, waiting for me to say something else, but I don't.

"Let's talk about your relationship with Adam."

"What about us?" I pick up my water, feeling anxious.

"Did you meet him after your dad died or before?"

"After. I'd just come out of a broken engagement."

"I see." Eva scribbles down a note.

"My ex-fiancé and I weren't right for each other. It was good we found out before we got married. He put me down a lot. He wasn't a kind man."

"Is it fair to say your self-esteem was low when you met Adam?"

"I guess so." I remember running into the sea, trying to hide my body.

"How would you describe your relationship?"

"Amazing." Did that sound fake?

She holds the silence until I break it. "We have our ups and downs, of course, all couples do, don't they?" Still, she doesn't speak. What does she want me to say? "We'd been having some problems." I look at my hands.

"Tell me about them."

"We'd been trying for a baby for a long time. It created a bit of a wedge between us." I pick at my nails. "A lot of a wedge."

"In what way?"

"He's never said anything but I think he blamed me."

"You think?"

"We don't talk about it. We don't talk about much anymore."

"Why not?"

I take another drink. Wishing I could wash away the image of us lying on the beach when we met. My leg hooked over his. His thumb stroking mine. The way we opened up to each other.

"I think...I think I love him so much it was unbearable to think I'd let him down. I didn't want to hear him say it."

"But you don't know how he feels?"

"No. But he doesn't have to say; I can tell by the way he forgets to do things I ask him to or accuses me of nagging if I ask when he's going to do some DIY. I'm trying to create a home and he doesn't seem to *care*. The books are stacked on the floor when he could easily build the bookcase and..." I stop. Suddenly feeling a sickness deep in the pit of my stomach. Adam could be *dying* and I'm complaining he doesn't do enough around the house.

Eva gives me a moment to compose myself. "Does Adam ever indicate that he wants to talk?"

I shake my head.

"Why do you think that is, Anna?"

Because he doesn't care.

Because he doesn't care *enough*.

"Because..." I think of Adam treading water while I clung to the yacht. "*Jump,*" he had shouted, panic in his voice. "*I won't let you fall. I promise I'll catch you.*"

"Because he's scared."

He's scared. I'm scared. I cover my face with my hands and Eva allows me the indulgence of tears. Eventually I raise my face to hers.

"We've so much to say," I whisper. "So much we should have said. We didn't talk. We didn't *listen*. If there's the slightest chance I can put that right... Please. Let me."

She puts down her pen. "I'll go and fetch Oliver."

CHAPTER FORTY

Oliver

Anna's psychological assessment has gone well. Eva is willing to sign off on the paperwork on the condition she gets to chat to Anna every day.

"Sofia has taken Anna to the medical wing for a physical," he tells Nell, who is nursing cold coffee. "There are certain conditions we need to be mindful of when using magnets, which would rule Anna out of participating in the study. She shouldn't be too much longer."

"What sort of things?" Nell asks.

"Pacemakers, any metal in the body; plates, screws that sort of thing. If Anna is pregnant."

Nell sighs. "She was. Anna had a miscarriage after the accident."

It is both shock and sadness that steal Oliver's words. Anna has been through so much more than he had imagined.

"They had been trying for a baby for five years," Nell says.

"Do *you* think she's ready for this?" Oliver respects Eva's opinion but Nell knows Anna better than anyone. "If you don't think she's up to it, I'll call it off now." Science is everything to Oliver but even he knows that people . . . people have to come first.

"I think she needs this," Nell says.

They sit in silence until Sofia brings Anna back to them. Immediately, Nell rushes toward her friend, wrapping her arms around her. Murmuring in her ear. Oliver glances at Sofia. She gives a slight nod.

"Anna." Briefly he touches her shoulder.

"I want to see Adam." Wearily she turns around.

"Of course. Right away. All the tests are fine so if you want to, we can bring him back here?"

"Today?"

"Only if you're comfortable with that. You could sleep here tonight. Both of you?"

"I've got an early flight," Nell says. "I don't want to disturb Anna by getting up at a ridiculous hour."

"I can arrange for a car to pick you up from the apartment first thing and drop you at the airport," Oliver says.

"I think that would be best. Is that okay with you, Anna?"

"I don't…I guess…Would we begin the trial tonight?"

Oliver hesitates. His head and his heart battling it out. His heart wins. "Not today, we need time to settle Adam in." They don't, but Anna looks fit to drop. He knows she'll push herself through it but he really wants her to get some rest. "In the morning though."

On the way to the hospital, Anna dozes, her head resting against Nell's shoulder. Nell keeps a palm pressed to Anna's cheek so her head doesn't loll when the car turns a corner. The Institute's private ambulance follows them. Oliver feels his excitement beginning to brew.

But that's until they reach the hospital.

Until they walk into Adam's room.

CHAPTER FORTY-ONE

Anna

My glare is steely. "Dr. Acevedo, what do you mean I *can't* take Adam? He's my husband!"

"And *my* patient." Dr. Acevedo doesn't look away. "I don't think it's in Adam's best interests to be moved."

"You think he's going to wake up imminently then?"

"In my experience Adam's chance of recovering is—"

"Three percent, yes, I know. It shouldn't matter if I move him then, should it?"

"Anna—"

"Mrs. Curtis."

"Mrs. Curtis. I'm familiar with Oliver—"

"Dr. Chapman," I correct. I'm behaving terribly but I can't help it.

"I'm familiar with Dr. Chapman's work and while I commend his research into neurological disease, I can tell you now what's in Adam's mind. Nothing."

He's always been more pessimistic than I'd like, but his opinion is still a punch to the gut.

I glance at Adam. When I had sat by his bedside talking to

him, I had longed for him to be able to hear me but now I hope he isn't listening to *this*.

"Dr. Acevedo." Oliver steps in. "I can return with the Institute's solicitor if you'd prefer, but can we perhaps talk outside?" He pushes his glasses nervously onto the bridge of his nose. I don't hold out any hope that he can talk Dr. Acevedo around but when they come back into the room, Dr. Acevedo has Adam's release papers and a pen. My hand is quivering. It takes me three attempts to scrawl my signature.

"You're doing the right thing," Nell says.

Adam is wheeled along the corridor, with me once again trotting at his side. This time the doctors from the Institute are speaking in English, chatting to me, trying to put me at ease. It's so different to when we arrived, but the fear... the fear is still the same.

Am I going to lose him?

Once Adam is settled at the Institute, I return to the apartment to pack our things.

"You do think I'm doing the right thing?" I ask Nell for the hundredth time as we eat our last dinner together.

"Absolutely. I was reading this thing online—"

"Please. No more science." My head's throbbing.

"Sorry. It's just so fascinating. I might train to be a neuroscientist. Imagine that! I could win the Nobel Peace Prize."

"I think you could do anything, Nell, and Dr. Stevens has a nice ring to it." I spear a piece of fish with my fork. "I wish you weren't going home tomorrow." Everything seems manageable with her here.

"I wish I didn't have to, but it's only for a few days while Chris sorts out cover at work and can look after the kids. I'll fly out again next week."

Next week. By then everything might have changed.

Or nothing.

"Anna, you could always wait until I'm back to start the trial?"

"I'll think about it." We both know I won't. We're painfully aware that time is precious. That it might be running out.

A 3 percent chance of recovery.

"He'll come back to me, Nell, won't he?"

She squeezes my hand.

The car Oliver sent to fetch me winds around the coastal road. Out of the window I see nothing but darkness. Night has settled, merging the sea with the sky. It's odd to think of Nell sleeping in the apartment, alone in the double bed Adam and I should be sharing. Tomorrow she'll be back in the UK, but I won't be alone. I'm grateful for Oliver and his support.

Back at the center, in front of Adam's door, I am introduced to Luis.

"He'll be Adam's main nurse," Oliver tells me. "There'll be somebody with Adam at all times but if you have any concerns and Luis isn't on shift, he will likely be in his room just across the corridor. You can call him anytime, day or night."

"I'll be checking on Adam regularly, Mrs. Curtis, whether I'm working or not." He shakes my hand.

"Call me Anna, please, Luis. So . . . what happens if something goes wrong? At the hospital there was an alarm. So many doctors and nurses."

"We've a large medical team, please don't worry," Oliver says. "Adam will receive state-of-the-art care here."

"I know but…" But I'm having second thoughts. It's too quiet here without the clatter and chatter I've become used to.

"Here." Oliver pushes a button into my hand. "Press it."

My thumb presses down and immediately a siren blasts, orange lights strobe. Within seconds the corridor is filling with people. Oliver taps on his phone and the siren falls silent, the lights stop flashing.

"Feel better?" he asks kindly.

"Yes. Thanks. I think I'll go to bed now."

"Do you want me to come in with you? Your luggage is already inside. I could help you unpack?"

I shake my head.

Everyone slips away until it is just me, my fingertips on Adam's door handle, steeling myself to go inside and when I do, disappointment bites. There's still the flash of the monitor. A nurse stationed in the corner. My eyes fill with hot tears. It's ridiculous I had harbored an expectation that it would be different here. I'd felt a bubbling hope under the surface of my skin that perhaps moving him would trigger something. That now I'd have found him sitting up in bed, reading. The lamp blazes—and I hate myself for all the times I'd complained that he was keeping me awake. Our last row was only a few days before Adam had booked our holiday.

"The light's too bright. I'm trying to bloody sleep." I had sat upright, shielding my eyes.

"I can't read without it. Sorry, I won't be—"

"Why can't you just buy a Kindle like normal people?" I had made a show of thumping my pillows, throwing myself back down with a sigh.

"I like the feel of a paperback in my hand." He had turned the page.

"You wouldn't get that bloody rustling with a Kindle either."

"Christ, Anna. Next you'll be saying I breathe too loud."

I had muttered under my breath.

"Is there anything I do lately that doesn't irritate you?" Adam had snapped.

I had remained silent and when Adam slammed his book onto his cabinet and clicked off the light, I had lain rigid with anger long after he'd fallen asleep. I had thought I hated him. I had thought I didn't love him anymore.

"I'm so sorry." I crawl over the safety rail on the bed and lie beside him. "I'll make everything better, if you just wake up."

We need to learn to communicate again; my session with Eva has taught me that. I try to remember the us that used to talk for hours. Lately we'd passed Grandad's coin back and forth instead of using words. I loved the sentiment behind it but it made us lazy. It made us think that was enough.

It wasn't.

I have been unhappy these past few years. That hasn't always been the case throughout our marriage, but in this moment when I try to think of Adam, remember why I fell in love with him, this is the Adam that now comes to mind. The one with tubes and wires, skin as pale as the sheet he lies upon. But still, I want him back. Surely things will be different now I've had a glimpse of life without him?

Will they? Will our problems have magically disappeared?

I'm exhausted with it all. I curve my body against his and rest my head on his shoulder. I can't believe that I'm questioning us. Still unsure of who we are and who we'll be when Adam wakes up. Who Adam will be. If I was questioning if I loved Adam before, how would I be if he were a stranger? If he couldn't talk.

If I had to wash him, feed him, dress him every single day. Would he even know who I am?

My thoughts should be full of love and hope and positivity, but they're not. I feel lost and scared and confused.

Tomorrow.

Tomorrow I'll find out what's inside Adam's head.

My last waking thought is that I hope it's better than the doubts filling mine.

CHAPTER FORTY-TWO

Anna

My breakfast has been brought to me. The breeze is soothing as I sit at the table by the open window, pushing an egg with a sunshine-yellow yolk around my plate. It feels wrong to eat solid food while Adam is meters away being fed through a tube. I'm not hungry. Nerves are squirming in my stomach. Later this morning Oliver and Sofia will be here and the clinical trial will start. For the millionth time I question whether I'm doing the right thing, not just for Adam but for me. Yesterday I hadn't thought beyond what might be in Adam's mind but today I'm worried about me. Am I being selfish? How will Mum cope if something happens to me? The letter I left with Oliver doesn't seem enough. All of a sudden, I feel the urge to talk to Mum. I'd intended to ring her before Adam's cardiac arrest but, distracted, I still haven't called and told her about the accident.

"I'll be back soon." I kiss Adam and slip out of the door.

The beach is almost empty. It's still early but the sun is already throwing out warmth. The sky is brilliant blue and cloudless; it's going to be scorching later. I sit. The sand is damp beneath my cotton sundress. I kick off my flip-flops and cross my legs under me. It takes several deep breaths of the salty air before I can dial Mum's number. I know she'll be up, pottering around her kitchen, checking her wall planner to see what she's filling her day with.

"Hello, love. I didn't expect to hear from you while you're away."

Her voice renders me mute. Overcome with the emotion of needing her.

"Anna, what's wrong?"

"I don't want you to worry but—"

"Oh God, it's terrorists, isn't it? Are you somewhere safe?"

"It isn't terrorists—"

"A tsunami. You need to be somewhere high—"

"Mum! It's Adam." I pause to let that settle in. "There's been an accident." Slowly, reluctantly, I tell her, not everything—not about the baby or the clinical trial—but enough.

"But he will wake up?"

I close my eyes. She sounds so close it's as though I can reach out my hand and touch her. I wish that I could.

"His original doctor, Dr. Acevedo, said that typically comas last between two and four weeks." I keep the details as vague as I can.

Two years. Twelve years. Twenty years.

"A month! Oh, Anna. I'll come. I'll book a flight and—"

"You can't. Nan needs you."

"*You* need me." I've never heard her sound so strong. So determined. After Dad died, every single decision she had to make took forever as she endlessly deliberated. Constantly asking my opinion. Leaning on me the way she'd always leaned on him, sometimes too much. I was grieving too.

"I'm okay. Adam's got a great new doctor, Oliver Chapman, and Nell's coming out in a few days—she rang a few moments ago to see how the holiday is going." I lie to spare her feelings. She'll be hurt that Nell knew several days ago and had flown out straightaway.

"I can be there—"

"I know. And thank you, but let's give it a few days and see what happens. Adam could wake and we'll be home before you get here! I'm coping."

"I've no doubt about that. You've always been a tough little thing. After Dad…you did so much. Too much. I wasn't in a good state, but I'm okay now. Please don't feel you have to keep things from me."

"I won't. Mum, about Dad. Is there anything you wish you could have told him when he was in hospital that you didn't get to say?" We had all thought he'd recover. None of us said goodbye.

"Yes," Mum answers straightaway. "I talked to him while he was unconscious. I don't know if it's possible he could have heard me. The doctor and one of the nurses said he couldn't, but there was another nurse who said she believed he could. Anyway, I told him that I'd be changing his diet, swapping sticky toffee puddings for fruit and that we'd dig out his golf clubs from the garage, make sure he got some exercise. But what I didn't say, what I should have said, is that I'd be okay without him. Not because I wanted to be without him, or I believed I would be okay, but because…" She falters. "Because if he could have heard me, it would have reassured him. Made letting go that little bit easier. He always worried so much and I hate to think his last thoughts were wondering how I'd cope alone."

She sniffs and I know she is crying too.

I'm doing the right thing.

What comfort Oliver's work could have brought Mum.

Knowing that Dad could hear her would have made such a difference. Would have allowed her to say all the things she needed to make it easier for him. For her.

"I've got to go, Mum, but I'll call you soon."

"I love you, Anna."

"I love you too."

And leaving my doubts and fears on the beach, I head back up the incline to the Institute.

It is time.

I shuffle out of my bedroom, self-conscious in the gown Sofia has given me to put on. All of my bras have underwire and because I can't wear anything with metal in the scanner, I'd had to take it off. Self-consciously I cross my arms across my chest as I pad, in socked feet, to find Oliver.

Again, he shows me the console room where he and Sofia will be watching me, both through the glass and via the computer screen. Luis settles Adam on the patient table, as I now know it is called.

"The scanners are notoriously noisy," Oliver tells me. "Unfortunately the knocking sound you'll hear is something we couldn't entirely eradicate with our new design but you'll be wearing noise-canceling headphones. I've a microphone in the console room and I'll be able to speak to you. There's a mic within the machine so you can talk to me. I want you be comfortable and if you're not, just say and I'll get you out as quickly as I can."

"Okay." Nerves writhe around my stomach. "There is enough air in the machine for both of us?" Oliver's new design may be larger than usual but now I'm about to go inside it, it seems impossibly small.

"Absolutely. Some people can experience anxiety in a confined space but, again, we can get you out at any time."

I don't care how bad it gets or how panicky I feel. I won't ask to stop. This is possibly my only chance to do this.

"We'll be timing you for thirty minutes and then we'll call a halt. Potentially it might feel much longer; I'm sure you've had dreams that seem to have lasted an extraordinarily long time, but when you woke up, you might only have been asleep for several minutes?"

"Yes."

"In a dream state, the processing speed of our subconscious mind is much faster than the conscious mind. An event that in reality might take hours can be experienced in just seconds in the subconscious mind."

"Last night I dreamed about the time Adam and I stayed up all night on the beach talking, seven years ago. I woke thinking it must be morning but I'd only been asleep for twenty minutes." It was all so vivid. The taste of cheap wine like vinegar on my tongue. The setting sun burning orange. Clicking our love lock to the fence. The smell of salt. The feel of Adam's skin under my fingers. Tracing the map-shaped birthmark staining his arm.

"That's because your brain understands how long that night took and used your real-life experience to simulate the passage of time. Minutes can seem like hours."

Hours with Adam is what I want more than anything right now.

"If there's anything in Adam's consciousness we're hoping to record it, but again, this is a prototype and its capabilities on paper may not match the reality. I don't want you to get your hopes up."

I try to force a smile. My hopes are sky-high. "I know. Can we just start, please?"

"Okay." A smile stretches across Oliver's face before his features settle into serious scientist once more. I can't blame him for being excited. This is his life's work. His big dream. Suddenly I am heavy with the weight of responsibility that I might let him down.

I settle myself on the table next to Adam, linking my fingers through his. Sofia slips the goggles onto me and then the headphones. There's a jerk and then we're sliding into the scanner. I'm not claustrophobic but the sense of heat, of being closed in, is uncomfortable, and if this wasn't my chance of seeing what Adam is thinking, I'd be tempted to scramble out. There's a hiss and then Oliver's voice sounds through the headphones.

"Okay, Anna?"

"Yes." My voice sounds inaudible to me.

"I'm going to count down from ten and then we'll begin."

Ten

Am I doing the right thing?

Nine

I am terrified there'll be nothing there.

Eight

Terrified there'll be something there and it will be unbearable.

Seven

What if he's thinking he doesn't love me anymore?

Six

What if he knows I've been questioning my love for him?

Five

I can't breathe in the machine.

Four

My heart is racing too fast.

Three

I want to stop. I've changed my mind.

Two

I have to know.

One

Adam, I'm coming for you.

CHAPTER FORTY-THREE

Oliver

Oliver stares at the scanner through the window, his senses on high alert as he listens for signs that something is happening, watching to ensure Anna isn't trying to climb out of the machine in panic, but she is still and silent.

"Sofia?" he asks quietly. He knows his assistant is studying the computer screen, while he stares through the window—he can't tear his eyes away from the machine in the other room.

"There's nothing."

"Nothing as in it's not recording or nothing as in the equipment isn't doing what we thought?"

"Either? Both? I can't tell."

"What are you seeing?"

"Darkness. Nothing but darkness. But we can't expect it all to run smoothly the first time, can we? You know what Edison said: 'I haven't failed, I've just found ten thousand ways that didn't work.' Let's leave her for the thirty minutes and see if anything changes."

But it doesn't.

The computer screen remains black.

CHAPTER FORTY-FOUR

Anna

My head is spinning. I'm dazed, disorientated. There's a sense of having been picked up and dropped somewhere else entirely, and in a way I have. I am back at home in the UK. In bed. On the wall is the black-and-white framed photo of our wedding day. Adam's forehead touching mine. My flower crown circling my head. On the bed next to me, my husband.

"Adam." I burst into noisy tears.

"Hey." He scoops me into his arms. At first I am stiff. Scared that if I move, Oliver will take it as a signal that I want to be brought back but I can feel my body is still, the movement only in my mind.

Adam's mind.

The place where we've met in the middle.

I cling to him and he rhythmically strokes my back.

"It's okay," he says, but that only makes me cry harder. It isn't okay. It isn't okay at all. I try to calm myself. I've lost all concept of time, unsure how long I've been here. How long I have before I'm back in the Institute with my husband. My husband who can't talk, laugh, move. Who can't press me close to his body and whisper my name into my hair. I don't want to waste a single second.

"Adam." I wriggle backward so I can see him properly. My fingertips brushing his face, his collarbone, his chest. Tracing the map-shaped birthmark on his arm, reassuring myself he is here, he is real and solid. I search his eyes for a sign that he knows that us being together is only fleeting, that this is not our reality, but there is nothing.

"Adam, I..." What can I say? What should I say? What would be the point of telling him that this version of him, of us, is one his mind has conjured. That his real body lies broken in Alircia, kept alive by machines. I look around the room. The Yankee candle I always burn in the evenings is flickering on top of the drawers. I inhale; instead of the sterile smell of the scanner—bleach and disinfectant—there's the aroma of lavender. It's so real. I am incredulous that it isn't. I tug the corner of the duvet toward my face to wipe my tears; it smells of Comfort fabric softener.

It smells of home.

"Anna?"

A hint of a frown passes across Adam's forehead. My throat tightens. Normal, I must act normal.

But I can't.

For the second time, I wind my arms around his neck and press my body close to his. He hasn't shaved and his chin scratches against my cheek. Before, I would have complained at this but instead my laughter merges with my sobs until I am hiccupping, not sure what I am feeling.

I am feeling *everything*.

I pull away from him, giggling.

"Okay. Tears I could understand, but laughter? Should I be

paranoid?" He adjusts his boxers. "Nope, nothing hanging out there. Want to share the joke?"

"Sorry…I'm just…happy." It's too small a word to describe how utterly joyous it is to be with him at home where everything is so…perfect.

"Right. Well, happy. Yeah…me too." He grins. "Still hasn't sunk in, has it?"

"Ummm. No?" For one horrible second I think he is referring to the accident. That would explain his "tears I could understand" remark. While I wait for him to speak, I wipe my eyes with my pajama sleeve.

"Not for me either, but the book told me your moods would be up and down. Crying is normal."

"The book?" I'm not following him at all. There's a book about yacht accidents?

"Yeah. I know you told me to stop reading it since I told you it said it will take nine months to get your extra weight off, but I know seesawing emotions are because of your hormones. It's only to be expected in your condition." He smiles as he places a hand on my stomach.

"In my…" A movement in my belly knocks the air from my lungs. I place my hand on top of his, my eyes straying down toward my bump.

My bump!

"That's all it is, isn't it, Anna? Hormones." His eyes darken as he studies me. "Everything's been better since Alircia, hasn't it? Or since this little one?" He gently pats my tummy. I begin to cry again, shifting myself up to sitting so I can reach a tissue and mop up my tears.

"I'll go and make you a tea." He swings his legs out of bed.

"No." I grasp his wrist, not wanting him to leave me, however momentarily. I remember what Mum wished she'd said to Dad. "Adam, I…I would cope okay without you, you know. I'd be okay on my own."

He turns and studies me. I can't remember the last time we properly made eye contact; not fleeting glances at each other while we talked about the mundane, but properly drank each other in. In this moment I feel so connected to him, but when he speaks his tone is clipped and I realize I have inadvertently upset him.

"I know we've had a tough few years and the pregnancy isn't a sticking plaster; we have to work at healing the wound but—"

"Christ." I cut him off. "Where did you get that analogy from? The book?" Automatically I fall into the defensive. Why does he take everything the wrong way?

"So what if I've been reading up? Some of us want our family to work."

"I want our family to work!" I'm crying again. I can't believe we're bickering.

"So what's all this 'I'll be okay on my own' bollocks?"

"I just…I don't know. I just wanted you to know that if anything happened to you…I wouldn't want you to worry."

"Ah. This is antenatal anxiety—"

"I love that you've researched all of this. Really. I'm sorry." I take his hand. I don't know how much longer we have and I don't want to waste a second.

"Don't be. It's really common. Let me go and make a drink and we'll have a cuddle."

"I don't want—"

"It's okay. I remember you're off caffeine. I picked up some more chamomile on the way home." He unpeels my fingers and I am left alone as his footfall thuds down the stairs. I'm terrified I might never see him again. While I blow my nose, I scan the room. In the corner, the chair heaped with a pile of Adam's T-shirts. His red Coca-Cola one. His faded brown Oasis tour T-shirt. The sight of my jewelry box causes my fingers to flutter to my neck. I'm wearing my star pendant. The one I'd packed away when Adam and I started going through a bad patch. When I was unable to conceive. I trace the curve of my belly with my fingertips.

I'm pregnant.

I try to gauge how far along I am. Six months? Seven? Eight? It's impossible to tell. My body feels heavy. I pad over to my drawers and lift out the tissue paper–wrapped parcel. Back in bed I gently unwrap it, lifting out the tiny lemon sleepsuit and the Percy the Parrot cuddly toy.

Adam saunters back into the room in his familiar green tartan pajamas, carrying two mugs, a packet of chocolate digestives tucked under his elbow, the way he always used to before my love for him turned bitter and cold and I'd bitch about the crumbs in bed. The chocolate stains on the duvet. It's as though we've regressed back to our honeymoon phase but instead we've moved forward.

We are having a baby!

My heart sings.

Happily I drape the sleepsuit over my bump while Adam examines Percy the Parrot with joy.

"I'd almost forgotten about him!" he exclaims.

"It seems so long ago since we were first in Alircia," I say.

"It seems so long ago that we were last in Alircia." Adam rips open the biscuits and takes one out, biting it in half. Crumbs scatter onto the duvet but I don't tut and dramatically brush them off. Instead I reach for a biscuit and snap a piece off, placing it on my tongue and letting the chocolate dissolve. "We need another holiday! We'll have to go back once this little one makes his appearance."

"His?" I ask.

"Or hers. I'm glad we never found out at the scan. What do you say to the three of us on a beach?"

"I'm in no rush to go back to Alircia." If I never see the island again it will be too soon.

"Why?" His face falls. "It's our special place. It's because it was a different sort of break, wasn't it?"

"Different? How?"

"You know. With you being in the first few weeks of pregnancy and me not letting you do anything. No sightseeing. No yacht trips. No coach journeys to tourist attractions. Were you bored?"

The space in my throat constricts. He has created a fiction that kept me safe, him safe, us safe. Our lives carrying on in the way they probably would have done had the yacht accident never have happened.

"I wasn't bored," I whisper.

"Good, because I have plans for the three of us. I think we should go traveling. Take the trip I'd planned before I met you."

"I don't know. With a baby? Is it safe?"

"You're always safe with me, Anna. I'd never let anything happen to you."

I think about the way he'd twice risked his life to save me. If only he hadn't gone back to help that elderly woman. His thumb traces my cheekbone. I turn my head to kiss his palm. He smells of coffee and chocolate and Adam.

"Oh God. You're not going to cry again, are you? Christ,

woman, we'll never be able to go anywhere because we'll have spent all our savings on bloody tissues."

"No, I'm not going to cry." I take a deep breath. "We can go anywhere you want to, Adam. Do anything."

"You hear that, Percy?" He lifts the parrot to eye level. "A world trip awaits us. In the meantime, Mrs. Curtis…" He waggles his eyebrows and I feel a frisson of excitement. A desire to be touched.

"Yes, Mr. Curtis."

"I'm going to finish this chapter before we go to sleep." He twists around and picks a Kindle up from his bedside table.

"Adam…" I feel incredibly sad for every mean thing I've ever said. Incredibly regretful. "Why don't you read a paperback tonight?"

"Are you kidding me? You've converted me to e-readers now. I love that you fall asleep on me and I don't have to worry my light is keeping you awake." He turns and clicks off his lamp and I do the same. He wriggles an arm under my shoulders and I mold my body around his. By the glow of his Kindle I study his face, the movement of his eyes as he scans the page, the twitch of a smile.

It's a perfect, perfect moment until it's spoiled by Oliver's voice, deep and cutting.

"I'm going to bring you back now, Anna." Panic bites. I want to remain in this make-believe world where the accident never happened, where our holiday continued without tragedy, I didn't lose our baby and everything is as it would have been in the life we almost had.

Ten

I hold Adam's hand tighter as though I can prevent the glue holding us together from becoming unstuck.

Nine

As though I can somehow prevent Oliver bringing me back.
Eight
Adam.
Seven
Anna?
Six
My lips press against his skin.
Five
I love you, I whisper.
Four
I love you too. He turns back to his book.
Three
Oliver, don't make me leave him.
Two
Don't bring me back.
One

The air is cooler as I am brought out of the scanner. The goggles are lifted from my face, the headphones from my ears. I twist my head to see Adam's motionless body beside me.

I begin to cry.

It takes a few minutes for the dizzying sickness to pass and then I sit up. There's a throbbing in my head. Blood streaking from my nose and Luis dabs at it with a tissue. Sofia presses a glass of water into my hand and I take a sip.

Oliver tries to be patient but he can't help firing questions at me I am not yet ready to answer. I want to be alone. To hold the pictures that are fading too fast from my mind and cherish them.

Normal. It was all so normal.

Adam could have been drifting in his consciousness through

Belgium, Italy, Thailand. All the places he'd dreamed he'd go. Instead he is at home with me. A child still on the way.

And we are happy. The version of us who are excited and hopeful and preparing to be parents.

On some level, in Adam's mind, we are together and we are happy.

CHAPTER FORTY-FIVE

Oliver

Anna is pale. Agitated as she twists the corner of the tissue in her hand into a sharp point before dabbing at the blood still leaking from her nose.

"We couldn't see anything on the screen," Oliver says again.

"I'm not making it up," Anna insists. "I can see how you might think I'd be so desperate to talk to Adam again I might have fabricated it all, but I didn't. I was back at home and everything was...normal."

Oliver scratches notes on his pad. Usually he'd type on his laptop but the way his computer had let him down by failing to record the trial had left a desire to go back to basics. Computer readings were often wrong or missing during trials, but it didn't make it any easier knowing that.

"If I'd imagined it," Anna says, "I wouldn't have imagined it that way. There was a point when we were bickering the way we used to but...I was there. He was there." Anna's expression is so earnest that Oliver believes her. The computer may not have recorded it, but it has worked. Despite his years of research, Oliver is staggered that it has. On the outside he is composed, studiously documenting Anna's account of her journey, but on the inside he is singing. Dancing. Frothing open the champagne. This is revolutionary. He has built a bridge between the subconscious and the conscious. It really will change lives.

Clem would be so proud of him. She'd also tell him he should be looking after Anna. Oliver feels a pang of shame as he notices the droop of her eyes. The yawn she's stifling.

"Do you want to go and have a lie down?" he asks.

"Yes, please." She stands, her shoulders rounded as she begins to shuffle away. "Oliver?" She turns, their eyes meet and then hers flicker away from his. For a second he is tense. Certain she is going to ask for arrangements to be made for Adam to be flown home. Instead she says, "How soon can we repeat this?" He relaxes.

"Luis will check Adam over again and you need another physical and to talk to Eva. I want to be certain that there are no delayed reactions and we'll take it from there, okay?"

"Okay. But…when?"

"I'm concerned about your nosebleed, Anna. The throbbing you've described in your head." Her face shadows. "I'm glad you've told me your head hurts. It's important that I know these things. Let's take it step by step. Get some rest and I'll come and see you later."

It is dusk when Oliver taps on Anna's door.

"How are you feeling?"

She yawns. "Fine. I can't believe I've slept. I saw Sofia before I crashed but I haven't spoken to Eva yet. Is she still around?"

"She's finished for the day. Don't worry, you can see her in the morning. Join me downstairs for dinner? We can talk."

"Give me a sec." Anna crosses over to Adam and kisses his lips before moving the coin on his bedside table closer to him.

In the cafeteria, Oliver asks, "What's the coin for?"

"It's the coin my grandad used to win my nan's heart." Anna laughs at the expression on Oliver's face. "No really." She explains about the jukebox. About the coin passing back and forth between her grandparents and now back and forth between her and Adam. "Did you and Clem have any rituals?"

"No," Oliver began. "Yes, actually. She used to press a finger against her lips. It was her way of telling me that she loved me when she couldn't say it. From across a room, that sort of thing." Oliver fiddles with the salt pot. "It was the last thing she ever did."

"Oh, Oliver." Anna rubs the top of his arm. "You must miss her terribly."

"You think you know how you'll feel when you lose someone you love, but you don't. You can't possibly imagine it. She's everywhere and yet she isn't here. Her absence makes her more present in a way. That doesn't make any sense, does it?" Oliver can recite facts and figures but he has never been good at expressing his emotions.

"It does. She fills your mind."

Oliver nods. "Yes, that's it. And I haven't just lost her but I've lost everything else I wanted to be. A father. A grandfather. We hadn't planned on having kids for another few years but we would have done. Eventually."

"A child would be a comfort," Anna says.

"Sorry. That was insensitive of me." Oliver is horrified at his thoughtlessness. "I know you've suffered a miscarriage recently. Do you want to talk about it?"

Anna scrapes her hair back with both hands before letting

it fall free again. "There's not much to say. We'd wanted a baby for such a long time and now…" She looks sorrowfully at her flat stomach. "Now I'm left with that empty, unbearable sadness that I'll never get to meet them. Him or her. Harry or Charlotte."

"I'm so sorry, Anna."

"I…I was pregnant today, when I went back. About seven or eight months, I think."

Oliver processes this for a moment.

"I didn't tell you earlier because…it's personal. My life and yet"—she shakes her head—"it isn't my life." She sweeps her arm around the room. "This is my reality, unfortunately."

"If I could change things for you, I would."

Their food arrives and the conversation lightens to the tourist attractions on the island. Anna tells him about the lava caves she had visited with Adam when they first met.

"Have you been?"

"No," Oliver says. "I'm a bit all work and no play, I'm afraid."

"It was incredible. Each one was a themed room with furniture and everything. All underground. There was even a dance floor."

"Ah, now I definitely won't go. Nobody needs to see me dancing. Clem said I resembled somebody with their finger stuck in a plug socket." He makes jerky movements with his arms.

"Adam thinks he's Kevin Bacon in *Footloose*." Anna smiles. "Stick on the soundtrack and he'll be up there doing his thing."

"I've never seen that film," Oliver admits.

"Adam would be *horrified* to hear that. He's obsessed with Eighties music and movies."

They finish eating, lingering over coffee.

"So…" Anna looks at him intently. "Can we…can I take part in the trial again?"

"I don't know, Anna. I should probably take it back to development stage and check everything is safe. Something isn't right with the computer not recording and then there's your nosebleed and headache."

"How long would that take?" Anna asks.

"Months." Oliver wants to be truthful.

"It may be too late for Adam then. For me. Oliver...I was pregnant."

"I think perhaps we could try again, but this time I have to be the one taking part."

"No! Oliver, you promised I could try."

"And you have, Anna. I need to see for myself."

Emotions slide across Anna's face. "I appreciate you've spent years working toward this and of course you want to try it but... not yet. Soon, but I'm still adjusting to all of this. It's okay for you. Science is your job. Your passion. You understand its capabilities. A few days ago, I didn't know anything about consciousness and Adam, he isn't...he isn't just a subject to me. Today seems like a dream almost. I want to do it again."

"Anna, I think I made a mistake letting you try. I didn't think about the effect it would have on you mentally, when you had to stop."

"But you did consider that on some level. You wouldn't have insisted on me seeing Eva otherwise. You're a good man."

Is he? Oliver wonders if he was just following procedure. Ticking boxes. There is no checklist for morality. Was he playing God?

Anna leans toward him. "I've signed a disclaimer; you don't need to worry—"

"I'm not worried about being sued." Oliver is indignant. "I'm worried about you. You haven't seen Eva yet. We agreed."

"I'll speak to her first thing, but I'm okay. You want me to trust you, Oliver, and I do. Please trust me. Everything was fine. I'm fine. Let me be the one to try again, not you."

Oliver is torn between his head and his heart. He sees Clem press her finger to her lips. He sees her lying delirious in a hospice bed. He remembers his despair.

"Okay," he eventually says. "Tomorrow. If Eva is happy, you can try again tomorrow."

CHAPTER FORTY-SIX

Anna

It is the morning light pushing through the window that stirs me. Ever since the accident I've been waking every thirty minutes, skin clammy, heart pounding, but last night I slept for seven hours straight.

Adam.

I rush through to his room, praying that the trial has somehow brought Adam back. Properly back.

It hasn't.

Luis is writing his notes.

"Is everything okay?"

"No change," Luis says cheerfully. "Eva says she'll see you at ten."

I am hopeful I'll be allowed to take part in the trial again. My headache has eased and for the first time in days I feel able to cope—seeing Adam has given me strength. I wander outside. The sun casts sparkles onto the aquamarine ocean. It is only nine o'clock but there are children digging in the sand with brightly colored spades, parents stretched out on candy-striped beach towels.

I sit on a large flat rock, stretching my legs out in front of me. A girl of about eighteen hurries past me, head down, self-consciously clutching a towel against her sarong-covered body. I remember how anxious I had been that first day on the beach when I felt Adam's eyes on me. Worried he was judging me, the girl with cellulite speckling her thighs, clad in a black swimming costume amongst a sea of neon bikinis. I was convinced that if I could lose ten pounds, my life would be perfect. If only my body were my sole worry now. It's Adam's body, limp and unresponsive, which makes my blood run cold. Yesterday, seeing him, hearing him, *touching him*...It's all so hard to process.

My mobile has been off all night—I switch it on and call Nell.

"It worked," I blurt out before I have even said hello.

"Fuck. Tell me *everything*."

"It was like...not watching a movie but being in one. It wasn't some elaborate fantasy in Adam's mind where he was conquering Mount Everest or starring in *Back to the Future*, it was...normal. We were home. Eating biscuits in bed. He mentioned our holiday here but we hadn't been on the yacht. It was as though we were living the life we would have if we hadn't been on that trip. Nell, I...I was still pregnant."

"Oh, Anna. That sounds unbearably sad."

"It was." Spending time with Adam in a world I couldn't stay in was excruciatingly painful, but oddly comforting too. It has unplugged something, making it easier to remember the good memories—and there are so many of them—before they became sullied and sharp from the years of trying for a child. Just that brief glimpse into the ordinary life that could have been ours has been enough to strengthen my resolve. Whatever happens with Adam, whatever care needs he might have, I will be steadfastly there for him, the way he has always been there for me.

"Do you think…" Nell slows down her speech and I know she is carefully choosing her words. "I know it must be tempting to want to do it again, but…I don't know. Maybe you should quit while you're ahead? You've seen something wonderful and next time…"

"I know." There is a part of me that has thought the same thing. If I go back again, I'm risking spoiling the memories of the first time, but how can I not?

"It's a lot to cope with, Anna. Emotionally."

"I'm okay. Honestly." I was devastated when Oliver had brought me back, sorrowful and angry, but now, talking it through with Nell, remembering how it felt to lie next to Adam, elation is my overriding emotion. Excitement at doing it again. I am missing him horribly; not the Adam that lies in the bed being pumped full of nutrients but the Adam as he was, and now there's a baby! All I ever wanted is so close and yet frustratingly out of reach. "I told Mum yesterday, not about the Institute but about the accident. Adam's coma."

"How did she take it?" Nell knows my mum doesn't cope well.

"She was amazing. She offered to fly out but I've told her to wait. Are you still coming back next week?"

"Yep. Chris is taking over with the rug rats. I'll be glad of a break, actually. Oh God. I didn't mean. Shit. Sorry. I know it's not a holiday."

"Don't worry about it." She's tired and not thinking straight. I know how that feels.

"Have you told Josh yet?" she asks.

"No." But I must. "I think I'll do that now."

"Good luck. Love you, Anna."

"Love you too."

*

Before I call Josh, I plan my side of the conversation in my head. I won't need to sugar-coat Adam's prognosis the way I had to with Mum, but it will hit him hard. The first few times I'd met Josh I hadn't understood why he and Adam were friends; they were polar opposites. Adam quiet and sensitive, Josh loud and raucous. I assumed it was their shared history that bound them together. On Adam's side, gratitude that Josh's parents had taken him in. For Josh, a friend that paled into the background, allowing him to take center stage.

I was wrong.

They genuinely enjoy each other's company. Enjoy their differences. They're like brothers and it pains me that I have to be the one to break the bad news. I press dial and when the call connects, I say, "Josh. Is this a good time to—"

"What's wrong with Adam?" He knows I wouldn't be ringing him from Alircia otherwise.

"He's in a coma." I get straight to the point. "There was an accident." I tell him about the yacht. Sometimes he cuts in and asks questions but mostly he just listens while I let it all pour out.

"Stupid twat always has to be the hero," Josh says after I've finished. Tears thickening his words. "I'll book a flight."

"Thanks. But there's really nothing you can do here right now."

"There must be some way that I can help?"

I pause. Josh will need something practical to occupy him or he'll be jumping on a plane, whatever I say.

"If you can carry on looking after Hammie, please, that would be great? And you could also keep an eye on the house. Make sure there isn't any post sticking out of the letterbox. Water the plants."

"Yeah, I can do that. Is…is he getting the right care over there? Wouldn't you be better off in the UK?"

"We'll be back at some stage, but there's nothing anyone can do to wake Adam up."

"But he could just wake up, couldn't he?" Josh sounds like a small boy.

A 3 percent chance of recovery.

"Of course." I am the adult. I am good at pretending. "At any time."

"And then he'll be fucking unbearable. You know how he gets when he has a cold. Going on about it weeks later. We'll never hear the end of a coma."

I smile. "You're right. He's never great when he's sick. A few months back I had tonsillitis and felt terrible. I took myself off to bed. Adam came in and laid down next to me. Said he'd sneezed and was worried he'd was getting the flu. Asked me what was for dinner."

"I can believe that. Did he ever tell you that when we shared a flat he had a cold and convinced himself he'd never recover? I wouldn't indulge him so he dragged himself to the chemist and asked for some euthanasia tablets. 'Don't you mean echinacea?' the pharmacist asked. 'I know what I mean,' Adam had said."

We both laugh and it feels good.

It feels hopeful.

"I've got to go, Josh, but I will keep in touch. Is there anything you want me to tell Adam?"

"Yeah, tell him a one-legged, half-blind ape could save more goals than he does nowadays..." I hear how painful this is for him. "Tell him...tell him that I love him." He cuts the call, leaving me with the dial tone in my ear and a lump in my throat. I don't think Adam quite likes football as much as he used to, but he kept going so he could spend time with Josh.

Shades of shame color me. I recall the times I'd nagged him for trailing dirt over the floor after practice, for leaving his kit—damp with sweat and crusted with mud—on the bedroom floor. I should have been grateful Adam was keeping fit. Keeping in shape. It will give him the strength to fight this. The human body is powerful, resilient. Something to be respected and admired. My brief glimpse yesterday into Adam as he was reaffirms my faith that he can recover.

I can't allow myself to think otherwise.

Nevertheless, Dr. Acevedo's "3 percent chance of recovery" drives me to my feet. Impatient to repeat the trial again.

Not because I think Adam won't survive.

But still there's an urgency to my pace as I stalk back up the hill to the Institute.

CHAPTER FORTY-SEVEN

Anna

Eva studies me, playing the silence game once more. We are waiting to see which of us will be the first to break.

It's me.

"Okay, maybe I am embellishing how good I felt afterward so you give the go-ahead for me to do it again today, but yesterday was mostly a good experience."

"Mostly?"

"There was a part where we started to argue. It was almost automatic. I was so pleased to see him. Pleased is an understatement but somehow we began to bicker. We stopped though, moved on."

I pick at my nails, suddenly feeling close to tears. Life should have been easier in the reality Adam created, shouldn't it? If we didn't have perfection there, what does that say about him? What does that say about us?

"We talked a little bit before about the communication in your relationship," Eva begins.

"The lack of," I say.

"Yes. It's interesting that yesterday in Adam's mind you're

pregnant but, understandably, you have years of bitterness that built up during your infertile spell. Without that being addressed, there's always likely to be underlying resentment."

"But…" I don't know what to say. It's like having the chance to create your ideal box of chocolates and yet putting in one that you hate. A rogue Turkish Delight amongst a plethora of strawberry creams and crunchy pralines. "I felt…I felt upset but I wanted to move past it quickly and make the most of the time we had. Is it odd it felt so real?"

"No. Oliver hoped it would. That's why he wanted a direct connection rather than viewing images through a computer. The ultimate virtual reality as though you were really there, experiencing it all. Anna." Eva leans forward. "You do know that this isn't real? That this isn't a permanent solution for you to be with Adam?"

"Of course." But I can't help second-guessing what my next experience will be like. The one after.

"Oliver will only need you to repeat this a few times before he'll need to find other participants. It can't be a balanced trial with only your results."

"I know." Oliver keeps telling me this but every time it's hard to hear. The thought of being shipped back to the UK and left to sit by Adam's bed, wondering what he's thinking while I wait for him to wake up, is unbearable.

Two years. Twelve years. Twenty years.

"But you're happy for me to try again?" I ask.

"If you're up to it, then yes."

I rush out of the room to find Oliver, a "thank you" trailing in my wake, before Eva has even put the lid on her pen.

*

Again I am lying on the patient table next to Adam but this time I'm more excited than scared.

"We're almost ready," Sofia says. "We still haven't got to the bottom of why the computer didn't record, so in the event that it happens again, we're relying on you to remember as much as you can." She slips the goggles on me and then the headphones. The table slides into the scanner and I wait for Oliver to speak.

"I'm going to count you down now, Anna," he says. I wait impatiently for the count of one.

I am back at home. In the bath. My fingers instantly stray to my stomach. I'm smiling when I feel my bump, under the coconut bubbles. I place both hands across my belly.

"Hello, little one." The water ripples. There's a twisting inside of me. Something hard pushing into my skin. It's such a joyous feeling. I trace the shape of it—an elbow? A heel? Before I can identify what it is, there's a shift and my stomach is a smooth, hard mound once more. "I've waited for you for an awfully long time," I whisper. "I can't wait to meet you. You are so loved. So very loved." I haul myself out of the bath, unused to the weight of my body. I want to find Adam. While I dry myself, I continue talking in hushed tones. "There's Great-Nan. She's a little forgetful but you don't need to worry about that. You're unforgettable. Then there's Grandma—that's my mum— she'll be knitting you Christmas jumpers until you're my age most likely, but you can allow her that because she's the best baker. Wait until you taste her scones." I flap the towel toward my feet in the vain hope it will absorb some water because I can't bend to reach them. "There's Aunty Nell. If you're a girl, she'll teach you about boys, and if you're a boy she'll tell you what girls want." I shrug on my dressing gown. "And then there's Uncle Josh. I dread to think what he'll teach you."

I open the bathroom door and step outside, stubbing my toe on the bookcase that still waits in pieces on the landing to be built. Some things never change.

"Adam. I've almost fallen over that bookcase again," bursts out of me before I can keep it in. I hobble downstairs, trying to keep the irritation out of my voice. "Adam?"

He's prone on the sofa. Picking at a bowl of Kettle crisps that rests on his stomach. A can of lager on the floor.

I hover, midway on the stairs, the pain in my toe disappearing.

My husband.

I waddle toward him, awkwardly drop to my knees and cover his face in kisses. His lips taste of cheese and onion.

"If that's because I bought you Philosophy bubble bath rather than Asda's own brand, then you're welcome."

"It's not because of that. It's because I love you." I can't stop smiling. "Josh does too, even though he said to tell you a one-legged, half-blind ape could save more goals than you do nowadays. We, umm, spoke the other day."

He laughs but admits, "I do feel a bit old to be part of the team now. I think I'll give it up."

"Don't give up," I say decisively. "Don't ever give up on anything."

"I thought it would make you happy?"

"You being fit, strong. That's what makes me happy."

Idly, I run my fingers over his wrist. The space where his watch used to be. He never wears one anymore.

"I'm waiting," he says.

I look up at him quizzically.

"For my rollicking over the bookcase?"

"No, it's fine," I say, but then I think of Eva explaining to me that Adam and I bottling everything up has led to our underlying resentment. "Actually, it isn't."

"Here we go." Adam sits up.

"I don't want a row." Time is too precious. "But can we talk?"

"Yeah." He shuffles over to the corner and pats the cushion next to him.

"Do you think I nag you?" I keep my tone soft.

"A bit." He glances at me. "You go on about the bookcase a lot. I get it. It's because you're pissed off with me about...other things."

"It isn't that at all." I make a mental note to come back to the "other things." "Sometimes when I complain the bookcase hasn't been built, it's because I actually want a bookcase to be built."

"I think we both know that—"

"I've got nowhere to put my books," I finish, gently. "Adam, I'm perfectly capable of building the bookcase. I'm perfectly capable of repainting the kitchen. I'm perfectly capable of decorating the dining room—"

"You wanted wallpaper in there." There's exasperation in Adam's voice and I remind myself to keep calm. Part of me wonders whether it's even worth having this conversation, what good it will do. If... *When* Adam wakes up, he's not likely to remember it but still, the thought that I can repair our relationship on some level brings me comfort. It's a positive step, I think.

"Okay, so I'm perfectly capable of paying someone to wallpaper the dining room." I take his hand. "It's not important to me how things get done, but it seems to be important to you. Every time I offer to help or say I'm going to hire a tradesman, you get pretty shirty."

"Yeah, well, I'm the man and I should—"

"Don't give me that sexist bullshit. This isn't the 1950s and you're all for equality in every other sense. Why does it mean so much to you?"

"Because. I feel that I should be able to...provide certain things."

"Things?"

Adam moves my hand. "Want a cuppa?"

"No. I want to talk. Adam, *please*." I don't know how long I have with him.

"I don't know what to say."

"We're going to be a family soon. We need to learn to communicate."

"We talk."

"Not properly. Not like we used to. Remember when we met?"

We fall into silence. Both of us back on the beach.

It is me who speaks first. "What do you feel you aren't providing, Adam?"

"A baby." And there it is. *Other things.* The thing we never talked about. "I couldn't get you pregnant—"

"Because of my endometriosis. It wasn't your fault."

"I still felt you blamed me."

"Why?" My chest aches. How had I made him feel that way?

"Because you were so snappy with me. Every month."

"I was...sad. Sad I wasn't pregnant and feeling guilty that it was all my fault. I thought you blamed me."

"I didn't. I felt...helpless. It all got so overwhelming. I just thought I was letting you down in so many other ways, what was the point? Painting a wall or digging a border in the garden wouldn't change anything in the big scheme of things. It seemed so trivial. I can't give you a baby but I've fixed the leaky tap." He waves jazz hands.

"I wish you'd fix the leaky tap." I smile to show I'm joking. "I'm sorry, Adam. I genuinely am that you've been blaming yourself, feeling inadequate."

"I'm sorry I didn't realize it was how you were feeling too. I've been a bit of a knob."

"I've been a bit of a bitch."

"A bit?" He raises his eyebrows. I nudge him with my shoulder.

"At first I thought it would happen for us and when it didn't..." He is serious. "Every month...The disappointment turning to despair it wasn't happening. Fear it would never happen and then suddenly so much time had passed it seemed odd to bring it up and because you'd never broached the subject either..."

"I was afraid of what you might say. What you might think of me," I say quietly.

"Same."

Our fingers find each other.

"Are we okay?" he asks.

"Yes. But we need to do this regularly. Talk. Not try to second-guess what the other is thinking. Let each other know what we need."

"I need you."

I kiss him, my fingers sliding under his T-shirt. It feels... right. I find his belt buckles, the button of his jeans. Our kisses are hot, hard. My breath ragged. This...this is how I used to feel. Overcome with longing. With passion. This wasn't a perfunctory task to be performed because the app tells us it's the right time. We have already made a baby. This is because as he runs featherlight touches over my body, tracing the outline of my bra, I feel I might die if he doesn't touch me properly. I feel the way I used to feel for him.

"Adam"—our faces are inches apart—"I want you. I want you to—"

But I don't finish my sentence because suddenly there's a searing pain in my head and Adam is slipping away.

Everything goes black.

CHAPTER FORTY-EIGHT

Oliver

"What went wrong?" Eva asks. She studies Oliver intently. She's sitting close to him. Oliver shifts away uncomfortably.

"I'm not sure." Oliver runs his fingers over his beard. "A blip in the power supply perhaps. We're checking everything over. Is Anna okay?"

"She's upset at being snatched away from Adam without warning and I don't like the sound of her headache, and that nosebleed was nasty."

"I don't know if the magnets and the processors are too strong in the scanner or if the addition of senses recognition to the VR goggles is just too much. She was checked over by Sofia though. She's exhausted but fine physically. I mean is she okay...emotionally."

"She was...excited."

"Excited?" Oliver thinks it's an odd choice of word.

"Excited that she was able to put into place some of the communication strategies we'd discussed."

"So that's a good thing?"

"It's...odd."

"How so?"

"This is Adam's consciousness. Adam's dream as it were. How can it be that he's thinking of the exact same thing I'd just discussed with her that morning?"

"The way they connect must give her a degree of influence and their bond means she is more of a participant than, say, I would be."

"Are you positive that's what's happening? That this is Adam's consciousness, not Anna's imagination?"

"No, but then that's the point of a clinical trial. To establish patterns. Facts."

"If it's Adam's thoughts, how did Anna start off alone in the bath, without him there?"

"We all have thoughts and dreams featuring other people and we're not always present. Anna often has a bath. Adam could easily recall that, re-create that. It was sweet the way she was talking to the baby."

"Yes, the baby. She's getting too attached. As we spoke, her hands were over her stomach as if she is really pregnant. She'll be devastated when her part in the trial is over. It will be like the trauma of miscarriage again."

Oliver is silent for a moment. "I don't think I understood the implications on an emotional level of allowing Anna to take part in the trial. It seems cruel now to have allowed her to connect to Adam, to be with him again on some level, and then send them both back to the UK without access to the equipment. I like her. I'm not as detached as I should be." He runs his hand over his beard. "Have I messed up? Caused her irreversible trauma?"

"I don't know. This isn't exactly a scenario we covered in my training but I'm not convinced your invention is doing what it should."

"What do you mean?"

"I think possibly Anna is imagining how she would like things to be. That she hasn't really connected to Adam at all. She wants a baby more than anything, and suddenly she's pregnant again."

"They both want a baby. Don't forget, Adam is unaware of the miscarriage; it's not too much of a reach to think that he—"

"So you believe it's working?"

"I believe that Anna believes it. I think so. I hope so."

"But you can't be sure?"

Oliver removes his glasses and rubs his eyes. "No, I can't be certain. I still can't get the computer to record for a start. It's one thing to capture still images from a person's mind but the computer can't cope with images that move at lightning speed the way the subconscious plays things out. I should have done the trial myself and then there'd be no question as to whether it was a success or not. But…" He sighed and slipped his glasses back on.

"Clem," Eva said softly.

"I remember what it's like. That waiting. Wondering. Anna reminds me a little of Clem. A little of myself. That makes it harder now."

"How so?"

"Anna thinks she's seen something amazing and I have to be the one to take that away from her." There's a burning behind his eyes. He has approached this so very wrongly. He looks to Eva for answers but she doesn't speak. "I think we need to stop. Figure out why the computer isn't recording. Sofia is actively seeking out another suitable candidate. There's a woman in St. Barnabas's Hospital we think is ideal. I'm going to talk to her next of kin. I'll be the one taking part in the trial with the next participant."

"What about Anna?"

"She's going to take it hard."

"Of course, but it isn't fair to let her carry on if it isn't working. It's a form of delusion almost." Eva taps her pen against her clipboard. "But then it doesn't seem fair to pull her out of it, if it is working."

"That leaves us in a quandary. There's no definitive way of knowing at this stage."

"Yes, there is. You'll have to do the trial, Oliver. With Adam."

Oliver pushes up his glasses. "Even though Anna is against it?"

"Especially because Anna is against it. Why doesn't she want you to try it, Oliver? On some level does she know it's all in her head?"

Oliver mulls this over. "You're right. I'm going to give it a go myself. Let's find out, one way or the other, whether it's working the way Anna says it is."

"And if it isn't?" Eva asks.

It pains Oliver to say it. "I'll have to send them both home."

CHAPTER FORTY-NINE

Anna

"No." I can't believe what I am hearing. "I told you that I don't want you connecting to Adam yet, Oliver. I won't give you my consent."

"Anna, after yesterday, I can't let you try this again."

"I'm fine. It was a shock coming back without hearing you count down but I'm okay. The headaches aren't getting any worse." They are but I'm not going to tell him.

"I don't believe you. You keep holding your head. Something is wrong."

"Other than my husband only having a 3 percent chance of survival?" I struggle to gain my composure. "Look. This means so much to me, Oliver. More than you know." Adam and I can have the relationship I always wanted, a three, not a two. Open and honest. Sharing our feelings. I won't back down. "You *owe* me. If I hadn't come here, you'd still be congratulating yourself for having designed something on paper that you had no idea would work in the real world."

"It's a bit more technical than that—"

"I don't *care* about the technicalities. The design process. All of your facts and figures. I *care* about my husband." I lower my voice. "I need to be with him."

"I...I'm not sure you are actually with him." Oliver pushes his glasses up once more. "What you're seeing, describing is..." He rubs at his beard while I wait, wishing he'd hurry up. Wanting to shake the words out of him. "It's possible that it's not...not Adam's consciousness but your own projections. The things—"

"Everything I have told you is true."

"But I haven't been able to see them for myself."

"I *know* that." He's not telling me anything new. "That's why I remember *everything* and tell you *everything*." My hands stray to my stomach. "I've held nothing back."

"Anna, the thing is, without being able to record where the images you describe are coming from, there's no guarantee they are from Adam. You share the same life, you want the same things." Oliver studies me while I process this. "The only way to tell if it's working is for somebody else—"

"Absolutely not." I shake my head furiously. "No one else is delving around inside my husband's mind. The things I'm seeing, feeling, they're Adam's thoughts. I know they are."

Oliver leans back. Nudges his glasses, which are slipping down his nose again. I want to rip them off his worried face and smash them. I take a breath. Force myself to calm down.

"It *is* working." I am fighting back tears. "I won't give you permission to connect to him yet."

"Anna..."

"If you want to carry on, you'll have to use me again." I know he doesn't want to give up. "It's not like you have anyone else if I take Adam away, is it?"

There's a pause. Another nervous rub of his beard. "I told you there would be numerous participants; we can't base our findings purely on Adam."

"But..." I feel sick with panic. "You don't have anyone else yet, do you?"

"Not yet, no. But you need to be aware it's something we're working toward. You being here, doing this, it isn't a long-term plan, Anna. You knew this."

"But..." I glance at Sofia; she can't meet my eye.

"I've always said that after we've collected the results that we need, I'd cover the costs of flying you home, pay for Adam to be assessed by a private doctor in the UK."

"Fine." Anger has dried my tears. "Do you want us to leave now or do you want to carry on and let me try one more time?" My heart thuds. I call his bluff.

It works.

Soon, my fingers are laced through Adam's. Oliver begins counting backward. I'm not as tense as the first couple of times, expecting again to effortlessly slip back into my life, into my home. I feel myself falling, falling and I wait.

Instead of the slight dizziness and disorientation I felt before as Oliver reaches the count of one, pain rips through me.

Pain like I've never experienced before.

CHAPTER FIFTY

Oliver

Oliver is disappointed in himself that his desire to carry on with the trial has overridden his resolve that he should be the one taking part this time. Despite his assurances that it was a power failure last time that had wrenched Anna back too early, what if it wasn't a one-off blip? Oliver isn't convinced this is safe. He is nervous about what experience she might have this time. He watches her carefully as he counts down. Sees the way her feet jerk as he reaches one. He hears her breath through his mic, it's fast.

Too fast.

CHAPTER FIFTY-ONE

Anna

The tidal wave of pain slams into me once more. I screw my eyes tightly closed while I grapple with my brain to lift my arm. Oliver needs to bring me back. Something is wrong.

Very wrong.

"We need to get you to hospital." Adam's voice reaches me. I try to tell him we're already in the hospital but the pain comes again, snatching my breath away. "Fuck." I can sense his panic. "The contractions are getting closer together. Let's go or you'll be giving birth in the car."

I open my eyes. I am sitting on the stairs at home. Adam swims in and out of focus but his presence calms me, my breathing leveling out.

"Are we...We're having a baby?" I ask.

"We sure are. Your maternity bag is in the car. Are you okay to walk?" He supports my weight.

"But...but I'm not ready." It wasn't supposed to be like this.

"You've had nine months to get ready. Little Gregg is coming, whether you like it or not."

"We're not naming our son after a bloody sausage roll." I grit my teeth, shuffling out of the front door.

"Better than after a boy wizard who had a pet owl." He smiles. Another contraction grips me and I want to wipe the smile off his stupid face. I want to cover his stupid face with kisses.

We're having a baby!

At the hospital we're settled in our room and introduced to Helen, our midwife. She reads my birth plan, smiles and tells me to just ask if I change my mind about drugs.

"I'll come and check on you in a bit," she says.

"Wait. What? You can't *leave* me." Panic is thick and heavy in the room—mine, Adam's.

"You've got a while yet, don't worry. Press the buzzer if you need anything." And then she is gone.

"We'll be okay," Adam says uncertainly. "I've got something for you."

He rummages through his rucksack and brings out a Tupperware of sandwiches and cartons of my favorite pineapple juice. He roots around again and I hope he doesn't pull out a camera, but when he turns back to me, he has a purple velvet pouch in his hand. Inside, a silver pram charm dangles from a delicate chain.

"The charm was handmade by the little shop by the cove in Alircia. I bought it the morning after you told me you were pregnant."

The day of the yacht accident. I'm too overcome to speak.

Worried, he carries on talking. "I had seen the charms when I bought the love lock. When you told me we were having a baby, I knew I had to go back and get a baby-themed one. Give it to you when little one decided to make an appearance. Do you like it?"

I nod, the lump in my throat still keeping my words contained, but I like it. I like it very much.

The night seems endless. Oliver's words sometimes drift into my mind that the subconscious can stretch time. That thirty minutes can feel like an eternity but still, I am exhausted, wracked with pain. My head is swimming from the gas and air I have been sucking on. I'd refused all other drugs, knowing they can slow down the process and I'm longing for the labor to be over. The fear that Oliver might bring me back before I have met my child leads me to grip Adam's fingers tightly, grit my teeth and push.

"Not yet," Adam says. "The midwife says..."

"I don't fucking care what Helen says." I cannot stand this pain a second longer. "And you can fuck off too." I shake my hand free of his, and when he tries to take my hand once more, I slap him away, before grabbing his wrist. "I'm sorry. I'm sorry. Please don't leave me."

"I can hardly drive home." He cradles his hand. "I think you've broken my—"

"Are you kidding me?"

He gingerly flexes his fingers. "It really hurts, Anna."

"Adam!" Our eyes meet and simultaneously there is a lull in the pain and I find myself laughing. I take another suck from the gas and air, this time for kicks.

"Can I have some of that?" he asks. I pass the tube over to him. He takes a deep breath in and a smile stretches across his face.

"Wow. That's some good shit right there. Are you sure you're not dragging this out so you—"

"I'll get someone to drag you out in a minute." I take back the mouthpiece and draw another lungful. "Josh would love this."

"Don't tell him. He'll be getting some poor woman knocked up just for the legal high."

"Do you think he still carries a torch for Nell?"

"Yeah." Adam mops my forehead with a damp towel. "You know, when he first met you, I think he thought he was in with a chance."

"Really?"

"Don't you remember the way he kissed your hand when you were introduced? *A beautiful name for a beautiful woman.* Smarmy git."

"Well, if that was his best move..." I wince. Wait for the contraction to pass before I pick another ice chip from the polystyrene cup on my bedside table. Place it on my tongue.

"Oh, I warned him off making any moves."

"You did, did you?"

"I loved you the instant I saw you, Star. Hey, that's a good name for a girl!"

"We're not calling any potential daughter a name you've called me during sex!"

"Good point. Josh thinks if it's a boy we should name him Joshua."

"God no."

"I've told him he should think himself lucky we're trusting him to be godfather."

"We are?"

"You haven't changed your mind? He's said yes."

"As long as he doesn't get drunk at the christening."

"I've told him it's not like a wedding where you get dibs on the chief bridesmaid if you're the best man. He doesn't get to shag Nell because she's the godmother."

"He didn't get to shag Nell when she was chief bridesmaid!"

"No, but they had their first snog—"

"Their only snog. Fuck." Another contraction hits. The pain is getting worse.

"Breathe through it." Adam takes slow, comical breaths but at a loss for anything else to try, I match my breathing pattern with his. The pain begins to ease.

The door swings open and Helen bustles back into the room. "Let's have a little look at you." She snaps on gloves and I let my knees flop apart; I lost my dignity hours ago.

"You're almost ready." She pats my thigh. "I'll be back in another ten minutes or so."

"Shit. Ten minutes." The harried expression on Adam's face makes me forget my own discomfort.

"You'll be an amazing dad, Adam."

"I don't know…"

"I do," I say firmly. "You are brave and selfless and—"

"I can be a selfish git—"

"Shut up." I sit up and reach forward, holding his face between my palms. "When it comes down to it, you always put others before you, even…" My voice cracks. "Even if sometimes I wish you didn't, you're my absolute hero. I'm so proud of you."

"Anna." His finger lightly runs across my wedding ring. "My wife. I love you so much."

"I love you too and I'm sorry we had a rough—"

"It's not important. The here and now. It's all we have."

I nod, too overcome to reply. If only he knew how true that was.

"Right." Helen bustles back into the room. "Are you ready?"

"Wait!" Adam rummages around in his rucksack and pulls out

a CD. "On the tour of the maternity unit we were told we could bring music?"

"Yep. You could have had it on earlier."

"No. This is just for now." Adam smiles as Helen slips the disk into the player. I'm half expecting a mix of Eighties music, a selection of the terrible songs that played in the bar in Alircia the night that we met. Madonna singing "True Blue" as Nell handed me a bright pink cocktail decorated with umbrellas and pineapple. Instead, Elvis croons "Love Me Tender," our wedding song.

"Oh, I love this!" Helen says.

"You might not if Anna doesn't push this baby out pretty damn quickly. The track's on repeat for ninety minutes."

"That wife of yours might be tempted to throw the CD player at your head. Right." Helen has a quick check. "Ready? You will shortly become parents."

My body is splitting in two. I huff and puff. Panting when Helen instructs me to, Adam panting beside me. Pushing when she says it's time, squeezing both of Adam's hands in mine. This time he doesn't complain. "Love Me Tender" is still playing, so it has not yet been ninety minutes. It feels like ninety hours. Helen and I definitely have different definitions of how long the time span "shortly" should cover.

I'm tired now. Sweat slicks my skin, the sheet under me drenched. Sporadically, Adam smooths my tangled hair away from my face. Runs a damp flannel over my lips. The ice chips have long since melted.

"I. Am. Never. Having. Another. Baby." I don't even have the energy left to cry. "I can't do this. I can't." My hands cling to Adam's T-shirt. I give him a feeble shake. "Make it stop now."

"Anna—"

"I've changed my mind!" I am shouting now. Trying to swing my legs down. Wanting to walk away from it all. "I can't do it." My chest is heaving with dry sobs. I feel a complete and utter failure.

It's too hard.

Too painful.

Too everything.

"One last push, Anna," Helen shouts.

"You hear that, Anna? One more and it will all be over. We'll meet—"

"If you say Gregg, I'll fucking kill you."

"Get ready," Helen barks. "Deep breath and…push!"

I screw my eyes, grit my teeth, use the last ounce of my strength to push. Just when I feel my head will explode with the exertion, there's a give.

"Take a break, head's out."

"Did you hear that, Anna?" Adam's excitement is palpable. "It has a head! Can you tell if it's a boy or girl yet, Helen?"

"If I could tell that from the head, you'd make medical history," she says. "Ready, Anna, you're doing really well. Deep breath and…push."

I clench my hands into fists, the room swimming from lack of air until Helen tells me to take a break again.

"One more push should do it," she says.

I prepare myself and when she tells me to push, I do until she tells me to stop.

"Good girl. It's all over. You've done brilliantly. Two seconds and…"

A sharp cry fills the air.

A baby.

My baby.

"Well done, Anna. You were amazing." Adam presses his lips hard against mine. He's crying. I'm crying. His face is shining with joy. His eyes bright. Again, he is the boy I first met. The boy from the bar. The intervening years where we bickered and took each other for granted melt away. I am twenty-four once more. Falling deeply into a love that is absolute.

"I love you," I sob.

"I love you too." He wipes my eyes, his eyes. "I was doubting it would ever happen." He slapped both hands on top of his head. "I'm a dad!"

And I am a mother. So many emotions battle for prominence inside of me and while I am trying to unpick them, Oliver's voice penetrates my blur of exhaustion and exhilaration and pain—he's begun to count down.

Ten

No!

Nine

"Quick." I beckon for Helen to bring my baby over.

Eight

Hurry!

Seven

I have to see my child.

Six

Hold them.

Five

"Is it a boy or a girl?"

Four

"Congratulations, Anna." Helen takes a pause.

Three

"You have a perfectly healthy…"
Two
"…baby—"
One
I am back.

CHAPTER FIFTY-TWO

Oliver

"No!" Anna shouts as Sofia tries to help her off the patient table. She wrestles to snatch the goggles back, her nose streaming with blood. "I have to know. Send me back. Send me back right now!"

"Anna." Oliver hurries forward. Sofia steps back, rubbing her wrist while Anna glares at Oliver with pure hatred.

"I understand that—" he begins.

"You don't understand *anything*. I was just about to find out. One more second. Why couldn't you have waited? One. More. Second."

Oliver passes her a tissue. She presses it against her nostrils. Instantly, it turns crimson.

"Anna, let's go and talk."

She shakes her head and winces at the movement.

"Please come with me." He offers his hand to help her down. She brushes it away and Oliver is ashamed as he watches her struggle from the table, her face pinched with pain. He had lost sight of the unquestionable truth that love is something science can't predict. Can't control. How could he have been so stupid as to think this would be a nice experience for Anna, visiting Adam the way you would visit a friend? Happy to see them, okay to leave them. He thinks he has, perhaps, made a dreadful mistake.

"Let's get some air," he tells her.

They sit on a bench outside the Institute, facing the sea, watching the gulls soar and swoop. Listening to their call.

"Seagulls mate for life," Oliver says. "They return to the same nesting space year after year. Every species wants to make a connection. To find their home."

"Adam's my home." Anna raises a bottle of water to her lips and drinks.

"I'm so sorry," Oliver says, taking her hand. She holds it. For a time they both stare into the distance. Oliver knows that Anna isn't taking in the towering cliffs, the sunflower sun hanging high in the sky—all there is for her is Adam. He clears his throat. "There's a percentage of the population who oppose scientific development, whether for religious or moral reasons. Those who believe that humans shouldn't interfere with the natural order of things. It has always seemed so black and white to me. If there's a disease we can find a cure for, why not create the necessary treatment? If a person needs blood, where's the harm in transfusing someone else's blood? I think…I think what's right and wrong is subjective. I believed it was a good thing, creating the means so that those who couldn't communicate, whether it be because of locked-in syndrome or a coma or something else entirely, would be able to share their thoughts and feelings. Express what they need. To take comfort in, to bring reassurance to their loved ones that they still…exist. It can be the cruelest thing when the body of someone you love is in front of you but their mind…their mind…"

"Do you wish you hadn't developed the technology?" Anna still can't look at him.

"I don't know." Oliver doesn't know how he feels. What he should have done. What he should do now, moving forward.

"Today…" Anna slowly exhales. "Today, I had a baby." She turns to Oliver with tears in her eyes. "I might never fall pregnant again. I might never again experience how it feels to give birth. I might never feel that immense…intense love that was instant the second my child came into the world. I felt that today because of you. Thanks to you."

"No wonder you were so distressed when I brought you back."

"The midwife was just about to tell me whether it was a girl or a boy. Oliver, will I ever find out?"

"I just don't know."

He expects her to push for a proper answer but instead she says, "I'm going to see Adam."

Oliver watches her leave. There's a stoop to her posture. A weariness. He stays on the bench. After a while Eva joins him.

"In twenty-five years as a clinical psychologist I've assessed, diagnosed and treated so many emotional, behavioral and mental disorders. I've enabled patients to deal with chronic conditions. To cope under extreme pressure. This…this is something else entirely. I don't feel equipped for it, Oliver."

"Me neither." It is the sad truth.

"I'm afraid Anna will break if we carry on. I'm afraid Anna will break if we stop."

"Me too." What are they going to do? "She gave birth to a baby today—"

"She *thinks* she gave birth to a baby. Oliver, I can't be involved with this anymore. I'm sorry."

They were all sorry.

"Could you possibly do one last thing for me?" he asks. "Could you take Anna for her post-trial evaluation and keep her with you for an hour? I'm going to try the equipment for myself."

"Has she given her permission?"

"No."

"Is that ethical?"

"Is any of this? At least… at least we would know one way or the other if any of this has been real."

Eva stands. "An hour. No more."

Sofia expresses her disapproval. "This isn't right without Anna's consent."

"I'm not proud of what I'm about to do." Oliver isn't proud of any of it. His life's work. His biggest dream. Every time he measures his previous expectations with the reality, it leaves a sour coating in his mouth. He hasn't changed the world, and he knows if he doesn't let Anna connect to Adam again he will have made her world unbearable. Science should enhance, progress, improve. He forgot it also had the power to destroy. He has to know if the equipment works. If he can utilize it in a different way. Without hurting people. Without hurting Anna.

He slips on the goggles. The headphones. It's warm inside of the scanner. Claustrophobic. He waits, forcing his breathing to slow as he listens to Sofia count.

Ten

Please work.

Nine

His life's dream.

Eight

I'm sorry, Anna.

Seven

This is for Clem.
Six
For Adam.
Five
For everyone who has ever sat with an unresponsive patient.
Four
For anyone who has ever wondered if there is anything else.
Three
Clem.
Two
Clem.
One
Nothing.

There's nothing.
  Fifteen minutes, nothing.
  Thirty minutes, nothing.
  It doesn't work.

CHAPTER FIFTY-THREE

Anna

Eva was different during our session today. Uncomfortable. She frequently looked at the floor to avoid making eye contact.

Oliver is much the same as he leans against the wall in front of Adam's room, studying his shoes as though they're some sort of miraculous scientific discovery.

"I need to go and rest," I say. Something is clearly wrong but I can't face another conversation about the trial right now.

Oliver has other ideas. "I'm so sorry, Anna. I've decided to put an end to the trial. To go back to development stage."

"But outside...we sat on the bench...I told you about the baby. I need to know the sex of my child. I thought you understood."

"There is no baby," Oliver says sadly.

"There is. There..." He can't look at me. Something has happened. "What makes you so sure there isn't a baby? Before you didn't know whether the equipment was working or not."

"I...I've concluded—"

Immediately I know. "Oh my God." I step backward. "You tried it. You tried it when I was with Eva." He doesn't have to answer. The expression on his face tells me I am right. "How *could* you, Oliver? I *trusted* you. I thought that we were friends."

"We are friends. It's because I care about—"

"You don't care about me." The thought I might never hear Adam talk again, hear his laugh, feel his hands on my skin is torturous. "You don't care about anything except yourself and your dead wife. What would Clem think of you now, Oliver? Going behind my back. Lying to me." I squeeze my hands into fists. "I don't care what your experience was in the scanner. It works for me. Don't stop it."

"I have to. It's my final decision and the right one, despite how it seems. That's what testing is for. We try and try again until we get it right."

"And how long will that take? Until you're convinced you've *got it right*? In time for me? Adam?"

Oliver opens his mouth and closes it again without speaking.

"I thought not."

"I'm so sorry, Anna."

"Fuck you." I push past him and run into my bedroom, throw myself onto my bed and cry as though my heart is breaking.

As though my heart is breaking again.

I've been holding Adam's hand for hours; my fingers tingle with pins and needles but I don't let go of him for a second. I'm in despair that Oliver has given up on us. It's only a matter of time before he sends us home. A few days ago I'd been searching for a way to fly us back to the UK but now the thought of being in a crowded NHS hospital, with overworked nurses who have the best intentions but not enough time for their patients, is horribly depressing. I know Oliver will initially send us to a private hospital but he can't fund that forever, can he?

Two years. Twelve years. Twenty years.

Here, with this large private room, with Luis and the team, Adam is in the best hands. Will he even survive a flight?

I have never felt more alone.

Oliver cracks open the door.

"Anna, do you want to talk?" he asks, but I don't reply. Anything I say would come out in a rush of anger or a rush of tears and neither would be helpful. When he said his decision was final, I knew that he meant it. There is nothing to say that we haven't already said. If I'd thought things looked bleak before, now they are desolate.

"Anna?" Oliver says again, but I do not answer because he has taken all the words. He has taken all of my hope.

"Night then." He slips away. Luis is dozing on a chair in the corner and I am alone once more with too much time and too many thoughts.

It is quiet. At home Adam would always be streaming Spotify. Oasis would be "Supersonic," the Arctic Monkeys asking "Do I Wanna Know."

Oliver has connected to Adam and seen nothing. Has all of this been only in my mind? My desire manifesting a happy marriage, a baby. Conversations flowing with kindness and respect. The trial had made me fall in love with my husband all over again but have I fallen in love with him or an ideal my mind has created? The version of a life I so desperately wanted. I close my eyes and try to recall the details of giving birth, but it doesn't seem real.

What if it wasn't?

But I can hear the cry of my child that I never got to hold. Never got to find out if it was a boy or a girl.

Now Oliver has said we can't try again, I will never know.

The room, which had fallen into shadows, slips into darkness. The only glow a soft yellow lamp angled toward Adam's bed. Luis sneezes.

"Excuse me."

"Are you okay?" I whisper. He's been quiet today.

"Coming down with a cold, I think."

"Should you be near Adam?" I'm alarmed.

"I think I'll find someone to cover me. Get some rest."

"It's late," I say. "Go and have a lie down in your room. I'm not going to sleep."

"Adam can't be alone."

"He won't be. I'm here. The alarm will sound if there's a problem and I'll call you if I'm worried, I promise."

It's a minute before he answers. "Okay. I'm going to crash for a couple of hours. I'll set my alarm but come and get me if you need me in the meantime."

He slips out of the room. My mind races.

Thirty minutes.

That's all I am allowed to be connected to Adam for. After that time my nose streams with blood and my head throbs. What would happen if we stayed connected for an hour? Two? Three? Adam's condition is spider-web fragile, his mind and his body, but what about mine? Would my brain cope with prolonged exposure to the tech? Or would there be no recovery for me?

Behind my eyes are spikes of tiredness but I can't stop wondering.

What if.

What if.

What if.

Everything I need is in the next room. Oliver has demonstrated how to set it up. How it works. How to set the timer. Somewhere in the muddle of my mind, one thought burns brighter than the rest.

I could connect to Adam again. Here. Now. Before Luis comes back and Oliver comes to send me home.

Thirty minutes.

Or the rest of the night.

The rest of my life.

If it is too much and my mind can't cope, perhaps there is a chance I would stay with Adam. That our consciousness can be together, even if our physical bodies can't.

I know there's a chance that this might be dangerous. That mentally I might never come back from this. But somewhere, Adam waits for me. My baby waits for me. I imagine dressing their tiny body in the lemon sleepsuit covered in bears, still wrapped in tissue paper as fragile as my heart. I can do this, I can. I am steadfast in the belief that there is something beyond the realms of our imagination. Something extraordinary and incomprehensible to us as we live out our too-short lives on this planet we call home. I know there is something; I've been there and there has to be a way I can stay there for good. Here, there is nothing for me because a world without Adam doesn't make sense to me. My need to be with my husband. My child. It overrides everything else. So what if I die trying? What I'm doing now, the way I'm feeling, is hardly living.

I'm going to find a way to reach Adam without Oliver.

I'm going to find a way to stay with him.

CHAPTER FIFTY-FOUR

Anna

I had waited for twenty minutes before creeping into Luis's room. He'd been flat out on his back, snoring. I switched off the alarm he had set. Hopefully his fever would keep him asleep for hours. It had been a struggle to slide Adam from his bed onto a trolley and from the trolley onto the table but love, the thought of being with Adam once more, had given me strength.

I hold Adam's hand. Praying I have fixed everything up properly.

I must have done, because suddenly I am falling. Dizzy. Disorientated.

Scared and confused, until…

A baby cries.

It has worked.

"Your turn," Adam mumbles, nudging me in the ribs with his elbow. I sit up, ecstatic. Eager to take this turn, every turn. My heart bursting with happiness.

It has worked.

By the dim nightlight plugged in under the window, I see the outline of a Moses basket. Inside it, a small face screwed up with rage, damp curls plastered to a forehead, tiny hands fisted, is a baby.

My baby.

The room starts to spin and at first I am terrified I'm going to find myself back in the Institute. I steady myself, one hand resting on the wall, realizing I'm not going anywhere. I am, however, completely swamped with a rush of new emotions.

"Hello, you," I whisper. I don't yet know whether I'm mum to a boy or a girl, but a pure, unfiltered love sweeps through me, snatching my breath. A balance of tenderness and strength. A sudden knowing that I would lay down my life to protect theirs. It's incredible that I feel all of this and more within seconds of becoming a mum.

A mum!

Then, another sound. The bark of a dog. My eyes are drawn to another wicker basket, this time by the door. A golden puppy clambers out with huge floppy ears and a wagging tail.

I scoop my child into my chest as Adam says, "Shush, Dug. It's just Harry, hungry again."

Harry!

Adam clicks on the lamp. His eyes are shadowed with black circles. He yawns as Dug dances around the bed, looking longingly at the door. "Want to go out, do you, boy? We might as well have a cuppa, now we're *all* up?"

"Well, you thought it was a good idea getting a dog." I try to keep my tone light but I can hear the wobble in my voice. It's a lot to take in.

"Yeah, well, we could hardly give him back when he was a baby gift from Josh. Anyway, you know all the books said as long as baby is here first, Dug will know he's not in charge." Adam sighs as the puppy happily chews Adam's slipper. "Who am I kidding? He's *totally* in charge."

"I can go downstairs, so you can sleep?" I offer, jigging up and down while Harry continues to cry.

"Sleep? What's that? Nah, it's okay. While I'm still on paternity leave, I can catch up in the day tomorrow. I'll go and make myself useful with the kettle. I can't feed the baby, can I?"

Adam pads downstairs, Dug at his heels. Carefully I climb back into bed, holding Harry as though he is the most precious thing in the world.

And he is.

Nervously, I undo the buttons on my pajama top, feeling I haven't done this before, but of course some version of me must have because there's no way a baby could cry as loudly as Harry without being healthy and well fed.

"Here you go, little one." I draw Harry hesitantly to my breast but that's all I need to do because he latches on all by himself. I rest back on my pillows and gaze in wonder at the rapid sucking movement of his cheeks.

Harry.

He's named after my grandad and for the first time I have a prickle of doubt. Would Adam have picked that name?

"Too wizardy." He really wasn't keen. Is this my dream?

But I don't think it is. Harry is dressed in a white sleepsuit with "Future England Player" printed on it in red. Probably another gift from Josh. In my ideal world, my baby wouldn't be wearing this. There wouldn't be a puppy in the same room as my newborn, in the same house even.

I'm still feeling an odd sense of vertigo. Exhausted in a way I haven't felt before but I don't close my eyes for a second. I can't stop looking at Harry. Counting his tiny fingers. Marveling at his paper-thin nails. His eyes roll and his mouth slackens, milk dribbling down his chin. I shift my weight slightly and he is wide awake again, feeding once more, until his eyelids begin to flutter again. He is dozing by the time Adam returns with our drinks. Soon he is fast asleep. I fumble with my pajama buttons with one hand and the movement wakes him. His eyes lock onto mine but he doesn't cry.

"Hey, little man. I've waited such a long time to meet you," I say, softly running my index finger across his tiny fist. He wraps his finger around mine and holds it firmly. He is surprisingly strong. I know if Adam were to turn the lights off, I would be glowing with happiness. Harry tightens his grip as though he's telling me he loves me. His mouth flickers into a smile before it becomes a grimace, his face turns beetroot. There's the sound of him emptying his bowels and the smell . . . Let's just say he takes after Adam.

"Nice one, son. Pass him here and I'll change his nappy." Adam holds out his arms.

"I want to do it." I want to do it all.

Adam passes me a packet of wipes and I ease Harry's legs out of his sleepsuit. The second I remove the nappy, an arc of urine sprays me.

"Still glad you volunteered?" Adam says. But I am.

"You change the sheets and I'll give us both a quick bath. We're soaked."

In the bathroom I run warm water into the tub and squirt in Johnson's Baby Bath. I ease Harry's arms out of his sleepsuit. Wide awake now, he watches me with deep blue eyes, Adam's eyes. I lay him on the bathmat, where he kicks his arms and legs and makes raspberry sounds while I strip off my own pajamas. My body has changed and not for the better; purple veins criss-cross over my breasts. Red stretch marks streak my stomach. But I don't care. I've grown a human. Right now, I feel like the cleverest person in the world.

"Let's get you clean." Harry doesn't protest as I slide him into the water with me. It's when I'm sponging his arms that I see it. The birthmark shaped like a map, almost an exact match of Adam's. I trace it with my finger.

"He's destined to travel." Adam leans against the door frame.

"Maybe." I grin. "But doesn't it feel good to be at home?"

I wake.

My eyes snap open. I'm terrified I am back in the Institute in Alircia, but I'm still in my bedroom. Adam snoring next to me. Harry cooing in his Moses basket, awake but content. A whole night. Perhaps this is it. Perhaps I am staying here for good. The thought warms me. I pad across our landing past the bookcase, which has now been built and is filled with paperbacks. A photo of Adam and me framed in silver on the top shelf. Smiling, I head downstairs and lift a frying pan from the cupboard. Bacon and eggs. On the fridge is a to-do list, the first few items crossed off, including the leaky tap. When breakfast is nearly ready, I gently shake Adam awake.

"What have I done to deserve this?" he asks as I set a full English in front of him. "You've just had a baby. I'm supposed to be looking after you."

"We can look after each other. We're a team." Finally, we feel like it.

We eat in bed, our baby nestled between us. Afterward, I lie on my side and feed Harry.

"This...Harry," Adam says. "Us...It's just..." His eyes fill with tears.

"I know." I smile at my husband, knowing he is feeling exactly the same things that I am. Loved. Wanted. Happy. All of the things we had thought that we weren't.

After breakfast, we lounge on the sofa, watching *Up*. More than ever, I feel sorry for the old man and his wife who never got to have children. I can't believe how much my life has been enhanced and Harry has only been in it for a day.

Adam's hand dips into a box of sweets. "Toffee?" He noisily unwraps the foil. Instinctively I begin to say no, conscious of the waistband of my yoga pants digging into soft flesh. Knowing I'm the biggest I've ever been, but then I chide myself for being so ridiculous. Of all the things I've come to realize are important, worth worrying about, my weight is somewhere near the bottom of the list.

"Please." I open my mouth. Adam pops the toffee onto my tongue.

My eyes flicker constantly between the TV and Harry's sweet face. He is fast asleep on Adam's chest. After the film finishes we remain in the same position, reluctant to disturb him, until he begins to stir. While I feed him, Adam clears up the kitchen. When he steps back into the lounge he's carrying a dog lead.

"I'm going to take Dug out for a walk," Adam says. "Want to come and get some air?"

"It might be too cold for Harry?" I peer doubtfully out of the window. Clouds bunch in the sky but it isn't only the weather that's holding me back. Home is the only place I want to be. The only place I've ever been to in Adam's consciousness. What would happen if we stepped outside these four walls? I'm reluctant to risk it. Adam doesn't let it drop.

"We'll just go down to the park on the corner and back; Dug's puppy legs can't take too much exercise."

"I think we'll stay here." Amongst my own things, safe and familiar.

"Anna, you've got to go out sometime. I know it's daunting because Harry is constantly hungry and, to be blunt, he shits himself more times a day than Josh, but I'd feel better when I go back to work knowing you've ventured further than the kitchen. We've got to take him outside sometime. This is our life now."

Our life. It's our home. The same and yet somehow not. It's like the hopscotch Nell and I used to play as kids. Each time the rain would rub out our chalk marks, we'd scratch them onto the pavement again. At first glance they looked exactly the same but it's impossible to re-create exactly the same thing twice. There's always a subtle difference. It is all here. Our furniture. Our clothes. But there is something missing.

The underlying anger we'd been carrying.

The disappointment.

The way we usually skirted around each other.

It's gone. All of it.

I smile. "You're right. I'm just nervous."

"Don't be. I've got you."

It's ages before we're ready to leave. I've changed Harry's nappy and the second I get him dressed, he fills it again. He's now wrapped in so many layers he lays stiff in his pram, unable to kick his limbs.

"A snowsuit is a little extreme?" Adam says cautiously. "No, it's fine," he quickly says when I begin to lift Harry up. "Don't change him. Honestly, Anna, it's taken you an hour so far and we're only going to be out for ten minutes."

"I just want…" My voice thins. "I just want everything to be perfect."

"And it is." Adam wraps his arms around me, his chin resting on the top of my head. "Now, come on, we can be back by three."

"What's at three…Oh." Football, but oddly this doesn't irritate me. I might even watch the match myself.

Adam pushes the pram into the hall and opens the front door. "Right, let's do this. Little man, meet the world." Adam maneuvers the wheels down the step. "It might seem big and scary but it's pretty awesome. Like your dad actually."

I roll my eyes and step outside, and that's when it happens.

The world tilts and blurs and I can feel myself slipping away.

"Adam!" I cling on to the door frame and stretch out my arm. Adam rushes back down the path toward me. He takes my hand but I feel his fingers fading from my grasp.

I feel myself fading.

I feel nothing.

CHAPTER FIFTY-FIVE

Adam

Falling. Twisting. Weightlessness.
  Fighting to breathe.
  Fighting to move.
  Choking.
  Choking.
  Choking.

CHAPTER FIFTY-SIX

Oliver

The siren blares. Oliver half falls out of bed and grabs his glasses. Runs barefoot down the corridor wearing his pajamas.

Orange flashing lights blink on and off. On and off. The noise builds and builds as he approaches Adam's room.

"Quick." Sofia beckons him inside. He can't believe, after everything, they are losing Adam. Anna will be devastated. Oliver has come to deeply care about them both.

He rushes inside. Adam's bed is empty. Oliver is momentarily confused until he notices light shining through the open door to the scanner room. It's a sudden sickening realization.

No. Anna. No.

In there, Luis is hunched over the patient table.

Doing what he can.

No.

Oliver draws nearer and sickness thuds deep in his stomach as he realizes it isn't Adam at all who is in trouble.

It's Anna.

CHAPTER FIFTY-SEVEN

Adam

Drifting. Drifting.
Body heavy.
Can't think straight.
Noise. Whooshing? The waves?
Hissing. The sound of the sea?
Something else?
A siren.
A voice.
Somebody calling Anna's name.

CHAPTER FIFTY-EIGHT

Anna

"Anna." Hands shake my shoulders. "Anna." Fingertips press into my pulse point on my wrist. "Anna. Wake up." But I don't want to. Instead of Harry's crying and Dug's happy barking, there is the blare of the emergency siren.

I am in the last place I want to be.

Blood streams from my nose, down my throat. I choke but I don't care. Without Adam, Harry, I am nothing. I am rolled onto my side, something pressed under my nostrils.

"Anna." The voice won't stop talking. I prize open my eyes and the light feels like a laser slicing through my brain. "Thank goodness." Oliver's concerned face looms toward me. I close my eyes once more.

I don't want to see.

I don't want to speak.

I don't want to feel.

CHAPTER FIFTY-NINE

Oliver

Oliver sits by Adam's bed. Partly because he had promised Anna that he wouldn't leave Adam while she slept, but mostly because he still wants to be close to her in case she needs him.

When he'd found her earlier, pale and still, blood pouring from her nose, guilt and panic had thrust through Oliver's veins. He had thought for a second they'd lost her and he'd felt genuine sorrow for her. Then the feeling of relief that she'd been okay. The relief that he wouldn't be held culpable for leaving the scanner room unlocked, the equipment unsecured, only came later and he hated himself for it.

He wasn't the most important one here.

"It was never supposed to be like this," Oliver tells Adam. He has spent the last hour telling Adam all about the trial. It's a relief Adam can't respond. He knew how he would feel if somebody had put Clem in a similar situation.

"I wish you'd wake up, mate," he tells Adam before self-consciously pushing his glasses onto his nose. The word "mate" unfamiliar on his tongue, but Oliver doesn't feel comfortable around men; he doesn't feel comfortable around people. "If you'd wake up there's a chance you could make it all real. Give Anna a baby. She's become so attached to Harry, it's blurred the lines between what's real and what's not. She won't accept that her mind has fabricated him." Oliver sighs. "Survivor's guilt is so common. She's okay and she's taking the guilt she feels and channeling it into this fake life she's created where you're all so happy."

Oliver studies Adam. It's hard to imagine him talking. Laughing.

"I wish... I wish it had been real. I wish I could have met you properly. I think I'd have liked you. I'm not sure what you'd have made of me. Anna thinks you'd be horrified I haven't seen *Footloose*. There's the thing. You have likes and dislikes. Hobbies. Passions. You love. You feel. I put it all second, all of those things that make us human. I made the science more important than the emotion. I'm sorry for what I've put Anna through. What I've yet to put her through."

When Anna wakes up, Oliver needs to tell her some more bad news.

CHAPTER SIXTY

Adam

Words. Sentences. Snatches of a one-sided conversation that makes no sense.

Harry isn't real?

Anna has survivor's guilt.

If Anna's the survivor, what does that make me?

I try to move, but I can't.

CHAPTER SIXTY-ONE

Oliver

"I've booked you flights back to the UK for the morning. A private ambulance will meet you at the airport to transport you both to St. Agnes. It's a private hospital."

"Oliver…" Anna begins to cry. Oliver feels his heart shatter.

"I'm so sorry."

"Is there anything I can say to make you change your mind?" Anna wipes her eyes with her sleeve.

"You could stay but the trial is over. Don't you think you'd be better off at home, with your family and friends?"

"I thought you were my friend," Anna says in a small voice.

"I'd like us to stay in touch. I've grown very fond of you, Anna. Of you both. Do you hate me?"

Anna considers the question. "No, I don't. You've shown me something wonderful. Something amazing. I wish it could carry on but…no, I don't regret coming here. That chance to spend some more time with Adam, to see the life we almost had, I feel… I feel incredibly sad that it's over, of course."

"Nothing lasts forever, unfortunately."

"Love does." There's a confidence to her words. "I had thought

315

a few weeks ago that I didn't love Adam anymore, that our struggle through infertility was too long, too hard for us to recover from, despite my pregnancy. The resentment too deep. If you hadn't given me the opportunity to speak to him again, perhaps I'd always have felt that way. Now I know. Nothing is insurmountable if you want it badly enough. Adam is my…"

"Seagull?" Oliver suggests.

"Not quite as romantic as I hoped, but yes. My seagull. My mate for life. My everything."

"If there's ever anything you need. Anything. Just call. More than anything, I want you to be happy. I hope Adam recovers, Anna. I really do." Adam only has a 3 percent chance of recovery but Oliver is rooting for him. He's a scientist, but he still believes in miracles.

Oliver opens his arms and Anna steps into them. This is goodbye.

CHAPTER SIXTY-TWO

Anna

"We're going home tomorrow," I tell Adam.

I'm trying to stay positive. Oliver's right. I've a support network waiting for me at home: Nan, Mum, Nell, Josh. Together, we'll all keep the faith that one day Adam might recover.

Two years.

Twelve years.

Twenty years.

Without the help of Oliver, I worry how long I'll be able to keep alive the vibrant Adam who lives clearly in my mind. But I vow I will. I can't ever let him become a memory, vague and fading.

"So…" Usually I fill the silence with chatter, recollections of times past or plans for the future but now I cannot think of a single thing to say. I feel lost. As though I've forgotten who I am and why I'm here. As though I have failed my husband, failed us both. The thought of our little family slipping away, of never holding Harry in my arms, is heartbreaking.

Outside it is gloomy. For the first time since we arrived on the island, the sun isn't beaming down. Clouds slip across the sky like ghosts.

Intermittently I doze.

Each time I wake, I remember we are leaving soon and I feel desolate once more. A ripple of a memory stirs, just outside my grasp. There's something important, something that will change everything. I try and force it to the forefront of my mind but my recollection is slow and muddied.

I lay my head on Adam's chest and whisper, *I need you*.

CHAPTER SIXTY-THREE

Adam

Anna's head is on my chest. It's impossible to gauge whether she has her eyes open or closed. I need to move. Speak. Do *something*.

Trying to raise my finger is like trying to lift a two-ton weight. Mentally draining and physically impossible. My eyelids are equally heavy and my frustration builds; even babies can blink.

Anna.

I am incredulous that she can't hear me calling her name. That she can't see the shape of it leave my lips.

CHAPTER SIXTY-FOUR

Anna

"Anna." Adam's voice is warm and soft.

"You're awake?" A sunburst of happiness. I touch his face. His lips. Feel his mouth crinkle into a smile.

"Yeah. Sorry. Have I been asleep long?"

"Too long."

"What have I missed?"

Everything.

Nothing.

Me.

"Happy anniversary, husband."

"Happy anniversary, wife."

I have to fetch Oliver. Ring the buzzer and summon Luis, but I can't let go of Adam. I won't let go of Adam.

He holds me close. "Anna." His voice a whisper in the breeze.

I jolt awake.

Neck stiff and eyes sticky with sleep. Drool crusted around my mouth. The disappointment that Adam hasn't really woken is crushing. I had spent last night pressed against him. My sleep light with fear, not allowing myself to fall too deeply in case I inadvertently dislodged a tube. A wire. I am heavy with sadness. That might be the last time I share a bed with my husband; it won't be possible in a regular-sized hospital bed—if Adam survives the journey home.

If.

I wish I could step inside his consciousness and tell him good-bye. I wish Oliver would change his mind. But he is adamant the trial hasn't worked.

As I think this, there's another sliver of something I can't quite put my finger on. I close my eyes and try to will the thought to form but it doesn't take shape.

Sofia taps on the door. "The car will be ready in two hours to take you to the airport."

I still need to pack but first I want to make the most of this quiet time. Adam and me in bed. The sound of the waves outside. The sun beating through the window.

"So before we go home I want to remind you of a few things."

I begin to tell him the story of us, just so he doesn't forget how much we love each other.

I will, never, ever forget that again.

I've covered our meeting, his proposal, am onto our wedding when I think his hand moves slightly under mine. I hold my breath. Wait.

But nothing happens.

It's wishful thinking, I know.

I carry on talking.

CHAPTER SIXTY-FIVE

Adam

Her fingers stroke mine, slowly. Rhythmically. Under hers I try to move my own but it's fruitless.

She's telling me about our wedding day. About Josh's speech.

"What can I say about Ad?" Josh had said as he shuffled awkwardly from foot to foot, pausing to down yet another glass of champagne. I was already cringing. Already second-guessing the content of the speech he hadn't let me read.

Adam's a twat for giving up his dreams and marrying so young.

He wet the bed until he was seven.

He didn't lose his virginity until he was eighteen.

He's been known to cry at Disney films.

So many things he could say about me, and I didn't want him to say any of them.

Instead he cleared his throat, studied his shoes, before raising his head and beginning to speak quietly.

"I'm amazed Adam asked me to be his best man. Those of you who know me will know that I can be a bit of a dick. I'm not good with words." He refilled his glass and took a sip. And when he spoke again it was louder. "The thing is, I've known Adam almost all of my life. I've listened to him bang on about all the places he wanted to go to, all the countries he wanted to visit. He used to have a cork board in his bedroom with cuttings from holiday brochures. I admit when he first told me he was giving it all up for Anna, I thought he was a bit of a—" I cleared my throat loudly. I had warned Josh to keep it clean because of Anna's nan. "A bit of an idiot." Josh swayed and for one horrifying second it looked like he was going to topple over but he caught his balance. I waited for the punchline with bated breath. "But he wasn't... an idiot. The truth is I've never seen Adam look at a map the way he looks at Anna." Laughter rippled around the room. "It might seem that we don't have much in common anymore. With him settling down and me still shagging everything that moves. Sorry... I mean... making love to. Is that better? Shit. Sorry, Anna's Nan."

"It's okay!" Anna's nan's voice had warbled toward the top table. "I have heard of sex, you know. Done it myself once or twice."

Josh had raised his glass while a mortified Anna covered her face with her hands. "But I'm still... exploring my options because I haven't met anyone who makes me feel the way Adam feels about Anna and after seeing the two of them together, I don't want to settle for anything less than what they have." He turned to me. Almost-empty glass raised. "Adam, I love you, mate. And even if we're heading in different directions, I'll always have your back."

"And I'll have yours." I stood quickly to give him a hug. His eyes were glistening too.

"To Adam and Anna. May you have a long and happy life." He had raised his glass. And I recall thinking then how happy I was. I recall thinking then that I had it all.

"Do you remember," Anna says now, "that Nell was so moved by his speech they had a snog."

I remember, I want to tell her. But I can't. The words are in my head but I can't speak. I can't move. I can't take my wife into my arms and tell her that I thought it was impossible to love her any more than I did on our wedding day and yet, somehow, I do.

I can't say any of it.

CHAPTER SIXTY-SIX

Anna

The suitcases are stacked by the door. I've double-checked our rooms to make sure nothing has been left. Grandad's coin is now back in my purse.

"Do you want me to come to the airport with you?" Oliver asks.

"No. I do want to say goodbye—"

"Of course, we'll—"

"Not to you." I look pointedly at Adam.

"Anna...I can't..."

"It's our wedding anniversary today. Wouldn't you want to see Clem on your anniversary?"

"That's not fair."

I know it isn't but I'm running out of options. "It will absolutely be the last time and then we'll get on the plane, I promise. It'll be my goodbye. Closure."

"But last time...You could have died, Anna. You weren't in a good state when you came back."

"Because I wasn't supervised. You'd be here. I need this."

Indecision slides across Oliver's face. I wait. I whisper.

"Please."

CHAPTER SIXTY-SEVEN

Adam

"Please." Anna trails off and I know she'll be staring into the distance, nipping her lower lip between her teeth in that way of hers when she's struggling to find the right words.

It's our anniversary and I can't move, I can't speak. I can't tell my wife that at the bottom of my suitcase under the clothes I'll never unpack is a wooden box—the traditional five-year gift. It's impossible for me to explain that inside are small rectangles of colored paper on which I've written the words that best describe her. I haven't got it right the last few anniversaries; I know somewhere along the line we stopped making an effort but I wanted to...I *want* to show her how much she means to me, still.

Always.

This year, I hoped I'd hit the nail on the head. Anna is way better at the gift stuff than me. On our first anniversary I arrived home with a bouquet of roses, a huge box of chocolates and a takeaway menu I had picked up from the new curry house on the corner. I had thought it was enough. I knew I could never match the star I had named after her for our first Valentine's but, looking back now, I hadn't really tried. The house was lit with flickering candles; it was like walking onto a film set. "Love Me Tender" was playing from the Bose. The smell of paella—always our "special occasion" meal—drifted out of the kitchen. Anna hesitantly came down the stairs, smoothing her black dress over her thighs, tucking behind her ear a tendril of hair that had escaped her complicated up-do. She looked beautiful.

She always looks beautiful.

"Happy first anniversary, husband." She kissed me softly, her lips sticky with gloss. "This is for you." She held out a small present and I took it, awkwardly pushing the flowers and chocolates into her arms. We moved onto the sofa, where she opened her card and exclaimed how gorgeous the flowers were while I tussled with the red ribbon wrapped around the turquoise gift box. Inside nestled a pair of cufflinks. I looked questioningly at her.

"The first anniversary is 'paper' so I bought you some paper airplane cufflinks so you never forget your dream to travel."

"Anna!" I felt overcome with emotion. A bit of a dick for not researching anniversary rules; I should have known there would be some. I lifted the cufflinks from the box.

"They're great."

"They're useless without this." She slid out another box from under the sofa and placed it on my knee. I tore off the wrapping paper. A shirt.

"Strictly speaking, that's cotton for next year but I know you don't have the right shirts for wearing cufflinks, so..."

I kissed her hard, wanting my mouth to convey what my gifts

hadn't. That every single one of the 365 days of our marriage I had felt like a lucky bastard.

Now she takes my hand. "Oliver, I absolutely have to be with Adam on our anniversary."

And despite everything, I still feel like a lucky bastard.

CHAPTER SIXTY-EIGHT

Anna

While I'm waiting for Oliver to decide whether he'll let me say goodbye to Adam, it hits me.

"It was real!" A whoosh of excitement rockets from the tips of my toes to my scalp. "It was real!" I am fizzing with relief that I have remembered the one thing that had been gnawing at me. The single thing that will convince Oliver I had been speaking the truth. "Oh my God!" I clutch his arm, I'm shaky but am grinning so wide I can feel the stretch of my cheeks. "It happened just as I said. All of it. I can prove it." I rush off to my room. Adam's case is ready to leave in the corner where I left it. I unzip it and begin to dump his clothes on the floor. At the bottom of the case is a box. "You Are..." is painted on the outside. I tip out the contents; red, yellow, orange pieces of paper float to the floor.

Gorgeous, says one.

Soul mate, another.

Kind.

Coming around to loving Eighties music.

A far better cook than me.

My best friend.

Emotions burn behind my eyes. This must be Adam's anniversary gift to me. But I can't allow myself to become distracted by the sentiment. It isn't what I'm looking for.

Think! Where would he hide something from me?

I stick my hand inside his left trainer, empty. His right. And there it is, shoved in the toe. Triumphantly I rush back to Oliver.

"Look!" I wave the purple velvet pouch in my hand.

"What's that?"

"That," I say as I tip out the delicate silver chain with the pram charm onto his hand, "is the bracelet Adam gave me after I'd given birth to Harry. Remember? I *told* you about it when you brought me back. You *wrote* it down. Adam had said that he had bought it the morning after I had told him I was pregnant. That was the morning of the yacht accident. He told me that he bought it with the intention of giving it to me the day I gave birth. He *did* save it until the day I gave birth."

Oliver turns the bracelet over in his hand but he doesn't speak.

"If I'm not really in Adam's consciousness, but fabricating the whole thing with my mind, how could I have known to include this bracelet in my imagination? I didn't know it really existed until today."

"It could be something you've brought here from the UK."

"It isn't. The charm is handmade by the little shop by the cove near our hotel. You can check."

"Adam could have given it to you before the yacht accident and you'd forgotten."

"He didn't."

"You could have seen it in his case after the accident."

"I haven't had reason to go in his case." Why can't he see it?

"It's *real*. Somewhere. Somehow, whether it's a world Adam has manifested through his consciousness I don't know, but there *is* another world with Adam in it. A place where I have visited. A place where he gave me this." I tap the charm on Oliver's palm.

"Anna, I understand that's what you want—"

"It's real."

"It isn't...it didn't work."

"It *is* real," I say again. "All of it. It's like we both exist in some alternative reality away from here. We're living a life. A good life. The life we almost had."

"Scientifically—"

"Fuck science! What about the bracelet? How do you explain that?"

"On some level—"

"On some level you think everything can be explained with science?" I am calmer now.

"I do."

"You don't, or you wouldn't be researching consciousness in the first place! You told me we don't know everything. That Dr. Acevedo was narrow-minded. Closed. If you didn't believe there were other levels, things outside of what we know, things that push the boundaries, defy the realms of our imagination, you wouldn't...you wouldn't be *scared* right now. Scared that Clem is living another life somewhere else entirely. A life that may or may not include you and the fact that...the fact that you can't connect to her is..." I am crying now. "You wouldn't just give her up, would you?"

"The bracelet doesn't definitively prove—"

"Look, it sounds crazy, but you sounded crazy when you came to me with your proposal. I gave you a chance."

Oliver meets my eyes. His are full of doubt but I know he'll say yes.

He might not believe I can really connect to Adam, but love— he has faith in love and that will be enough.

It has to be.

CHAPTER SIXTY-NINE

Adam

It is all moving too quickly. I can't process what is going on.

"But last time... You could have died, Anna. You weren't in a good state when you came back," the man had said. Oliver, Anna calls him. But some of the other voices who frequent my room have referred to him as Dr. Chapman. He had sat with me once, telling me about some trial, but I couldn't make sense of it at the time. I'm trying to make sense of it now. What's happened to Anna? Why does she want to put herself at risk again?

For me.

My heart begins to gallop. Even if I couldn't feel it gathering pace inside my chest, it registers on my monitor. I can sense Oliver crossing to my bed. Feel his fingers press against my pulse. I want to shake my hand free. I want him to tell Anna no. He can't risk anything happening to her. She's too precious.

The trial. I need to figure it out. My head hurts. I try to remember past conversations, pain drumming deep inside my skull. It was something about consciousness.

My consciousness.

Anna's and Oliver's voices crash around me like a choppy sea and I have experienced a rough angry sea recently, haven't I?

A yacht?

I desperately try to work out what is going on, to piece it all together. But it's when I remember something Oliver had said about a state-of-the-art fMRI scanner he'd invented, software, VR goggles, so Anna could experience what I have been thinking, that my blood runs cold.

Could he really connect our minds somehow? It sounds terrifying.

It sounds dangerous.

I have to stop this.

Stop her.

CHAPTER SEVENTY

Anna

Finding the bracelet had swept away any doubt I might have had that my experience with Adam wasn't real.

Oliver is doubting himself now too; I can see it in his face.

"You believe me," I say softly and then louder. "You. Believe. Me."

CHAPTER SEVENTY-ONE

Adam

"You believe me," Anna tells Oliver.

She's talking him round. She's persuasive, that wife of mine, I know that. If she wasn't, we wouldn't have a purple dining room. He doesn't really have a chance. But still, I'm willing him to stand firm. Not put her at risk.

I long to get up. To walk away from Dr. Fucking Frankenstein, but I can't. The proverbial lab rat.

"I know why you want to go back, Anna," Oliver says. "But I have explained to you when I connected to Adam in the scanner there was nothing to see. Harry...Harry isn't real."

At this, my heart splinters. "He's real," I want to shout. But suddenly I'm not sure. Have I imagined it all too?

I think back to the day he was born; Elvis crooning "Love Me Tender."

Isn't it real?

Isn't he real?

But he must be. My arms remember the weight of him, my nose the smell of him—talcum powder. His dark blue eyes trained on mine.

If Anna's seen him too, then the tech must work? It must let us be together, but at what cost?

"You nearly died," Oliver had said. If it takes living without me to keep Anna safe and alive, then that's what she must do.

They are standing either side of my bed. I feel like a bloody tennis net as objections are served and batted away. A game that nobody can win.

A scream builds inside of me but I can't let it out.

"I know that there comes a point where..." Oliver's voice catches. "Where we have to let the ones we love go."

Again, Anna grasps my hand with both of hers. She squeezes. I squeeze back but she can't feel it.

I'm back in Alircia when we first met. Watching Anna's anxious face as the bird is placed on my arm. Feeling my fingers fumble against the chain that tethers it. Watching the parrot soar into the brilliant, blue sky. But I'm not there.

I'm here.

I'm at home with Harry.

I don't know where I am.

I don't know who I am.

My head hurts. My body hurts. My heart hurts.

Anna sniffs. She doesn't let go of my hands to find a tissue. Her tears drip onto my forearm. I can't wipe them away.

"I won't give up. Adam wouldn't want me to give up either," she says.

But she's wrong.

Her sitting day after day in this room, living out a life, a fantasy almost, that can't be real, no matter how solid it feels, means she's missing out on the outside world because of me. Putting her health at risk.

You could have died, Anna.

This isn't what I want at all.

I summon up every ounce of energy in my body to tell her this, but my voice remains silent when I speak.

Anna, don't kill yourself over me. I'm not there, I'm here.

I'm everywhere.

I'm nowhere.

But no matter where my mind hops to, my heavy, unresponsive body remains in this bed.

A 3 percent chance of recovery, I had overheard.

If you love someone, set them free.

She needs to let me go.

I need to let her go.

I won't let her destroy herself, miss out on living her life to the fullest because of me. I love her too much for that.

"One last time," Oliver says. "Just to say goodbye."

He's caved. I knew he would but it doesn't matter. I know what I have to do.

CHAPTER SEVENTY-TWO

Oliver

Oliver knows Anna's right. He'd want the chance to say goodbye to Clem, it seems only fair. He's shaking as he watches Sofia help her with the goggles through the console room window.

One last time.

Thirty minutes.

He's here to monitor every second.

Nothing can go wrong.

Can it?

CHAPTER SEVENTY-THREE

Adam

My body is slid onto a cold hard surface. I want to shout no. To tell Oliver that he can't let Anna keep risking everything for me. I am not the same person. I no longer feel like me. I am not aware of my body. I cannot move, can't force my eyes open, but love? I still feel love.

If I were to stir, Anna, then what? You'd spend the rest of your life caring for me and I'd spend the rest of my life not being able to tell you how I feel. You've lost the husband you had. But Harry... the son that shouldn't exist and yet we have somehow brought into being, is a light shining in the darkness. Your guiding star, just as you are mine. It isn't fair for you to be wrenched away from him time and time again. It is too painful to bear and it will be your ruin.

What I'm about to do is for you. Please forgive me.

Brief snatches of the life we almost had is too cruel. If I could find a way to give you it all, I would, but I can't. But there's something I can do for you.

If you love someone, set them free.

Remember, Anna?

For one last time, I wish I could take your hand in mine. Look deeply into your eyes and tell you that whenever things seem impossible, they aren't.

There is always an ember of hope quietly smoldering if you know where to look.

There's always a miracle waiting to happen.

Love *will* find a way.

CHAPTER SEVENTY-FOUR

Anna

For the last time I allow my body to relax, my mind to fall. Adam's hand in mine.

Instead of being in the UK, I find myself back in our apartment in Alircia.

Alone.

"Adam?" I'm hesitant. Suddenly afraid but unsure why. "Adam?"

Why aren't we at home? Where is Harry?

Perhaps we are back on the island, celebrating an anniversary. Or Harry's birthday? Despite hoping I will find Adam and Harry napping on the bed, I still enter the bedroom with a sense of unease. The hairs at the back of my neck prickling.

Something isn't right.

The room is empty. White duvet pulled up over the pillows. I pull it back and touch the sheet with my hand. It's cold.

"Adam?" His suitcase is on the floor, lid open. His clothes strewn around it haphazardly. I open a drawer; my shorts and tops are neatly folded. There are no baby things. No travel cot. My chest tightens as panic courses through me.

Where is Harry?

The longing to see my son is painful. I try to slow my breathing. Regulate my pulse. I can't have Oliver bringing me back yet. The thought I might not get to say goodbye to my husband and child causes a crack to appear in my heart. Where are they?

The bathroom is empty but steam lingers from the shower. The scent of musky shower gel hanging in the air. He's been here then, and recently.

In the kitchen, a pen and pad rest on the worktop. An address scrawled on the top page. Upper Harringdon. It's a town about thirty miles away from our home in the UK. Adam is always chatting to the other hotel guests about football. Perhaps someone had given him their address to keep in touch, but that doesn't explain where he is right now.

Another sheet of paper catches my eye; it's stuck to the fridge with the "I love Alircia" magnet.

Anna, meet me at Pacifico Beach and remember I LOVE YOU xxxxx

My anxiety increases, remembering the disaster that struck last time we were at Pacifico Beach. How could he possibly think I'd want to go there? How could he want to go there? But then I remember in Adam's mind the accident never happened. He doesn't know. But still, my nerves are jangling. Why are we here? Has his mind forgotten Harry? I just can't figure out what's going on.

A fierce desire to find my husband, my son, propels me out of the door.

My arms feel empty, my heart full of dread. Shockwaves travel up my shins while my sandal-clad feet pound the pavement. By the time I get to the beach, my sundress is plastered to my back with sweat. When I see what's waiting for me, it's like running into a wall. Shock slamming the breath from my body.

It's exactly the same.

Pacifico is a riot of noise and color. Music and laughter. Red and green bunting hanging between wooden poles that have been pushed into the sand.

It's exactly the same.

A BBQ sizzles the scent of beef. On the makeshift bar rest goldfish-sized glasses filled with milky pina colada, garnished with chunks of pineapple, straws and pink paper umbrellas.

Boy George's voice drifts from the speaker. "Do you really want to hurt me?"

It's exactly the same.

"Ma'am?" asks a voice to my left. I turn to the man in the navy polo shirt with the red "WLY" logo, who offers me a leaflet. "Free trip? It's the launch of Webster's Luxury yachts. We're dropping people off at the island over there, and collecting them later. Trips are every forty-five minutes. You're too late for this one but—"

I glance at my watch. It's almost eleven. The yacht sank at eleven.

It's exactly the same.

"Adam!" I scream, running across the beach.

The yacht is leaving. Even before my eyes frantically seek out the *Maria* in black cursive script, I know that it is the same one.

I pelt into the frothy waves until they cover my thighs, my hips, my waist.

"Adam!" I shield my eyes against the sun and stare at the yacht. He's there, just as I knew he would be. Leaning against the railings, his eyes locked onto mine.

"Please"—I turn toward the beach—"the yacht is going to sink. Somebody make it come back. Please." But nobody hears me. "Listen!" I scream so loudly the skin of my throat throbs in protest. "Help!" A girl wearing a navy polo shirt with the "WLY" logo splashes toward me.

"Are you all right?"

"No." I cling to her. My knees threatening to give way. "The yacht is going to sink. My husband's going to die. You have to call it back."

"Ma'am, have you been drinking?"

I shake my head. Squeezing her arm with my fingers.

"Have you been out in the sun too—"

"No." I'm a mass of tears. I'm going to lose him. I'm going to lose him all over again. "Adam." Grief pushes me forward. The sea splashes salt into my open mouth. Wets my tear-damp cheeks. I'm yanked upright by the back of my T-shirt like a marionette.

"Ma'am?"

I shake her hands off me.

The yacht moves further away. My breath is coming in frightened gasps.

I can just make out Adam as he raises his arms to the sky. He links his thumbs together, forming wings with his hands. He mimes flying free.

"No!" I collapse. Feel arms around my waist pulling me from the sea, but Adam is the one who needs to be dragged from this nightmare Groundhog Day. I already know how it ends.

"Adam! Adam!" I fight for freedom. Wade back into deeper water. Hating myself for not being able to swim to him. Not being able to save him.

He doesn't want to be saved.

He is still watching me. His hands still miming what he wants. He wants me to set him free.

"Something wrong with the yacht!" someone behind me shouts.

This is it.

I watch in horror as the yacht begins to sink.

This is it.

I throw myself forward, not caring that I might drown trying to reach him. Not wanting to live without him. Hands are on me once more, but not the girl's.

Oliver's.

He has brought me back and over my own choking sobs I hear it. The continuous beep.

Adam is flatlining.

CHAPTER SEVENTY-FIVE

Adam

For the second time there's a blow to my skull. The taste of blood in my mouth. Colors bright and dull. Light and dark. A kaleidoscope of pain.

Water, in my mouth and eyes.

Water, in my nose and ears.

My arms and legs flail. I'm sinking deeper and deeper. Dizzy. Disorientated. My lungs burn, chest feels tight.

The water turns from blue to gray to almost black. I'm spinning. Twisting in the sea. Everything feeling like it's about to explode. My skull. My rib cage. Body burning.

Anna.

It is the thought of her that prevents me fighting for air. Stops my legs kicking their way to the surface.

I'm sinking. Heavy. A mass of pain and fear but not regret. Not this time.

If you love someone, set them free.

I'm heavy and weightless and here but not.

Anna.

Drifting. Drifting. My arms and legs are splayed.
A feeling of calm washes over me.
Anna begins to fade away.
And then I feel nothing at all.

CHAPTER SEVENTY-SIX

Anna

We are yanked out of the scanner with force. Sofia pulls me from the table so Oliver can reach Adam. Blood is streaming down my face. My head is splitting, the continuous screech of the machine screaming what I already know.

Adam has gone.

Anxiety grips me tightly. I watch Oliver shake Adam by the shoulders. "Adam, Adam, can you hear me?" But of course Adam doesn't answer.

He can't.

Oliver is going through the motions like he's performed this a hundred times but the pallor of his face, his hesitation, tells me he hasn't. Oliver gives a cursory check of Adam's airway while Luis cuts open Adam's T-shirt and begins chest compressions. Sofia runs to the trolley and picks up two paddles that look like irons and passes them to Luis.

"Clear." He places them on Adam's chest.

Adam's body jerks.

"Still in VF," shouts Sofia.

Oliver continues with chest compressions.

Adam's eyes locked onto mine. His thumbs linking together, forming wings with his hands.

The machine continues its beep. Oliver and Sofia exchange a worried look.

"Please." But I am not sure what I'm pleading for. For them to save the man I love, or let him go.

"Clear," Luis shouts for the second time. Again, Adam's body jerking.

"Still in VF," Sofia says.

The bird he had rescued soaring high into the sky. "He's happy now," Adam had said. "He's free."

Oliver places his hands back on Adam's chest.

"Let him go." My words are thick, my tongue too big for my mouth. My lips unwilling to move. But still I try again. "Oliver."

Adam's wishes are ever-present. Impossible to ignore. They whisper and roar like an orchestra, building to a crescendo, which forces me to acknowledge the cutting truth.

I have lost him.

Oliver meets my eye.

"Stop," I say. "It's time." Oliver's face crumples in pain but he holds out a hand to Luis. "Wait."

In three strides Oliver takes my hands. For a second I think he's going to tell me he has to treat Adam. Has to bring him back even if there's nothing to bring him back for other than a hospital bed and an inability to communicate. Is any life better than no life? Instead, he asks, "Are you sure, Anna?"

In truth, I'm not sure, but I know this is what Adam wants. What he was showing me as he stepped onto that yacht for a second time, knowing how it would all end.

Pain sinks its fangs sharply into my heart.

"Yes," I say quietly.

The beeping stops. Machines are quickly pushed aside. Luis fetches a sheet and pulls it over Adam's chest while Oliver checks his watch and scrawls on Adam's notes and then the room empties.

Slowly, hesitantly, I approach the table.

"Adam?" I know he will not answer. He is not here. My only hope is that he is running free with Harry and Dug. That they will look after him. That he will look after them.

I touch his cheek. It's losing its warmth.

I've heard it said that once you've passed, it looks like you are sleeping.

It doesn't.

In sleep, Adam was always moving, fidgeting. Slinging his arm over his head, sticking his leg out from under the duvet.

Breathing.

Now, there is nothing.

My boy from the bar is no more.

PART FIVE

"If you love someone, set them free."

ADAM CURTIS

CHAPTER SEVENTY-SEVEN

Anna

When I think of funerals I think of gray skies and thunderous clouds. Crashes of lightning and rumbles of thunder. Not this. A beaming sun and bright yellow daffodils poking their hopeful heads through the earth, a painful reminder that life goes on.

Most days I wish it didn't.

This is the church we married in five years ago. Instead of my gorgeous cream wedding dress, I'm wearing a black skirt and blouse. Instead of carrying a bouquet, I am weighed down by my heavy heart.

I step inside. Beeswax and roses. The temperature is startlingly cooler than it is outside. I am alone, but not. Adam's parents said the journey would be too much for them, his mum not coping with the shock, but those closest to me are here: Mum, Nan, Josh and his parents, Nell and Chris. Oliver has flown over with Eva, Sofia and Luis. And Adam.

I can't bring myself to look at the coffin.

I won't.

I've been staying with Mum. Unable to bear sleeping alone in the bed that me and Adam once shared. She has been feeding me soup, baking scones I cannot eat. Sitting for endless hours with me, holding me when I cry. Offering to sort out the funeral if I couldn't cope with it, but she had already been through the trauma of arranging Dad's.

It was my turn.

It was torturous making the arrangements. My head fuzzy from the short course of sleeping tablets my doctor had prescribed. Making Josh and Nell check and double-check the details, convinced there was something I was forgetting. Something niggling at the edge of my mind.

Nell slips her hand into mine and whereas before she had followed me down the aisle, holding my train, today we make the journey down the red carpet stretching toward the front of the church, shoulder to shoulder. I feel eyes on me but instead of meeting the sea of familiar faces with jolly smiles like the last time I did this slow walk, I stare at the floor.

We sit next to Mum and Nan. The benches cold and hard. The vicar isn't the same one who married us. He speaks about Adam as if he knew him before he introduces someone who actually did.

Josh clears his throat. It's the first time I look up. I'm grateful he's agreed to speak. I have a million words tying themselves in knots inside me, but I know if they rose in my throat they would choke me.

"When Adam and Anna married, I was scared about giving a speech," Josh begins quietly. "Today, I feel much the same but this time it isn't because the thought of public speaking terrifies me but because the thought of a world without Adam terrifies me." He pauses. I can hear someone sitting behind me sniffing but I'm holding myself together. Just. Because I know if I allow my sobs to break free, I will never stop crying. Around my neck is the pendant Adam bought me for our first Christmas. I pinch the star between my fingers until the sharp edges penetrate my soft skin, which allows me to feel something other than the solid ball of grief that is expanding in my chest.

Josh carries on, "I've thought long and hard about how Adam would want to be remembered. A husband. A friend. Almost a brother to me. A son to his parents who sadly couldn't be here today, and a second son to mine." At this I hear an anguished moan from Josh's mum. "He was many different things to many different people, but I think this one story sums him up."

There's a beat. Josh tightens his grip on the lectern. I have no idea what's coming. He had asked me if I wanted to hear what he was going to say but I couldn't bear the thought of sitting through it twice. Once is almost destroying me.

"Adam adored his grandad, Ted. It was because of him that Adam wanted to travel the world. See all the places Ted had visited during his time with the navy. Before he died, Ted gave Adam his watch. Adam treasured it. It was an antique, valuable, but he didn't care about the monetary value, just the sentimental value. Adam wore it every day. He didn't have time to take it off all those years ago when he had rushed into the sea to save Anna. The watch wasn't waterproof. It stopped working that day."

I remembered it so clearly I could almost taste the sea water in my mouth, my throat. Coughing as we sat on the beach, thoughts clouding my mind of what might have been if Adam hadn't saved me. Adam asking me questions about my relationship I didn't want to answer and me changing the subject by running my fingers over the face of his watch. "I hope that's waterproof?" I had diverted the conversation away from me. "It looks old?"

"It will be okay," he had said.

"When we got home," Josh continues, "I had it repaired for him and again he wore it every day until, some months later, I noticed he didn't. 'Where's your watch?' I asked him. 'I've sold it,' he said. He'd sold it to buy Anna's engagement ring."

I twist the diamond ring around on my finger. Where it once felt like a sign of love, it now felt uncomfortable. I'd have been happy with a plain ring, a candy one even. Why had he done that?

"'What did you do that for you tw– you idiot?' I asked him. 'Because,' Adam had told me, 'once I had asked Grandad the story of how he'd met my grandma. He'd been docked at Southampton and the second their eyes met they knew they were right for each other. Knowing Grandad had to leave in a few days, they tried to pass it off as a holiday romance, the same as me and Anna. When it was time to say goodbye, Grandad had tried to picture the future without Grandma but he couldn't. He knew she felt the same after she'd given him the watch because on the back she'd had engraved *Love will find a way*.' Adam's grandad had told him, 'We both knew that somehow it would all work out and it did. You'll know too when you've found the love of your life because the thought of not seeing her every single day will break your heart. When you find that, you don't let her go. You *do* anything, *give* anything, to keep her.' Adam had said that was the way he felt the instant he met Anna. The thought of life without her was impossible. He knew that his grandad would approve. Selling his watch to pay for Anna's engagement ring made Adam feel that Ted was part of their new life. Involved. That thought made him very happy."

The sparkle from my ring is blurred by the tears that film my eyes.

"And that was Adam," Josh says. "Thoughtful. Generous. Loyal.

Open and…certain. He was certain that what he'd found with Anna would last the distance and I know his only regret would be that it didn't last for longer."

I am crying now. Josh steps down and I stand, opening my arms and we hold each other while "Love Me Tender" begins to play, the music barely audible over the sound of raw grief. Many of the mourners had watched Adam and me take our first dance to this song.

The pallbearers balance the coffin on their shoulders as though it weighs nothing and for one, perfect second I believe that Adam is not inside the heavy wooden box after all, wearing his cotton anniversary shirt and his paper-plane cufflinks. That all of this has been a mistake.

It hasn't.

Outside, I blink in the brightness. It still isn't raining and I hate that the sky isn't crying for Adam the way that I am crying for him.

"You're doing amazingly well." Nell hooks her arm through mine, as Josh does the same to my left.

I stem my tears as we stand at the graveside while Adam is lowered into his final resting place. I just need to hold it together for a little longer but the world is spinning. I feel my knees buckle and, if it weren't for Nell and Josh, I would fall.

"I'll always catch you, Anna," Adam had said. But he isn't catching me now and suddenly I hate him for leaving me, and then I hate myself for feeling that way.

"Anna," Nell whispers. I am offered a red rose from a bucket; I'd chosen not to have soil. Heat spreads through me as I fight the urge to tip the flowers on the grass—if we don't pay our last respects to Adam, surely they can't fill in his grave?

"You don't have to do anything you don't want to," Josh says, but today I am doing everything I don't want to.

I am letting go of the man I love.

My face is fire. Tears burning behind my eyes, pressure building in my nose. My forehead throbbing with the emotion I'm trying to contain.

Slowly, reluctantly, I unhook my arm from Josh's and I pluck a rose from the bucket and step forward, holding it between my fingers.

"Be free." I let the flower fall as I say goodbye to my husband, to Harry, to the life we almost had.

To all of it.

I stuff my hands into my pockets, rooted to the spot, unwilling to leave him. In my pocket I find a coin. I pull it out. It's *the* coin. My grandad's. I hadn't remembered putting it in my coat and, after running my finger over it one last time, I kiss it and let it fall into the grave.

I'll be thinking of you, Adam. Always.

It is when I turn away that the circling thought that there is something I need to remember stills and becomes as clear as the bright blue sky.

The day Adam died, before he took the fateful yacht trip for the second time, he had scrawled an address on a notepad. An address I can't clearly remember.

It was a message for me. It must have been.

But what?

CHAPTER SEVENTY-EIGHT

Anna

The wake is held in The Star. I haven't been here for years. Adam would be pleased to know they still have the same pool tables. I step inside onto the forever-sticky floor and it feels like stepping back in time. Dark wooden beams striping the ceiling. Round mahogany tables wobble on spindly legs.

I hover uncertainly by the bar, unsure of what my place is here. What I am supposed to do. Both unwilling and unable to mingle and join one of the conversations that are too loud. Too jolly. Voices dripping with relief that the ceremony is over, and laughter. People are laughing.

"Anna?" An elderly lady I don't recognize stands before me, a much younger man at her side. "I... I just wanted to say..." Her opaque eyes fill with tears, and then I know.

"You were on the yacht." She was the one who Adam had tried to save.

"I'm so sorry." She waits for me to speak. I don't. I can't.

"I know it's no consolation," the man speaks now, "but Grandma is the heart of our family. We'd all be lost without her. I'm so sorry about your husband. Adam. But we're all very grateful to him. If he hadn't noticed Grandma had been left behind and gone back to rescue her, no one might have noticed she was stuck. He was a brave man. A good man."

What can I do but agree with him? Adam was a good man. The best. Hating the old woman who shakes in front of me won't bring him back.

"He would be happy to know you are okay." I touch her briefly on the arm before I walk away.

Nell thrusts a gin and tonic into my hand. I take a long drink, wanting the warm bloom of alcohol to numb me. On the bar a TV displays a slideshow of pictures of Adam. Most of the photos are Adam as an adult. I had asked his mum to email some baby ones but she said it was too painful for her to look through them.

"You don't know how awful it is to lose a child," she had said. Memories of Harry rendered me mute and I cut the call.

The smell of him.

The feel of him.

"Are we okay to bring the food out?" the landlady asks me and I nod, not caring either way. Knowing my knotted stomach won't let me eat.

A plate of towering sausage rolls is placed on a trestle table, warm meat and flaky pastry. My eyes meet Josh's. I know he has chosen the menu carefully.

"I'd like to name our son after Harry, my grandfather," I had said to Adam.

"I'd like to name him Gregg," Adam had replied.

"Is he a relation?" Adam never talked much about his family.

"No, but he makes a bloody good pastry." Adam had grinned.

Bowls of Twiglets next.

I can hear Adam's voice, *"Sticks of marmite, I'm in actual heaven."*

Slices of pizza laden with greasy pepperoni and stringy cheese.

"I can't wait for Italy; the food alone will be spectacular."

A trifle sprinkled with hundreds and thousands.

"Proper English food that I'll miss when I travel the world."

Josh fiddles with his Bluetooth speaker and Simple Minds sing "Don't you forget about me." The mood lifts as, just for the next few hours, the mourners shake off their grief by tapping their feet while they queue for the buffet and just like that, this becomes a celebration of Adam's life. He'd appreciate music and laughter more than he would tissues and tears.

"You need to eat, Anna," Nell says.

"I will. Soon." I can't focus on anything except the fragments of the address Adam left on the pad, which are swirling around my mind like leaves in the wind. I can't seem to catch them and rearrange them in the right order. The knowing that it must have been important causes my temples to throb.

I slip outside into the beer garden for some fresh air, craving silence and peace but not yet ready to go home and be alone. Clouds are gathering in the sky. The light's fading and the day has lost its warmth. A patio heater glows red and I slide onto a wooden bench. An ashtray piled with cigarette stubs is before me and I inhale deeply, welcoming the hit of tar in my lungs. I've never smoked but I'm tempted to start.

What was the address?

I close my eyes, traveling back to that day, back to the apartment, but all I can see is the note telling me to go to the beach. All I can feel is my panic building. The bunting. The yacht. The barbecue. The smell of sausages and burgers will always take me back to that time. Still, I can hear the music. My own anguished voice screaming for Adam to get off the yacht.

To stay.

I rub my eyes, desperate to replace the image with something else. Harry springs to mind, as he often does. As painful as it is, I push him away too.

Think.

The apartment was empty. Before I saw the note on the fridge, I had looked at the notepad.

I know I read the address. I know the answer is nestled within my consciousness somewhere. More than anyone, I understand how powerful the mind can be.

I take a deep breath. Clench and unclench my fists, my jaw. Slide my shoulders from their tense position near my ears to where they should naturally sit.

Relax.

The first spots of rain hit but I don't move. Instead I feel them on my skin, the wetness, the temperature.

Relax.

Upper Harringdon.

The words spring from nowhere, but now they are here, I remember wondering why Adam had written down the name of a town about thirty minutes from where we live. There was more, I know. Something about a saint. St. Jude? St. Agnes. St. Mary! St. Mary Street or Road or something. I feel a prickle of excitement. I try not to force another memory. The rain pelting harder now.

62.

Number 62. St. Mary's something in Upper Harringdon.

Immediately I am opening the taxi app on my phone. Summoning a cab. Momentarily I think about slipping back inside the pub to tell Nell and Josh where I am going but they would only insist on coming with me. But whatever is waiting is the last new thing I will ever find out about my husband and I want to be alone. Besides, I can't face an endless round of goodbye hugs, of sympathetic smiles and tear-filled eyes, not to mention the "if there's anything you need."

This.

Going to Upper Harringdon is what I need.

CHAPTER SEVENTY-NINE

Anna

During the journey to Upper Harringdon, I deliberate over what I might find waiting for me. A shop? But it's a long way to come to buy something you could probably get online. A pub? A restaurant? Adam loved to eat. To try new places. Perhaps he was jotting down a recommendation. My mind veers from the mundane to the unimaginable. Adam had a secret girlfriend. A secret family. Children he'd never told me about. I dismiss this but the thought keeps creeping back in. What if I'm about to come face-to-face with his other woman? A part of me, a large part, thinks this notion is ridiculous. I knew Adam better than anyone and he would never cheat on me, but then I feel Ross's lips on mine. I remember I contemplated leaving Adam more than once. There are things he never knew about me. Can we every really properly know what goes on in someone else's head? What secrets they carry?

The last thought, as we pull into Upper Harringdon, is that I might find an empty building. Nothing at all. This would be the hardest to bear.

"This is St. Mary's Street, but there's a St. Mary's Road, do you want me—"

"No." I shove too much money at the cab driver and stumble out of the car. I need to find out the truth and put an end to my black thoughts once and for all.

Speculation is dangerous. I need cold, hard facts.

Rain pours down the collar of my blouse. I run the length of the road. Lungs burning. Disappointment bitter in my mouth. The highest-numbered building is 48.

There is no 62 St. Mary's Street.

Google Maps tells me that St. Mary's Road is a five-minute walk in the opposite direction. I spin around, skid on the wet pavement and a sharp pain circles my ankle as the heel on my shoe snaps. I fall forward onto the concrete, slamming hard onto my knees. My tights are torn, my skin grazed and bloodied. I wrench off my shoes, and carry them in my hand as I limp. Hair plastered to my face with rain. I am freezing cold, and frustrated tears are not far away but I try to keep them inside. I can imagine my mascara streaking down my cheeks. In the unlikely event I am about to come face-to-face with Adam's secret girlfriend, she will only need one quick glance to wonder what he ever saw in me.

By the time I find St. Mary's Road I am soaked to the bone. These are all three-story Victorian homes, most of them converted to businesses. I pass a dentist. A solicitor. An optician. I hobble slowly, checking the numbers carefully. Number 62 doesn't have a bronze plaque outside and I wonder whether it's a family home. Blinds shield the windows.

This is it.

My ankle and knees sting. I climb the six steps before I am standing in front of an imposing black door with a silver lion's-head knocker.

Before I can change my mind, I rap three times.

It seems an age before I hear heels click-click-clicking down the hallway.

The door cracks open. "Yes?" The woman before me is probably around my age. Pretty in her vintage A-line polka-dot dress, her dark brown up-do and deep red lipstick. Her eyes sweep from my hair, dripping with rain, to my torn tights, the blood running down my leg.

"I'm here for…" I falter. What am I here for? "Adam. Adam Curtis." I study her carefully. There isn't a flicker of recognition on her face when I speak his name.

"There's no one here called Adam."

"This building? What is it? What happens here?"

"Do you have an appointment?"

"I…" I think about saying yes but know I'll be caught out right away.

"No."

"Then I can't help you." She begins to close the door.

"Please." I step forward, my foot over the threshold preventing the door from closing. "Please. I…" I don't know what I can say. What I should say. It sounds crazy. It is crazy but Adam wanted me to come here, I know it. "My husband. Adam. He's…" I try to stop myself from crying but I can't. Wiping furiously at my cheeks while I try to steady my voice. "My husband died. We buried him… today. I've just come from the wake." Her face softens. The pressure against my foot eases as she stops pushing the door toward me.

"I'm so sorry for your loss."

"I… it's hard to explain all of it but Adam, he… he wrote down this address on a piece of paper and left it for me to find. It was the last thing he wrote." I have fished a tissue from my pocket and am dabbing at the tears that won't stop falling. "There's something here that Adam needed me to see, or someone he wanted me to meet. Please..."

"It's against the rules to let anyone in without an appointment," she says, but she doesn't ask me to leave. I can feel her wavering.

"Look." I rummage in my bag for my phone. I hold it up. My screensaver photo is of our wedding day. "This is Adam...was Adam. I have to know why he wrote this address. I *have* to."

"I don't know—"

"Please. I've lost my husband. My son."

"Your son?"

Her eyes meet mine. I see pity. Indecision and something else. An understanding. She has lost too; I can sense it.

After a moment, she nods. Pulls the door open wide. "I'm Nancy. You'd better come inside."

CHAPTER EIGHTY

Anna

My stomach jitters with nerves. I step into the hallway of 62 St. Mary's Road. I have no idea what I'm walking into. I stamp my feet on the doormat, trying to dislodge the raindrops that cling to my skin, my clothes. I can sense that I am being watched. Nancy must have some idea of why I'm here. When I'm as dry as I can be, I raise my face to see her eyes are still filled with sympathy. For a split second I think about running away, unsure if I'm strong enough to cope with what she might reveal.

"Come on through." Nancy leads the way into a small room to our left and gestures for me to sit on a dark wooden chair. I perch on the edge of the seat, not wanting my wet skirt to dampen the deep green velvet cushion. She pulls out a chair from behind the impossibly shiny desk and sits opposite me. Waiting for her to speak, I lick my dry lips, tasting the furniture polish that lingers in the air.

"Can I fetch you a hot drink?" she says. "You look freezing."

I am torn between demanding answers and wanting to delay them.

"Please."

Rather than leaving the room, she crosses to the short bookcase under the window where there's a kettle. She flicks it on. I look around for some sort of indication of what this room, what this building is. There's nothing other than a gold cross on the wall. Neither of us talk while she spoons coffee into mugs and splashes on boiling water.

"I can fetch some milk—"

"I take mine black," I lie. The wait has become unbearable. I need to know what happens within these four walls with the burgundy flocked wallpaper and too many secrets. Why Adam had either been here or was planning on coming here.

Nancy hands me my drink. I wrap my hands around the mug, trying to still the trembling in my fingers.

"I lost my daughter," she says simply. Her words are steady, firm, and instinctively I know she's said them many times before. Her eyes are filled with pain. "That's what led me here."

I nod, but I don't understand. I can't. I'm shaking so hard I put down my mug.

"Her father, he...he wasn't around. I had no interest in another relationship. I had no interest in anything. It was three years after...after Lucy that my mum suggested I come here. It wasn't that I wanted to replace her, but..." Momentarily she closes her eyes while she inhales deeply through her nose before huffing out the air. "In the end I couldn't do it, but I began to volunteer and...it was healing. Now I'm the manager but it's more than a job, it's a vocation and...it's enough for me."

She leans forward and takes my hands in hers. "Your husband... Adam. I don't know why he wanted you to come here but the fact you've lost a child..." She doesn't finish her sentence. Again my eyes sweep the room for clues.

"What is this place?"

"It's a children's home."

"It can't be." I draw my hands away from hers, looking around wildly for signs of children. Listening for sounds of children. There aren't any.

"They're mostly all in school." Nancy senses my confusion. "We don't put a sign outside because some of the children have come from difficult homes and we want to protect them. Give them some privacy. Some dignity back. You wouldn't believe what some of these kids have been through. Wherever we can, we place them with new families, of course."

"I…I'm sorry." And I am. Sorry for her loss, sorry for the children who find themselves without stability, security, but most of all I'm sorry for myself. I had come here for answers but now all I have is more questions. Why did Adam lead me here? It makes no sense.

"I…" I trail off. I can't speak. Can't think. Can't breathe. I stand up, my chair toppling back. I rush for the door. I have to get out of here. It was a mistake to come.

"Anna!" Nancy is seconds behind me but I don't stop. My chest is in a vise. I don't know what I expected to find but it wasn't this.

My hand is on the front door handle when I hear it.

A cry.

A cry that tears at my heart.

A cry I recognize.

Choking back a sob, I spin around. Push past Nancy, heading for the stairs.

"Anna! You can't go…"

But I am halfway up the flight, my feet barely touching the ground.

The cries grow louder. Nancy's footsteps thundering behind me.

"Anna! Wait!"

But I don't. I can't. I run full pelt toward the door at the end of the landing and throw it wide open.

There are so many things I feel as I approach the cot. Fear. Excitement. Disbelief. Relief. Confusion. Pain. But everything I feel is overridden by a crushing anxiety that I might be wrong, but my heart tells me I am right.

It's Harry.

His face flushed red. Curls damp against his scalp.

It's Harry.

Small hands scrunched into fists.

It's Harry.

On his arm, the birthmark shaped like a map that matches Adam's.

"You shouldn't be in here," Nancy says, but her voice is soft.

"It's...it's you. It really *is* you," I whisper.

At the sound of my voice the baby stops crying and studies me with deep blue eyes. Adam's eyes. Gently, I scoop him up and hold him against my chest. The familiar weight of him. The smell of him.

"Poor little mite has barely stopped crying since he was left on the steps outside ten days ago."

But she doesn't have to tell me he was left the day Adam died. She doesn't have to tell me because I know.

However impossible, this is my child.

This is Harry.

PART SIX

"Love will find a way."
EDITH CURTIS—ADAM'S NAN

CHAPTER EIGHTY-ONE

Anna

Twelve months later

It took almost nine months for me to adopt Harry. The wait was torturous. During that time, I lived in constant fear that someone else would swoop in and take my boy away. I hadn't been on the waiting list to adopt, of course, but thankfully Nancy had recognized the bond between us and rather than placing Harry with foster carers, which would have broken my heart, she continued to care for him while she championed my application from beginning to end. It was her expertise, her patience, that allowed me to untangle the red tape and bring Harry back to where he belonged.

Home.

"I don't know what it is about you two," she had said, watching me during one of my frequent visits. "He cries almost constantly when you're not here." On cue Harry released one of his infectious giggles while I blew raspberries on his tummy. "And yet with you he's happy. Content. It's like you were meant to be."

Sometimes she would raise her eyebrows, an inviting of

confidence, and I'd smile, and nod, and tell her yes. It did feel like Harry was mine. Once. Just once she asked me why I thought Adam had left me the address of her care home.

I had shrugged. "I can't say for sure but I'm very grateful he did." Never sharing that I could say, but didn't. There was no logical reason for Harry being left here while Adam lay dying across the other side of the world. How a baby, my baby, who scientifically speaking had never existed, now lies contentedly in my arms as though he belongs there.

And he does.

Over time, I have stopped trying to figure it all out.

"There are more mysteries to the universe than we can ever unravel," Oliver had said. "Things that are beyond the realms of scene, of probabilities." Hearing this allowed me to stop endlessly googling neuroscience and consciousness and trying to find a rational explanation.

There isn't one.

From time to time, I spring awake in the middle of the night. Sheets tangled and drenched with sweat, heart pounding as I wonder what would have happened to Harry if I hadn't remembered the notebook. The address. But generally I don't allow my mind to go there.

"I'll stick this one in my boot and drop it at the Parkinson's charity shop in the morning." Josh hauls the box I've labeled "Donations" into his arms. "I think that's the last one." He pounds downstairs.

"Thank God for that." Nell wipes her forehead with her sleeve. "I'm knackered. You ready, Anna? We'll be late."

I shake my head. I'm not ready and yet... "Can you give me a few minutes?"

"Of course. Come with your aunty Nell." Nell stretches out her arms and Harry crawls across to her. His dungarees are filthy at the knees. I was mortified at the amount of dust that had been uncovered when the furniture was carried out. Nell scoops him up and plants a kiss on his check. He giggles. He loves her so much. Again, I question whether I'm doing the right thing, tearing him away from his bedroom with the yellow ducks marching around the walls, his home.

"Let's get you strapped into the car, little man," she says. "I'll give you another lesson on girls."

Her footsteps recede. The front door closes and I am alone with my memories.

"Do you remember the day we moved in, Adam?" I murmur into the empty space. We had felt so grown up that we could afford a house with a spare room.

"For guests," I had said.

"Like who?" Adam had asked. "Nell and Josh live minutes away and so do your family. And my mum and dad . . ." He didn't have to finish. I knew it was a source of sadness they didn't know him properly as an adult, that they weren't around to see the man he had grown into. No matter how old we are, I think that ultimately we all crave the love and approval of our parents, don't we?

"I suppose you want to turn it into some sort of man cave?" I had lightened the mood. "A games console and a mini fridge stocked with beer."

"Absolutely not." Adam had slipped his arms around my waist and nuzzled the back of my neck. "You can't fit many cans in a mini fridge; I need a full-sized one, and a pool table, and a Pac Man and—"

"Umm, you have seen the size of the room." I had spun around and gestured with my hand. "But then you do overestimate the size of things." I backed away with a smile. Mock outrage crossed his face.

"I *would* tell you what's enormous." Adam had sprung forward, tickling my ribs until my knees buckled and we were both lying on the rough, hessian carpet. "But you'd never believe me."

"What," I had laughed. "What's so enormous?"

"My love for you." He was suddenly serious, holding me with his eyes.

"Adam, I…" I didn't know what to say. I had never felt so happy. So content. So complete.

"And you know what would fit perfectly in this room?"

I shook my head, maintaining eye contact.

"A cot." He had dipped his head, his lips feathering over mine. "This will be a nursery." His hands undoing the button on my jeans, his jeans. In that moment we had no doubt that our lives would be exactly what we wanted them to be: long and happy. Together.

Now, I wipe my eyes. There has been too much time for sadness. I conjure another image, determined that all my tears today will be happy ones. I wander into our bedroom. There's a dark rectangle on the carpet, where our bed—now dismantled and in the removal van—used to rest. The memory of our first night here brings a smile. We had bought a double air mattress while we saved for the wrought-iron bedstead I'd coveted.

"Be careful it doesn't burst," I had said as Adam's foot furiously worked the foot pump to inflate the air bed.

"It's nowhere near full." Adam's T-shirt had been damp under the arms.

"I didn't mean the mattress might burst. I meant your head. Your face is bright red! For someone who plays football—"

"I'll have you know I'm in the best shape of my life," Adam had said breathlessly, taking a break. "All muscle." He patted his stomach.

"All pizza and beer," I had joked, but I didn't mind that he'd gained a few pounds since we'd met.

When he had finished inflating the bed, I'd lain on it while he put the pump back in its box. Then he'd flopped down next to me. As he landed, his weight had propelled me into the air and across the room. My arms and legs flailed for something to grip but there was nothing. I had landed with a thud, facedown on the carpet.

"Anna!" Adam's hands had touched my heaving shoulders. "Are you okay? Please don't cry—"

"I'm not." I had rolled over, tears of mirth streaming down my face. "Best shape of your life..." I had howled with laughter until my ribs ached.

"It's not because I'm fat that you went flying through the air, it's...physics!" he had said, but he was laughing too. "You never did understand science."

I still don't.

As I wander from room to room, I remember, I remember it all...

Texting Adam that I was wet and miserable after my first experience running with a local keep-fit group. When I had eventually staggered through the front door, he said, "Told you you'd hate it. Never mind, I've something that will warm you up." He had pushed a piece of paper into my hand. On it a sketch. "I've drawn you a bath!" He laughed.

"Thanks for nothing." Unamused, I had stomped up the stairs, into the bathroom. My eyes filling with grateful tears when I saw the steaming bubble bath waiting for me. The tea lights flickering on the windowsill. The glass of chilled wine on the edge of the basin.

Downstairs, I recall the time I had come home to find the kitchen in a state, and Adam's face in a mixing bowl.

"What on earth—"

"Anna." He had looked up, his face dripping with milk. "I tried to make a curry but I got chili seeds on my fingers and rubbed my face. It's not funny. My eyes. My skin!" He, too, was laughing. We had ended up with a takeaway.

As I sift through our time, instead of sadness and regret I feel a sense of gratitude for the years we were together.

That despite our ups and downs we were happy.

And this is what I take from the house as I lock the door behind me for the very last time, the knowledge that life isn't always perfect—I am not always perfect—but there are times you have to fight for what you want, and times you have to let go.

Today I am doing both. I climb into the car where Josh and Nell are singing "The Wheels on the Bus" to Harry.

"I'm ready," I say, and instead of looking back as Josh pulls away, I keep my eyes fixed firmly forward.

CHAPTER EIGHTY-TWO

Anna

Our leaving party is at The Star; it seems only fitting. Rather than wearing black clothes and reminiscing about the past, today the guests are wearing bright fabrics and looking toward the future.

Everyone is here, Mum, Nan. Josh's parents have driven down. Oliver, if it weren't for him, Harry wouldn't be here, and Nancy, who allowed him to be mine once more. Nell's Chris has brought their children and the pub is filled with happy chatter.

"Shall I bring the food out?" the landlady asks, and my stomach growls in response. I'd been so busy packing up the house that I missed lunch and now I'm ravenous.

"Please."

Trays are carried out of the kitchen, laden with some of Adam's favorite foods and some of mine.

Harry sits on my mum's lap, a plate of Marmite soldiers on the table in front of him. He picks up a piece of bread and squishes it into his fist before aiming it at his mouth.

"Marmite!" I say to my son, opening my eyes wide and slapping my hands either side of my cheeks.

He giggles, white teeth and gummy gaps—Adam would be so proud—before smearing his buttery fingers all over Mum's skirt, but she doesn't seem to mind.

"You know," Mum says for the umpteenth time, "even though you adopted Harry, he looks so much like Adam. It's astonishing."

She'll never know just how astonishing it all is.

"I'm so glad you brought him into our lives, Anna." She kisses the top of Harry's head. "Being a grandmother is just as wonderful as I'd always hoped."

I flit between the people I love. The people who love me.

Chris is telling Josh about a friend of his who has recently broken up with her boyfriend. "You've got loads in common. I could set you up?" he asks.

"Is she hot?" Josh asks when what he's really asking is, "Is she anything like your wife?"

"Yeah. She looks a bit like Nell, actually."

Josh smiles. "Yeah, cheers. Why not."

"Now, are you sure you're okay for money?" my nan asks.

"I'm absolutely sure," I reassure her. Last week she'd tried to give me five hundred pounds again. "Adam's life insurance is more than enough for us to live on for now."

"We'll miss you so much, your mum and I. And your dad." Her eyes fill with tears as she speaks of her son. "If he were still here, your dad would be..."

"I know." I hand her a tissue. "I'll be back before you know it, and until then we'll FaceTime." Nan has bought an iPad especially. "Excuse me for a minute."

In the corner, Oliver nurses a lemonade, awkward and alone.

"Thanks for coming," I say. "I know social engagements aren't your thing."

"I wouldn't have missed it."

We've become good friends. Aside from Nell, there's no one I can really talk to about what I went through except for Oliver. Many nights we've spoken on the phone until the early hours. Poring over everything again and again. He's still at the Institute, still trying to make the world a better place, but concentrating on disease for now. He's more cautious.

"Will you carry on with your research into consciousness, one day?" I ask.

"I still can't decide. I don't know if there are some things we are perhaps better off not knowing." There's a question in his eyes that I can't answer. I shrug.

"But"—his face brightens—"we've had a breakthrough with our research into Parkinson's. Every day we're getting closer and closer to a cure."

"Clem would be proud of you but…" I hesitate, not sure if I'm speaking out of turn. "She'd want you to step out of your lab occasionally and live. Perhaps even love."

"Eva did…" His cheeks redden. "Eva did ask me out to dinner. There does seem to be some chemistry."

"You and your science." We both laugh. "Be happy, Oliver."

"You too, Anna."

Across the pub I notice Nell gesturing at her wrist. I check the time. Not long left. I pick up a fork and tap my glass and when the room quietens, I begin to speak.

"I couldn't have got through this past year without the support of everyone here. It hasn't been an easy decision to leave the home I shared with Adam, but I don't want to be living in my memories, yearning for the life we almost had. I want to make the most of every precious second of the life I have right now.

I feel…" A hot lump rises in my throat. I take a sip of my drink to wash it back down before I can continue. "I feel Adam will be with Harry and me as we make our trip. The world trip he always planned. Following the route he'd mapped out. Visiting all of the countries he'd wanted to go to. It seems the perfect tribute to the man I love." I wipe the tears from my cheeks. "The man I will always love." I raise my glass. "To Adam."

"To Adam," is chorused back at me.

"And Anna and Harry," says Nell. "To the adventure of a life-time." Our eyes meet and I know she's remembering making the same toast as we flew toward Alircia for the first time eight years ago.

It's almost time for my taxi to arrive. There had been several offers to drive me but I'd declined them all, not wanting any emotional airport scenes. I had been there. Done that.

"Anna, we've made this." Josh's dad hands me a scrapbook. I flick through it. It's full of photos of teenage Adam, with mad frizzy hair and terrible clothes. He's on a dance floor somewhere doing his John Travolta, *Saturday Night Fever* pose and I can't help but laugh. There's a cutting from the paper when his football team won an amateur league. His arm is looped around Josh's neck and they are both grinning wildly at the camera. You'd think they had won the World Cup rather than a trophy so tiny I can hardly make it out. There are Adam's A Level results; of course, he passed geography with flying colors. The last page contains a photo achingly familiar. It is Adam and Josh raising a glass to the photographer. In the background, through the glass wall, I can see a plane. They are wearing shorts and T-shirts I recognize. I don't need Josh's parents to confirm that this was taken before they flew to Alircia.

"We thought you might like to show it to Adam's mum and dad when you reach Australia, so they can catch up on the years they missed," Josh's mum explains.

"Thank you." I am touched by the thought they've put into the scrapbook, and appreciate how painful it must have been to make. Adam's passing must have felt like losing a son to them. I hug them both tightly before tucking the scrapbook inside my tote bag, which is crammed with nappies, wipes, teething gel and all the other paraphernalia a tiny person needs to travel. In my suitcase is an envelope of photos of the adult Adam. The first stop on our trip is his parents' house so they can meet Harry, and I can affirm what an amazing, special man their son grew into. It was always such a source of sadness to Adam that they'd drifted apart. On the phone they'd sounded delighted I'd be coming.

"We regret…we regret lots of things," his mum had said. "We shouldn't have missed your wedding, for one, but perhaps most of all we regret not flying over for the funeral. I'll dig out Adam's baby photos before you come."

I can't wait to see those but can already imagine them. I see Adam every time I look at Harry's face.

"I've something for you too." Josh looks uncertain as he holds out a box. Inside, a watch.

"It looks like Adam's old—"

"It is."

I take a deep breath, lifting it from the box. "But how?" How on earth had Josh managed to trace Adam's grandad's watch that he'd sold to buy my engagement ring?

"I've been looking on eBay for ages to try and find something similar for Harry and I found this. The engraving on the back says *Love will find a way*. It's the same one, Anna."

Josh studies my expression while I turn it over, tracing the inscription with my finger as my eyes blur with tears, wishing I could bend and shape time. Wishing we'd had more of it.

"I'm sorry, Anna. Have I upset—"

"No." I look up and smile. "I'm glad you found it. I'm just a bit overcome."

"It's such a coincidence," he says.

"It's a miracle," Nell says.

Another one, I think, looking at Harry, almost asleep against her shoulder.

From outside, the sound of a car horn. Chris picks up our luggage—we're traveling light—and everyone bundles outside to wave goodbye and I promise them that I will see them soon, even though I know there are no certainties in life. All we can do is appreciate the here and now. I give everyone a hug and a kiss and I tell them that I love them because, although we always think there'll be a next time, another chance, sometimes there just isn't. I never put off doing anything I can do today. That's why I'm not waiting until Harry is older to make this trip. God willing, there'll be a chance for us to do it all over again, when he'll remember it too.

On the way to the airport, Harry dozes, his long lashes dark against his pale skin. His arms clutching the Percy Parrot that Adam had chosen for him years before he ever came into being. Where his sleeve has ridden up, I see his birthmark. The map.

Again, I open the box Josh has given me and ease the watch from its velvet cushion before fastening it around my wrist. One day I'll give it to Harry and tell him the incredible story behind it.

Behind us.

Love will find a way.

Ours wasn't a typical love story, Adam, but it was our love story, and although I'm not yet ready for it to end, *still* not ready for it to end, in Harry I've found a new beginning as well as discovering the answer to my question: Can love really be eternal? Of course it can—is there any other way?

Adam, this is my promise to you: one day I shall tell Harry everything. I'll teach him that sometimes you set something free and it comes back to you, and sometimes it can't...

...no matter how much it longs to.

CHAPTER EIGHTY-THREE

Adam

Anna, while you add Harry's name to our love lock in Alircia, I am the gentle kiss of the ocean breeze on the back of your neck.

I am the whisper in the leaves as you traipse through Italian vineyards.

I am the golden sand that tickles Harry's toes in Thailand, making him collapse into giggles.

The white feather that drifts into your yurt in Hawaii, that's me.

As you sit in the mountains in Canada, gazing at the stars that twinkle in the sky, I want to tell you that your star still shines the brightest of them all, but I think you know that.

I hope you know that.

I am with you, Anna.

Always.

Reading Group Guide

Warning: Contains Spoilers

Dear Reader,

Hello. Thanks so much for choosing to read *The Life We Almost Had*. I hope you fell for Adam and Anna in the same way that I did writing them. It's been exhilarating, heartbreaking, but ultimately exciting writing and publishing my debut contemporary fiction novel.

This story felt very personal. It was inspired by the time I spent with my wonderful brother-in-law, who sadly has Parkinson's dementia. As anyone who has experience with dementia knows, it is the cruelest of diseases. If you're interested in learning more about why I wrote this story and how I approached it, there is an essay after this letter explaining my thought process.

In the book Oliver questions whether he has put science before emotion and the moral implications of the technology he invented. I'd love to hear what you think, and you can send me your comments at AmeliaHenley.co.uk, on Twitter or Facebook, or Instagram @msameliahenley.

Amelia x

Discussion Questions

1. "I made a mistake." Anna writes to Adam during the prologue of the book. What did you think might have happened between them?

2. Adam discovers "There's less than a 50 percent chance of couples staying together in a long-distance relationship, and out of those couples who don't make it, the average time they were together was four and a half months." Have you ever been in a long-distance relationship? What was the reality for you?

3. Did you think Nell and Josh would end up together? Were you pleased or disappointed with the way their relationship progressed?

4. When Oliver meets Anna, he offers her a life-changing experience but with the possibility of harrowing consequences. What would you have said in Anna's position?

5. Oliver questions whether he is playing God. "*There's a percentage of the population who oppose scientific development, whether*

for religious or moral reasons. Those who believe that humans shouldn't interfere with the natural order of things." Discuss.

6. When Anna shows Oliver what she believes is proof that her experiences were real, did you believe her?

7. Adam makes a heartbreaking sacrifice for Anna. Did you understand why he did this? Was it selfless or selfish?

8. When Anna visits the address Adam had written down near the end of the book, she stumbles across something truly astonishing. How did you feel when Anna made her discovery?

9. At the beginning of the book Anna questions whether love can be eternal; by the end she has her answer. What do you think?

10. Is a second chance at first love worth risking spoiling the precious memories you have of that time?

Out of Tragedy Comes Hope

Consciousness is something without a firm definition. Scientists and philosophers are unable to agree on what it actually means. To me, consciousness is, simply, being aware of our existence. This is something I spent many years exploring following a car accident that left me with severe compromised mobility and chronic pain. It was during this gloomy period that my grim thoughts drove my mood, trapping me in a vicious cycle of negative thinking. I felt I was a failure, both as a mother and as a human being. Being confined to a wheelchair in my thirties was humiliating and distressing, and shortly after my enforced change in health circumstances, I found myself in the clutches of clinical depression.

It wasn't until I discovered mindfulness that I began to climb out of the metaphorical hole into which I'd fallen, focusing what I was thinking and experiencing in the moment, which enabled me to be fully present and consciously aware. I spent hours learning how to observe my thoughts rather than being consumed by them. To be able to release them rather than letting them control me. Over time I was able to reduce my antidepressants until, eventually, I was able to stop taking them completely.

While I was rebuilding my life, slowly learning to bear weight and walk again, I read as many books as I could on the mind-body connection and really began to appreciate how powerful the brain is, and how little I actually knew about it.

It was around this time my beloved brother-in-law developed Parkinson's dementia. Dementia is such a terribly cruel disease, and I and the rest of his loved ones watched helplessly, hopelessly, while he slipped further away from us.

Often, he wasn't fully aware of the present; he was living out a different life, in a different time. He talked frequently of events that happened some thirty years ago, and yet he generally asked after my children, who weren't born during that time. His mind had created its own timeline, its own narrative. Sometimes when I visited, he fell asleep, and it was during one of those times that I watched how relaxed he became. He was smiling as he dozed, and I wondered what was going on in his mind. Where was he? Who was he with? As a family we had the heartbreak of watching his decline, but sometimes, just sometimes, he was happy in the world he had created and I was desperate to discover what that world was. I thought, Wouldn't it be wonderful if we could step into that world? If my sister could spend time with him inside of his mind-made fiction?

If they could be together, and be happy?

For a long time I had wanted to write a love story with a difference, and although I knew it was too soon, too raw for me to write about dementia, I began to think of a couple who were separated, possibly through a medical condition, desperate to reach each other, understand each other, but they couldn't. Tentatively I began to write, but my writing was self-conscious, unsure, and lacking in confidence. I didn't feel I could make it work.

For both my plot and my own personal circumstances, I began to research brain science. Magdalen College in Oxford, UK, is a leading center for the study into consciousness, and after contacting them and explaining what I wanted to do, I'm grateful they permitted me to go along and sit in on some lectures. There I met several neuroscientists who all specialized in their own field, and after classes I chatted with one of them, Daniel Bor, about my brother-in-law and asked him, despairingly, whether we would ever really know what's going on in someone's mind.

He opened up his laptop and showed me the work of Yukiyasu Kamitani, who is referenced in this book, and I was astounded and excited.

Kamitani had carried out a trial that resulted in visual cortical activity being measured to reconstruct internal imagery. We could, in a fashion, see what someone was thinking as a still image. This opened up the possibility of patients with conditions such as locked-in syndrome being given a chance to communicate.

Later, I also learned that there were plans for a mobile MRI to try to record the movement of speech and images from the dreams of sleeping subjects. There are also some goggles being developed for the purpose of telepathy, although, at the time of writing this book, few details were available.

Nevertheless, concepts that I'd have previously dismissed as "sci-fi movie–esque" were suddenly tangible and credible, and a whole new world of possibility opened up to me.

I spent weeks reading research papers, some of which were beyond my comprehension, and asking questions. Every study I read about brought a hope that, although the technology being developed wouldn't be in time to help my brother-in-law, the future of brain science is progressing in life-changing, life-enhancing leaps and bounds, and I feel privileged to be able to witness these developments in my lifetime.

It was shortly after, on holiday in Lanzarote, that I stared out into the sea, and Adam and Anna came to me as full, rounded characters. I saw the scene with the yacht play out before my eyes like a movie, and instantly, unusually, I knew their complete story. I couldn't wait to write it. I felt Anna's heartbreak. Adam's despair.

Beginning my book again, I wrote quickly because I'd lost the fear that being able to reach someone inside their consciousness was incomprehensible, improbable.

Initially the tech I used were electrodes connected to Adam's skull that then fed into a helmet with a screen that Anna wore. This meant the couple could lie side by side, holding hands, giving it that romantic feel, that sense of unity. They are in it together. When I'd finished writing the first trial, I sent it over to Daniel, who pointed out all the reasons this tech wouldn't work. He suggested using an fMRI, or functional magnetic resonance imaging scanner, which has stronger magnets.

After I'd rewritten with this in mind, we talked through the control room scene and I admitted I was worried about needing the equipment to fail. "I know that wouldn't happen in a high-tech lab," I said. He told me that faulty equipment and sketchy results is par for the course. And so with the technology plausibility in place, I could really delve into the relationship between Adam and Anna.

I do hope you enjoy reading about them as much as I enjoyed writing about them.

Amelia x

In Conversation with Amelia Henley

Q. You're known for bestselling psychological suspense books written under your real name, Louise Jensen. What made you decide to write a romance?

A. I love love! As much as I adore the intricacies of writing thrillers, the mystery, the twists, I found spending my days thinking of terrible things that people could do to each other, writing about secrets and lies, was taking a toll on my mental health. After losing my mobility very suddenly several years ago, I suffered with depression and I could see myself slipping back. I wanted to take a break so I could come back fresh to thrillers, but I didn't want to stop writing altogether. The idea for the plot and for Adam and Anna as characters came to me very suddenly, and I felt a surge of excitement knowing that I had to write this book, and it brought me so much joy. Afterward I began a new thriller with a sense of elation rather than a sense of dread. Writing both romance and thrillers is the perfect balance, and I feel immensely grateful I can juggle both.

Q. After numerous suspense books, you must have an established process for writing one. Did you use it for writing this book?

A. The process has been completely different. With thrillers I can't think ahead. I have so many twists that I find it impossible to figure them out beforehand. During a first draft I have constant low-level anxiety that the story won't work out. With romance I see the entire story, including the ending, play out in my mind before I write it. I have been able to integrate some of the techniques from my thrillers, though. Leaving each chapter on a mini cliffhanger. Throwing in some surprises. I didn't want this to be a typical love story.

Q. Several of your novels have a scientific basis for the plot. What draws you to science? Were there particular challenges in crafting a love story imbued with nonromantic, scientific elements?

A. For this plot I'd already been researching brain science because my beloved brother-in-law had dementia, and I'm fascinated and encouraged by the leaps and bounds science is making. I think that because of my own complicated medical history, I work through a lot of my emotions in my books regarding health and science. It's very therapeutic.

That said, every time I write a medical or science-based book, I say never again because the research is so difficult and time-consuming, and finding experts with the time to help can be a challenge. But I learn so much I find it really rewarding when it all comes together.

Q. You and your husband have been married for eight years. People would call that a success and inspirational. Did you draw from any real-life experiences when writing about Anna and Adam's relationship?

A. Ha! My husband is fabulous, and although I love him dearly, he is the least romantic person I know. With Adam and Anna I had a chance to explore the romantic side of relationships, and it was lovely. That said, no relationship is perfect and we all have faults, so it was important to me to make Adam and Anna as flawed and as fallible as the rest of us.

Q. Anna takes extreme measures to connect with Adam after his accident. That brings up questions about fate and choice. Are you more likely to accept the hand that life deals us, or are you a "do not go gentle into that good night" type? Do you think Anna would have taken the same extreme measures if she and Adam had been married five years or ten years?

A. I'm all about hanging in there and fighting to make a change. After my accident I was written off by most health professionals, but I never gave up. When I eventually fell into the care of my wonderful specialist, he said he was amazed by my drive and determination to regain as much of my mobility as I could.

I believe it doesn't matter how long Adam and Anna had been married; she'd stick by him as he would by her. Love endures.

Q. What's one thing you want all your readers to know about you?

A. That I strongly believe in fate and that everything will be okay in the end. If it isn't okay, it isn't the end.

VISIT **GCPClubCar.com** to sign up for the **GCP Club Car** newsletter, featuring exclusive promotions, info on other **Club Car** titles, and more.

 @grandcentralpub @grandcentralpub   @grandcentralpub

ACKNOWLEDGMENTS

Firstly, huge thanks to my agent, Rory Scarfe, for encouraging me to write the story that was in my heart. My fabulous editor, Manpreet Grewal, who instantly fell in love with Adam and Anna, understood what I wanted the story to be, and helped me shape it with a gentle hand. The inspirational Lisa Milton—I'm very grateful for the belief you have in me.

The wonderful Forever family—in particular Kirsiah McNamara, Jodie Rosoff, and the production team. It takes so many people to bring out a book and I'm very thankful for the help I receive.

The support from my early readers, who took Adam and Anna into their hearts when I wasn't quite sure what the story was or if it was working, was invaluable. Fiona Mitchell, Lucille Grant and Emma Mitchell, I'm not sure if you realize just how much your kind feedback and encouraging words meant to me. Darren O'Sullivan, for listening to my angst over coffee and too much cake while I tried to keep the story straight in my head.

I'm so appreciative that Magdalen College in Oxford allowed me to sit in on lectures in consciousness given by leading neuroscientists.

Thanks to David Luke for taking the time to speak to me during an early draft. Daniel Bor, who has been so patient answering endless questions over the past year, and contributing ideas to bring Oliver's technology to fruition in the story. Of course, I have taken artistic license in fictionally developing the technology that is currently available to fit Adam and Anna's experience. It's been so fascinating to learn about the developments in science, the current trials and the technology out there (not a million miles away from the tech that Oliver has created), which I'd previously thought could only have existed in sci-fi movies. The future is exciting. To everyone involved in brain science research who is working tirelessly toward eradicating neurological disease, my heartfelt thanks. You really are changing the world.

Louise Molina, for all your medical expertise—any mistakes are purely my own.

All the book bloggers who work so hard sharing their love of good stories. In particular Linda Hill, whose romantic relationship with her husband, Steve, made me long to write about a love like theirs.

My friends who, like Nell, are always there for me when I need them, no matter how much time has passed; in particular Sarah, Natalie, Hilary, Kuldip and Sue.

My family: Mum, Karen, Glyn, Bekkii and Pete. I love you all immensely, along with my husband, Tim—thanks for your unwavering support.

Callum, Kai and Finley, who make me infinitely proud every single day. I would cross worlds for you three. Always.

And Ian Hawley. Forever.

Amelia Henley is a hopeless romantic who has a penchant for exploring the intricacies of relationships through writing heartbreaking, high-concept love stories.

Amelia also writes psychological thrillers under her real name, Louise Jensen. As Louise Jensen she has sold over a million copies of her global number one bestsellers. Her stories have been translated into twenty-five languages and optioned for TV as well as featuring on the *USA Today* and *Wall Street Journal* bestsellers list. Louise's books have been nominated for multiple awards.

The Life We Almost Had is the first story she's written as Amelia Henley and she can't wait to share it with readers.

YOUR
BOOK
CLUB
RESOURCE

VISIT
GCPClubCar.com

to sign up for the **GCP Club Car** newsletter, featuring exclusive promotions, info on other **Club Car** titles, and more.

 @grandcentralpub

 @grandcentralpub

 @grandcentralpub